Book O

CW00435427

South V

by

C L Larson

Prologue

The tall green grass was waving in the breeze that swirled in the small valley. It was mid-morning; the sun was just topping the trees behind him and bathed the forest on the far side of the valley with light. A flock of starlings drank from a small spring feeding the creek that flowed south through the center of the valley. Thom caught the faint smell of flowers as the cool breeze blew from the valley floor.

Something startled the birds and they took to the air reminding Thom why he was here. His army of five thousand was gathered and waiting silently in the forest behind him.

He occasionally saw the glint of steel in the forest on the far side of the valley. The force he was here to fight was barely half the size of his own and his scouts had confirmed there would be no reinforcements. He wondered at the wisdom of their commander; this was a fight he could not win.

Both armies started to gather within sight of each other on either side of the valley. Two men stepped from the enemy ranks. One wore the uniform of a captain with the setting sun of the Western Territory emblazoned on his chest. The other man wore a breast plate, helm and a large shield, that was blinding when it caught the sun. The two men began walking toward the center of the valley.

"Perhaps we can avoid this slaughter after all," Thom muttered to his captain before he began making his way to the center of the valley.

Thom approached the commander and his companion and stopped within talking distance, but out of easy striking range. The captain was young but imposing; he stood a half a head taller than Thom. His blonde hair hung loose to his shoulder, his face was shaven except on his chin and that was nearly the length of his hand.

"I am Captain Derrick, we ask that...," the enemy commander began.

Thom barely heard him, he was distracted by Derrick's companion. The man's armor appeared to be made entirely of polished silver. His helmet was shaped like a human skull. His breastplate and shield also had life-sized skulls embossed in their centers. His sword, which seemed at least a foot too long to be useful, he held easily with one hand. It had a small skull with what appeared to be rubies in the eye sockets on its pummel.

Derrick cleared his throat, bringing Thom's attention back to the business at hand.

"Your companion," Thom asked, gesturing toward the man in plate.

"Not important. He is simply here to make sure you don't try anything stupid," Derrick stated.

Rather than let the young captain continue, Thom interjected. "On behalf of the governor of the Southern Territory, I am authorized to offer you quarter. If you surrender, I will personally ensure that you and your men will not be mistreated, and, when John and Governor Edward come to peaceable terms, you will be returned home."

Derrick's tone was dismissive when he replied, "You are either stupid or your arrogance has blinded you. You stand before me unprotected, with an inferior force at your back and you seek my surrender? Tell me why I should let you walk from this field!"

Thom was confused by Derrick's assumption of having the greater force but he did not let it bother him. "I am neither stupid nor arrogant. I have at least double the number of soldiers on this field as you. You have no reinforcements available, and, if you kill me now the outcome of the battle will not change save for the fact that you will have given my men one more reason to kill you.

Judging by your reaction to my offer I am to infer that you mean to die with all your men today and I will not be able to talk you out of it. I hope to meet you personally on the field of battle to find out which of us is arrogant and which is confident." Thom turned without waiting for a response and made his way back to his waiting forces.

The battle started as he would have expected, both armies met in the center of the valley and the killing began. As the day wore on everything became a blur of blood and exhaustion.

The battle was taking too long, the enemy should be dead or in retreat.

Sometime later--how long he did not know--the roar of battle seemed to have quieted some. He took a moment to assess. He noticed most everyone was gone; all that was left was about thirty of his men surrounding what was left of the enemy army.

One man stood before him. He looked ready to fall from exhaustion and was covered in blood and pieces of flesh. The large bearded man must have killed dozens of men by the amount of blood that covered him.

The man looked him in the eye and said without a hint of emotion. "It looks like you will get your wish General. Here we are; let's see who is the better man and put an end to this day." With that comment Thom realized he stood before Captain Derrick.

Thom was too tired to comment. He simply raised his sword and began his attack. The larger Derrick seemed to easily counter everything he tried. He was too tired, his sword seemed to weigh as much as a horse and his eyes were full of crusted blood. He knew he could not continue much longer, so he backed off to catch his breath.

Derrick did not let him rest for more than a moment. His attack came high and fast, meant to take off Thom's head and end the battle quick. Thom brought his sword up to parry, or at least that is what he intended, but he stepped back onto the head of one of the fallen and twisting his ankle, fell flat on his back. Derrick, caught off guard by the disappearance of any resistance to his swing, lost his balance, slipped on the blood-soaked ground and fell toward Thom, who reflexively lifted his sword to block the falling man and impaled Derrick's head through his left cheek and exited the back of his head. Derrick's blood felt hot as it ran down Thom's arms to mingle with the blood of thousands of others who had fed the grass of the valley.

Thom managed to get back to his feet. His ankle was only an annoyance, like the many injuries he had received. As he scanned the battlefield his heart sank. The valley was covered in the bodies of the fallen. The greatest concentration was just south of the spring, where the creek was damned by bodies creating a small pond, thick with the blood that had accumulated there. Few if any on the ground moved with life; the slaughter was indeed very thorough.

There were twelve of his men still alive and they surrounded a single enemy soldier. His men seemed hesitant to engage the man. That was when he realized that man was captain Derrick's protector. It was at that same moment that the man with the skull helmet lifted the front of his helm and said something to the men around him. They were too far away for Thom to hear, but it was clear that his men used this opportunity to attack. He could not comprehend how, but the man with the skull helmet seemed to move as quickly and smoothly as a naked man with a full day's rest...and he swung that too long sword as if it were a thin reed. The result was within moments, what was left of his army was in blood-soaked pieces, lying on the ground.

Before the head of his last foe hit the ground, the man in the skull helm started walking toward Thom. Thom then felt the exhaustion of the full day of battle. His whole body began to shake and he had a hard time not emptying his stomach.

As the man walked, Thom was distracted by the call of a raven. He turned to see the bird land on the face of his second in command. For some reason he could not recall his name.

The raven began to pull the man's eye out with its beak. He thought to scare the bird away but could not seem to move, so he brought his attention back to the strange man. The man was covered completely with the gore of the day except for his helmet and the embossed skulls on his chest and shield, which struck Thom as being very odd and out of place.

The man approached and lifted his visor. Thom lifted his sword. The man raised an eyebrow, that simple gesture filled Thom with fear and shame; if the man meant to kill him, he would have kept his visor down. If his men had taken the gesture correctly, they would be alive still. Quickly, Thom tried to throw his sword away but only managed to drop it at his feet. He stared at his sword a moment as if confused by his inability to throw it, then looked at the man before him. Thom was struck by the man's appearance--he was utterly ordinary looking. His hair was the color of dry dirt, his eyes a light blue. He expected after what he had seen there would be some great personage behind the mask--a face from a great legend, a hard face that demanded respect or... something. It would be a face he would never forget. Nor would he forget the blood on the man's face or the tears that mingled with that blood and dripped from his chin.

"General, tell your governor what happened today, so we don't have to be a part of more pointless death." His voice held none of the emotion that was plain on his face.

"We will do what has to be done to protect ourselves from Edwards advances into the Southern Territory." Thom said with as much confidence as he could muster, which wasn't much.

The man looked at Thom thoughtfully for a moment. "We have not been making advances into your territory. We have been getting reports of Southern Territory soldiers burning and looting border towns. Captain Derrick believed your presence here proved the reports true."

Thom looked over the battlefield covered with thousands of dead. Both armies were completely destroyed. The wounded would lie amongst the dead and painfully join them one by one.

All of them had died for a lie.

"Our reports and our assumptions were the same as yours. Who would want us at war and why?" Thom asked.

"Politics are beyond me. I don't know nor do I care who or why," the strange man said. Turning to leave he added, "Regardless of the cause, a war with us will be the end of the Southern Territory. Convince John or we will be here again soon."

The man in the skull helmet hadn't gotten but a few steps away when Thom asked, "What is the name of the man who spared my life?"

The man stopped, but did not turn and said in a cryptic tone. "I did not spare your life. Fate spared you and it would have been better for you to have died on Derrick's sword than to live with this memory haunting you 'til old age takes you." He paused, put the sword into the scabbard on his back and started walking up the western slope of the valley then said, "Like Captain Derrick told you before, who I am is not important."

Thom watched him leave then turned to leave himself...and fell flat on his back. He remained there for what seemed like an eternity in and out of consciousness fighting off the crows that picked at his flesh.

Thom woke in a cold sweat vainly fighting crows, that were no longer there. It had been five years since that day in the valley, yet he still re-lived it at night every couple of months. This was the second night this week though. The dream was always the same but different slightly from the real day. The day of the battle there was strategy, orders given, friends dying and people with names that he no longer re-membered. The most obvious to him was the raven that was eating his second-in-command's eye, there weren't any ravens until after the battle had ended. Also, he had never been able to understand why the skulls on the man's armor had been clean in the dream. The man had been completely covered in gore, there was no hint of polish once the battle had ended. Thom also knew the man in the silver armor or he at least knew of the man by reputation. He was the Reaper's Hand. The dream was accurate. He had asked for the man's real name. He had never cared to know his name before that day, because be-fore that day the Reaper's Hand was a monster: a creature from the depths of hell--he was not a man. Then he saw the blood streaked tears, the concern in his eyes and he realized he was a man. A tortured man, that had far too much blood on his hands and he hated it.

His musing was interrupted by a continuous pounding on his door which must have been going on since he was asleep. "What! What do you want?"

"The governor is requesting your immediate presence, sir, and I have been trying to wake you for some time now," was the response.

"Tell him I will be up as soon as I can get some clothes on," Thom muttered just loud enough for whoever was out-side to hear, his annoyance very evident in his voice.

The room that Thom called home was small with a small window up near the ceiling that let in the morning light. Judging by the angle of the light it was mid-morning, hours after he normally woke. On either end of the room were two large tapestries that helped warm the atmosphere but not the air. One was a mountain waterfall scene; the other was Southport at sunset. The walls and floor were stone and there was a small fireplace in the corner that he rarely used because it did little to warm the place.

He did not want to leave his warm bed. The dream always left him exhausted, as if he had actually fought the battle rather than just dreamt it. As much as he dreaded it, he pulled himself up and began putting on some clothes. He wore a simple pair of black cotton trousers and an un-dyed long-sleeved cotton shirt that buttoned up the front. He rarely wore a uniform anymore, usually only when the governor required it. "I wonder what's got him in a lather today? He'll probably make me come back for my uniform… ahhh to hell with it," he muttered to himself as he splashed some water on his face, ran his wet hands through his hair to try and look somewhat presentable. Then he left his room.

The route to where John would most likely be was a meandering trek through the lower levels of the Keep. If you hadn't been there several times the likelihood of finding his room, even with good directions, was slim. That is why he chose it. He could have had a large suite in one of the upper levels, but he did not see the point; he had few belongings and he did not do much here but sleep anyway.

When he got to the balcony where John usually ate his breakfast there was nobody there. "Damn it, where is he?" he asked the empty balcony.

"He is in the audience chamber, sir," a meek female voice said behind him.

"Ahh shit!" he exclaimed as he spun to see the unseen

speaker. "Don't sneak up on me like that girl," he said more harshly than he intended. The girl before him seemed to shrink as he spoke. "Sorry for speaking harshly but you nearly made me wet myself. A man my age can't retain his fluids as tightly as one would like," he joked, trying to lesson her fear. "Do you know what all the fuss is about this morning?"

"No sir, but everyone is either sad or very angry, and nobody seems to think I need to know anything," she said with a hint of irritation as she started piling dishes from the table to a cart.

"Are you busy?" Thom asked.

"Sir, I am nearly done cleaning up breakfast but I was told that anything that you, the governor, or the wizard needs was more important than my regular duties. So, I'm at your service, sir," the girl said expectantly, standing straight and looking him in the eye.

"I need two things. First, is there any toast or a pasty left from breakfast close by? If there is, could you go get it? Second, I need someone to talk to as I walk. Since I don't know who you are, you would be perfect for the job," he said, hoping a little light conversation would help get his mind off his dream.

"Yes sir, I'll be right back," she said with enthusiasm.

Thom didn't wait for her to get back before he started for the audience chamber. His destination was on the opposite side of the Keep and he was sure John was already mad at his absence.

She caught up to him just outside the room. He was quite pleased to see she had found him a sweet roll and a large glass of milk. He took the glass and reached for the plate with the sweet roll on it

"I'll hold the plate for you, sir."

"Yes, that will probably work better." He picked the roll off the plate and took a bite.

The girl walking beside him was more a young woman than a girl. Her hair was brown and her eyes were light blue. She stood nearly to his shoulder, which was average for a woman. Thom would not have called her pretty...kind of cute maybe, but she wore her simple servant dress well.

"What's your name, girl?" he asked, after washing down his first bite.

"Lisa, sir. I do prefer my name over *girl*." An unsure smile on her face.

"I'm sure you do. I prefer my name over *girl*, also," he said smiling down at her. "What part of Southport are you from Lisa?"

"I'm not from Southport, sir. I am from Elk Valley."

"Elk Valley? You're far from home, aren't you? What brings you so far south and to serve in the governor's household no less?" He was genuinely interested.

"My parents insisted I come live with my aunt. She works in the kitchen, so I've been helping her."

He could tell she was purposely leaving the most important part out and he was not going to let her off the hook. "So, there is a young man in Elk Valley that your parents disapprove of, I take it."

The sadness in her eyes when she looked up at him, told him he was not far off. It also told him he was done with personal questions. All he needed to make his day was a young lady crying on his shoulder about lost love and unjust parents.

They walked in silence for a moment while Thom ate his breakfast. Thom noticed as they walked that Lisa obviously had something on her mind.

"Spit it out girl," he said through the last bite of his roll.

"What?" she asked.

"I've been a general for a long time. I can tell when somebody has something to say, but doesn't know how to begin, so just spit it out. What's the worst that could happen?"

Lisa looked up at Thom, obviously still unsure of herself.

Thom frowned down at her.

She looked to her feet then blurted out almost too quickly for him to understand. "I was wondering if I could do more work for you, sir? My aunt said that if you gave me things to do, I wouldn't have to do as much for the wizard."

He looked down at her, brows furrowed. "And why do you think working for me would be better than working for Andarus." he asked, knowing that if she spent much time with Andarus things would turn bad for her. The last servant girl He had taken an interest in had jumped from the tower. But he also did not want to alarm her.

"My aunt says you're a good man... and would understand," she said slowly, looking into his eyes at the end.

"Who is your aunt?" He asked, but after the look she just gave him, he already had a pretty good idea.

"My aunt is the head cook, sir."

Thom chuckled, he had been right. He and Cynthia had helped each other through the loss of her husband--his second in command--at the battle he had just dreamt of. He owed her a great deal and would have to find a way to keep this young lady out of the hands of the wizard. He would not be able to save them all, but he would save this one.

They turned the last corner on their trek to the audience chamber. In front of them were two guards, insuring no one entered that were not meant to enter. Both men saluted the general. The guard on the left said, "They are expecting you, sir," and went to open the door for him, Thom held up is hand and the guard stopped.

Thom turned to Lisa and said just loud enough for her to hear. "Go finish cleaning up breakfast. Then try to avoid Andarus as best you can until I can find something for you to do. If he does find you, tell him that you are already busy doing something for me and whatever that something is, I don't want him to know what it is," he said with a wink at the end and then entered.

The room was large with a row of seven red cushioned wood chairs in the front of the room, ten tiered rows in the back that faced the front with a walkway down the center of the ten rows and a space of four strides between the rear tiered and front seats. There was a wood rail that separated those seven chairs from the open space between. The center chair was occupied by the governor. Andarus was seated to his right and Amber, the governor's daughter, was to his left. Standing before them were two soldiers and behind them there was several members of the keep staff. The door Thom entered was to the right of the row of seven chairs, so those seated did not initially see him.

"...so that is why I think we should be mobilizing a force to...," Andarus was saying, until he noticed Thom's presence, then said, "Nice of you to finally join us, General."

John turned, his face going from a mix of sadness and anger, to one of near rage. "Damnit Thom! Where have you been and why do you look like the son of a goblin whore?"

I should have worn my uniform, Thom Thought. "Sorry sir, I was told my presence was required as soon as possible, so I did not bother with the uniform." He walked toward the two soldiers.

"What has happened?" Thom asked the governor while circling the two soldiers.

"The governor's son was attacked on his hunting trip by Edwards's men," Andarus said with contempt.

Thom's heart sank, he was quite fond of Petre. "Is there news as to Petre's well-being, sir?" he asked with sincere concern.

"There is no word on Petre; he may be dead or captured," Andarus answered.

"I did not ask you, Andarus... but since you want to answer questions, perhaps you can tell me who these two soldiers that do not salute their general are?" Thom was still eying the soldiers.

"They witnessed the attack and managed to escape to let us know what happened. As to why they don't show you respect, I am not the general. You tell me," he snidely said.

"Enough of this petty shit. My son is missing or dead and the two of you bicker like children," John said, more sad than angry.

"Your sword?" Thom asked the soldier on the right, his hand held out in expectation.

"Sir?" the soldier asked, looking to the governor and Andarus before unbuckling his sword and handing it to Thom.

"What is this about, Thom?" John asked.

Thom did not answer, but addressed those not sitting in the front. "Everyone, leave now," Thom said with the authority of a general--which in spite of his disheveled appearance caused everyone to start and quickly begin leaving, including the two soldiers.

"Not you two," the general said to the soldiers.

"What is this about Thom?" John asked, demanding an

answer this time.

"Sir, I have some questions for these men that should not be heard by everyone." Both men started fidgeting nervously. "First, I chose the men that went with your son and I did not choose either of them. Second, this sword is not a Southern Territory issued sword."

"I lost my sword in the battle and picked one up to defend myself, sir." the soldier quickly replied, before the general could continue.

"I did not finish my question!" Thom yelled, inches from the man's face.

"General?" Andarus interjected. "I may be able to shed some light on your concerns."

"I'm sure you can. Please, do then." His exhaustion evident in his reply.

"Well, I did not know that you had personally picked the men to go with Petre. There seemed too few in my opinion to protect him, so I had him take a few more men. These may be them."

Thom seemed to be thinking about what Andarus had said, but his mind was on the dream and the fact this was the second time this week. There was a reason for the dream, but what was the reason? Pulling himself back to the business at hand, he drew the sword from its scabbard and looked at it closer. This sword did not have the mark of Edward's men either. Where were these men from? What was Andarus' role in this? It was at this point he realized he had shown too much suspicion. If Andarus was involved, he was now in danger. Oh well, no going back now.

"Thom!" John yelled.

"Yes, sir," he replied quietly, not realizing the governor had been trying to get his attention.

"What has been the point of this? Regardless, Edward will pay," John said with conviction.

"The point, sir, is that Edward did not do this," he said as calmly as he could muster. Thom was slowly walking around the two soldiers observing them closely. One seemed very nervous, but the other--the one whose sword he held in his shaking hand--was more confident and kept glancing toward Andarus when he thought nobody was looking.

His decision made, he said, "My soldiers are trained to fight until they can no longer fight for those they are ordered to protect. These men should have died ensuring Petre's safety. Yet they stand before you without any major wounds. If these two are soldiers in the service of the governor I would know their names. I do not. This sword does not bare the mark of Edward's men. Tell me, are you a soldier in the service of the Southern Territory sworn to protect the governor and its people?" Thom asked the soldier whose sword he held.

"Yes sir, I am," the soldier said with confidence.

Thom stepped in front of the man between him and those on the stand. The sword moved so quick that the soldiers look of smug arrogance was still on his face when his head hit the floor. The man's knees buckled and his body fell backward on the floor. Blood pulsed from his neck into a growing pool on the marble floor. "I hereby sentence you to death for abandoning your duties," Thom said, barely loud enough to be heard.

The soldier that was next to him, his face covered in the spray of blood, paled, swayed and nearly passed out. Then his urine was mixing with the blood on the floor. Thom stepped in front of the second soldier, his body shaking with anger and exhaustion. "I will question you later. Guards take him away and get someone in here to clean up this mess."

The whole gory scene happened so fast, those sitting

were just starting to let out their held breath when they started taking the man away.

Thom turned to those seated before him and pleaded, "I will get to the bottom of this and if your son lives, I will see him returned safely, but please don't run to war until we know all the facts." When he finished talking, he nearly fell over, so one of the guards came and helped him to a seat. Everyone sat quietly for a few moments while a couple of men carried out the dead man.

Finally, John spoke. "Thom I can see some merit in your concerns. I will be very interested in what the other soldier has to say."

"Sir, if I may?" Andarus interjected. "I am not going to say the general is wrong, but there is just as much merit to the story of the two soldiers. Just because they were cowards doesn't make them liars and the fact, they left the scene before they were killed allowed us to know what transpired. Without their story, your son may have simply never come home and we would have never known why. They may be heroes instead of villains if you look at it with an open mind, instead of from the strictures of military dogma," Andarus said calmly, his voice smooth as silk. "This being said; however, I do not begrudge the general his judgment upon one of those under his authority."

John turned to his daughter. "Amber, what do you think should be done?"

Amber thought for a moment, looked at Andarus then to Thom. "I think it would be best if we prepare for war, but wait until we know for sure what has happened. We only have the word of two soldiers and the evidence of their treachery. For all we know, nothing has happened at all, and my brother could arrive home in a week or two wondering what all the fuss is about."

"I agree. We will start preparing for an assault on Edward," John said to everyone present, then looked to Thom. "Thom, I want you to choose someone to take your place as general."

Thom noticed Andarus's eyes light up. "Sir...," Thom began, but was waved to silence.

John continued, "Hear me out. I'm not retiring you. I feel that if you had been there with my son instead of here, he would be safely home. It appears in his concern, Andarus may have inadvertently had spies sent with my son. So, your new job is to protect my daughter as if she were your own. I want you to do whatever and choose whomever you see fit to watch over her. I don't want her alone, ever."

"Father, I already have guards--I don't need any more babysitters," Amber complained, sounding too much the girl, not enough like the now possible heir to the second largest province in the empire.

Thom watched the exchange between John and his daughter. She still looked sick from the bloodshed of a few moments ago. He was already formulating a plan to keep her safe. He glanced toward Andarus. The man was looking sick himself. The apparent joy at the news Thom would no longer be general was gone.

1 - Ulrick

Ulrick was lying on his back on the cold, moist ground. The sun was warm on his face and chest. The contrast between the sun and cool ground felt wonderful. The air was calm, cool and thick with the sweet smell of decaying leaves and fallen aspen trees that had just recently emerged from the winter snow. The sun was much closer to the horizon since he had lain down. He had been exhausted after their climb up the slope of the mountains earlier this morning.

To the left of him, still asleep, was his cousin Vincent. To the right was his good friend Eramus. Today had been one of the hardest days of the three-month trek. It had been their job to clear rocks and trees that had fallen during the winter and push the wagon through the mud and up the steep sections of road, while Vincent's father David, drove the wagon. David had continued on after they got to the top. His trip wasn't over today. Tomorrow he would be continuing south to Smithville, to sell what he had bought in the Western Territory.

"What do you think Eram?" Ulrick asked conversationally.

"I think we should probably get going so we can be home before dark." Eram sat up and started brushing the leaves out of his shoulder length brown hair. "It's still cold after the sun goes down up this high"

"I think you're just scared of those goblins, you kept imagining," Vincent said mockingly, obviously not asleep.

"Everyone saw them but you, so it is you with the bad eyes. Even your dad thought he saw one yesterday just before dark. Anyway, I'm more concerned about the mountain cats and wolves than puny goblins." Eram climbed to his feet, shouldered his pack, and started down the road toward home.

"So, you admit to being scared?" Vince called.

"Shut up, Vince. Why do you always have to be an ass?" Ulrick said, just loud enough for Vince to hear.

"Why did you have to convince my dad to bring him along this year? You know I can't stand him," Vince said a little louder than Ulrick was comfortable with.

Ulrick had convinced David that having Eram, who was an apprentice blacksmith along, would save some money if they had problems with the wagon and he would be able to help judge the quality of the iron they would be buying to sell in Smithville. Ulrick had, however, just wanted his best friend to see a little of the world. Before this trip, Eram had never been out of Elk Valley.

"Come on." Ulrick grabbed his pack and jogged to catch up to Eramus.

They had a couple hours of travel left before they reached home; most of it was spent kicking rocks and walking in silence. As they walked, Ulrick developed a strange feeling in his chest. It felt as if there was a string attached to his heart, and that string was tied to a small rock...that trailed somewhere behind him. As he continued, the pressure increased as if the rock tied to the string was getting larger. He also noticed that when the road turned the string tugged a different direction through his body.

The smell of burning pine told them they were nearly to the summit that overlooked Elk Valley; the small mountain town they called home. Near the top, Ulrick slowed his pace, and then stopped. When he stopped, he could feel the stone on the end of the string still moving... and it seemed to be getting closer.

"Hey we're nearly there, what's the problem, Ulrick?" Eram must have sensed his unease.

"This may sound odd, but I think someone is following us," Ulrick whispered.

"Probably just goblins. Let's go," Vince muttered sarcastically.

Ulrick grabbed Vince's arm and stopped him. "I'm serious don't ask how I know, but I'm sure somebody is following us. The feeling has been getting stronger over the last hour."

Eramus pretended to be looking in the bushes on the side of the road, while looking behind them. "I don't see anything".

"Of course, you don't. There isn't anything there." Vince's tone, was dismissive.

"Wait, there is somebody, he's just coming around the bend about a quarter mile back. It looks like he is walking his horse, but it is hard to tell." Both Vince and Ulrick turned to look.

The man seemed to be looking at the ground as he walked. A moment passed as the three just watched. Then the man looked up, saw them, stopped and started getting something off his horse. All three looked at each other at the same time, no one needed to say anything; each started running toward town.

The road became a series of switchbacks as it descended toward the small town. Vincent was the first to leave the road and head straight down the hill. Ulrick and Eram ran side by side for a moment. "I will meet up with you in the morning," Ulrick called as he left the road and started sliding down the hill.

When Ulrick got home, he fell into one of the chairs on the front porch. It was just over a mile through rough wooded terrain, on top of the already long day had worn him out and it would be a few minutes before he would want to go inside.

The cold evening air felt good after the run.

"Aren't you going to come inside? I haven't seen you in three months and you don't even bother to come in when you get home." There was kind annoyance evident in the voice that startled him from his near sleep.

"Oh, Sara! It is good to see you." Ulrick stood and gave her a hug. "I would have come in, but I ran down from the pass and I wanted to cool off before I came in."

"Where is Vincent?" Sara handed one of the two cups she held to Ulrick.

"He's not here yet?"

"No, I haven't seen him. Wasn't he with you?" she asked, her concern rising.

"Sara, don't worry; he'll be here soon, I'm sure. I'll wait out here 'til he gets here then we'll come tell you about the trip."

"Okay, but don't be too long. I've missed you boys." She shivered and went back inside.

Ulrick considered Sara to be his third mother. He only had vague recollections of his birth mother and some of those may have been his imagination after hearing stories of her. She had died when he was barely four. His second mother was his mother's sister--and Vincent's mom. She had raised him after his mom died. Then a few years ago, Vincent's mother had been killed. Sara had been hired as a maid to help David with the house and kids so he could still run his trading business. David and Sara never married, but they now lived as though they were.

Ulrick was nearly asleep again when he heard Vince's boots hit the wood floor of the porch. "Where have you been?" he sleepily asked.

"I stopped off for a drink." Vince sat in the chair next to

Ulrick.

"How did you know we were being followed, Ulrick?"

"Why, the interrogation?" Ulrick was a little annoyed by Vince's tone. "I don't know how I knew, but I still know. I can feel him like he is tied to me with a string." Ulrick glanced north with a distant look in his eye.

"If you can still feel him, where is he now?"

Ulrick's answer came after a moment's thought. "Precisely, couldn't tell you, but I would bet he is at the inn," he said sarcastically.

Vince ignored the sarcasm. "How long would you say he has been at the inn?"

"Oh... about an hour." Ulrick was starting to lose interest.

"He was not there when I was getting a drink. That was ten minutes ago, but he's been there an hour? I think you don't have any idea where he is and you just got lucky with the whole, we-are-being-followed bullshit!" Vince eyed Ulrick skeptically.

"I don't care what you think or believe or where this guy is. The question I have is why you care so much to begin with? Never mind. I don't care why you care. I'm going to bed." Ulrick left Vince sitting alone on the porch.

The next morning Ulrick woke a little late, but feeling good. He didn't notice the pull of the string until he got out of bed, but then every movement he felt the pull--distantly, from the direction of the inn. He did not give much thought to Vince's strange behavior from the night before. Instead, he headed out to meet Eram where they always met.

"Where are you headed off to? Aren't you going to eat breakfast?" Sara asked before Ulrick got to the door.

He slowed his departure. "I'm going to meet Eram. I am already late, so I plan on eating breakfast at the inn."

"I've been dreading this day," Sara said sadly.

"Why? What's wrong?" Ulrick's brows furrowed with concern.

"Well, it's just I'm losing my two boys and I'm having a harder time with it than I thought I would. Vince left sometime during the night and you are leaving now, and I have a feeling after this spring, I won't see either of you again. It's what boys do... they leave." She tried to hold in her emotion, but a single tear betrayed her.

"I won't be long this morning and I'll try to get Eram to come over for lunch and we can tell you about our trip," he said as he closed the door behind him. He did not like leaving Sara sad, but he also did not want to let Eram wait for him too long. Eram's father would probably be mad as it is.

The morning was cold, but clear. The sun would not reach the valley floor until mid-morning. Set between tall hills, the sun comes up late and sets early in Elk Valley. Ulrick was glad to be home. He enjoyed his winter trips with his uncle and cousin, but after three months he craved the comfort and consistency of home.

There is a big old pine next to the creek in the center of town, its trunk would take two large men holding hands to reach all the way around, and, it is probably hundred and fifty feet tall. There is a bench under the tree that faces the creek. It is at this tree that Eram and Ulrick always met.

As Ulrick approached the tree, he noticed Eram was already waiting. He was leaning against the tree, looking like a beat dog, like usual. Eram was a little taller than Ulrick, but because of his thin frame and poor posture, most thought him the shorter of the two. Ulrick had noticed that Eram's demeanor had improved on their trip, but now that he was home, he was back in the same old rut. "I see you made it home last night," Ulrick said as he approached.

"Yah... everything's back to normal. My dad has got a stack of shit for me to do and was bitching when I left," Eram said bitterly.

"Well, I won't keep you then. I just wanted to make sure you made it okay."

"Where are you headed now?"

"I'm on my way to breakfast. Want to come with me?" Ulrick expected a refusal.

Eram perked up. "I've still got a few grains, why not?"

"Won't your dad be upset if you don't get back soon?" Ulrick asked as they started off toward the north end of town.

"I'm counting on it," Eram said with a big grin. "Do you still have the strange feeling?"

"Yes. That is why I'm going to the inn."

"That's what I thought." Eram seemed more interested by what they might find than Ulrick did.

They stepped inside the door to the inn and looked around. The room had five tables with five chairs at each table. There was a fireplace on the right that was not burning well, filling the room with smoke. The innkeeper's son, Jonah, was working to remedy the problem. To the back was a bar, and behind that, the kitchen. There were a few customers sitting at the tables and a large man sitting on the far-right side of the bar with his back to the room.

"Hey, could you guys leave the door open?" Jonah called. Everyone in the room turned and looked their way.

Leaving the door open, they made their way to the bar and sat in the middle. "Do you think that is the guy?" Eram whispered, nodding toward the man at the end of the bar.

"I don't think so. I think he is in one of the east rooms." Ulrick whispered back.

"Ahh... you boys are back. It's good to see you," the middle-aged innkeeper said as he came in from the kitchen. "Eram, how was your first trip away from home? Did you have any luck with the ladies?"

"There is no place like home, Ben. I'm not just saying that either--there really is no place like Elk Valley. As for the ladies, I had about the same luck as I do here... not much luck at all," Eram responded.

"Well we're glad you boys are back. What can I do for you two today?" Ben cleaned the counter in front of them.

"Eggs with cheese for me and apple cider, if you've got it," Ulrick replied.

"And you?" Ben looked at Eram.

"The same, thanks."

Once Ben had left for the kitchen, Eram leaned in close to Ulrick and whispered. "The guy at the end of the bar was pretty interested when Ben mentioned our trip."

Ulrick watched the man out of the corner of his eye for a while. The man was big--not just tall, but thick as well. His hands and arms were covered with scars and it looked like there were a couple fresh wounds as well. His hair was shoulder length and black, except for some grey on the sides. He had a short black beard with grey on his chin.

"What do you mean, she's gone?" Eram's outburst brought Ulrick's attention back to Ben, who was setting plates of food in front of them.

"She left for Southport when the road south was passable; that was about a month ago," Ben replied.

"Do you know why?" Eram's voice turned sad.

"Not sure, but I heard it was because she was pining for one of you and her parents were not happy with the prospect of her ending up with one of you scoundrels." Ben smiled.

"Who are we talking about?" Ulrick asked.

"Lisa," Eram quietly deflated.

Ulrick could not help feeling bad for his friend. Lisa had grown up not far from Eram's home and they had spent a lot of time together when Ulrick and Vince were on their annual trips to the western territory. Eram had never thought of Lisa in a romantic way, until this last winter when he went with them. After the first week, he came to realize how much he missed her and by the end of the trip, Lisa was all he talked about.

In his concern for his friend, Ulrick had not noticed the man at the bar leave. He also did not notice him return, until he had pulled up a stool and sat down right next to him. The realization nearly knocked him off his stool.

"Ulrick?" the man asked, facing Ulrick in such a way Ulrick knew if he tried to run, he would not make it far. He would not have normally contemplated running, but the combination of the strange pull and the violent look of the man, had him ill at ease. The thought of fighting the large man was fleeting. Putting fight out of his mind, he did not know whether to answer or run--he was about to run.

Eram answered before Ulrick could do anything. "I'm Ulrick. What do you want?"

Ulrick looked at Eram, and there was his normally meek friend, standing shoulders back, staring the man straight in the eye, daring the man to try something.

The man instead of taking the challenge shook his head and chuckled. "You're Eram. And based upon your reaction, the young man before me, is indeed Ulrick." The man stopped chuckling and said seriously, "Ulrick you have nothing to fear from me. I was a friend of your father's. I was with him when he visited you ten years ago, and, I was with him when he died last fall."

Ulrick did not remember much of his father. If anyone asked, he would not even be able to say what he looked like. He also thought he was over the bitterness, but with the mention of his father, he felt nothing but anger.

"I don't know what you're talking about. I have no father," he said bitterly. He thought of getting up and leaving at this point, but he suddenly didn't have the energy.

The man just ignored his statement and continued. "My name is Kramdon. I have three things to give you: a letter from your father, an item of some... sentimental value, and the third I will give you when we've dealt with the first two."

Ulrick was about to continue his denial and refuse anything from this man. Obviously, Eram knew what he was thinking and interjected. "Ulrick, this man is not your father, he is simply delivering a message. When he is done, you can still hate your dad and he can get back to doin' whatever he does, which by the looks of it, is killing things... I've got to get going." Eram stuffed the rest of his eggs in his mouth and downed his juice, and then got up to leave.

He hadn't made it two steps when the large man stepped in front of him and put his hand out and said sincerely, "Ulrick's father would have been very pleased to know his son has friends like you. It has been a pleasure meeting you. I'm sure I will be seeing you sometime in the future."

Eram's brow furrowed in thoughtful surprise at Kramdon's strange statement. "Unless you frequent the Elk Valley blacksmith shop, I doubt you will ever see me again." Eram shook his offered hand and left.

"You are lucky to have that man as a friend." Kramdon

sat back down next to Ulrick.

"He was a fool to think he could survive a fight with you though."

"He knew he didn't have to fight me. His bravado was to keep you from running and making a fool of yourself." Kramdon pulled a folded paper out of his pocket and slid it in front of Ulrick.

Ulrick looked at the paper. It was folded in three with a seal on the front. The seal was a skull pressed into wax. He sat and looked at the paper and thought of what Eram had said. He realized he had looked like a foolish child.

"Do you know what it says?"

"Yes, I penned it for your father as he lay dying," Kramdon replied, as he pulled another item from a bag at his side. He set the item in front of Ulrick, to the side of the letter. The item was egg-shaped, with a smooth surface, flat on the bottom so it would not roll and was hinged in the back. "What you seek is inside. The container simply protects you from the pull."

Ulrick realized he had not felt the string attached to his heart since just after he had sat down. He looked at the letter and egg-shaped box contemplating which he would open first.

They both sat in silence for a while, then Ulrick reached over and pulled the box closer and started opening it. As soon as the lid was cracked, the string reattached to his heart with some force. He closed it back up for a moment, took a deep breath, then opened it quickly. What sat before him was a silver ring--shaped like a skull, with what appeared to be rubies in the eye sockets.

As soon as Ulrick saw the ring, memories from ten years ago came flooding back to him. He remembered being excited to see his dad for the first time. He remembered his father cutting his finger, then putting the ring on him. He remembered his dad did not stay long and he remembered him giving him a hug and saying goodbye with tears in his eyes when he turned and left. That was the first and last time he remembered ever seeing his father.

Ulrick wiped tears from his eyes and put the ring on his left middle finger. As soon as the ring was on, the pull disappeared, but he also felt weak for a moment, and the rubies in the ring seemed to darken. Ulrick looked at Kramdon expectantly, hoping for some explanation.

"Did you get your father's sword?" Kramdon asked.

"I think so. Some man came to the house at the end of last summer, handed my uncle a sword, and told him that it belonged to me. I haven't done anything with it. I couldn't even get it out of the sheath and it weighs as much as a horse, anyway."

"You may find that it is a little more useful now."

Ulrick looked at the letter. "Can I read the letter privately, later?"

"No, I promised your father that I would deliver the letter and make sure it was either read by you or to you."

Ulrick picked up the letter, broke the seal and started to read.

Ulrick,

Let me start by saying, nothing I say here is meant to be an excuse for my absence in your life. I regret the life I chose. My father had been a great man, and, in my haste, to be a great man like him, I made commitments to people that were not as noble as they seemed. As you will find, the items I inherited from my father made me highly sought after as a soldier. The pay was good and I was able to choose who I fought for, which kept my conscious clear.

I was on one of these missions when I met your mother and then my perspective changed. I had already made enough money to retire from fighting and buy a farm. I had always loved to watch plants grow and I had had enough death. So, I bought a farm just inland from Oyster Bay. The first year was great, you were born and I had a family. Then people from my past kept showing up wanting my help. I turned them down over and over again. I managed to stay out of conflict for several years. Then Edward came to me asking for my support in his bid to be governor of the Western Territory. I turned him down at first. When I did, his opposition took that to mean that I would support them. They were, however, not willing to take no for an answer. They killed your mother when I was in town picking up supplies. Luckily, I had taken you with me, or all I lived for would have died that day. The day after your mother was killed, I took you to your mother's sister, Jenna. I gave her all my money and told them to move somewhere that is far removed from conflict and politics. I then pledged myself to Edwards cause.

I tell you this now because you deserve to know the truth, now that you are old enough to understand. I told Jenna and Dave not to tell you any of this. I wanted you to grow up as normal as was possible and without the anger and hatred that filled my heart for years. I wanted to tell you in person, but there are sinister forces at work in this world and they are stronger than ever. I am dying, poisoned.

I've asked Kramdon not to tell you who was behind my death, because even though you probably have no love for me, I don't want you seeking revenge for me.

I have also avenged your mother; all that were involved are dead. This, like so many things, I am not proud of. I tell you so that you know there are none left to hate. Please son, don't let hate rule your actions.

I tell you my story not for your sympathy or your love, but out of my love for you. I hope my story will help you make better choices than I made.

I also want to give you some advice. Don't pledge your loyalty to anyone. The energies of the ring sometimes make your words binding. Don't go seeking fame or glory--the simple life is better. Keep your relation to me as secret as possible. Use the power you now possess only when absolutely necessary.

The ring Kramdon has given you is the key to the sword you hopefully already have. The sword is useless without the ring and the ring is useless to anyone, but you. I give these things to you hoping you will never need them, but there are those that know you are my son and there will be times you may need to defend yourself and those you love.

I pray that you may find love, happiness and peace.

Your father,

Ulrick

Ulrick put the letter down, wiped the tears from his eyes and looked at Kramdon. "It was easier to hate him for not being here."

"I know. Hate is easier, but it also exacts a higher toll."

"Here is the third item I am to deliver," Kramdon said, as he put a leather pouch down on the bar in front of Ulrick.

Ulrick opened the pouch and looked inside. It was about fifty imperial gold coins.

"Your father was never a big spender, so he tended to accumulate money. This is actually the smaller part. He gave a lot of his coin away before he died. This is what was left when I went through his things after.... I also used a little for travel expenses," Kramdon said matter of fact.

Ulrick ran his hands through his short dirty blonde hair and exhaled sharply. He had never even seen a one hundred grain imperial gold coin. He had seen one of the smaller fifty grain territorial gold coins. He could buy the biggest house in Elk Valley... no, with this much money he could buy the inn and still have some left over.

"Your father did not want me to tell you who was behind his death and I was going to honor that request, but as I drew closer to Elk Valley, I was attacked on the road by several groups of goblins. I believe these forces are aligned with the same group that killed your father and he believed his killers were sent by Edward of the Western Territory. I can't say why, but I will tell you the peace your father hoped for you may not come for a while. Choose your friends wisely and keep your own council. It was your father that helped me find peace; that is why I agreed to be his messenger.

That peace is now threatened," Kramdon said, then looked around to make sure no one was close enough to hear then leaned in closer and whispered, "I am being hunted. I expect an attack here tonight. I need your help to get out of town safely. I'm leaving today as unseen as possible. All I need for you to do is tell anyone that asks--and I mean anyone--that I am leaving tomorrow. Will you do this?"

Ulrick was quite surprised by Kramdon's change in demeanor. "I will do it, of course, but are you sure there isn't anything else I could do to help?"

"No, just that. Be sure to tell no one I left today," Kramdon whispered, got up and went to his room.

Ulrick sat at the bar, contemplating what he had learned. In the time it took to eat breakfast, his whole world had changed. He looked closer at the ring. The detail was precise--it looked just like a miniature version of a skull, even on the sides and the back, the whole thing. It looked like a skull with his finger going through it. The red gems in the eye sockets changed color slightly as he watched, going lighter then back to darker again. He could also feel the color fluctuation or the color fluctuated with how he felt...he could not tell which.

There was also something written. The writing started on the side, went across the forehead, and ended on the other side. The writing looked familiar in that he could make out some characters, but it was a more flowing script than he had seen before, so he was unable to read it.

He stopped looking at the ring and looked at Ben when he noticed he was watching him. Rather than have to answer any of the questions, he could tell were about to begin, he said, "Thanks for breakfast." Leaving three silver grains, he stepped outside.

Outside, the sun had finally climbed high enough to bathe the town in warm sunlight. Insects buzzing, and the distant sounds of people going about the day's chores, filled his ears as he made his way back to the large pine in the center of town, seeking solitude and some time to absorb the day's events. When he got there, he was relieved nobody was there. He sat on the small bench facing the creek. Out of habit he tried to see if he could spot the trout swimming in the small stream.

He tried to make sense of his feelings. There was still some lingering bitterness, but he felt like a weight had been lifted from his soul. He could be proud of his father for the first time that he could remember, but with that came guilt--for the bitterness and all the times he had traveled to the western territory and had never even thought to look for him. He then thought of the last memory he had of his father, saying good-bye for the last time, with tears in his eyes. He could not contemplate how hard it had to have been for his father to leave his son, knowing he might not ever see him again, for some reason he thought he could feel the sadness of his father's deathbed regrets seeping into him. At this point Ulrick put his face in his hands and sobbed.

After his emotional breakdown, he just sat for a while

watching the fish and listening to the sounds of the world. He felt better, and ideas for his future were starting to fall into place. There was a girl he wanted to marry. Her father owned one of the inns they stayed at, sometimes for a couple of weeks, waiting for the pass to thaw. Naomi had been closer to Vincent until the last two years.

Vince, the last couple of years, had spent a lot of time hunting in the hills rather than with her, so she had spent a lot more time with Ulrick. Ulrick had never liked hunting. Sure, the thrill of the hunt and the kill was exciting, but the cleaning of the kill always made him sick. This last trip, she had told them that she would marry whoever came back first and asked her. Ulrick knew it was him that she was really interested in, but since Vincent still professed his love every chance he got, she included him, which also gave Ulrick a way out. But he intended to go back as soon as possible, now that he had some money.

A strange noise pulled him out of his contemplation. It sounded a little like a dying dog-- he could not be sure, because he had not been paying attention. That is when he noticed it was already near midday, and he had forgotten to tell Eram to come over for lunch. Forgetting about the noise, he hurried off to get Eram for lunch.

Ulrick arrived a few minutes later at the Elk Valley Blacksmiths Shop. He went inside. The annoying clanging on the outside, was deafening on the inside. Eram was hammering what looked like a shapeless hunk of glowing metal into something a little more, square. Ulrick hated this place. It was loud, dirty and stank of wood smoke, oil smoke, oil and metal. He also did not care much for Marcus; that is why they would meet at the tree in the center of town.

"Eram," Ulrick called, obviously not loud enough, because there was no reaction. "Eram!" he yelled louder.

Eram stopped pounding and turned around. His face

and hair were wet with sweat, his arms were covered with scale that would fly every time he hit the metal, and his leather apron was black. Eram tossed the hammer and gloves on a table nearby and walked over to Ulrick, who hadn't bothered to come in any further than the door.

"Hey, how did it go after I left?" Eram asked.

"I'll tell you on the way."

"On the way? Where are we going?" Eram couldn't hide his interest.

"I promised Sara I would bring you over for lunch so we could tell her about our trip." Ulrick smiled.

Eram started taking off his leather apron. "I probably should stay here. My dad will shit nails if I'm gone when he gets back." He picked up a clean cloth and wiped his face, trying to get it as clean as he could, without being able to see it.

"Where is your dad?"

"He went to get us some lunch." Eram chuckled as he used the same cloth to brush the scale from his arms and clothes.

"You should probably stay here then. I'll let her know that you're busy and you'll be over for dinner instead." Ulrick didn't want Eram to get in trouble with his father.

"Like hell. I've been trying to come up with a reason to be done for the day anyway." Eram made his way out of the shop, obviously in a hurry to be gone before his father got back.

"No wonder you don't get along with your dad when you do shit like this." Ulrick was frustrated with his friend's behavior.

"Since you don't have any experience dealing with a father, your opinion is not valid or wanted. Are we going?"

Eram's tone conveyed none of the spite his words seemed to convey.

They walked for a while in silence, both a little irritated by each other's comments. It was about a mile from the Blacksmith shop to Ulrick's home. About halfway there Eram finally broke the silence. "Let me take a closer look at your new ring."

Ulrick took the ring off and handed it to his friend. "Don't take too long--it is uncomfortable to have it off. Apparently, I was not feeling Kramdon following us. I was feeling my dad's ring. I've got a box that when the ring is in it, I can't feel it, but the rest of the time it feels like it is tied to my heart."

"This is great. The workmanship is better than anything I've seen before. It obviously is magic. Do you know what it does? Do you know what kind of stones are in the eye sockets? Do you know what the writing says?" Eram gave the ring back.

"Huh... no, no, and Kramdon said it works somehow with the sword I got last summer." Ulrick was unable to keep from chuckling over his friend's excitement.

"You got a sword last summer? How come you never told me?" Eram asked, exaggerating his hurt feelings.

"When I got it, David told me not to tell anyone I had it, and to keep it hidden. I can't use it anyway. It won't come out of the sheath and it is too heavy."

After Eram was done asking about the ring. Ulrick took out the letter his father had written and gave it to Eram to read. Then he told him everything Kramdon had told him. Everything except that Kramdon was leaving today. They walked in silence for a moment as Eram read.

He said nothing about what was written, obviously knowing Ulrick would talk about it when he was ready. So, when he finished reading, he asked, "Where's Vince?"

"I have not seen him since last night after I got home. Sara said he left again before light this morning."

"Hopefully he is still gone. I've had more than enough of him this winter. If I have to hear another of his lies, I think I'll beat him in the face with a big stick"

Ulrick had nothing to say about that. He did not understand why Vince hated Eram so much, but he did understand why Eram hated Vince. Vince treated Eram like shit the whole trip, and Ulrick wasn't sure why Eram hadn't done anything about it.

When they got to the house, Sara was waiting on the porch with some boiled eggs and fresh baked bread. "I was starting to think you boys weren't going to find time for lunch today."

"I got a little side tracked, but we're here now." Ulrick picked up a piece of bread, stuffed it in his mouth. "Eram, go ahead and eat. I will go get the sword," he said around the bread in his mouth and went inside.

The house he lived in with his uncle, Sara, and Vince was bigger than most in Elk Valley. There were three bedrooms and a main living area that included the kitchen table with chairs, bench by the front door, and a wood burning cook stove in the center. Ulrick made his way to his room and located the sword, where he had put it under his bed. He pulled it out and looked at it. The sheath appeared to be lacquered wood, but he wasn't sure--the design was odd. There were what appeared to be joints down the sides. It looked as though it would just fall apart, but it didn't, and as much as he had tried before, he could not get the sword out. The hilt was large enough to use two hands, barely. It was wrapped in gold wire and the pummel had a skull on the end with gems in the eye sockets--just like the ring, but instead of bright red, they were lighter almost clear. The cross-bar appeared to be silver and was nothing fancy.

When he took the hilt in his right hand, his world changed. His sight went black for a moment and the sword felt heavier, causing him to almost drop it. He could feel a connection between the ring on his left hand and the sword in his right. It seemed as though something was flowing to the sword from the ring. The gems in the ring were dark, but now were dimmer, and, the gems in the sword were almost the same color and getting darker. When the gems evened out and stopped changing, the sheath clicked and the sword came loose. Instead of sliding out of the top though, it pivoted in the middle of the sheath. Then, to get it out, he only had to pull half the distance of the blade. He had previously thought the sword nearly useless, unless you were eight feet tall. There was no way he would have been able to pull the blade free--it was too long, and if he were to tie it to his hip which was usual, the tip would drag the ground. He realized now that he would have to tie it to his back.

He pulled the blade free. The sword was no longer as heavy as it was before; he could actually hold it out straight. He put the blade back through the center of the sheath, then pivoted it back into the sheath. He heard a *click* and it was back tight. Excited to show Eram, he hurried back out to the porch.

Ulrick stepped out onto the porch and handed the sword to Eram. Eram looked it over and ran his hand over every inch of it. "This is beautiful. The design is simple, but the quality is superb. It is heavy though...there is no way you could use this affectively," he said.

"Just wait. Go ahead, take it out," Ulrick urged.

Eram tried to pull the sword free, but was unable too. But he did not give up. He looked for a latch, then he inspected the seams down the sides. Finding no way to remove the sword, he looked to his friend and shrugged.

Ulrick picked the sword back up, readied himself for the jolt this time, and then grabbed the hilt. He didn't feel anything. The sword clicked free. He pulled it clear and handed it to Eram.

Eram sat there in awe, looking at every surface. Then he took the sheath and inspected it. "Genius. That's all I can say. Truly genius. The scabbard--how it opens up, the steel used for the blade--I've never seen before. It is perfect, like it has never been used. And the polish...I could never polish steel that smooth and sharp. The writing down the center of the blade looks the same as the ring, is it?"

Ulrick looked at the ring, then the sword. "Yah, I think it says the same thing. What's a scabbard?" he asked.

Eram looked up at his friend like he was stupid. "This is a scabbard." He held up the sheath.

"I thought *that* was a sheath."

"A sheath is usually made of leather and is more flexible. A scabbard is usually made of wood... or something rigid," Eram instructed.

The whole time Ulrick and Eram were looking at the sword, Sara just watched with a sad smile "I can tell you what the writing on the sword says".

Both boys turned to her, surprised. Before they could say anything, she continued, "It says, 'Honor, Family, Peace.'"

"You can read this language?" Ulrick was surprised by how little he knew of the woman that had been like a mother to him for years.

She smiled, understanding his confusion. She had been a simple cleaning lady after all. "It isn't a different language. It is an old style of writing no one uses anymore. I can't read it either. Your father told me what it says."

Her last statement hit Ulrick like a rock to the head. How could she know his father? She was not in Elk Valley the last time his father was here. Nothing in his life was as it seemed.

The shock actually affected him more than anyone could have anticipated. He took the sword from Eram and walked quickly around the back of the house. Then he ran into the woods behind his house. Ulrick didn't know how far he had gone, but he didn't feel tired--and tired is what he wanted. He didn't want to think anymore; he didn't want to talk to anyone. His mind was exhausted and confused, but his body was on fire with energy.

He slowed his run and swung his sword at a tree about as big around as his leg. He didn't care if he ruined it, he just needed to release his frustration.

The sword did not even slow down as it passed through the trunk of the tree. He did, however, find himself in the path of a falling tree. He stopped just in time for the tree to miss him. Standing there in the middle of a grove of aspen trees, he started chopping down trees as fast as he could. The smaller ones, he could not even tell he had hit anything. Sometimes swinging through, he could cut down all the trees in reach of his sword. Coming to a tree nearly as thick as he was in the chest. He swung. The sword sunk in most the way, but stopped just short of exiting the other side. He stood there staring at the tree.

He had been in the forest, but now he was in a small clearing filled with fallen trees. He should be exhausted, but he felt less tired than before he started. He looked down at his ring. The gems were a deep blood red and so were the gems in the sword. Frustrated, he grabbed his sword and made to leave, but his sword was stuck. He pulled harder. It didn't budge. So, he sat down on a fallen tree, looked at the ground and thought of nothing but the sound of his breathing and the light breeze through the leaves of the large tree he sat by.

2 - Eramus

A cool breeze made the already pleasant afternoon even more so. Eram and Sara sat silently for a while on the porch after Ulrick had left. Eram peeled another egg and ate it. Eram had always thought Sara was pretty for an older lady, and being alone with pretty ladies of any age made him nervous. He wanted to say something to end the uncomfortable silence, but he had nothing to say that didn't pertain to Sara's relationship with Ulrick's father. So, he sat there avoiding eye contact, eating eggs and bread until he didn't think he could eat anymore.

Unable to sit there in the silence any longer and unable to eat any more eggs, he finally said, "Ulrick will be fine by morning... I think. You make good bread Sara."

Sara laughed and shook her head. "Eram, I can see you have questions you want to ask, don't bother. Ulrick can tell you after I have had a chance to tell him everything."

"I understand... you wouldn't want Ulrick to find out that you had told me before him, about your relationship with his father. Obviously, those that were trying to control him found out about the two of you. So, he had to make you disappear before they could use you against him. That is when he sent you to Elk Valley. He probably asked you to watch over Ulrick for him while you were here." Eram paused for a moment, but then continued before Sara could say anything. "I only have two questions for you. Does David know? And, what is your real name?" Eram asked, never looking up from the floor until the last question, then he looked into Sara's blue eyes and held her gaze.

She was frowning at him, eyebrows together, trying to gage if he was just guessing. He did not know if any of what he suspected was true until he saw her reaction, then he knew he was on the right track. He smirked and looked back at the floor.

"Shit, damn, hell!" she cursed.

Eram had never heard Sara curse before or seen the look she was giving him. It seemed she was transforming into who she really was right before his eyes.

After a moment, she sighed. "My real name is Melisa." She knew she could not pretend any longer. "I think David would know if he thought about it, but his mind is always on the deal. This sort of thing is not important to him." She had a distant sad look.

They sat there in another uncomfortable silence for a while, before Melisa finally said, "You know Eram, you see too much. I think that is why you are such a sad person." She was not going to let him get away with manipulating her without a cost.

"I'm not a sad person."

"Then why do you never smile?"

"I smile plenty." He gave her a toothy grin.

"Yes, you smile, but that smile never reaches your eyes. In fact, the only time I've ever seen you happy is when you're with Lisa." She smirked at him.

Eram did not take the last comment very well at first, then he realized she was just paying him back. He laughed. "I think I might like Melisa better than Sara. I'm sure Melisa makes good bread, too." They both laughed at their previous discomfort.

They talked for quite a while, mostly about how Melisa was going to explain things to Ulrick. Then, as the sun drifted below the western hills, their conversation turned to the trip to the Western Territory, Eram gave her the details of the ups-and-downs of the trip. He told her about Ulrick's plan to marry Naomi.

After a time, they just sat waiting for Ulrick to return. Melisa brought out some hot cider to fight the chill that came as the sun went down. Sitting there drinking his cider, Eram started feeling uneasy. "Do you ever get the feeling that something bad is about to happen?"

"You feel that way now?"

"Yes, it's like a sick feeling in my gut." He looked around nervously.

"Typically, when I get that feeling, I ignore it and go to bed, but it's been my experience that when two people in the same place and at the same time get the feeling, something bad does happen." She got up and quickly headed for the door.

After what she said Eram was even more nervous. He stood and pulled out his dirk.

"Eram, stay here and stay alert. I'll be back." When she returned, she was wearing a chain shirt and wielding a short sword.

Eram looked at her questioningly.

"What, did you think Ulrick's dad met me at a ball? Is that all you've got?" she mocked, pointing at his little dirk.

Eram's nerves were getting the best of him so he remained silent.

"Do you smell that?" Melisa asked.

Eram smelled the air. "Yes, it smells like old man Higgen when he's particularly ripe."

"That's what I thought. We've got goblins to kill tonight. Stay close, but don't get in my way, and try to stay on the porch so they can only come at us from three sides." She threw the chairs off the porch, giving herself more room to move.

"Why don't we make our stand inside the house?"

"They'll just burn it down and move on. We've got to kill as many as we can to save as many of our neighbors as possible."

3 - Ulrick

The shadow of the western mountains was just covering the eastern mountains and Ulrick was still sitting and staring at the dirt. He was aware of nothing except the sound of the breeze blowing the leaves of the trees he hadn't chopped down. The distant sound of a hound dog baying did not catch his attention until the sound ended suddenly. Then the memory of the sound of a dog dying earlier, along with Kramdon saying he was being hunted by goblins made his gut clench.

He got up and headed for town. He made it ten paces, then he felt the pull of the sword-- not on his heart like the ring, but on the ring. He hurried back for the sword, grabbed the hilt and pulled. It would not budge. He yanked it as hard as he could, almost pulling his arm out of socket, but the sword still didn't move. He had to get back to town, so he could warn people if it wasn't already too late. So, he left the sword and started running for town. He made it about fifty strides and stopped. The pull was so strong that his left arm was actually being pulled back. His temper flared. "Fine!" he yelled at the sword.

He stalked back to the tree and put his shoulder against it and pushed away from the cut he had made. He let up and pushed again. He did this over and over again, each time he managed to get the tree to sway just a little more. He took hold of his sword, pulled as he put all he had into one last push. The sword pulled free. He wasted no more time--he had to get home before it was too late.

4 - Eramus

Eram and Melisa were waiting for the attack to come; they could hear goblins out in the woods. To Eram it seemed like there were hundreds of them, but he knew it had to be his imagination and fear that made it seem like there were more than there was.

"Cowards! What are you afraid of? A girl?" Melisa yelled to whatever was out there.

The taunt worked. Two goblins came out of the trees into the clearing in front of the house. Eram had never seen a goblin this close before, if at all. He was surprised by what calmly walked before them. They were short, about five feet tall. The skin on the one closest to him was black as ink. Its eyes were close together and slightly too big. Its black oily hair hung down to past its shoulders. It carried a club half as long as it was tall. It wore no clothes and it was obviously excited to see Melisa.

Other than being the same size, the other goblin looked nothing like the first one. Its skin was pale and greenish. It had no hair, and its ears were long and pointed. It carried a short sword and wore what looked like dog skin draped over its shoulders and tied with a rope around its waste. To Eram's horror, the skin was still dipping blood and dragging behind was the dog's head not completely severed from the skin. What bothered Eram the most though, was the fact that they looked like really ugly children. Both goblins were grinning big, eyeing Melisa with lust.

Eram started forward.

"Let them come to us. They will move in slowly, then attack fast. They will probably both come for me. Watch for an opening, then strike hard. These don't look too smart, but they are strong little bastards." Melisa said quietly, motioning Eram back to the porch.

She was right. They came closer, weaving side to side slowly, then both ran at her at the same time. Spinning out of the way of the one with the club, she extended her sword out as she came around and caught the other goblin in the face, tearing open its cheek and dislodging its jaw. The one with the club turned to come at her from behind.

Eram saw his opening. With his dirk held in both hands, he stabbed down to the side of its neck, just behind its collar bone. The scream the creature let out was wet with blood. Covered in blood, his hands slipped off his dirk when he tried to pull it free of his foe. Still alive somehow, it turned on him swinging its club for his head. Injured as it was, its swing was easy for him to duck. The club passed over his head; as it went by, he straightened back up and kicked it with everything he had between its legs.

The goblin dropped its club, then went to its knees. Not wasting any time, Eram picked up the club and smashed it into the side of the goblin's head with a sickening thud that forced its head into the wood post holding up the porch roof. The impact from both sides crushed its skull, spilling blood and brain onto the wood floor. Eram reached down and dug his fingers under the crossbar of his dirk and yanked it free of the dead goblin. Then he kicked it off the porch.

Dirk in his left-hand, club in his right, he looked for his next foe. Melisa was standing there watching him. "Not too bad, but slice with your dirk when you can. I know it's made for stabbing, but you don't want to lose it again."

The goblin that Melisa had hit had run off a few strides into the yard. As they waited for whatever came next, Eram could not help watching the goblin kneeling in the dirt, trying to put its jaw back in place--its tongue just dangling from the hole in its face. The sight turned his stomach, causing him to puke up the eggs he had eaten earlier.

The next half hour continued much the same. Melisa

managed to kill five and Eram killed two...and acquired a sword.

It was fully dark now. Whenever they had time to catch their breath between foes, they could hear fighting in the distance. The worst was the screams of women and children.

Eram stood shaking; he was exhausted and didn't know how much more of this he could take. He could no longer hold back the tears that came with the loss of blood lust.

He nearly pissed himself when he saw what came out of the trees. The beast was easily seven feet tall. He wore leather armor and carried a huge sword.

"You should run Eram--go to the inn and get help. I'll deal with him," Melisa said calmly.

Eram ignored her; he wasn't going to leave her.

The goblin--if that is what the beast was--looked around the yard. Then looked at the injured goblin still trying to put its jaw back. He calmly walked over to it and kicked it over, then stepped on its head. The small goblin's head held his weight for a second, then popped, squirting gore in a circle around his foot.

"Drop your weapon, woman. I am here to make sure you don't get killed," the giant goblin said, his voice a smooth baritone so deep Eram could feel it as much as hear it.

"Don't be offended if I don't believe you," she responded. "What about him?" She motioned to Eram.

The beast pointed to the goblin whose head he had just stepped on and said, "That was my son. Someone will pay for his death." Then he pointed at Eram. "This one will pay. He will suffer before he dies."

"Run, Eram. He's not going to kill me. Go to the inn and get help." Melisa seemed too calm.

"He might not kill you, but there are things worse than death, and I will not let that happen!" Eram yelled, more to the giant than to Melisa as he stepped up next to her.

"Boy, give up and I will not defile the woman." The giant's smooth speech seemed odd coming from such a large, ugly creature.

Melisa attacked.

She was not going to let Eram even think about giving up. Her first strike was easily blocked. She then started side-stepping, hoping to get the beast between them. The giant turned slightly toward Eram. This gave Melisa an opening. Knowing that going for the beast's body would do little to stop it, she rolled toward the rear, and as she came up, she extended her sword out and caught the beast's leg just above his heal.

"Hhrrg… you little bitch," he said as he backhanded her. She was far enough away and quick enough that the blow only managed to bloody her lip.

Eram, seeing an opening, went for the beast's sword arm, but before he could land his blow he was hit hard from the side. His sword flew from his hand as he fell hard to the ground.

The small, weaponless goblin that had hit him, started pounding on his face. Eram had a hard time seeing through the tears and blood. He did manage to get his hands free and was blocking most of the punches to his face. If he didn't do more though, he knew he was dead. It was then that time seemed to slow down; everything became clear and he felt no pain. Every punch seemed to come slowly, the pattern became predictable. He let the next punch hit his face, then grabbed the goblin's left arm with his left hand and pulled it out and away, turning the goblin away from him. He let the goblin continue to try and hit him with his right hand as he wrapped his right arm around the goblin's neck and started to squeeze as hard as he could.

It started thrashing, trying to get away. Eram just squeezed harder. The thrashing started getting weaker.

Eram saw the second goblin with a club just before the first hit came. The club hit his right forearm. Pain exploded and his sight went dim. Then more blows came one after another. He could no longer think or see.

His world was pain and blood.

Melisa realized her mistake when she saw Eram get tackled, and a giant goblin stood blocking her ability to help him. Her attack on the giant had not severed the tendon. So, he was effectively keeping her at bay while she watched as the goblin with the club started beating Eram. She had to do something. Eram would soon be dead. Hoping that the goblin was really trying not to kill her, she attacked.

5 - Ulrick

Ulrick encountered several goblins on his run back home. Apprehension rising, he simply sliced through them without hardly slowing.

He rounded the corner of the front of his house just as Sara's sword cut deep into a giant's knee. Instead of swinging its big sword and cutting her in two, the giant goblin punched her hard in the chest, knocking her onto her back several feet away. Sara saw Ulrick, "Save Eram!" was all she could get out with what little air was left in her lungs.

That is when Ulrick noticed a man-sized goblin pounding on his friend with a club. The goblin never saw him coming--Ulrick cut its head off. The angle of his sword sent the creature's head flying, hitting the giant in the back.

The beast turned, looked at Ulrick, hesitated for a moment, then ran as fast as it could manage with both legs injured. Ulrick started after it, but then thought better of it. He went to check on Sara first. She was starting to get up. Seeing him, she yelled at him. "I'm okay! Go help Eram!"

Eram looked like a pile of pulverized meat. Ulrick, shocked at what he saw, didn't know what to do. His friend was obviously dead. Sara arrived and started pulling the dead goblin off of him. "Help me!"

He grabbed the headless goblin and rolled him off to the side. Sara grabbed a second goblin and rolled it off the other side. Then she was leaning over Eram's face. "He's still breathing!" she exclaimed, relief flooding her face.

Ulrick breathed a sigh of relief. He realized now that most of the damage he had seen was the goblin on top of Eram--not that Eram looked good. One of the bones was sticking through the skin on his right arm and bleeding a lot. One of his eyes was swollen so badly that the skin was tearing.

His nose was broken and his lips were a mass of torn skin and blood. To Ulrick's surprise, Eram opened his one eye slightly and asked, "Is Melisa ok?"

"Who...?" Ulrick started to ask.

"I'm here and I'm fine." Sara had tears in her eyes.

Eram mumbled something and passed out.

Sara cut a strip of cloth from her pants. "Give me your shirt."

Ulrick quickly removed his shirt and handed it to her. Ulrick watched as Sara pulled Eram's arm straight, setting the bone back under the skin. Then she bandaged it using his shirt and then tying it to his body with the strip of cloth from her pants.

"Help me get him inside," she said, voice shaking almost as much as her hands.

They managed to get him inside and onto Ulrick's bed. Sara cut off all of Eram's blood-soaked clothes and looked for more bleeding. Other than his torn-up face, his broken arm and a massive amount of bruising about his chest and left arm, he seemed okay.

"I'll stay here with Eram; you go see if they need any help at the inn. Kill as many of those bastards as you can on your way. Once you get to the inn, have Ben send someone to get the wizard. Tell whoever he sends to hurry--if we don't get help for Eram tonight, he will probably die." Sara's tone was seriously urgent.

Ulrick wasted no time. He ran from the house and made his way to the inn, killing any goblins that he caught sight of. He slowed as he approached the inn. There were at least fifty dead goblins strewn about in front of the inn.

Hoping for the best, but ready for the worst, he entered the inn, sword ready. The main room was quiet, save for the sobbing coming from Ben's wife, Paula, whose face was dirty and streaked by tears.

Jonah was pacing, and Ben was looking after someone that had been injured, lying on one of the tables.

Kramdon was sitting in a chair looking out one of the front windows.

Ulrick wasted no time getting to the purpose of his presence. "Is there anyone that can ride out to get the wizard? Or does someone have a horse I can use so I can get him? Eram has been severely hurt--without the mage's help, he won't live through the night."

Jonah stepped up to Ulrick and calmly said, "I will go get him," then walked toward the kitchen's back entrance.

Ulrick was relieved because in his over excited state he realized he had offered to go but didn't know where the wizard was.

Kramdon looked up. "Ulrick, it looks like you've had your share of the fun tonight," he said without any joy in his voice.

"Fun? You call this fun!" Paula screamed. Standing, she started toward Kramdon with murder in her eyes. "If you had left earlier, it would have just been you dead instead of who knows how many innocent people!"

Ben hurried over and grabbed his wife and pulled her into the kitchen, still screaming.

Kramdon shrugged. "I kill dozens of goblins--saving who knows how many, and this is the thanks I get," he said dismissively, waving toward the kitchen. "The battlefield is a lot easier to deal with than this shit," his disgust plain on his face. "That bitch tried to kill me twice already. She said it was me they were after, so if I were dead, they'd leave. She said that after trying to knife me in the back!" Kramdon yelled the last statement, then under his breath said "I should have left today."

"Why didn't you leave? That was your plan, wasn't it?"

"I told four people I was sneaking out today and swore all to secrecy with the idea at least one of them would tell somebody. Then, whoever's behind the attack would have been looking for me somewhere in the mountains instead of here," Kramdon answered.

"But why didn't you just leave?" Ulrick asked again.

"Let me see if I can explain so you can understand. First, if I had snuck out of here unseen, then the goblins would have attacked looking for me and causing much more damage than with me here to help. If I had left and everyone had seen me go, then I would be dead out on the road somewhere. I wasn't in favor of that, but to get them to believe I was leaving, anyone I told would have to believe I was leaving… obviously the plan had holes, but I didn't have many options."

Ulrick decided he had better go help Jonah get ready to leave, but before he got to the kitchen Jonah returned with the wizard following close behind.

The wizard definitely looked the part. He wore a robe with a hood that he rarely put over his mostly bald head. What little hair he did have was white and unkempt. He walked erect and with strength, taking away any hint of frailty.

"That didn't take nearly as long as I thought it would" Ulrick's relief was plain.

"Where is Eramus now?" the wizard asked.

"He is at my home. I'll show you the way."

"Kramdon, why don't you come with us? We will probably want to bring young Eramus here. I'll need your help with that and you won't have to worry about a knife in your back if you come with us," the wizard said as he exited the inn.

On the way, Ulrick explained what he had seen of Eram's fight and the injuries he had seen. After hearing what Ulrick had said, the wizard started running for Ulrick's house.

They hurried through the house to Ulrick's room. Sara had brought a chair in so she could sit next to the bed. She got up as soon as they entered, allowing the wizard room to look at Eram.

He removed the blanket and looked him over then put his hands on his head and closed his eyes.

Kramdon motioned Ulrick out into the main room. "Help me make something to carry him on."

Ulrick went outside to cut some limbs. Kramdon had a large blanket laid on the floor when he got back. They rolled the limbs in the blanket from each end until it was just wide enough for Eram to fit. When they brought the stretcher into the room, the mage was still standing over Eram. He stood like that for what seemed a lifetime; the only sound in the room was soft gurgling whenever Eram exhaled. If the wizard was using magic, Ulrick couldn't tell. He would have thought there would have been something more spectacular to see.

Finally, the mage lifted his hands off Eram's head and turned to those in the room, "I've done what I can. He's got some swelling on his brain. If he makes it through the night, I think he'll live, but we need to get him to the inn, because if he does survive, he will not be about for several weeks."

The trek back to the inn was uneventful. It seemed that any goblins that still lived had left. Ulrick and Kramdon carried the stretcher while the mage and Melisa kept an eye out for any threat.

They entered the inn. Paula, having calmed down some while they were gone, motioned for them to put him on one of the tables. "Oh, you, poor boy" Paula said as she inspected Eram's swollen eye. Then she hurried into the kitchen and brought out a pan of warm water and a rag so she could wash some of the blood off of him. "Do you think he will be blind, when this heals?" She looked at the wizard.

The wizard thought for a moment. "It's hard to say for sure, but it is likely if he isn't blind in that eye, his vision won't ever be the same."

Everyone was quietly watching Paula carefully clean the blood from the uninjured parts of Eram's face. The exhaustion everyone felt had them glazed, except for Ulrick. He felt more awake than he ever had before. He was pacing, unable to focus his mind on anything but anger.

Paula stopped washing and said quietly--almost to herself, but loud enough for everyone to hear, "It's just terrible what happened to Eram, but I'm sure glad it was him and not my Jonah, Vincent or Ulrick."

Paula's comment shocked everyone out of their stupor. Kramdon looked like he was going to say something, but decided it wasn't worth it. Melisa looked like she was going to be sick and went into the kitchen.

"Kramdon, will you and Ulrick go out and search the town for people that may need help and let Eramus' parents know that he is here?" the wizard asked.

The sound of wood being chopped and the unpleasant smell of eggs being over cooked, woke Ulrick from his light sleep. He had fallen asleep on a chair looking out the front window of the inn. Some of the men from town were throwing the dead goblins on a pile of wood. Soon the smell of burning goblins would make the eggs smell pleasant, but the thought of eating them more repugnant.

Seeing Ulrick awake, the wizard pulled up a chair next

to him. "Interesting how events unfold. If I had not been here, this would have been much more tragic. The goals of those that sent the goblin men would most likely have been achieved, and that would have been unfortunate."

The wizard's comment caused all kinds of questions to swirl about his head. Like, who was behind the attack? What were their goals? But it was too early to get into all that, so he was going to ask the wizard what makes wizards so strange, but instead asked, "Why are you here?" The wizard rarely came into town and Ulrick was surprised and relieved he had been here the night before.

The mage's eyebrows raised and he smiled. "Ahh... of all the questions you could have asked, you asked the one question I am prepared to answer."

Ulrick sat looking at the wizard, waiting for the answer. He was about to ask again when the wizard started speaking. "I was planning to come get you later this spring, but about a week ago I had a dream. In that dream I was sitting on a peak of the mountain looking down on the pass you take into the western territory. The pass was covered in snow when the dream began, but as I sat and watched, it all melted away. So, I came earlier."

"Why..." Ulrick began, but was interrupted.

"I decided to leave home to arrive here last night, getting a room, drinking some wine and sleeping in a little." He looked at Ulrick purposefully and continued. "I even envisioned sitting in this very spot, eating some eggs, discussing our arrangement. Of course, I did not envision a battle with goblins, a sleepless night, or having no appetite for eggs."

"What were you coming to get me for?" Ulrick hurried to ask before the wizard could say anything more.

"I came to train you," the wizard replied, slightly annoyed by the interruption.

"Train me… for what?" Ulrick was confused.

The wizard looked at him like he was stupid. "If a wizard comes to you and says he's going to train you, what do you think that training might be… horsemanship? No! I'm going to train you to be a wizard." Shaking his head, he added more quietly, "Although I am pretty good with horses."

"I…," Ulrick began.

Again, the wizard interrupted. "It's not so much training though; it is more like some guidance to get you started. Training comes with time and use and will take the rest of your life."

Ulrick sat there, looking at the strange man. He had grown up seeing the wizard from time to time, but he had never before talked to him at any length. He found he was not enjoying the conversation much, and he did not want to go anywhere with him. He had plans. He was going to head back to marry Naomi, then maybe he could learn some wizardry or something, but not until he was married and settled. Having made up his mind and had given the wizard plenty of time to finish whatever he was going to say. "I have pla…"

Once again, the wizard interrupted. "Another thing, Ulrick, the eighth of that name, son of Silverskull, Hand of the Reaper who was son of Silverskull the Peacemaker, who was son of Silverskull the Goblin-Slayer, who was son of Silverskull the Liberator and so on… when a wizard comes and says he is going to train you, your plans change. You come from a long line of great men. Some great for the good they did, some for the death they wrought.

"I promised your father I would see that you would learn of your heritage and learn *from* your heritage. You were born with the ability to become a wizard. Your father was not. You have the potential to be much more powerful than your father. Your father is credited with killing ten thousand men and many more goblins than that. If you think for a minute that I will let someone with that kind of power walk into the world with no guidance..."

The wizard had started getting a little angry. So, he paused to compose himself, drink a little water and then he continued. "I'm sorry, I was getting a little ahead of myself there. Your father was a good man that found himself in a very bad situation. There are things about that sword and ring you just acquired that nobody alive knows, but me. You would be wise to take my offer for training." The wizard smiled fatherly at Ulrick.

Ulrick did not know what to say. He had heard of 'Silverskull Hand of the Reaper,' but he had never known that was his father. Now that he knew, it made sense and he felt stupid for not realizing earlier. He knew nothing of the other men the wizard had mentioned. He wanted to learn of his family, but he felt he needed to get back to Naomi, just in case Vincent thought to go back for her. He was going to explain to the wizard why he was hesitant, but he knew if he started talking, the old bastard would just interrupt, so he just sat there looking at the goblin pyre.

Finally, after several minutes of both of them watching bodies burn, the wizard finally spoke. "Ulrick, you may now speak your mind, but know this before you begin: I want nothing but the best for you. I was close to your grandfather and I knew your father better than most. But if I feel that your path will end with you being a threat to the empire or the lives of those I care for, you will not leave this inn today."

Ulrick was shocked by what the old wizard had just said. He'd never had anyone seriously threaten to kill him before.

The first impulse he felt was to quickly kill the wizard, before he had the chance to kill him. His sword was sitting on his lap--it would be simple to just do it, and then he could do as he pleased. The thought of the old man's blood splattered across the room seemed enticing, and sent a thrill up his spine.

He noticed, however, the wizard had become brighter and looked to be shimmering, after he looked at his sword. His next impulse was disgust at even the idea of killing the old man. Why had that thought even come to his mind?

Ulrick's thoughts were interrupted by an argument Eram's parents were having with Sara and Ben. "I'm not going to pay for last night and I'm certainly not paying for any more nights," Eram's father Marcus was saying.

"You can't take him to your house. He shares a room with two other people and sleeps on straw. He will die if you take him from here," Sara said, having a hard time not crying as she spoke.

"Look Sara, I've got a business to run. I can't have one of my rooms occupied by someone that isn't paying. If Marcus is not willing to pay, then he is going to have to leave. I feel bad, but that is how it will have to be," Ben said with as much regret as he could, but it was obvious to Ulrick, he did not care half that much.

"And who is going to feed and bath him? Certainly not me," Paula chimed in.

Ulrick looked to the wizard. "I'll be right back," he managed to say through a growing lump in his throat. Then he stood, sword in his hand, shaking with anger. He looked to the sword and paused for a moment.

He could vent his anger... *but not with this*, he thought as he dropped the sword point down. The blade sank several inches into the floor. He walked over to the bar where they argued and slammed an imperial gold coin down on the bar between them.

"This should be more than enough to pay for any care

Eram may need until he recovers." Then he looked at each in turn. "You people make me sick. I'm leaving town for a while." He turned and yelled, "When are we leaving, Wizard?"

"I can give you a couple days, if you need it."

"I'm leaving town tomorrow. If I find out that you mistreated Eram in any way I will want my money back with interest." Then he went back to his seat next to the wizard.

"My name is Bob." The wizard said after Ulrick got back to his seat.

"What?" Ulrick looked confusedly at the wizard.

"My name is Bob. Well, actually it is Robert, but I prefer to be called Bob. If we are going to be spending some time together, we can't have you yelling 'hey wizard' every time you need something, can we?" the wizard Bob said off hand.

Ulrick was having a hard time with the events of the last two days, nothing seemed real. It was like he was living a dream. He found out yesterday that his father was dead and was a better and worse man than he previously thought. He received a magic ring that makes him nearly unbeatable in a fight. His uncle's girlfriend somehow had a relationship with his father. Then, his best friend is nearly killed by goblins, which until yesterday, he had never seen up close if at all. Today he found out that he is a wizard. His best friend's father would rather his son die, than spend a little money. His father was responsible for the deaths of more people than he thought was possible of anyone. And to top it all off, he was going to be the apprentice to a great wizard named Bob...that threatened to kill him.

The laughter started slow and low but quickly became hysterical, and it became hard to tell if he was laughing or crying.

Bob motioned Sara over. "Help me take him to a room."

They lead Ulrick to one of the rooms and laid him on the bed. "Look in his pouch and see if you can find a small egg-shaped box."

Sara pulled it out. "Is this it?"

"Yes. Take his ring off and put in the box."

As soon as the ring was off and, in the box, Ulrick fell asleep.

When Ulrick woke it was still morning, but nearly noon. He stayed in the bed for a while after waking, to get his bearings. On the table next to him was the egg-shaped box and leaning against the wall was his sword in its scabbard. Somebody must have gone to his house to get the scabbard, because he was pretty sure that is where he left it.

He got out of bed. His clothes were still on and he smelled bad. The blood from last night's battle was dried and crisp. He picked up the box with the ring, put it in his coin pouch that was still tied to his waist, grabbed his sword, and went out into the main room of the inn.

Bob the wizard--he chuckled a little at that, but didn't get hysterical this time--was sitting in the same chair as earlier and was eating eggs.

He motioned Ulrick over. Ulrick sat down next to him and looked out the window. The goblins were now just a smoldering mass of ash.

"They burned pretty quick, didn't they?"

Bob looked at him, one eyebrow rose. "It's been a full day and a night."

"I slept that long?" Ulrick was subdued.

"Yes, you did. I think this little incident should illustrate why you need some training. That ring you have can cause some interesting things to happen to your emotions and your energy levels. You add the sword to the mix and then you can end up in a lot of trouble or dead." The wizard's eyebrows were still skewed.

"How do you do that?"

"How do I do what?"

"How do you do that thing with your eyebrows?" Ulrick looked at the old man's forehead with interest.

"Oh, you mean this?" he said as he raised one eyebrow and lowered the other, then raised the lowered and lowered the raised. "Years of practice. It's pretty effective, isn't it though?"

Bob finished the eggs he was eating. "Now that you are of right mind or as right as you've ever been, we can get back to what we were talking about yesterday."

"You don't have to threaten to kill me today. I decided to go with you." Ulrick interjected, before Bob could continue.

"I was referring more to our conversation about expectation. You see, I told you about my dream and of how I expected to be sitting in this chair, eating eggs after drinking wine the night before and sleeping in. Well, I was only one day off. Your inability to keep a level head after my disappointment remedied that disappointment." Bob stood and brushed the bread crumbs off his robe, then sat back down. "All joking aside, I think it is time for your first lesson...while yesterday's emotions and thoughts are still somewhat fresh in your mind." He stopped to pick something out of his teeth. "After I threatened you, you contemplated murder, did you not?"

Ulrick was suddenly on edge; he did not know how he should answer. He didn't want to admit to murderous thoughts, but the wizard obviously could see the truth. "I did," he finally said, but did not elaborate.

"If you had young man, you would have succeeded, but you would have also killed yourself and most of the people in the room with us. I had gathered enough energy within myself to insure your death and if you had killed or injured me, I would no longer have been able to restrain that energy and it would have been released in one great blast." Bob looked seriously at Ulrick.

"That energy is that why you looked to be shimmering?" Ulrick looked at his feet, ashamed to look at the wizard.

"Indeed, it is. And that is how as a wizard, I always know who is or has the potential to be a wizard. No one else in the room could see the 'shimmer' but us. If you use magic, I can see it, and because I am practiced, it is much clearer than a shimmer. I can see what kind of energy you have manipulated and how much of that energy you currently have under your control."

Ulrick, while listening, had opened the box with his ring in it and was looking at it. He was about to put it on.

Bob leaned over and put his hand on his. "Don't put that on just yet. You need a break for a while."

Ulrick looked at him confused.

"To explain, I will have to explain the different types of energies a wizard can use. There is thermal energy that controls heat and cold. There is electrical energy. The most apparent manifestation of this energy is lightning. There is life energy. This is the energy your ring utilizes when you take a life with your sword, the energy that holds the physical body and the spirit together, is released and captured by your ring. A small amount or a lot, if you don't know how to use it, of the life force is transferred into you.

"If you are a mage that specializes in life energy, the energy can be manipulated so one can transfer life into others. You can't bring someone back from the dead but you can give them energy that can help hold their spirit and body together as they heal. And there is spirit energy. Spirit energy is similar to life energy, but different in that it actually steals energy from the spirit of a person or animal. The process is usually fatal and the energy is tainted, in fact the more tainted the more power.

"Spirit or blood mages as some refer to them, use items to store the energy stolen. This type of magic can be taught to and used by anyone. Most people don't have the stomach for it because the process of gathering the energy warps the soul-- and utilizing the energy also causes damage. Those that practice this are, or will be, quite mad." Bob paused to ask Ben for some water.

"So Ulrick, if your ring utilizes life energy, why would I not want you to put it on now?" Bob looked at Ulrick critically.

Ulrick sat thinking. He thought he had an idea, but he did not want to sound stupid. "I don't know."

"Think about it for a while, while you start getting ready to leave." Bob seemed disappointed in Ulrick's answer. "You still want to leave today or do you want to take another day because you slept through yesterday?" Bob got up and started toward his room, stopping to wait for Ulrick's answer

"I would like to leave tomorrow instead, if that's okay." He got up also and made his way to Eram's room.

Ulrick didn't want to disturb Eram's sleep or that of Eram's mother if she was in there. So, he cracked the door and peeked inside. The room was just big enough to fit a bed, a small table with just enough room to put a chair to either side of the bed. Opposite the door was a small window that faced east.

The chair on the right side of the bed was empty. Sara sat in the chair on the left. She was holding Eram's hand; her head was bowed and her eyes were closed. Ulrick did not want to wake her, so he started closing the door. "Come in, Ulrick. I'm not asleep, and I would like to talk to you before you leave," she said just loud enough for him to hear.

"I'm not leaving until tomorrow, I can come back later," he whispered back.

"No, I need to talk to you and you might be too busy later." She was more insistent.

Ulrick entered, quietly closed the door, and sat in the empty chair. Eram had always had a little thing for Sara. He had always said there was something different about her that had him fascinated. He had always said it was the way she walked and the look in her eye, like she knew something that no one else knew, and that something was funny.

Ulrick had never seen what Eram saw, but after the other night--when she took control of the situation, making sure Eram was taken care of--he got it. The look she was giving him now had reminded him of Eram's fascination; he could tell she was trying to find the right words for what she had to say.

Ulrick really did not want to talk about his father anymore; he had heard more than enough. So, he asked, "how is he doing?" motioning to Eram.

"I think he will be okay. Most of yesterday, I wasn't sure." They both sat in silence for several minutes.

Sara was dressed differently. She usually wore a loose dress. She wore leather pants and a loose-fitting shirt today. Her brown hair, instead of being held up on top of her head, was down around her shoulders. She looked younger. He realized he did not know how old she was. He really did not know anything about this woman who was like a mother to him.

Ulrick realized Sara was waiting for him to start the conversation. "Sara, was my dad a good man? Kramdon liked him, and the wizard said he was a good man trapped in a bad situation, but can anyone called "the Hand of the Reaper" be a good man?"

"First, my name is Melisa, not Sara. Now that your father is dead there is no reason to pretend anymore." Melisa looked at Ulrick, searching for the right answer to his question. "Was your father a good man...?" she repeated to herself looking to the ceiling. "No, your father was not a good man. He was good to me and he was good to Kramdon, but who isn't good to their friends? The wizard is like so many people that equate feelings of friendship with goodness. A good man is honest when it is hard to be honest. A good man sacrifices himself for the good of others. Your father did the bidding of an evil man. He told himself that he was stuck and had to do it, or you and others he loved would suffer. But how many other families suffered so his wouldn't. The truth is, your father was afraid of not being able to be someone great like his father. That fear is what made him exactly what he feared he would be: a dark shadow of his father." Melisa paused, taking a deep breath to calm her increasing emotional frustration with a man she had loved--a man that was dead and she missed badly.

Ulrick let her settle herself--he could tell this was going to be harder for her than it was for him. He was feeling a little ashamed about his behavior when he had found out that she had known his father. "By your definition, do you know any-one that is a good man?" He wanted to change the subject from his father.

Melisa took a drink of water, then poured a little into Eram's mouth. Most just ran out the side. "At least it helps keep his lips moist." She put the cup back onto the small table be-side the bed.

"Most men don't fall into the category of good; some,

because they are not good. Others may not have had the opportunity to prove themselves--to test their character. Eram is a good man. I have never heard him lie, and he had his test the other night. When that giant came out of the woods, I told him to run. Most the men I have known would have already been gone. I was hoping he would run, so I could injure the beast and run myself, but instead he stayed. He had to know he had no chance; he's not stupid. That was no ordinary goblin--that beast could take on ten well trained soldiers without much effort. Eram stayed because of me." The last statement she said through tears. "Now he is barely alive and the people of this town don't care." Tears turned to anger.

Melisa, still emotional continued. "You are a good man or you have the potential to be a good man. Your future is whatever you want it to be. Be something your dad wasn't; use what power you have to help those that can't help themselves." Melisa ran her hands through her hair, took a deep breath, and let it out slowly. "I know your father is a little bit of a sore subject for you right now. So, let me begin by telling you a little bit about myself and how I met your father.

"I was born in a small town in the northern territory. I don't remember the name--if it even had a name. My father beat my mother and his kids, including me. I was a little rebellious and decided I could find a better life for myself by myself. I left home when I was twelve. I lived in the woods and hills, stealing what I could from farms and people traveling between the cities. This was actually working out pretty well. I had found a small cave to shelter in during bad weather, and I only went hungry during the first winter.

"I quickly learned, however, that I was not the only young person doing what I was doing. There was a band of thieves that patrolled that same area. I had escaped their notice for the first summer and winter, but that first spring, I was caught stealing by them. The penalty for stealing in their territory was to join their group or die.

"I joined, of course joining wasn't pleasant. Girls tended to have only one use in the group, as you can imagine, but I was not going to let myself become a whore. I practiced with my knives every day and got a couple of the lower level boys to help me learn how to use a sword. I got pretty good. Perhaps I had more reason to excel or I had a natural talent. Either way, I was good enough for some of the more difficult jobs. That meant I no longer had to be a whore.

"I did this for several years. Then a mercenary group came through 'cleaning up the crime' in the area. Rather than find myself on the end of a spear or hanging from a rope, I joined them. It was a few years after joining the mercenaries, I met your father. Actually, it was after your father had--with a much smaller force--slaughtered us. We were down to just a few of us, when your father came to take my head. I went to my knees. That sword of yours clipped my helm, sending it flying. Before he got his next swing in, he noticed I was a girl and he stopped. Apparently, he did not make it a habit of killing girls.

"When I met your father, he had just gotten back from visiting you. That was ten years ago. I joined his army--of course, it was that, prison, or worse."

She got up, went to the door, opened it and called for Ben, asked him for some sugar cubes and water, then returned to her seat.

Ulrick was speechless; he would have never imagined Sara... or Melisa to be a thief, let alone a whore. He found himself feeling sorry for the life she had led, and a little guilty for the ease of his own life. He knew it was stupid to feel guilty, but it made his problems and complaints seem selfish and small. He remembered all the times she had sat and listened to his problems and giving him advice. He found himself embarrassed by those memories. He didn't know what to say. There were so many things he could ask, but he asked, "How old are you?" instead of saying something intelligent.

"I don't know for sure, but I think early thirties."

She answered the light knocking at the door. Ben handed her a cup and a small bowl with some sugar in it. "I don't have cubes--hope this will work for you." Ben never looking at Ulrick directly, asked, "Do you want anything, Ulrick?"

"No, I'm fine thanks."

Ben closed the door and Melissa sat back down and mixed a little sugar into the water and dripped it into Eram's mouth.

"You see, until yesterday, you would have said Ben was a good man; now you know the truth," Melisa said, with just a hint of the anger she felt. "Before I met your father and got out of the 'business,' I would have stuck a knife in that man for refusing to help a friend of mine." Her matter of fact tone, was a little disturbing to Ulrick.

"How did you do it? I mean, be 'Sara' for all these years?" He regretted it, as soon as the question left his mouth.

Melisa could see his regret, but gave him an icy stare anyway. "When you work with thieves, you learn to play roles. It's not just waylaying people on the road. We ran scams and played on people's sympathies. I was one of the best at it, but really it wasn't hard. I had always wanted to be a mother and a wife-- live the quiet life. Also, the only deception these last few years was concealing my past. Sometimes I try to forget that I'm not really your mother." She gave him a warm smile. "These last couple years have been the best of my life."

"Why do you have to quit pretending if you like it here so much? Nobody really knows who you are."

Melisa looked at him for a while before answering. "No, I can't do it anymore. You and Vince are leaving, and even though I care for David, I don't love him and he doesn't love me. We have a relationship of convenience. There is nothing for me here anymore. I think I will be moving south to warmer weather, maybe Southport," she said reflectively, then added, "I, of course, will not leave until I know Eram will be fine. So, don't worry while you're gone with the wizard."

"I have one more question for you. I don't want to know any details about your relationship with my father--it doesn't matter, but the wizard doesn't want me to wear my ring for a while. He expected me to understand why. You knew my father for several years; maybe you could give me some insight so I don't look so stupid next time he asks?"

She contemplated her answer for a few moments. "Your father always spent several hours alone after a battle. Most men get together, drink and tell stories to make everything seem okay, even though they feel terrible inside. I asked him why. He told me that the ring draws its power from the death of those he kills and with that power comes a residue of the emotion they felt at the time of their death. He said it had taken him some time to be able to separate his feelings from those of the dead, and he needed time alone or he would get his feelings confused."

"Thanks, Melisa," Ulrick said with sincerity, but did not elaborate.

"For what?"

"For telling me the truth, but mostly for being my mother for these last few years--you will make a really great mother someday." He walked around the bed and gave her a hug. "What you were does not mean anything. It is what you are now that matters, and you are a good person by any definition." Then he let go of her, picked up his sword and started leaving. Just before he opened the door he added, "Let me know when he wakes up, if I'm still here."

Ulrick spent the rest of the day preparing to leave. He bought a horse and a couple of days' worth of food. He did not know how long of a trip it was, but he figured a couple days would at least get him to someplace he could buy more. He hadn't seen the wizard since their conversation that morning--of course, he hadn't gone out of his way to look for him.

He stopped by to check on Eram just after dark; there was no change, so he rode his new horse home. He did not have much experience riding so he figured he better start getting used to it.

Ulrick woke with a start. He had a strange feeling that he was being watched. He was facing the wall so he could not see if someone was watching. He didn't want to give in to his paranoia, so he did not move. Still the feeling was there, but he resisted turning to check. Finally, he turned to face the room. Sitting in the chair Melisa had brought in to sit next to Eram, was the wizard Bob.

"Good morning," Bob said. Ulrick started to respond, but the wizard interrupted. "Did you wear the ring yesterday?"

"No sir, you said not to, so I'm not going to, until you give me the word."

"I am giving you the word; put it on."

Ulrick turned the rest of the way over, picked up the egg-shaped box off the small table next to his bed, and braced himself for the pull that occurred once the box was opened. He opened the box, and even though he thought he was ready, the pull was so strong it took his breath away. He hurried to get it on, because he knew the discomfort would stop, as soon as he put the ring on. With the ring on, he looked at the wizard expectantly.

"How do you feel?"

Without hesitation, Ulrick a little louder than he intended said, "I'm a bit annoyed that you feel it is okay to just walk into my room and watch me sleep."

"I did not watch you sleep. I watched you wake up." Bob's smirk was infuriating.

"What the hell difference does that make? The problem is that you just walked in uninvited!" Ulrick said even louder than the first comment.

"Okay, take the ring off and put it back in its box."

Ulrick did as he was told, closing the box quickly to ease the discomfort of having the ring off.

"Now how do you feel?" he asked.

"Again, I'm a bit annoyed that you feel that it is ok to just walk into my room and watch me 'wake up,'" Ulrick said, a little more subdued.

"No. How do you feel? Not, what do you *think*," Bob corrected.

Ulrick thought a moment. "With the ring on, I felt like ripping your throat out and watching with glee as your blood pooled on the floor. Without the ring, I just want to throw you out on your ass. Is that better?"

"Much better. I think you now understand why you should be careful with that ring." Bob chuckled. "Are you ready to leave?"

"I think so; I got enough supplies to last a couple days. You weren't around, so I just figured a couple days would be safe," Ulrick said, annoyance still evident in his voice.

"I noticed you also bought a horse. That is good; it would have been hard for you to keep up otherwise," Bob said as he left.

Most of the morning was spent loading his gear onto his

horse, which he made more difficult than it needed to be. The wizard had left and told him to meet at the inn when he was ready. It was nearly noon when he got to the inn. The wizard had obviously seen him coming up the road and had come out of the inn to put the last of his things into the saddle bags, that sat on a beautiful white stallion. Bob had also changed his robe; he now wore a bright white robe to match the horse, and, he had the hood up covering his unkempt hair. He definitely looked the part now, almost respectable, even though his name was Bob.

Ulrick checked on Eram, and was disappointed that there had been no change in his condition. He said his goodbyes and then they got going.

From the inn, they traveled south along the road that ran beside the creek. Most of the homes in Elk Valley were in the trees to either side of the valley. The valley itself was tall grass with the creek, the main road, and a few trees here and there. As they passed the large tree with the bench, Ulrick thought of Eram and the time they had spent sitting under that tree talking of meaningless things, trying to catch the fish with their hands, while wading in the icy water and solving the world's problems. He was going to miss those days. Leaving now he knew he was never coming back, at least not to the way things were.

He hoped Eram would recover soon. Ulrick felt bad for his friend. Not just because of his injuries, but because his future seemed so bleak. He could not imagine spending the rest of his life working the forge. He had helped Eram a few times and it was miserable; the heat, the smell, and not to mention...it was almost impossible not to get burned regularly.

Before they had gotten back from the Western Territory, Eram had mentioned to him that at least he had Lisa to go back to. Eram figured he could handle life as a blacksmith as long as she was there with him. Now he did not even have that.

The tree was behind him a fair distance when Ulrick took one more look back, swallowed the lump in his throat, shook off the sadness, then looked forward both literally and emotionally.

"Where did you go yesterday?" Ulrick asked Bob.

Bob said nothing for a time. Ulrick was about to repeat the question thinking the old man hadn't heard him, when he finally answered. "Typically, what I do is my own business and I don't like to be questioned. If I want you to know something, I will tell you."

"Have it your way, old man. I was just trying to make some conversation, seeing how we're going to be traveling together." Ulrick didn't try to hide his annoyance with Bob's strange personality and mood swings.

Bob stopped his horse and looked at Ulrick seriously. "Ulrick, if we are going to get along, you're going to have to start listening. I said 'typically.' I was going to finish with an explanation. If you had some patience, I would have gotten to it. But you opened your mouth and made an ass of yourself."

Bob turned forward and started back down the road. "Ulrick, you may be the center of your world, but remember the rest of us are also the center of our own worlds. What is most important to you, is most likely not the most important to those around you, if important at all. I have lived alone for several of your life times. Conversation to pass the time is meaningless to me," the wizard said, his tone instructional condescension.

Ulrick said nothing, he just rode and listened. It was good he did not have his ring on or he may have gotten violent.

They rode in silence for several hours. Ulrick figured if they stayed on this road, they would be in Smithville just before dark. He did not know, however, if that was where they were headed and he did not care to ask.

The scenery had changed quite a bit. Instead of tall pines and aspen with snow covered peaks, they were in juniper covered hills. The air was a bit warmer also, which was a refreshing change.

Ulrick was just getting used to and appreciating the silence when Bob decided to continue their earlier conversation. "I was looking for my second pupil. You see, I did not come to Elk Valley just for you, there was another that magically is probably more valuable than yourself. But they were not there," Bob said, almost to himself.

Ulrick was now interested again. "Can I ask who this other person is?"

Bob looked at Ulrick for a moment, a mischievous grin on his face. "Can't you guess? Elk Valley is not a large place, after all." Seeing Ulrick's annoyance, Bob continued his tone instructional, but without the condescension of earlier. "The reason I ask you to reason for yourself, Ulrick, is because too many young people would rather just get the answer without work. You have lived your life with people that have taken care of you. When you ask, they answer, hoping to instruct... but really, the best instruction is for you to find the answer yourself. So, think about it. I know you can figure it out, then ask me if what you have figured is correct or not."

Ulrick thought a moment. Who was not there? He came up with two: Lisa and Vincent. He could not figure which because he had nothing to go on. "Is it Lisa or Vincent?"

"That was much better, but you could have figured exactly who if you had spent more time figuring, but I will spare you. Lisa is the other, and the situation has me...quite upset with her parents.

I had told them she had the talent several years ago, and that I would like to teach her when she came of age. I wanted to train both of you together. Kill two birds with one stone, as

77

it were, but they sent her to Southport instead."

Ulrick could tell this had been what was really bothering the wizard--and he had been getting the stick because of it.

They topped one of the larger hills. From the top he could see the town of Smithville. Ulrick had been to Smithville a couple of times. He did not care much for the town that got its name from the fact that most of the iron and steel products for the whole Southern Territory came from here. The sky above the town was marred by an orange-brown smudge caused by the smoke from all the forges.

"Okay, here is the plan. We are going to spend the night in Smithville. In the morning you are going to buy some new clothes, and then we will continue to my home, which will take most of the day tomorrow. I will teach you some basic principles--that will take about a month. then we are going to see to Lisa in Southport," Bob said.

"What's wrong with my clothes?"

"Time for lesson number two," Bob said with exaggerated excitement. "Nothing is wrong with your clothes in the normal sense, but as a mage you need mage clothes. I know what you are thinking. Why can't I be a mage and look normal, right?" He looked at Ulrick.

Ulrick shrugged and nodded.

"Because manipulating energy is not quite as easy as it sounds. Well, it *is* easy, but it is miserable at the same time. Every pain, itch or annoyance is multiplied by the amount of energy you are controlling. So, let's say the waist of your pants are too tight when you start gathering energy, that minor discomfort which you have learned to ignore is now excruciating. If you have a slight headache, again it compounds. Even if you are completely comfortable, the holding of energy is like an itch, and the release of that energy is like a sneeze. Once you need to sneeze, you just want to get it over with. The sneeze itself is somewhat pleasurable because it relieves the itch. So, you will want to wear soft comfortable robes, or the amount of energy you can gather will be minor before you give into the release of the discomfort."

Bob looked at Ulrick and gave him an evil grin, then continued. "Being just a beginner, the soreness in your backside from riding all day would make it impossible to even light a small campfire, if that was your skill." Bob took a long drink from his water skin. "Of course, we are going to have to get your ring and sword under your control before we get into any of the fun stuff. Speaking of your ring, how do you feel right now?"

Ulrick, while looking at the distant town said, "Actually, aside from my sore ass, I feel pretty good. I am actually finding some of your knowledge interesting."

"Good. Go ahead and put your ring on again, but remember how you feel now and remember the change in how you feel is not coming from you; it is coming from dead goblins."

Ulrick took out his ring and put it on. Instantly he felt angry, mixed with hatred of himself and everything around him.

"Take long deep breaths; try to separate the feelings. Focus on the feelings you had before you put the ring on," Bob encouraged.

"I have a ton of energy. I feel like I could run forever," Ulrick told bob. "What would happen if I just ran until the energy and feelings were gone?"

"That might help as long as you don't run too long. If you overdo it, once you take the ring off, you might sleep for two days--and you don't want to do that again."

"How much further is Smithville? If it's not too far, I could run beside the horses to town; my butt could use the break from the saddle anyway."

Not waiting for Bobs answer, he got off his horse, handed the reins to Bob, and started running down the hill. He could not wait--he had too much energy and anger. He just wanted to break something and kill. He unconsciously started looking for any animals to kill. He hoped something would cross his path so he could satiate his lust for death.

Bob caught up to him after tying the reins to his saddle. Ulrick was running faster than the horses could keep up with while walking, so Bob would walk a while, then trot the horses to catch up. The first time he caught up, he again told Ulrick to focus on his own feelings while he ran. Each time he would encourage him to not give in to the foreign feelings. Ulrick ran for nearly an hour when they started passing outlying fields and pastures.

"Ok, that is enough running," Bob called to Ulrick.

Ulrick stopped and waited for Bob to catch up again. "At first, running actually made it worse. I just wanted to kill something. But after a few minutes, the rhythm of my breathing and my feet calmed my need for blood. Actually, you giving advice from time to time helped also, but I still feel like I could run a few more hours."

"Now take the ring off, but before you do prepare yourself for immediate exhaustion."

Ulrick took a few more, long deep breaths, then took the ring off. He was surprised. He felt tired, but not like he thought he would have.

Bob was also surprised he did not fall over once the ring was removed. "If you think your emotions are stable and you're feeling okay, go ahead and put it back on. But if you happen to kill something with your sword, be aware that you may need to take it off again before you do something stupid."

Ulrick put the ring back on, climbed back onto his horse, and took a long drink from the water skin.

"Before we get into town, you need to cover the hilt of that sword. Remember your father was hated in the Southern Territory. Here, people will want to kill you. We could handle any trouble we may get into, but the best way to handle trouble, is to avoid it in the first place." Bob started moving again.

It had been a year since Ulrick was last in Smithville. Maybe it was the time of day or maybe something was indeed different, but the place seemed less friendly--if a town of blacksmiths and their laborers could have been considered friendly to begin with. Either way, he felt a kind of unease as they rode down the main road into town.

They stopped in front of an inn and tied the horses to the post and walked inside. The room they entered was small, with just enough room for a long, tall desk and a few chairs. The air felt close and musty.

The man at the desk looked up from a book he was reading, his eyes squinting, trying to focus on the two men in front of him. Once he was able to make out what was before him, he asked, "What can I do for you two gentlemen?"

"We need a large room with two beds." Bob looked over the room, hardly sparing a glance at the man at the desk. "We also need care for two horses until tomorrow afternoon." Bob still did not look at the man.

"I'm sorry sir, we don't have a room with two beds," the man said apologetically. "We do have two rooms next to each other, though," the man continued, his tone helpful.

"Doesn't the room at the east end of the second floor have two beds?" Bob looked at the counter in front of the man.

"Uh... that room is already rented, sir," the man said.

Bob's demeanor changed instantly. He leaned forward over the counter. "Huh... why is the key hanging on the hook there behind you then?" Bob's voice dripped with angry sarcasm.

Before the man could say anything, Bob continued, "You have lied to me twice, sir. I don't take too kindly to being lied to, so here is how you are going to make things right. First, you are going to give me the key to room 205. Then, you are going to get someone to take extra good care of our horses-- and you are going to charge us no more than the standard size room rate."

"I can't rent you that room for standard rate. We usually get one and a half the standard rate." The man was not backing down; his face was just inches from Bob's.

Ulrick could see the wizard's anger, even though from the side, Bob's face was not visible to Ulrick. The room got chill and so did the wizard's voice. "You don't have a room with two beds, therefore I will pay the standard price for room 205." Just as Bob finished his words the man's book burst into flame.

The man jumped back away from the counter, grabbed a rag and started trying to put out the fire.

Bob reached across the counter and took the key from the hook, then looked to Ulrick with just the hint of a grin. "Do you think you can handle both of our bags?"

"Yes, if you take this." Ulrick handed his sword to Bob.

When Ulrick returned with the bags, Bob was no longer there. The man behind the counter was assessing the damage to his book. "Up the stairs, end of the hall to your left," he said without looking up.

When Ulrick arrived at the room, he entered and set the saddlebags on the floor at the foot of the bed that Bob was not lying on. "I thought you wanted to avoid trouble?" He sat down on his bed.

"I'm afraid trouble may be unavoidable." Bob's tone was thoughtful. Ulrick was about to ask why, but Bob continued. "I have spent too much time studying the last couple years--things have deteriorated much faster than I would have thought possible. Hopefully it isn't this way everywhere."

Ulrick was lost; he wanted to ask a few questions, but knew as soon as he started the old man would just interrupt, so he just sat there looking at Bob, waiting.

Bob, lying there looking at the ceiling seemed to be deep in thought, then suddenly he looked at Ulrick. "I'll have to explain later. I need to find out more of what is going on, otherwise my explanation may be invalid."

Bob sat up and rubbed his eyes. "You hungry?" He didn't wait for an answer before continuing. "I know of a place not far from here that serves great beefsteak." Bob stood and stretched, popping his back. "At least I know of a place that used to serve great beefsteak--who knows now?"

Ulrick stood and started putting his sword under his bed. "You better bring that. We are going to find trouble tonight. How much and where we find it is the only question."

Their walk through the muddy streets to their destination was uneventful, though unpleasant. Ulrick never liked Smithville, but he was noticing that things were a little different from the last time he was here--and the difference was not for the better. The people they passed were just a little ruder; the women would give them a wide berth; the men's postures were challenging.

They got to the tavern Bob was looking for. It was still in business and the smell of cooking meat was strong in the air. A small engraved wood sign above the door read "The Golden Anvil." Bob motioned for Ulrick to enter first.

He opened the door to the sound of loud talking, laughing, and the clanging of cookware and dishes. The room he entered was quite large and open. It was crescent shaped, with the bar occupying the center inside edge. The outer wall had booths that offered a little privacy, and there were at least twenty tables. All but a few were occupied with dirty, drunk men.

The smell of cooking meat outside, turned to the smell of sweat and alcohol on the inside. The serving girls' clothes were designed more for accentuating the parts that should have been covered than covering them. And all but a couple looked more used than an old breeding mare. Their smiles forced or held malice, rather than joy. He unintentionally thought of Melisa and the pain she had gone through.

He hadn't made two steps into the room when one of the men behind the bar yelled something at him. He could not tell what he yelled because of the noise so he shrugged at the man and continued into the room.

The man said something to the other man and then ran around the bar and intercepted Ulrick before he made it far. "You can't bring that in here," the man said, indicating the sword he was carrying.

"Why not?" Bob asked from behind Ulrick.

"We don't want any trouble in here and having people we don't know bringing in weapons is a good way to cause trouble," the man answered.

"There are several men with swords in here," Bob said with a sweeping gesture.

"We know them."

"Ned, you know me also." Bob pulled back his hood to expose more of his face.

Ned looked closer at Bob. "Wizard, we knew you; we

don't know you anymore. And this kid with the sword, we never even knew."

"Ned is it? This sword is not really a weapon, it is more a family heirloom; it's too heavy to even use. See for yourself." Ulrick held his sword out for the man to hold. The man took hold of it and nearly dropped it.

"Damn that is heavy," Ned said.

"You see my dad just died recently and this useless thing used to just sit on the mantle above the fireplace. This is all the bastard left me, too. My younger brother got the house and the farm and I got this piece of shit. If my grandfather had not made it when he was an apprentice blacksmith, I would have just thrown it away, but you know it has some... sentimental value."

Ned returned the sword to Ulrick. "Okay, you can keep it but try to keep it as out of sight as possible." Ned looked around and then said a little quieter, "There are a couple of guys in here that look for any reason to start a fight, so stay close to the door and mind your business."

"We'll take the booth by the door." Bob headed for the closest booth.

"That will be fine." Ned returned to the bar.

Bob sat on the door-side of the booth and sat forward, slightly facing the wall. Ulrick leaned against the wall--put his feet on the bench and looked out into the room. He did not like people and places like this typically, but he did like to watch people and listen.

"Put your feet on the floor and face me." Bob's tone was like a mother scolding an adolescent.

Ulrick did as he was told, but gave Bob a look that conveyed his displeasure with being told how to sit.

Bob ignored the look and said quietly, "The way you

were sitting was asking for a challenge. People like this have a low opinion of themselves and don't like to be looked at by people they don't know. It makes them self-conscious, and to remedy their feelings of insecurity they feel the need to show everyone how strong they are by confronting you. That is what Ned meant by mind your own business." Strangely, Bob's explanation made Ulrick feel more embarrassed, but less angry at the old man.

"It's time for lesson three." Bob placed his hands on the table in front of him and looked Ulrick in the eye. "In this room there is someone that is manipulating energy. As someone who can do the same, you should be able to tell who it is. Don't look around--you won't see it with your eyes."

"When you did it, I could see you shimmering. Won't this person also be shimmering when I look at them?"

"When you saw me shimmering, it was not your eyes seeing it, if it was, everyone else could see it as well. Just look at me and listen. I am going to give you a lot of information that because of your limited education, will make little to no sense, but as you learn, will help you see the big picture. It is not your eyes, but a process that is linked to your vision. What you 'sense' will be visual in your mind, if you look at it with your eyes, it will be both pictures overlaid. When you are new at seeing it, this overlay will just confuse you because you really have been seeing it your whole life, but because what your eyes are seeing is dominant, you rarely noticed the other. Now look around the room; take in everything quickly." While Bob let Ulrick look around, he got the server's attention.

"What can I do for you?" she asked. Ulrick looked her in the eye. She gave him a tired embarrassed smile. She was still innocent enough to be embarrassed by the low cut of her cotton dress, at least in front of people she thought still had some dignity.

"I'll have a bottle of wine and the best steak you have--just warm in the middle," Bob said.

Ulrick, not really knowing what was available, just said with the warmest smile he could muster in this place, "The same as him will be fine."

"Miss, the young man will skip the wine. Juice or water will be fine for him. If you can move our order ahead, we'll make it well worth your while," Bob added.

"I'll do what I can, sir." She left.

After she left, Ulrick once again gave Bob a look of dissatisfaction.

"You know, I'm getting tired of having to explain every little thing to you, Ulrick. You will need to keep your head tonight--adding alcohol to the mix could by very disastrous for all involved." Bob's annoyance was plain on his face.

"Let's get back to it. When you looked around the room, did you see anything strange or out of place?" Bob asked Ulrick seriously.

"Well, everything to me is strange in this place,"

Bob exhaled growing more annoyed.

"Let me finish," Ulrick hurried to say before Bob could vent his displeasure. "I was saying everything is strange, but the big guy in the booth at the end seems to have a kind of darkness about him," Ulrick finished, self-satisfied by the look of hope on Bob's face.

"Good, you're right on track. Now close your eyes and picture the room in your mind. It should not be difficult. Focus your vision on the area near that man and describe what you see," Bob instructed, then was quiet.

Ulrick was quiet for a few minutes as he imagined the room. Then began, "I can see the room in my mind and the people at the tables; it all looks the same as with my eyes. Am I really seeing it, or is it just my imagination?"

"Where is our server?"

"She is picking up two mugs off the bar," Ulrick answered, a little unsure.

"You are not imagining it; that is what she is doing. Now focus on the man."

"I don't want to. Something is blocking me from looking at him and I really don't want to," Ulrick said a little fear creeping into his voice.

"Okay, open your eyes. You did better than expected for your first time. We'll eat, then you can try again."

Ulrick was having a hard time shaking his unease. Now that he had tried to look at that man in his mind and was blocked by something, he found it hard to look in that direction at all. And as time went, the unease was turning into an unexplainable fear.

Sensing Ulrick's distress, Bob put his hand on Ulrick's. "Be at ease--there is nothing in this room that can contend with us. I am the best wizard I have come across and you have that sword and ring. Together we could take on an army. The fifty men in here aren't a threat."

Luckily, the food showed up and helped distract Ulrick for a while.

"Is there anything else I can get you?" the girl asked.

Bob slid closer to the wall and motioned her to sit next to him. She gave him a cold look and started to leave. "It's not like that, Miss. I just have a question that I don't want everyone to hear."

She looked at him for a moment trying to decide if it was a good idea, then reluctantly sat down. "What do you want to know?" she said, making it clear she had no intention of doing anything but talk.

Bob leaned in a little. "Do you know the man in the far-left booth?" There were three men in the booth, but right away Bob got his answer without her having to say anything. The fear in her eyes and her shaking hands gave it away, and before she said anything, he said, "Never mind, child. I don't want you to put yourself in danger to satisfy my curiosity." He put a silver coin on the table. "Thanks for the great service."

Ulrick was struck by her fear, which did nothing to help his, but after seeing her so terrified he had to do something. He put his hand on the table palm down and leaned in close. "Miss, take this coin and leave town as soon as you are able, no later than tomorrow. If you don't think you have anywhere to go, head to Elk Valley. Go to the inn and ask for Melisa, tell her Ulrick sent you. If she is not there, the innkeeper's name is Ben--he will know where she is. Don't tell anyone you have this or where you are going."

The girl looked at Ulrick skeptically until he lifted his hand and she saw the imperial gold coin. She hesitantly took the coin, then she whispered, "Thank you." Then wiped the tears from her eyes and went back to work.

Bob didn't say anything; he just looked at Ulrick a moment, his expression unreadable. Then he started eating. They ate in silence and when they were both nearly done, Bob poured a mouthful of wine into Ulrick's empty water glass. Ulrick drank it and was thankful for the water.

"Ok, belly full?" Bob asked.

Ulrick nodded.

"Close your eyes again--do everything just as you did before."

Ulrick did as he was told, and, just as before, when he

tried to look at the man in the back booth, he couldn't. He wasn't sure if he was being blocked or if it was his own fear, but he could not look at him. "It is the same--I can't look at him."

"You're not being blocked really; it is fear, but it is not your fear--it is the type of energy he uses. It is meant to convey fear; it is fear this creature feeds on," Bob instructed.

"Creature?" Ulrick exclaimed.

Bob brought his hood back up over his head. "Maybe it is best if I explain what I think we are dealing with. It will be very difficult to explain in depth, I will do that when we get to my home. This 'creature' is not of this plane of existence. It has crossed from one of the lower realms and taken possession of the man in that booth. We are going to kill it before we leave here tonight. When you break through the fear, it will sense your ability. At that point we will have a fight on our hands."

"You want to do this right now?" Ulrick hoped the answer was no, then thought of another question. "What if it had sensed me earlier?"

"I had already done some experimenting. I knew it would take some effort on your part to break through. I wasn't too concerned. If he was facing us, he would have recognized my ability as soon as we walked in, and he probably would have left. Discovery is not in his best interest at this point," Bob said, then remembered Ulrick's first question and added, "No, not now, we will wait until we can do this with less collateral damage."

They sat in the booth long enough for their server to refill Ulrick's water cup three times and they found out her name was Abigail. Some of the patrons left, but most of the men were in it for the long haul.

"We are just going to have to do it now," Bob told Ulrick, then called Abigail over. When she arrived, he said, "Abigail, you and the other servers are going to need to find someplace safe to hide for a little while. There is going to be some trouble here real soon."

She looked at him with fear and hurried off.

"Okay, Ulrick, do just as before. Let me know when you are up against the resistance."

Ulrick did just as before, and just as before he encountered the fear. This time, having experienced it twice before, he noticed it was kind of a sphere. "Ok, I'm seeing it--it is like a sphere around him. I can look all around him, but not right at him."

"Good, are you moving within the room in your mind?"

Ulrick had not really realized that is what he was doing until the wizard had mentioned it. "Yes, it is like I am walking through the room. I can see all sides of everyone."

"Excellent, this is going to go quickly now. Don't be afraid--this creature is not physically here; it is just its spiritual energy. When we fight it, we will just be fighting a man with minor magical talent." Bob took a deep breath. "Now that your vision is moving freely in the room, move toward the man; don't look at him yet. Look to the ground, move slowly toward him and give me a nod, when you are within the sphere."

Ulrick once again did as he was directed. Once he got to the sphere of fear, he stopped. He took a deep breath, inched into the sphere, looking at the floor. His stomach lurched when he entered. Radiating from the man and running along the floor was a thick black fog; it filled the room in varying degrees, where voices were high with contention, the blackness was thickest. He gave Bob the nod.

"Take another deep breath and let it out slow. What you are going to see isn't going to be pretty," Bob instructed. "Ok now look at it."

Ulrick let his breath out slowly and looked up at the man. He just looked fuzzy, like there were two people sitting within each other. Then, he nearly pissed himself when one of the two looked at him. It was not ugly, like Bob had said it was going to be, it was a strikingly beautiful woman. It turned fully and stood. The man remained seated, so standing before him was the somewhat transparent image of a nude woman-- her hair dark red like drying blood, skin pale, but flawless, eyes a mesmerizing emerald green, and her form perfect.

She smiled at him...the smile held nothing but promised pain and the joy she would have giving it to him. Then it laughed--the voice not quite human and not quite female. Green flames that matched her eyes slowly covered her form. Ulrick could feel the warmth of it as if he were really standing next to her. "You went looking where you shouldn't have, sweetheart, now I am going to enjoy breaking your soul."

Ulrick opened his eyes and returned Bob's look. "Did you hear what she said?"

"She?" Bob asked. That was as far as they got, because there was chaos on the other side of the room.

The man on the other side of the room was standing and looking right at Ulrick. "Kill the old man. Knock out the boy and bring him to me," he said, sounding very much like a man now. Most of the men stood at his command, various weapons in hand. A few men managed to find their way out the front door before the fighting erupted.

All the drinks in the room froze instantly. Ulrick and Bob's breath came out in puffs of fog. Then several of the men closest to them burst into flame. Running and rolling about trying to put themselves out made it impossible for any of the other men to get close, buying Ulrick enough time to get his sword ready.

"Kill the creature as quickly as you can before it can escape!" Bob yelled, to be heard over the screams of the burning men."

Ulrick wasted no time, his too long sword started cutting into foes before they were close enough to hit him. With the death of each man, his sword got lighter and his speed increased.

Within moments it was over. The floor of the tavern was covered in blood and body parts. The possessed man's body lay in two pieces amidst a tangle of intestines.

Ulrick didn't feel any of the emotions of the men he had slain until it was over. Then it all came in a torrent, starting with the first man and culminating with the possessed. The emotions were a mix of annoyance, frustration, and some happy anticipation of violence.

The possessed, however, was different. The emotions of the man were subdued, but the emotion that came from the demon were of hatred so deep Ulrick could not fathom. Then, he became aware that it was not just residual emotion. The creature was still here and it was trying to control him. Ulrick's scream started as a low struggling groan then erupted. "She is trying to take me!" His body shook with exertion.

"Take off the ring," Bob yelled.

Ulrick's hands moved painfully slow, together. It took every bit of strength he had to get hold of the ring. His muscles were working against themselves. He finally managed to remove the ring. Relief and exhaustion took him to his knees.

He wasn't there long when Abigail and another of the serving girls were helping him to his feet. He turned to head back to his booth and saw the mess he had made for the first time. The scene combined with the smell of burst entrails caused him to add his meal to the blood on the floor. His retching and the sobbing of one of the serving girls was the only thing that broke the silence in the room.

"I hope they can line up a tub for us this late in the evening," Bob said as he headed for the door. They definitely wanted to get out of this mess as quickly as possible.

"Aren't you going to help clean up this mess?" Ned called, just before they got to the door.

"I would if I knew you better," Bob responded and left.

"You said she?" Bob questioned after they had left the tavern.

"She was beautiful, in a sinister kind of way." Ulrick was thoughtful. "She said she was going to enjoy breaking my soul. What do you think she meant by that?"

"I know exactly what she meant. There are only two ways that I know of in which a demon can take possession of someone. The first way is if you submit fully to the creature; the second is if you are broken. When a person is severely tortured, at a point the physical and emotional pain becomes too much to take and the spirit temporarily separates from the body, it is at that point that a demon can take possession. Although it appears there may be a third way. When you kill with your sword, it uses the energy from the severing of the spirit from the body. When you severed the demon from that man, the demon must have been able to use that conduit of energy to enter the ring and possibly take possession of you," Bob explained, his tone academic.

When they got back to the inn, the man at the desk seemed quite put out when Bob asked him for a tub. That was until he saw Ulrick covered in blood, then he became quite accommodating.

The next morning, they received better service from most the places visited. Ulrick found it strange that no constables were looking for them. He purchased a couple of robes in the style suggested by Bob. He opted for grey, also suggested by Bob. He had said it would not show the dirt as fast and it would not be as hot as the darker colors. It was just after midday when they finally got back on the road. They headed due west for a couple hours, then turned slightly north.

Ulrick was not up for talking much. He had never killed a person before last night, and he was trying to come to terms with his feelings. He had killed at least fifteen men. As far as he knew, none of them were innocent, but that was little comfort. Because of his mood, he rode far enough behind Bob to avoid eating any dust.

It was early evening when they came to a stream lined with cottonwoods. There were sandstone cliffs on the other side of the stream. They rode beside the stream for a while. Ulrick did not see that they were following any defined trail. Bob suddenly turned his horse and crossed the stream and made his way toward the cliffs.

When Ulrick cleared the trees, he saw a small shack built up against the cliff-face. "Is that your home?" he asked Bob skeptically. He hoped he wasn't going to have to spend a month or more in that small shack with Bob.

"Yes, it is," Bob answered with obvious pride.

Ulrick looked at him like he was insane, but kept any comments he had to himself.

6 - Vincent

Vince was sitting on a stump, inside an old barn southwest of Elk Valley. Dust twinkled in the air were the sun sent shafts of light through the barn. Tied to a post was a man that had played an important role in his life. The man's name was unknown to Vince--in fact, he doubted anyone knew him by his real name, but here he was known as Jax.

Vince had met him just after Jax had moved to town. Vince was around eleven at the time and was out gathering rocks for his collection of 'pretty rocks'. Jax must have been watching him for some time, because he knew what he was looking for and showed him where there were quite a few very nice rocks to be found. Once he was there, Jax showed him a few other things. Vince hated the memory of that day, he hated what Jax had done to him and after that day he hated pretty rocks.

After that day Jax had become like a big brother. He had taught Vince many things. The most important was the knowledge of stealing energy from the torturing of other living things. Vince had shown quite a talent for the gruesome work. The knife he held in his hands was a testimony of his skill and his dedication to the art. He had made this knife the day he had killed his own mother. It was in this very barn several years ago that the deed was done. He hated the memory of that day. He had not wanted to do it, but she had found out about his relationship with Jax. Jax had also told him how much power could be had because of the great emotion involved--both his and his mother's. Jax had been right--the knife had given him great power over the minds of the dim.

The day he had killed his mother, he had received another great gift. It was that day that he had started hearing the voice of the serpent, making him an official member of the Brotherhood of the Serpent. He had later been called by the serpent to be marked. He had received a second mark during his last trip to the Western Territory. The first mark was on his right palm, the second mark was scarred on his chest. The mark on his chest set him apart from other members, as chosen. Vince knew of only two others that were also marked--Jax was not one of them.

Tied to the post, Jax looked even more pathetic than usual, if that was possible. Vince could smell his stink from where he sat, some ten feet away. Jax's graying hair was shoulder long and flat with grease. He wasn't wearing a shirt; all his ribs were visible, yet his belly still protruded past his sunken chest.

Jax had been asleep. How he could sleep tied to the pole, Vince could not fathom, but there were many things about Jax Vince could not fathom. Now that he was awake, however, he had a few things to say.

"What is this about, Vince?" Jax sputtered through the water that had been used to wake him up.

"I think you know, Jax, but in the interest of time, I will just tell you." Vince paused for affect, hoping to watch Jax squirm a little, then he continued. "I specifically told you to kill Kramdon and take what he carried before he got to town."

"I tried; the man is tougher than he appears and he appears pretty tough," Jax said through an innocent smile and a chuckle. He had gained a little composure since his rude awakening.

"I also told you not to send your 'minions' into town. I told you, Ulrick already had the ring and that we would have to move on to phase two of the plan." Vince was calm.

"You gave conflicting advice. Part of 'phase two' was killing Eramus." He puffed out his scrawny chest and continued. "Besides, since when do I do what you say? I don't answer to you. We both know as long as it doesn't interfere with the overall purpose of the Serpent, I can do as I please."

"As far as Titan is concerned, you are correct, but as far as I am concerned, you are not. I have been looking forward to this day for a long time and I had planned to draw this out-- make you suffer, but I don't have the patience for it. Give me one good reason and I might spare your life, otherwise... well, you know." Vince stood and walked over to the little man.

"It is decreed by the Serpent that we are brothers in the cause, and that as brothers we should support and defend others of the cause. You would be blacklisted, marked for death if you continue." Jax was confident. He felt he was right and protected. He had taught this principle to Vince, himself.

"Did you not wonder, Jax, why these goblins--your minions--disobeyed you and tied you to this post? Do you not see? I am no longer your equal in the Brotherhood." Vince undid the buttons on his shirt, exposing the mark on his chest.

Jax knew he was dead now. The pieces had come together for the old bastard. Seeing the end in Jax's eyes, was all Vince had wanted. Vince thought to use this death to increase his strength, but had changed his mind. He wanted to be rid of this foul creature for good and hoped to forget about his very existence.

Jax was about to resort to begging for his life when Vince brought his hand around the back of the old man and stuck his knife in the left side of his lower back. Vince knew this would not kill him fast but he knew he would surely die. Then Vince shoved a rag into Jax's mouth to smother the noise that was issuing from his mouth.

Vince then turned to the giant goblin that had been sitting against the outside wall of the barn. "HeadSmasher, that's what they are calling you now, right?"

The giant nodded.

Vince didn't understand why goblins were always changing their names, but he also didn't care enough to ask.

"HeadSmasher, bandage Jax's wound then take him where nobody will find him and tie him to a tree, high enough that wolves can't get him. We don't want him to die too quick." Vince cleaned his knife.

"Okay." The giant's deep voice resonated in Vince's chest.

"Okay what?" Vince asked.

"Okay, Master."

"I don't demand you call me master for my benefit. I do it so you will remember your place and remain alive longer." Vince left the barn.

7 - Eramus

Eram stood on watchman hill, overlooking Elk Valley. The air was dead calm. Behind him were the peaks of the Dragon range. It seemed he could see forever from where he stood. Below was the town he lived. He could see the great pine he and Ulrick had spent so much time. He searched the valley below; he could make out his house and not far from there, Lisa's house, which gave him a jolt of sadness. Beyond Elk Valley he could see the Brown smudge from the forge fires of Smithville. Beyond Smithville, there was an endless vista of rolling hills.

When he returned his gaze to Elk Valley it was shrouded in fog, which was not unusual, but how fast it had rolled in, was. Standing beside him was Lisa. He was glad she was back. "I missed you," he said to her.

She did not respond. So, he continued, "I love you."

Instead of responding, she started off down the hill.

Eram, devastated by her unresponsiveness, started after her, but was stopped by someone grabbing his arm. He turned to see who it was. It was not anyone he knew, but her face was familiar, like he had seen it in some past dream. Her look brought him comfort. Her green eyes made him feel warm and safe.

"She is the past," the woman said, pointing to Lisa as she disappeared into the forest.

"It comes, Eramus." Her voice was like music.

"What comes?" Eram asked.

"Your future." She turned to face the peaks.

Eram stood looking north, feeling the comfort of standing close to this beautiful unknown, but familiar woman. He felt as though he would like to stand there forever.

Eram cracked open one eye, the other would not open and the fire that radiated from the right side of his head was excruciating. He did not know where he was or how he got here. He could see three people silhouetted by the light coming through a door. It took him a few minutes to realize it was his parents and Sara...no, not Sara, Melisa.

"You can't stay here all day, waiting for him to wake up. You have responsibilities at home. It's his own fault. If he had been where he should have been, he would not be all beat up in the first place." That was his father speaking. Eram closed his eye, he did not want to face his dad yet.

Melisa ignored what Marcus had said and turned to Eram's mother. "Nell, I will send someone as soon as he wakes."

Eram waited until he knew his parents were far enough away that he would have a few minutes before they could be called back. He felt a little guilt because of the sadness of his mother. He heard Melisa moving around the room, then she moved next to him and stopped.

Eram opened his eye again trying to look at Melisa. The pain brought a hoarse groan from him.

Melisa was standing over him, looking into his eye. "Thank all that is good," she said. "I might be able to catch your mother, before she is too far."

Eram managed to shake his head enough to stop her.

"You heard what your father said, didn't you?" she asked, not needing an answer.

He managed another nod, which brought tears to his left eye and more pain to his right. He wished it was the pain from his injuries that brought tears to his eyes, but it wasn't. It was the pained look in Melisa's eyes that illustrated what he had always known, but tried to ignore. His father did not like him. He may love him as his son, but he did not like him as a person. Eram tried to ask what had happened but only managed a meager croak.

"Don't try to talk. You haven't had anything to eat or drink for a couple of days now." Melisa got a cup of water, holding it for him to drink, he managed a couple swallows. Then Melisa told him everything that had happened. Some he remembered, but he had been asleep for most of it. He was sad to hear that Ulrick had left before he woke up. Eram only managed a few more sips of water then he was asleep again.

"It comes, Eramus." Her voice was like music.

"What comes?"

"Your future." She turned to face the peaks.

Eram stood looking north, feeling the comfort of standing close to this beautiful unknown, but familiar woman. He felt as though he would like to stand there forever.

Eram woke to the sound of his mother softly humming. She stopped when she noticed he was awake. She was quick to get him some water. The room was dark except for the light that came from under the door. "What time is it?" he asked.

"It is around midnight. I'm so glad you are getting better. I was so afraid that you weren't going to make it." Her voice was quivering with held-back emotion.

"I'm sorry, Mom, for making you sad and I'm sorry for disappointing dad." Eram's voice was just above a whisper.

"You have nothing to be sorry for. Melisa told me you were brave--that you could have run, but would not leave her. I'm proud of you."

Eram knew he was not going to be able to stay awake

much longer. He was going to tell his mother to go home and get some sleep, but instead he said, "I'm going back to sleep. You can hum some more."

She had just begun humming and he was asleep again.

"It comes, Eramus." Her voice was music.

"Who are you?"

"Your future" She turned to face the peaks. "Beware, Eramus, danger is close."

Eram woke with a start.

Vince was sitting in the chair next to his bed. "Good, you're awake." Vince tossed his knife, spinning it into the air then catching it by the handle, then tossing it again over and over. "I'm glad I have this opportunity before I leave to let you know I'm sorry for how I treated you last winter, and hope you get feeling better soon." Vince seemed sincere.

"You know I can always see through your bullshit, Vince." Eram was barely understandable.

"I know, Eram, and that is why nobody likes you." He was still spinning his knife. "You know, I came here today with the intention of killing you."

Eram looked to the door, hoping someone would be coming in soon. His throat was too dry to yell.

"Don't worry, Eram, nobody will interrupt us. Your mother left a few minutes ago and Melisa, if that is her real name, is moving her things out of my father's house. He was not happy to find out she was Ulrick's father's whore."

Vince looked to Eram, hoping to see anger in Eram's eyes. "Like I was saying, I came here with the intention of killing you, but I changed my mind when I saw for myself how pathetic you are. Don't worry though, I won't forget about you. Even though I am letting you live, your life will be hell. I will come back through town every now and again to check on you. If by some miracle you've found happiness, I will destroy it." Vince chuckled, self-satisfied.

"Why?" Was all Eram could think to say.

"Why what? Why was I going to kill you? Or why am I going to insure your life is hell? Or why are you so damn stupid?" Vince mocked.

"Why do you hate me?" Eram managed to get past his dry throat.

Vince looked to the ceiling searchingly, then looked to Eram. "You know, I really don't know. I just do." Then Vince got up and went to the door. "Eram, I will give you one piece of advice before I go. Everyone lies and they like it when people believe their lies. It is the honest man nobody believes, because nobody wants to see the truth. Think about that for a while." Then he left.

Eram thought about his conversation with Vince, but thankfully he did not have the energy to think long before he was asleep again.

Eram managed to stay awake a little longer each time he woke and started eating better. His legs were fine, but when he tried to walk, the pain in his head and ribs made him nauseous. Melisa made him get up anyway--at least for a couple minutes every time he woke. She was relentless, but Eram appreciated the fact that she was usually there when he woke. Occasionally there was another girl there. He had never seen before; they called her Abby, but she did not say much.

It had been nearly three weeks since he had been injured before he was able to spend more time up than in bed. His arm was still tied to his chest. Melisa had told him not to move it at all, but to occasionally move his fingers. Moving his fingers hurt like hell, so he generally only moved them when she insisted. The swelling had gone down in his right eye enough to be able to crack it open, but everything looked fuzzy through that eye.

Eram woke one morning to Abby and Melisa talking. When they noticed he was awake, Melisa got up and started cleaning up the dishes from his dinner the night before. He had a hard time not watching her every move. *She really is a beautiful woman,* he thought to himself. He even liked her slightly crooked nose. It was minor imperfections that he found interesting in a woman. Ulrick never did understand. They tended to see women differently. Ulrick liked simple perfection, but Eram liked a fire in the eye--an inner confidence that was not born of outward beauty, but something from within.

His musing was interrupted by Abby. "I think Eram, here, is feeling better today because he hasn't taken his eye off your backside since you got up."

Eram gave her an embarrassed frown that hurt his head and brought a smile to Abby's face. Melisa didn't say anything; she just finished picking up and left the room.

"Why did you have to say that?" Eram asked, still embarrassed.

"Don't be a child, Eram. Be a man. You will never get what you want if you don't go for it. Women like a man that says what he feels and takes what he wants," she said seriously.

Eram felt rebuked, even though he had done nothing to deserve it.

Melisa untied his arm later that day and helped him move it a little. Then she made him squeeze the water out of a rag--which hurt like hell. They were in the main room of the inn, so he kept his complaints to himself. There was no use looking like a baby in front of everyone.

"Remember, Eram, I lived as a mercenary for years. I've

seen many men injured...some recovered, and some are use-less cripples. The biggest difference between the cripples and those that recovered is that the cripples babied their injuries and they stiffened up. A broken arm like you had could stiffen, making it impossible to hold a sword tight enough to use it. I know you think I'm being mean, making you do this, but if you don't, you will be useless as a blacksmith." Melisa's tone was professional.

Eram hadn't thought about going back to work yet. He knew he had to go back, but he did not want to think about it until he had to. She was right; there was no way he could do his job with his arm the way it is now. Without thinking any more about it, he just blurted out like his tongue was not his own, "I'm not going back to the blacksmith shop. In fact, as soon as I'm better, I plan to leave Elk Valley."

"Ha ha that's what I'm talking about, Eram. Say what you feel and take what you want." Abby chimed in from where she sat at the bar. Melisa gave her a disapproving look, but did not comment on what she had said.

Later that evening he was sitting by the fireplace. Keep-ing his arm warm seemed to help alleviate the ache a little. He didn't know where Abby and Melisa had gone. Ben was the only one in the room. He was just finishing cleaning up for the day. "Hey Ben, have you got a minute? I have to ask you a few questions."

Ben put away the broom, pulled up a chair and sat next to Eram. "What's on your mind?"

"Didn't you hike over the dragon peaks when you were younger?" Eram knew he would get the long version because Ben loved telling the story--and his wife wasn't around to hurry him up.

Ben looked at Eram skeptically--a little hesitant to tell the story. Ben had never told Eram the story, but he had overheard the short version a couple times. Eram noticed his hesitance. "I don't feel like sleeping yet and a good story would help get my mind off my worries, but if you're not up for it that's okay."

Ben relaxed a little and began his story "It was my brother and I... everyone had heard of the great dragon that lived in the valley. Being young and wanting nothing more than to see the fabled beast, we bought supplies for a week's trek over the dragon peaks and into the fabled Dragon Valley. I don't' know if you know it or not, but it was said that there was a valley just beyond the peaks and in the valley, there is a cave. It is in the cave that the dragon lives with his treasure-hoard.

We set out early summer--just late enough in the year to avoid the spring snows. We hiked through the pass, just west of the first peak. Even though we thought we left late enough we got into snow anyway. We managed to make it into the next valley, through the snow. Then we cleared the next two peaks--it had taken us a full week to get that far, so we had to start hunting for food or starve." Ben paused for effect.

That is when Paula called from the kitchen. Ben's annoyance was plain as he continued. "It looks like you get the short version.

"On a slope after the fourth peak, there is a cave, but it only goes in about one hundred feet. Then it dead-ends. Long story short: we hiked over the next peak and all there was is another peak after that. We had studied several maps and all the maps say the same thing. There are five dragon peaks and on the other side of the fifth is the Imperial city. We cleared the fourth and there was nothing there."

He finished and left to see what his wife wanted.

Eram got up, went to his room and got into bed. He had brought a rag with him so he could squeeze it until he fell asleep. Now that he had made up his mind not to go back to the blacksmith shop, he no longer needed to milk his injury. He needed to get better so he could go meet his future.

He was nearly asleep when he heard his door open and close. "Are you asleep?" Melisa asked.

"Not quite."

"Good," she said as she took off her clothes and started getting into bed with him.

Eram didn't know what to say. He thought to argue that this was a bad idea, but then decided who was he to argue with a naked woman that wanted to sleep next to him. He had no idea why Melisa wanted to be with him but before long he was glad, she did.

The next morning when Eram woke, Melisa was gone. He got up feeling better than he had since his run in with the goblins. He had decided he was going to go tell his dad he wasn't coming back to the shop. He had decided after Ben's story that he was going to find the dragon cave or if it really wasn't there, he would go see the Imperial City, but after last night with Melisa, he was thinking maybe he could stay with her. She had not told him she was leaving, but he had overheard pieces of conversation that made him believe she was heading south.

Hopefully she hadn't already left.

He got dressed, had Ben make him some eggs, and then headed home. He took his time. The day was beautiful and warm. He made it a point to stop at some of his favorite spots.

When he finally got home, he could hear his father working in the forge. He had left with all the confidence in the world, but now he was having difficulty facing what was before him. He decided to take the coward's way and bypass the forge and go gather some of his things and return to the inn--

then he could find Melisa and they could be off.

He had managed to get his things into a pack and was leaving through the front door when his mother asked, "Where are you headed?"

Eram hadn't seen her, so was quite startled and took too long to answer, because his father had apparently come in from the forge and had heard his mother's question from the kitchen.

"I think he is running off with David's whore and her tramp friend," Marcus said as he came into the room and walked toward Eram with purpose. "Am I right?" He stared his son in the face.

Eram was caught off guard by his mother and now by his father, but what his father had said clarified his purpose and fueled a rage that he did not know he had. Before he even realized what he was doing, he had dropped his bag and turned and faced his father. "You will not speak of my friends that way."

"I will speak of whom I will, however I wish to speak of them, and you will not speak to me in that tone. Am I right? You're leaving your responsibilities at the forge and going off with that whore?" Marcus stared his son down.

Eram had been belittled and bullied by his father his whole life, and that old habit of giving in and submitting to his father's authority almost took him again, but in an instant before he did, he recalled his dream and the beautiful woman that stood beside him. "I am your future," she was saying. He looked to the north, even though he was in the house. He could see the vision before him of the dragon peaks and the comfort of the woman that stood beside him. He knew at that moment he could not go with Melisa, but he could not stay here. He was leaving, and he was leaving first thing tomorrow.

"Are you going to answer me or are you going to stand there staring off into space, like the dumbass you are?" Marcus yelled.

The comment pulled Eram out of the vision, taking away the beautiful woman's comfort--returning him to the rage that now fully consumed him. Before his father could react, Eram hit him as hard as he could with his right fist. The pain exploded in his arm, nearly bringing him to his knees, but he managed to stay standing.

His father completely caught off guard, did not remain on his feet.

Looking down at Marcus, he said through tears of anger, pain and sadness, "You will never speak of my friends like that again, and if you do, I will kill you--and end the suffering you bring to everyone's life."

Eram picked up his pack and started back to the inn. His trip back to the inn was a blur of angry tears and the throbbing pain of his not-yet-healed arm. When he got to the inn, Melisa and Abby were sitting at one of the tables. He knew he could not hold back his emotions, so he avoided them, went straight to his room and lounged on his bed.

He was nearly asleep when he heard a light knock on the door. "Come in."

Melisa stepped into the room and closed the door behind her and walked slowly to the chair beside his bed. In spite of what he had been through today, he still could not help admiring how she looked as she walked.

After sitting for a few moments in silence, she finally said, "I'm leaving tomorrow."

"So am I," Eram responded.

Melisa's expression became pained; she seemed at a loss for words.

Eram knew she was conflicted. He figured she thought he was insisting on going with her and she was not sure whether she wanted that. "I'm not leaving with you," he continued easing her discomfort.

"Where are you going? Do you plan on meeting up with Ulrick?"

Eram was quiet for a moment, trying to put words to his plans that didn't sound crazy, but he found none, so he just said, "I'm going over the dragon peaks to find what lies on the other side."

"No, you're not." She chuckled, thinking he must be joking, but when she realized he wasn't, she continued, with not just a little concern. "You can't, you need more rest and everyone knows there is nothing there."

"Nobody knows there is nothing there. I have heard Ben's tale and I know when someone is making stuff up. He and his brother hiked up into the dragon peaks, but they didn't go all the way. They turned back when it got tough."

He rubbed his still throbbing arm, trying to feel if he had re-broken it. He could feel the lump where the arm had broken and had started fusing back together. He didn't think he re-broke it, but it was starting to swell a little.

Melisa watched him for a while. "What's wrong with your arm? Did you hurt it when you were out?"

Eram looked up at her--she had real concern. He wasn't sure if it was for his pain or because she thought he was going mad. "I hit my dad today."

"Why would you do that?" she asked, then continued before he could answer. "Well, I know your dad is an ass, but why now instead of all the other times you had good reason?"

"It doesn't matter," he replied, then asked, "Where are you headed tomorrow? I might want to look you up sometime."

Melisa looked at him for a long time, she seemed to be

trying to decide what to tell him. "Abby and I were thinking Southport, but if we don't like it there, we'll move on--to where, I'm not sure." Her expression was thoughtful, when she continued. "I'm not leaving tomorrow... not if you are planning to run off into the hills before you're all healed."

"Melisa, I have to go. I can't stay here, and I know I can't go with you. I need to do this. I can't say exactly why without sounding crazy, but I do know I need to do this."

"You can't say why you're going without sounding crazy, because most people that go into the mountains in good health and well provisioned don't survive the journey. You are thinking of doing it alone and nearly crippled. It's suicidal. You can't do it." She was desperate to change his mind.

Eram lay in his bed looking at the ceiling, searching for something to say that would ease Melisa's fear, but he found nothing. So, he said so quiet she almost could not hear him, "I'm leaving tomorrow morning. My mind is made up. Unless you tie me up--and if you do--you are no friend of mine." He looked into her eyes as he finished his statement and held her gaze for a moment. "Will you stay with me again tonight?"

"Yes, I will stay with you tonight, but it is just early afternoon. We need to get out and enjoy our last day in Elk Valley," she said, trying to sound enthusiastic even though she felt like it was a funeral.

"I agree we should enjoy our last day here together, but to tell you the truth with Lisa and Ulrick gone, I have only you and Abby. I have come to realize since Ulrick left that nobody here in this town cares much for me. It is like what Vince said, people don't like to see reality they like to see the fantasy and I spent too much time pointing out the reality and seeing through the lies and people hate me for it.

"Enough of my whining. I think we should hike to the top of Watchman's Hill and watch the sun go down," he said, a little of his enthusiasm returning.

The trek to the top of Watchman's Hill usually took a couple hours, but Eram found himself lagging behind the girls most of the way. His throbbing arm and the shooting pains in his right eye made the trip a misery. The fact that he had spent nearly a month in bed wasn't helping his ability to climb either. What was a casual day for Eram and Ulrick a year ago was turning into a trip he was not sure he could finish. He was now really starting to question his decision to head north into the mountains.

The last part of the hike was the hardest. The walking trail became more of a climb that required navigating through a cleft in the stone cliff that capped the entire top of the hill. It normally wasn't hard for a man to accomplish, but not being able to grasp the rocks with his right hand was making it extremely difficult; he nearly fell a couple times.

Melisa and Abby made it through a few minutes before he reached the cleft and were now taunting him from somewhere up above. Eram was annoyed. He knew they probably thought their teasing was helping him stay motivated to keep going, but really, he just wanted to leave and let them have their fun by themselves.

He was nearly through when the taunts came to an end and all he heard was the wind whistling through the pines below. The top of Watchman's Hill above the cliff had no trees at all. There were just a few tufts of grass that he could not recall ever being green. Above the cliff the hill was domed, with a flat spot about one hundred feet square. Once at the flat of the top, the view of the surrounding mountains and valleys was breathtaking. The silence from the girls told Eram they had finally reached the top. Neither of them had ever been; he was sure they were stunned by the vista. He only wished he could have seen their faces when they saw it for the first time.

Eram finally managed to drag himself from the cleft. His

left arm was bloodied and his right arm was on fire from having to use it to keep from falling, and his clothes were covered with dirt from wiggling on his belly the last couple feet. He made it though and he started walking up the rise to the top. He took his time; he wanted to catch his breath and dust his clothes so he wouldn't be the butt of any more jokes.

Melisa and Abby were standing close together, looking at the peaks to the north. They were in the center of the large flat hill which consisted of very massive cut stones that appeared to be the floor to some ancient building. Eram had always marveled at the stones because they were far too large to move by any means he knew, and, they were made of stone that was completely different than the stone of the cliffs.

Eram made his way to where the girls were standing and stopped just behind them. He was tall enough that he still had a good view of the massive peaks that rose up in front of them. The great mountains looked larger from this vantage point than any other in the area. One could stare for hours and still be awed by the enormity of them.

Looking at the peaks as he was now, brought to mind his recurring dream: the feeling was so strong he unconsciously looked to his side for the woman from his dream. He felt disappointed when he discovered no one was there. The feelings from the dream were still strong and an uneasy anxiety started building in his gut. The best way he could explain the feeling was a restrained urgency--a need for action he could not take yet. Yet looking at those peaks and knowing the action he needed to take was traveling through those mountains brought a great fear. He glanced again to where the woman of comfort had been in his dream, and without realizing he was saying it out loud he said, "I wish you were here."

When he looked back to the peaks, both Melisa and Abby were staring at him. Abby spoke first. "You have got to be the dumbest person I have ever met! You can barely climb this hill and you plan on wandering through those mountains tomorrow." She made a wide sweeping gesture toward the mountains. Then shaking her head in disgust, she said again under her breath, "Got to be the dumbest person I've met."

Melisa took his left hand in hers. "Who do you wish were here?"

"It doesn't matter." He only glanced at her, then looked at his feet. He could not abide the intensity of her look.

"That is the second time you've told me that today. I had decided when we talked earlier that as your friend, I would respect you enough to let you make your own choice. As you said short of tying you up, I would not be able to keep you from going." She paused, looked to the sky in exasperation then grabbed his face to force him to look at her. "Eram, if you want me to respect you and let you kill yourself in those mountains, after I just spent a month trying to keep you alive, then you are going to have to answer me two things--and I better like the answers or I will be tying you up. First, why did you hit your father today and who do you wish was here with you right now?"

His jaw clenched as he tried to hold back his emotions. He did not know if it was the exhaustion from the climb, the pain in his face and arm, or the enormity of the task before him and how intensely he knew he had to do it. Like Melisa he could not see how it was possible. In spite of his attempt to stop them, silent tears slowly made their way down his face. After a few moments he calmed enough to speak without breaking down. "I hit my dad because he called you a whore." The sadness in Melisa's eyes after his comment caused him to pause to re-gather the strength to continue.

"And who do you wish were here right now?" Her tone was just a little more patient.

Eram extracted himself from her grip and walked past

them toward the peaks; he stopped a few paces in front of them. Melisa let him go and patiently waited for his response. Without looking back, he started his explanation. "While I was unconscious, I had a dream. I don't know how many times I had the dream, but it was always the same." Eram sat down cross legged on the hard stone as he continued his story. The two women joined him, all three facing north. "It wasn't an ordinary dream. It was more real, even after I woke. I still have the dream nearly every time I sleep." He paused and brushed dirt off the stone in front of him. He did not want to tell them of the dream because it sounded crazy to himself. He could only imagine how it would sound to them.

"Well, what is the dream about?" Abby was genuinely curious.

"You will think I am crazy. I can't convey all the feelings with words. Without the feeling it seems crazy." He took a deep, shaky breath.

Abby laughed. "We already think you're crazy. I can't see how your dream is going to make you crazier."

"Okay, the dream always takes place here on top of Watchman's Hill. I am looking south. I can see everything, more than you can actually see. I can clearly see Elk Valley below. Then I look further south and I can see Smithville and the rolling hills beyond. When I look back to Elk Valley, it is covered in fog. I am standing next to Lisa."

"Who is Lisa?" Abby asked.

"Lisa is Eram's good friend. She went to Southport just before Eram and Ulrick got back this spring. Now let him finish without interruption."

Eram stood, looked south and motioned them to do the same. "As I was saying, Lisa is standing next to me, then she starts to leave. I try to go after her, but someone grabs my arm. I turn to see who it is and it is the most wonderful woman

I have ever seen." He looked sheepishly at the two women, but then continued. "She had the most beautiful green eyes and she made me feel peace and comfort. She said pointing to Lisa 'she is the past.' Then she turned to the north as she said 'It comes, Eramus.'" He turned to the north. "I asked 'what comes?' and she said 'your future.' Then I asked, 'who are you?' and she said 'your future.'"

After his explanation, he turned and faced the two women. "Like I said, it is hard to convey how I felt, but each time I woke, I knew that is my future," he said, pointing to the peaks. "I also know that for me to find this woman in my dream, I must first find the destiny that awaits somewhere in those mountains." Then more quietly he added, "To answer your question, it is the woman with green eyes that I wish were here right now, because if she were here, I wouldn't be so afraid of what I have to do."

At this point his whole body was shaking with suppressed emotion and fear. Melisa pulled him close and hugged him. He lost all control then and began to sob. "How can I do this?" he whispered on her shoulder.

The sound of Melisa putting on her clothes woke Eram. "What time is it?"

"A couple hours before dawn," she replied as she sat on the foot of his bed and bent over to pull on her boots. "I have a few things to do before I leave that is best done while most are still asleep." She buttoned her shirt and went to the door. "Go back to sleep. I will come back to see you before Abby and I leave." Then she was gone.

Eram was wondering what she could be doing that required her do it while everyone was asleep. Then he was asleep.

Eram found himself standing on Watchman's Hill looking south. He could see much farther than he normally would. He could clearly see Smithville and the hills beyond. He looked down toward Elk Valley. The town was shrouded in fog. Lisa was standing next to him, but she looked different now, she was thinner, her hair pulled back and she carried a long knife. She was looking intently south, then she started walking away. Eram knew he was dreaming, and instead of going after her, he turned to where the beautiful girl with golden hair and intelligent green eyes was standing.

She was watching him, her eyes piercing. "You know now." She turned north.

Eram turned north and asked, "What do I know?"

"Your future, Eramus".

"What is your name?"

She looked into his eyes, her eyebrows pulled together the intensity transfixed him. She did not answer his question. "It is time. You must go… you have to succeed or all is lost." Her comment burned with an intensity that caused his stomach to twist with anxiety. She looked north again.

"Who are you?"

She turned back, looked him in the eye again. This time with humor and a half smile. "Your future…" Then her look became sad and distant. "Or your doom?"

Eram opened his eyes to Abby staring at him, her face lit by the dim light of dawn coming through the window. The sight of her nearly startled him out of his bed.

"You had the dream again, didn't you?" Not seeming to notice his distress.

"What are you doing here? You scared the me half to death."

"The me?" She laughed.

"The inability to talk is the result of waking up to you creepily staring at me." Eram rubbed his eyes and yawned. "Speaking of which, why are you watching me sleep?"

"I wanted to talk to you alone, before you leave." She leaned forward putting her elbows on her knees. "The dream, you had it again?"

"It was different this time, but yes, I had the dream." He answered, distracted by the fact he could see down Abby's shirt.

"Really?" Her tone was disgusted as she sat back and crossed her arms.

Eram shrugged. "You would look too, if I was half exposed."

"I would be vainly searching for what Melisa sees in you." Her smile was mocking.

"What do you want to talk to me about?" He was too tired to intelligently respond to her teasing.

"Do you know why I came to be in Elk Valley?"

"I don't. I did overhear Ben mention you were from Smithville. I thought to ask a couple times, but never got around to it. I kind of just figured you were sent here to torment me." He tried to straighten his hair a little, sat up and leaned against the headboard.

"Of course, everyone is here for your benefit. Well I'm glad you at least had enough interest to *think* about asking." She smiled as she leaned forward and put her elbows on her knees again. Her pretty smile kept him from looking down her shirt, for a moment anyway. At least he kept his looks to when, he was sure, she wasn't looking.

"Ulrick saved me. There are strange things going on in Smithville. It is hard to explain...it is like the town just got darker, angrier. Ulrick and the wizard, I don't remember his name."

"Bob," Eram said.

"What?"

"Bob. That is the wizard's name."

"Right, Ulrick and Bob the wizard came into the Golden Anvil where I was working and Ulrick told me to leave town and to come find Melisa, if I didn't have anywhere else to go. Then he killed everyone in the tavern."

"What!" Eram exclaimed. "You must be mistaken. Ulrick would never kill anyone. He would sick up just gutting a fish."

"You got the sick up part right. He regurgitated everything he had just eaten. That is not the point, however." She turned her head slightly to keep the sun coming through the window out of her eyes.

"So, what is the point?"

"When I got here, I found that strange things were happening here also. I think something terrible is going to happen, and I have a strong feeling that Ulrick is needed to help keep it from happening. When he killed those men in the tavern, instead of being horrified and sad, everyone that was still alive just seemed to exhale with relief like some weight had been lifted."

Eram was starting to get annoyed. He could not see why she needed to tell him about it. He, of course, was interested in what Ulrick was doing, but it also brought up some feelings of jealousy. Ulrick had left without even saying goodbye and he was stuck here alone. Lisa had left; Ulrick had left; now Melisa and Abby were leaving and his only choices were to stay here and slave at the forge or get himself killed in the mountains. "I don't think you have gotten to the point yet." He was disappointed that he could hear some of the emotion he was feeling in his voice.

Abby looked into his eyes--for once there wasn't ridicule in them. "No, you're right I haven't. After I heard your dream last night, I had a very strong feeling that not only was Ulrick important, but that you are linked with him and just as important or more so." She sighed and continued, "Because I believe you are an important part of something big, I think I need to go with you and help you make it to wherever it is you are supposed to go." Abby cleared her throat, she seemed afraid of how what she was going to say next was going to sound. "I think Ulrick was inspired to send me here to help you."

"Do you realize how crazy all of this sounds? It is crazy that I am willing to throw my life away because of a dream, but for you to do the same because of my dream and some feeling of 'inspiration' is complete insanity." Eram chuckled bitterly. "I will be completely honest with you, Abby, but you must promise not to tell Melisa any of what I say." He looked at her seriously.

She mirrored his look. "I promise... I hope I won't regret it."

"Abigail, I don't expect to live through this and I really don't care if I do. You see I have nothing. I have no one that truly cares. Everyone that I thought cared has left or is leaving. Lisa, the woman I was going to ask to marry me, left without even saying goodbye. My best friend, the person I shared all of my hopes and dreams with, left. He didn't even wait to see if I was going to survive. Now Melisa is leaving too, and she made it obvious that I am not welcome to come with her." Eram wiped the one tear he was unable to stop from his cheek then continued. "Now you say you want to go with me. You'd think this would help my feelings, but it doesn't. You don't want to come with me because of a friendship we have, but because you see some higher propose. That purpose is a lie."

"The dream...it is nothing but delusion created from my pathetic existence. My waking mind needs this dream to keep me from throwing myself from a cliff. I only told Melisa so she could leave without guilt. I know she cares, but I'm not her responsibility. So, you see, this is why you can't come with me." Eram finished bitterly, unable to look at Abby.

They sat in silence for a time. Eram could feel Abby looking at him. He felt like a pathetic whining child, but once he started, he could not stop himself. He also didn't know which was more pathetic--his whining or the fact that he felt somehow justified in doing so.

"Oh Eram..." Abby got up and straddled him on the bed and took his face in her hands and forced him to look at her. "Melisa loves you more than I have ever seen anyone love someone before. She is leaving because she feels you have the potential to do great things and be a great man. She leaves because she feels for you to be that great man, she must not be around to hold you down. It is tearing her apart. I would never tell her what you said, because it would kill her. I am sure Lisa and Ulrick care for you just as much. It is like I said before: there are strange things about; I can feel it in the air. The lack of love for you in this town is not natural. There is a sinister power here. That is why you must leave. That is why Melisa must leave, and that is why I must go with you." She kissed him on the forehead briefly, then pulled back. "You can try and convince yourself that your dream is delusion, but I know what I felt when Ulrick sent me here. I know what I felt when you recounted your dream, and I am not delusional." She got up and left.

Eram sat in bed thinking about his conversation with Abby. He was going to have to find a way to get her to go with Melisa, not with him. The smell of cooking bacon roused him out of bed. He was cleaning up and getting dressed when he heard the front door of the Inn open. He recognized the voices, but could not make out what was being said. One of those voices was that of his mother. "Ugh, I hope dad didn't come with her." He said to himself.

It wasn't long before there was a knock on his door. "Come in," he said, and sat on his bed to pull on his boots. He expected his mother, but he got Melisa, followed by his mother, and then Abby taking up the rear. "I can take anyone of you by yourselves, but all three at once is not fair." The levity he was trying for didn't' quite make it into his tone.

His mother sat next to him on the bed and put her hand on his shoulder. "Eramus, Melisa has informed me that you are not leaving with her, but that you are leaving today." Eram started to say something, but his mother stopped him. "I am glad she came and got me so I could say goodbye."

"You are not here to try and stop me?" He was a little surprised.

"No, I understand why you have to leave. I have been fighting this for some time, I don't know what it is, but I know there is nothing here for you." She took his hand in both of hers. "I love you, son, and I hope the best for you. Know that we love you, even your father. I know it doesn't seem like it, but he does. I brought some more things for you to take with you." She gave him a long hug. "I am glad Abby is going with you." Eram gave Abby a dirty look. "I love you son, but I need to get going before your father misses me. Even though he loves you, we don't need his inability to show it right now. Goodbye." She gave him another hug then left.

"Abby, you need to go with Melisa. She shouldn't have to go south alone," Eram pleaded.

"I'm not going alone. Vincent is going with me."

Eram suddenly felt sick. "I don't think that is a good idea. Vincent is not what you think he is."

"Don't worry about me. I Know who Vincent is. It was not his idea anyway. I found out he was going to be going to Southport, so asked if I could tag along. He didn't seem too happy about it, but agreed after some prodding."

They all spent the next few hours preparing to leave. Eram tried to convince Abby several more times to go with Melisa, but in the end, she simply stopped replying and just followed him around until they left.

8 - Lisa

Lisa was in a room with no windows and no furniture. The air was warm and stuffy. It had been a month since Lisa had had her first conversation with the general. She had changed more in that month than any other time in her life. After spending the afternoon cleaning blood off the floor of the audience chamber, she was informed that she would be reporting to Thom, the no-longer-general for duty. He informed her that she was to start training--to be the personal bodyguard of the governor's daughter, Amber.

She had been unable to contain her excitement at the news. The very next day, she regretted the decision to take the job. She had, after all, been given a choice. A month of long hours in training, drills and torture, at least that is how she felt about it, had turned her soft womanly curves into hard muscle.

This morning she was crouched in the center of a medium sized room. She was blindfolded and was struggling to hear her instructor in the room somewhere, trying to visualize where he was. In spite of the cold marble floor under her bare feet, she was painfully aware of the sweat running down the side of her face, around her jaw, down her neck, then slowing slightly at the divot at the base of her neck, before making its way between her breasts and finally pooling in her navel.

She was also painfully aware of her nakedness. Zeek had said that blinding her senses with clothes, would make it harder to learn how to feel the presence and location of others. Lisa was of the opinion that he really just liked hitting naked girls with sticks. They had only been at this exercise for a couple minutes and she already had been hit twice. The second hit was definitely going to leave a mark.

"You're not focusing," Zeek chided from somewhere to her right. Lisa really did not like Zeek and she was going to have to tell Thom if she had to continue training with him, she would find another job.

"If you don't focus, you will never get this." Zeek's voice grated on her. How did he get to her left and rear without her hearing it? How could anyone move so quietly so quickly, she wondered.

"Why am I naked again?" she asked. "It is really hard to focus when I'm naked. I really doubt I'm going to be naked when I am fighting off assassins. If feeling them coming requires being naked, doesn't that make the skill nearly useless?"

"Once you learn the skill, you will know what the feelings are and you will become better at it, then you will no longer need to be naked." Was his response directly in front of her? Lisa quickly rolled to her left out of the way of the hit she thought was coming.

"You see, Lisa, you are trying to use your ears. I'm not going to hit you when I'm talking." This time he was to her left, and she apparently had almost rolled into him instead of avoiding him.

The next hit was so hard it brought tears to her eyes and left a lingering wetness. Her yelp of pain elicited a slight chuckle from Zeek. She gently touched where he just hit her and her finger came back wet with what she assumed was blood.

"It is only going to get worse if you can't learn this." His tone seemed to convey a hope of failure on her part.

After licking the blood from her finger, Lisa, with unveiled hatred and intense sincerity exclaimed, "As soon as I am able, I will make you pay for this."

"Little girl, you will never be able, and if you ever are, I will deserve whatever you deem necessary payment." Zeek's chuckled response held very little insecurity.

With the taste of her own blood in her mouth, she adjusted her focus. She stopped trying to feel where he was, to avoid being hit, but to find him and beat him until nobody could tell who he was. Then she would beat him some more.

She crouched back down in the center of the room. She did not know how she knew it was the center of the room. She did not even think about how she knew, it just felt right. Then she visualized the space and where Zeek was. She imagined him slinking around the room several feet out of range, leering down his oversized hawk nose at her naked body. The sour smell of old sweat permeated his clothes and left a trail through the air behind him. She hated this man and she was going to make him pay.

She imagined him, slowly stopping just behind and to the left of her. He raised his stick. She figured that the angle he was going for would be right over the last hit, inflicting more damage to the same spot.

The stick started its course toward her back, but she was ready. She ducked slightly, leaned right and lifted her left arm to stop the stick. Apparently, it was not just imagined, pain exploded in her left arm, but she was focused, all the pain was just increasing the pain she would inflict upon him. The stick slowed enough by the impact with her left arm to allow her to grab the end with her right. She then spun right as she stood up straight, pulling the stick straight out of Zeek's grip. She continued the spin, increased speed and extended the stick to impact where she imagined his head would be.

It connected solidly to the back of Zeek's head. He was lucky the stick was thin, designed more for whipping than bludgeoning, otherwise his skull would have cracked with the impact and her revenge would be complete.

Zeek was caught off guard by her move; his forward momentum combined with the hit to the back of his head, caused him to fall forward and slide on his belly across the marble floor. He did not stay there--he was on his feet quickly and facing Lisa, his knife out. Lisa took a defensive stance and stayed facing him as he thought to circle around to get at her from behind. Seeing that she stayed facing him he started his attack anyway.

"Zeek! Stop!" The command filled the room. Standing in the open-door was Thom. "Zeek, what in the three hells is going on here?"

Zeek calmly turned, sheathed his knife and faced Thom. "Sir, she abandoned her training and assaulted me." His tone was matter-of-fact.

"So, you planned on killing her?" He motioned to the now sheathed knife.

"Of course not, sir. The knife was simply to keep that stick from causing any more damage," he said calmly. Lisa hadn't noticed until now that Zeek was bleeding profusely out of the back of his head.

Over the course of the last months training, Lisa had learned one thing over all others--and that was when Thom was in general-mode, you did not speak until spoken to. So, she held her tongue while Zeek told his lies. She also knew he hated emotional outbursts. If you wanted him to make a fair judgment, you had to present your case calmly and logically. She took a deep breath and calmed herself so she could answer the questions she was sure he was going to ask.

Thom looked at Lisa. "Zeek, you're dismissed. I will have a talk with Lisa. Oh, and you might want to have someone look at your head; it's pretty bad."

Lisa was infuriated. How could Thom just let him go and he was going to have a talk with her? She almost forgot her training and told him what she thought. She almost forgot her training, but she didn't. She stood--back straight--and waited for the asshole to leave.

After Zeek left, Thom shut the door to the room and picked up Lisa's clothes that were lying on the floor. He then walked over to where Lisa still stood at attention. Her jaw clenched to keep from breaking decorum. He held her clothes out to her. "Get dressed." He then turned his back to give her some privacy and waited.

Lisa put on her trousers, but did not put on her shirt, she simply held it in her left hand while still holding the stick in her right. She was not going to feel ashamed of her bare breasts--they were bare because of Zeek, after all. It was his shame; she was keeping bared before him and she wanted Thom to know it. "Sir," she indicated she was done.

He turned back around. Lisa noted with satisfaction, his disapproving raise of his eye brows. He did not say anything, so she volunteered and explanation. "The wound on my back will stick to my shirt. I thought I would put some salve on it before I put my shirt on so it doesn't." Her tone was academic.

Thom just stood there looking at her for what seemed like forever. He didn't say a word; he just stood there. Finally, Lisa could not take it anymore. "Well, am I dismissed or are you going to have a talk with me about Zeek's lack of control?"

The last part about Zeek's lack of control brought a smile to his face. Lisa relaxed a little.

Thom still just stood there though, staring at her--at least he was polite enough to look her in the eye instead of elsewhere.

She could no longer pretend her nakedness did not bother her, so she moved her shirt up to cover her breasts; she looked disapprovingly at Thom. This finally got a response out of Thom. "Are you going to take off your blindfold before we leave?"

Lisa was shocked by the revelation, so much so, she forgot her shame, dropped both the shirt and stick and removed her blindfold with both hands and looked questioningly at Thom. "How is this possible?"

"How indeed...Cover yourself up and walk with me." He started out the door.

Lisa picked up her shirt and hurried to catch up to Thom. "Where are we going?"

He looked down at her. "First we are going to see Cynthia for some salve so you can put your shirt on."

Lisa was about to ask him about Zeek's behavior, but before she could, Thom looked down at her, his eyes sincere. "I'm sorry about what happened back there."

"It's not your fault. Zeek is a creep."

"Let me finish. I'm sorry you went through that, but I'm glad you did." He looked at her purposefully, almost fearful of her reaction not because he was afraid of her, but because he cared for her and did not want this to hurt their relationship.

Lisa was shocked by the statement at first, but she knew him well enough to trust his judgment, but she still wasn't going to let him off too easy. "Why are you glad... because you finally got to see me naked?" she asked loud enough for a man that was walking in the hall in front of them to overhear.

The man looked back to see the subject of the comment and seeing Lisa with her shirt held just barely covering herself did not look forward fast enough for Thom's liking. "Eyes on task, soldier."

The man made it a point to turn down the next side hall.

The look he gave her made her day. "I'm glad because I expected the military side of your training to take the better part of three months, but after your performance today, I think you are ready for the next step." She started to respond, but he stopped her with an upheld hand. "Let me explain why I am so proud of you today. First, you followed my orders to work with Zeek and do as he said, even though what he wanted you to do was ridiculous. I did not realize how ridiculous it would be," he clarified. "But after he got out of hand, you used proper judgment and took control of the situation." The look in his eyes was excited and proud. "The fact that you have the abilities you possess is of no small significance. Finally, after it was said and done, you stood there in great pain and waited, while he lied to me. You waited for my judgment and you still held your tongue, when that judgment seemed unjust."

They walked in silence for a moment before Lisa finally said seriously, "He was going to kill me. You know that, right?"

"I know he was going to try. That is where I went wrong today. I had planned on being there for your training, but I was held up. After seeing what he had planned for your training, I realize he had had me held up," Thom said, then continued very serious and subdued, "For that reason, your next duty in your training is to kill Zeek. It won't be today or tomorrow, but soon. As much as it pains me to have to bloody your hands, it can't be helped. As Amber's protector you will be required to do it at some point. Zeek's behavior today made me realize he is a danger to our goals and he will need to be eliminated, so it might as well be you."

"I held my tongue, because I trust your judgment. I knew when you asked me to do this job it would require my hands getting dirty. I figured Zeek just required a severe beating, but in this, I will also trust your judgment and do what needs to be done."

They were nearly to the kitchen when Thom stopped. "I'm going to let you go on alone. Cynthia will kill me when she sees that gash on your back. Since I feel somewhat responsible, I would let her. When you are done here, get cleaned up and meet me at Amber's room. I am going to be there most of the day going over what I expect from her. Take your time-- you've had a rough morning."

"I'm going to kill that old bastard." Cynthia, tenderly applied a thick, honey-like salve to the gash on Lisa's back.

Lisa's aunt had been going on and on for a while, but Lisa wasn't really paying attention. She would close her eyes and watch everything that was going on in the kitchen. Then she would open them to verify what she was seeing was really happening. She marveled at the accuracy. In fact, she saw more detail with her eyes closed than open, and the people in the room all seemed to have dim colors that surrounded them. The colors seemed to correspond to what type of person they were and what their mood was. She could also see things from every angle, like if she were walking around the room. But it was better than walking around the room, because there were no obstacles. Her perspective could move through solid objects. She could change her perspective from one side of the room to the other with a thought.

The fascination she had with her new-found talent, made her forget the pain entirely.

"Okay I'm done. You can run off and get yourself beat some more." Cynthia just shook her head as Lisa absently put her shirt on and walked out of the kitchen.

Lisa contemplated what her new role would entail as she walked toward the governor's daughter's rooms. She had actually never been into Amber's rooms. Even though she had taken the job to be her personal protector, she hadn't even had more than just passing words with Amber. As a kitchen helper, someone else was assigned to the governor's daughter.

As she made her way into less familiar areas of the keep, she found her new-found ability to be a little less spectacular. In areas she did not know well, when she closed her eyes, she could not see her surroundings; she could only see the colors of the people she passed. If she knew the person, she could see them clearly, but those she did not know or knew little of, she could only see the colors of their personality. What those colors meant, she had no idea.

The double doors to the governor's daughter's rooms were open and there were two guards one on either side of the door. The guard closest to the direction she came from told her to go in...and that Amber was a little annoyed that her breakfast was late. Lisa was suddenly afraid she may have forgotten to bring breakfast with her, but decided to continue and hope she was not in too much trouble.

When she entered, she was struck with how large the room was. There was a large fireplace on one wall, two very soft looking sofas, a small table between them in front of the fireplace. On the other side of the room was a door that Lisa assumed went into Amber's bedroom, and a small table made of a rich looking dark wood. The table was just big enough for four people to sit at close together. Two of the chairs were occupied. Amber was sitting in one of the chairs and across from her was the former general. Thom noticed her come in and motioned her to come over.

Amber turned to look at Lisa. "Oh good, you're here. I'm starving." Lisa slowed, but kept walking.

Thom noticed her discomfort. "Lisa is not bringing breakfast. She is the person we were just talking about."

Amber looked from Thom to Lisa, then back to Thom. "She is my new protector? She is not quite what I was expecting. Shouldn't she be a bit bigger and definitely... I expected someone more experienced. She does not look any older than I do, and, isn't she one of the kitchen help? I know I have seen her around before delivering food. Also, I thought that you said my new protector is a mage."

Thom chuckled at Amber's comments and the look of confusion on Lisa's face. "Sam…, Pete." he said, motioning toward the guards at the door.

"Yes, sir," they said in unison.

"You two are now dismissed to do what we discussed earlier. Pete, will you, however, stop by the kitchen and ask how Ambers breakfast is coming?"

"Yes, sir." They saluted and left, closing the doors behind them.

Thom was chuckling again. Both girls were just looking at him. Lisa refrained from comment because she knew her place, and Amber in what looked to Lisa to be confusion.

"So, are you going to explain or are you just going to laugh at both of us for the rest of the day?" Amber's tone was mock anger.

The look Thom gave Amber spoke volumes to Lisa. She realized the love this man had for the young woman he was charged with protecting. She had seen that look from her own father many times. This revelation was sobering for Lisa; she just realized the trust Thom had put in her and she was now feeling inadequate to the task. Also, *what was that nonsense about a mage?*

"Ok, I will explain so you can both be put at ease." He stopped laughing. "Lisa, has been training with me personally and with my most skilled at combat. She has done exceptionally well."

He looked pointedly at Lisa. "The point is, as I have told both of you before, the best protector is the one that nobody sees--or more to the point, the one everyone sees as something else entirely. Lisa fits this role perfectly; she is close to your same age so she can pass as a close friend or someone hired to ensure the chastity of the governor's daughter. She can also stay closer to you than any of the male guards, for the same reason." Thom paused to take a drink.

Amber used this opportunity to ask, "I suppose you expect her to stay here in my rooms? This is exactly the invasion of privacy I was talking about when I made my objections to increased protection, when my father suggested it. You said you had a solution we could both live with. I'm not sure this fits that promise."

Lisa's discomfort was growing, causing a cold sweat to mix with the blood from her earlier injury, washing the numbing salve away, causing sharp pain as salty sweat entered the wound.

Amber must have noticed the discomfort. "I'm sorry Lisa, I don't mean to be insulting. This has nothing to do with you or your skills--which I still doubt, but has more to do with me having to share my room with someone else, regardless of who they are."

Thom, all humor was now gone and his tone was what Lisa recognized as the end of any argument said, "This really is not up for your approval, Amber. I have done all I can to ensure you as much privacy as possible, but we have heard nothing of your brother in over a month, which points to assassination rather than kidnapping. The assumption I have made is that those responsible either plan on killing you or your father. If they leave you alive, they are counting on your incompetence. If they leave your father alive, it points to a hope for war with the Western Territory. They won't leave both of you alive because your temperance is the only thing that has stopped your father from marching to war."

Thom took a deep breath then softened his tone. "I have

been charged with your protection. It is currently my only purpose. If I fail at this, I have nothing left. I have spent a good deal of time with Lisa. I feel I know her pretty well. She is the best I could come up with since I will not continue to have Sam out here in your parlor...while you sleep." Thom smiled. "I know you have grown very fond of Sam and the thought of him out here while you sleep has brought you a great deal of comfort, and you hate to lose that, but both your father and I think the relationship has gotten too close."

"Really, Sam, how could you think such a thing?" Amber was indignant.

"No, not really, but I think I finally made my point," Thom finished as the knock came to the door announcing the arrival of breakfast.

Lisa had not realized how hungry she was. She was very thankful that Thom had ordered enough for all three of them. The food was good like always, but the selection brought to the governor's daughter was a little better than she was used to. for one thing, she had apples which were rare this far south, and was typically considered reserved for the well-to-do. Lisa refrained from partaking of the more expensive items and stuck to the standard fair of eggs and cheese, which she ate more of than either Amber or Thom.

When the meal was nearly done, Amber turned, picked up one of the two apples, and tossed it at Lisa when she thought she wasn't looking.

Without thinking or looking, Lisa caught the apple and held it out to Amber.

Smiling appraisingly, "She does have good reflexes. Lisa, eat the apple I saw you looking at it. And, if you are to look like a friend, and not some sort of bodyguard, you are going to have to start eating and dressing the part."

"She is right, Lisa. And after what you went through this

morning, you deserve it." Thom took the other apple.

Amber saw the shared look and said, "I did not think my comments were particularly harsh or out of line, but I apologize if I put you through an ordeal. Although, I still think you two had better give me some better assurances of Lisa's skills in regards to my protection."

Thom's tone was once again playful. "Amber, I don't think your comments caused Lisa any discomfort. You see, Lisa started her training for the day six hours ago--which included a pretty sound beating that concluded with the knocking of Zeek senseless."

Amber looked from Thom to Lisa. "You did that to Zeek? Zeek is an animal. I've seen him fight; you better watch your back. He doesn't like being beat, and if it gets out, he got beat by a girl, he will be doubly mad."

Thom winked at Lisa. "She not only beat Zeek, she did it unarmed, blindfolded, and naked," Thom serious once more added, "This information, of course, does not leave this room. Remember she is a friend, not your protector. She is simply an unassuming young woman."

Lisa ate the apple and enjoyed it.

Amber watched her for a time then finally asked, "I have not heard you say anything yet. Do you have an opinion in any of this?"

Lisa swallowed the piece of apple. "While on duty, I give my opinion only when asked."

Thom smiled with obvious pride. "Lisa, that stage of your training is done. From now on, your opinion is welcome; you should give it freely. Any insight to any situation in the future is welcome and required. Speak your mind."

Lisa turned toward Amber and put her apple core on the plate in front of her. "Amber, I am very honored to be given the opportunity to help you in whatever you need, and I will try to be as unobtrusive as possible. Though I feel the task may be above my current skills, I will continue to train and use whatever is in my ability to ensure you are kept safe." Lisa then turned to Thom. "Now, what is this nonsense about a mage?"

"I suspected you had the talent when Andarus had taken an interest in you, but after what you did to Zeek earlier, I now no longer have any doubts." Thom reached under his chair and brought up a book and put it on the table in front of Lisa. "This is the only book on magic, I could find without alerting Andarus to what I know. I don't know if it pertains to your particular talent, but as I understand it, there are things that pertain to all types of magic."

The book was not very thick, but it was of the finest quality. The cover was soft leather and the pages were gilded in gold. The title "The Manipulation of Life Energy" was gilded in silver. "But, how do you know I am a mage?" Lisa asked.

Amber seconded the comment both looking to Thom expectantly.

"Open the book to the first chapter."

Lisa opened the book to the first chapter, clearly written in silver gilding was: "Mage Sight, Advantages and Limitations as it pertains to the Life Mage."

"I read the first chapter after I first suspected the reason for Andarus's attentions. Your ability to see where Zeek was, is Mage Sight. You should read it as soon as you can. The first chapter should at least help you know whether you are a life mage or if your talent lies in some other energy form. If it is some other energy form, then I will see what literature I can find to help you learn what you can on your own.

"I've got a few things I need to get lined up for Lisa's transition to her new duties. Amber, show her around. Lisa, you are on duty. Stay alert while looking comfortable." Thom got up, drank the rest of whatever he had in his cup, then left.

The two girls sat uncomfortably silent for a few minutes, Amber absently twisting a piece of her golden hair. Lisa picked up the apple and gleaned as much apple as she could from the core. Lisa decided she needed to break the ice since she was the one intruding. She looked at Amber who was staring at her intently. Lisa was struck by the intensity of what she just noticed as unnaturally green eyes studying her. Not wanting to give into the urge to look away she said, "You should not toy with him like that. Thom really cares for you and only wants the best for you."

Amber smiled. "You noticed I wasn't serious about the whole privacy nonsense? I was wondering if it was obvious." Amber sighed. "You noticed I wasn't serious, but you thought he was really affected by my act. It is frustrating that he is so much better at it than I am. It was all an act. I know who you are. Everything was arranged weeks ago, but I wanted to practice our act to see if I was good enough to fool you."

Lisa looked at her in confusion. "Why?"

Amber got up and walked to the doors to the balcony and opened them, letting in a breeze of warm, humid air. "We have decided it would be better if I played the part of the foolish, pampered girl in public. The thought is that if I look incompetent, I will survive assassination attempts, because they are more likely to send cheaper, less competent assassins to do the job."

Lisa thought the idea sound on the surface. "But just because you look incompetent, doesn't mean your protectors are also...and wouldn't that make your father more of a target."

Amber looked at her seriously. "Yes, that is part of the strategy. I love my father, but he has an irrational hatred of the self-proclaimed king, Edward of the Western Territory, and that is what Thom believes is the motivation of the whole plot. He believes whoever is behind whatever has befallen my brother, wants war between the Southern and Western Territories. Thom thinks it is Joshua of the east, but I think it could be either the north or the east, but probably both. If the west and the south weaken each other, then either the east or north can take what they want from either of us. What do you think?"

Lisa was pondering all this new information. At this point her training had been physical. Thom had not gone into any details of why Amber needed such protection or any of the potential plots of the other territories. "Thom did not brief me on any of the political details of your situation, so I'm not sure I can venture an opinion yet."

"Well, that is enough of the serious talk anyway. Come, let me show you around." She went to the door, to what Lisa had assumed, was her bedroom.

Amber's apartment consisted of a parlor--which is where they had eaten breakfast, a small library, a large bedroom, a bath off the bedroom, and a small storage room off the library, they had set up as Lisa's bedroom. The parlor had a large balcony facing north. The library and the bedroom had large windows, also facing north. The apartment was on the third story of the keep, which made it impossible for any normal people from coming in from the balcony and difficult for those more skilled than normal. All of the rooms were tiled in white marble, furnished with plush furniture and light green curtains covered the windows and Amber's bed.

"You think this is all a little excessive for a bedroom for one girl, don't you?" Amber asked.

"You are the governor's daughter. I have no experience with what is, or should be, appropriate for someone of your station."

"That was a diplomatic answer. Well, I think it is quite excessive. Before my mother died a few years ago, I had a single room with rather simple furniture. I was perfectly happy with what I had, but my father said since he was not planning on getting remarried, and he did not want the rooms to sit empty, I needed to move in here."

Amber moved through the library then into her bedroom, opening the windows as she went. "The room we have set up for you is just for show. You will be sleeping on one of the sofas in my bedroom."

Lisa wandered around looking for anything that could be a security risk. Not that she was an expert, but she figured if she started thinking in those terms, she would someday be an expert, and hopefully there wouldn't be any trouble, until she was. "You know the apartment is very nice, and even though it might seem excessive, I think your father is right. The rooms are already here and there's no sense in having it go unappreciated."

"Oh, I forgot to show you the best part." Amber hurried back into the bedroom. "Come over here and tell me what you see." She motioned to the east wall, just to the side of her bed. Lisa looked at the wall for a minute.

"What am I supposed to be looking at?"

"So, you don't see it, do you?" Amber's excitement highlighted her young age.

"I don't know what I'm supposed to see."

Amber moved a little further down the wall and kicked one of the stones at the base of the wall. When she did, Lisa heard a click from inside the wall and a section of wall swung back revealing a hidden hallway. Lisa was amazed. "That is impressive. I really would have never seen it, but should you be showing me your secret passageway?"

Amber didn't respond, she just led the way into the passage and closed the wall behind them. She started down the hall, which turned right after about fifteen feet. The hall was illuminated by small vents at the top.

They continued down the hall until they came to a wood panel with small beams of light coming through it. "You can see into the library through those holes." Then she continued a few more feet to a dead end with some more holes. "You can see into the parlor through these holes and both panels have levers that open panels into to either room. There is also one into the hall outside of my apartment. You can't open any of the panels from inside the rooms, except the one in my bedroom."

Amber looked through the holes into the parlor to make sure no one was there, then opened the panel and stepped out. Once Lisa was through, she pulled the panel closed, and like the door in the bedroom, once it was closed, she could not tell it was there.

"Should you be showing me this?" she asked again.

"You are my personal guard. I think if anyone should know, it would be you...and I have been dying to show somebody. Having a secret passage is pretty boring if you are the only one who knows about it." She sat back at the table where they had eaten breakfast.

Lisa sat at the table and thumbed the book Thom had given her.

"What is it like?" Amber asked.

Lisa looked over to see Amber looking intently at her, eyes once again very intense and unnaturally bright green. "I just discovered I had any ability at all today. The only thing I think I have experienced is what the book calls Mage Sight."

Amber raised her eyebrows. "I already know that. I want

to know, what this Mage Sight is like." She smiled at Lisa. Once again Lisa was struck by her eyes and the beauty of the girl before her. Amber was one of those women that other women hated because they wished they could be like her. "Thom said you could see while blindfolded. So, close your eyes and tell me what you see."

Lisa closed her eyes and imagined her surroundings she was not really familiar with, but the short tour had helped, so what she could see was relatively detailed. "When I close my eyes, I can see in my mind everything in the room, as long as I am familiar with what was already there. Except people, I can see them as they appear normally or as colors if I don't know them."

"So, you can see everything in the room with your eyes closed. How do you know it is not just a memory of what you already saw?"

Lisa thought a moment. "I think it is just a memory of the area, because in places I haven't been before, I can't see the space very well, but people are different. For example, I can see Thom outside in the hall, talking to someone I don't really know."

Before Lisa finished, Amber was up, heading for the door. She opened it and shouted with unrestrained excitement. "That is so... I can't think of a word, better than great, better than grand, ahh magnificent. That is what it is: magnificent!"

Thom came into the room, followed by a young man that was carrying most of Lisa's personal belongings. "Jan, you can put that on one of the sofas and go get the rest of Lisa's things."

"Yes, sir." Jan hurried out.

Thom closed the door. "What is magnificent?"

Amber still excited, "Lisa could see you and Jan outside in the hall."

"You can see now how her ability is far more valuable than any muscle she may be lacking," Thom said absently, as he closed the balcony doors.

"Lisa was saying people she doesn't know appear as colors and she was just about to tell me what she sees when she looks at me with her mage Sight."

Lisa looked at Amber, confused. "I was...Oh, I guess I can." She closed her eyes. She could see both Thom and Amber and they looked normal except for an aura of color that surrounded each of them. "Both of you look normal, but I can make out colors that surround you. Thom has an aura of brown with blue highlights. Amber you are surrounded by purple... well, purple, only darker, and your eyes are green."

"I know my eyes are green"

"No, I mean they glow green. Now I know why your eyes seem unnaturally green to me."

"What do the colors mean?" Amber asked.

"I have no idea. I will have to read that book and see if it says anything about it."

Lisa sat on a sofa in the library, absently reading the book on energy manipulation. It was a couple hours before dawn. The rooms were all dark except for a lamp on a table sitting next to her so she could see to read. The day before had been filled with Thom going over her duties and getting her belongings transferred to Amber's rooms. She had taken a nap for a couple hours so she could be awake for part of the night.

About all she had been able to learn from the book in her hands was that she was indeed what they call a manipulator of life energy or Life Mage. She could read, but not really well, and this book was filled with descriptions of things she did not understand, and used words she had no idea of their meaning. She was tired of trying to make sense of the nonsense, so she put out the lamp and was about to go into the parlor to make sure everything was in order, when she heard talking from Amber's room.

Lisa entered the bedroom. The moon was bright and low on the horizon, so it bathed the room in a soft pale light. Once in the room, she realized the talking was Amber. *She must be talking in her sleep*, she thought. Amber was not talking loud enough for her to hear what she was saying, so Lisa moved closer to the bed. She could see Amber clearly now. She had stopped talking for a moment and seemed to be listening to something, Then Amber, with a playful half smile said, "Your future," then her expression turned sad. "Or your doom?"

9 - Ulrick

The day was uncomfortably warm, or it would be if Ulrick wasn't sitting in the shade of a large Cottonwood tree. The small stream that ran in front of Bob's shack was just a few feet away, and the calm breeze was cooled as it flowed over the small stream under the trees. The air was thick with cotton falling from the trees. He was sitting cross-legged with his back against the rough bark. Sitting before him on a piece of soft leather were three balls of wax about the size of large unhusked walnuts.

Ulrick was pondering what he was going to carve the three balls into, and why he had chosen to divide the lump of wax into three equal balls, instead of just using it all for a single item.

Bob crossed the stream using the stones sticking above the surface to keep from getting his feet wet. He was quite agile for an old man. He looked down at what Ulrick was working on. "Three, Interesting," he commented as he crouched down in front of Ulrick. "Well, I have searched everything I could think of that might give us some insight into how to remove the demon from your ring, unfortunately I have come up with nothing."

It had been a little over a week since Ulrick and Bob had arrived at Bob's "shack." Ulrick had been quite surprised by the little place. The inside was exactly how he would have imagined it, at least on the surface. A cot, some cooking implements, a deer skin hanging against the stone wall, and some makeshift shelves to put personal items, was all that was visible. Then Bob led him past the hanging deer skin into a hollowed space in the cliff. He then triggered a hidden switch that exposed a stairway that lead up into the cliff. When he reached the top, nearly fifty steps up, Ulrick was amazed by the immense room before him. It was at least fifty feet long and twenty feet wide with several holes in the long wall that overlooked the cottonwood trees outside. The room was set up as a kitchen, a library with more books than he had ever seen, and a workshop.

The first morning when Ulrick woke, Bob had showed him where everything was kept and told him to make breakfast. After breakfast he had brought Ulrick a large lump of wax and told him, "Carve this into something. Your family has a knack for somehow transferring energy and a little bit of yourself into items you wrought yourselves. The ring and the sword you carry were made by ancestors of yours. I don't know how or why it is possible, but it is."

Ulrick had just looked at the wax, confused. "I am supposed to make a magic item out of wax."

Bob didn't explain any further, he simply said, "I am going to research our little demon problem. You are going to make me my meals and stay out of my way. Carving something will help you stay out of my way, and make sure you don't put that ring on until I know you are going to be safe."

He then spent the week reading.

Since it had been about a week since Bob had so much as acknowledged his existence, Ulrick was taken aback by the comment and took some time to ask. "So, is my ring and sword now useless?"

"I hope not. While I have not found anything that would help us remove it, I have pondered the problem for quite some time and I think I have a solution we may be able to live with."

"Live with it?" Ulrick's eyebrows raised questioningly.

"What I'm thinking is that you have not given yourself willingly, nor have you been broken, so this demon should not be able to control you--so long as you consciously exclude it from being within you." Bob stood and paced back and forth.

"If it is captured in the ring and I can't remove it, how

147

can I exclude it? Wouldn't excluding it be the same as removing it?" Ulrick wrapped the wax balls up in the leather and put them into a pack he kept close by.

Bob was a long time answering. "I don't know, but we need to try something. Here is what we are going to do. You will need to put on the ring, but I want to have a hold of your hand so I can remove it if things get out of hand." Still pacing he continued, "Once you have the ring on, you need to use your Mage Sight and imagine the demon standing before you, like you did at the Golden Anvil. You said when you saw it there, it spoke to your Mage Sight projection, right?"

"Yes, she stood before me, separate from the man sitting at the booth and spoke to me." Ulrick pulled the egg-shaped box out of his belt pouch.

"My theory is that only you have the means to control the ring and it somehow feeds off of your will. Perhaps you can simply command the demon to do as you say. I know it sounds a little iffy, but it is worth a try."

Bob sat down beside Ulrick and took his wrist in his hand. "Now put on the ring, but make sure you keep your fingers extended so I can get it off, if there is a problem."

Ulrick hesitated for a moment before opening the box. He had opened it several times during his boredom of the last week. Each time the power of the pull of the ring was breathtaking. He had noticed that the killing of the goblins had had much less effect on the power the ring held than when he had killed the men in the tavern, but the goblin energy came with harder to deal with emotions. The anger and urge to kill was a difficult thing. He braced himself for the staggering power and opened the box.

The power seemed slightly reduced from the last time, but the effect was still breathtaking. He wondered if he would ever get used to it. He did not like the irritation of the pull, so he hurried and put the ring on.

The high-pitched scream that filled his head would have deafened him if it was an actual physical sound, but as it was, it was so loud within him, it caused a sharp pain in his head that rendered him physically incapacitated. It took all his will to yell, "Take it off! Take it off!"

Bob removed the ring. Ulrick sighed, hurriedly putting the ring back in the box. All the pain was gone.

"What happened?" Bob asked.

"I don't know. I put on the ring and there was a very loud high-pitched scream in my head that made my head feel like it was going to explode.

"Does it still hurt?"

"No, as soon as you took the ring off, it was like it had not happened."

Bob got up and paced some more, his brow furrowed in thought. "Okay, let's try it again, but before you put the ring back on, you need to visualize the demon in front of you, with a gag in its mouth."

Bob sat back down. "Get the ring back out, but don't put it on."

Ulrick pulled the ring out. "It is quite hard to visualize anything. The pull of the ring is quite strong and distracting."

"Interesting. your father had never described the pull to me. His father had told me of the residual emotions. So, you can feel the power within the ring even when it is off. I would think just holding the ring could help with your mage training, practicing your concentration while holding the ring could improve your willpower." Bob's tone was reflective.

"Okay, while holding the ring, I want you to visualize the demon as you saw it before. While you do that, make sure you include a gag in the picture you project." Bob sat back down and took Ulrick's arm again "Take your time and describe exactly what you saw and visualize pulling the energy from the ring and putting it into painting the picture you describe."

Ulrick held the ring in his right hand. He struggled to focus; the pull from the ring was intense. After a few minutes, he started to imagine the demon before him, and as he did, he described the scene to Bob. "The demon is standing in front of me. Her skin is smooth, milk white; her figure is nearly perfect. Her hair is the color of blood after it has sat for a few minutes, and her eyes are the color of wet spring moss."

Ulrick took a deep breath and wiped the sweat from his forehead, before it could run into his eyes. "She has a large dirty rag in her mouth. It is shoved in so tight, she can't move her mouth, and her hands are shackled behind her back. The shackles are steel and are not affected by the green flames that lick her naked body. "

Bob jumped to his feet and exclaimed, "Bloody sheep balls on fire! Ulrick, put the ring back in the box."

Ulrick did as he was told, relieved to have the ring back in the box. "Why? What is wrong?"

Bob was pacing, then took off toward his shack, not bothering to keep his feet dry--he just plowed through the stream, not seeming to notice or care. Ulrick was about to follow when Bob called back. "Stay there. I'll be right back."

Ulrick sat back down and wondered what could have affected the old man so strongly. The only other time he had ever seen Bob hurry, was when Eram was dying.

It was about an hour before Bob returned carrying a small book. "Sorry it took me longer to find it than it should have." He handed the book to Ulrick.

The book had a plain leather cover. The title was crudely stamped into the leather and said "The Green Witch." Ulrick opened the book and started reading. "You think I have the soul of the Green Witch trapped in my ring?"

"Here, give it back." Bob took the book back and opened it to the back page and held it up for Ulrick to see. "Does that look like what you saw?"

Sure enough, somewhat crudely drawn and doing no justice to her beauty, was a depiction of what had stood before him at the tavern.

"You know, I met her once. She was quite beautiful like you describe. If she wasn't completely insane, she was some-one I definitely would have liked to have spent more time with." Bob handed the book back to Ulrick. "She was a genius when it came to manipulating thermal energy. But she wasn't satisfied with that power. She had to experiment with blood magic and it destroyed her sanity." Bob sat back down. He had a sad smile as he reminisced.

"Uh... you could not have known her. This book says she died one hundred and seventy years ago," Ulrick said, once again reading the first page.

Bob chuckled. "Let's try this again. I think we might have an advantage knowing who we are dealing with. If you end up having a conversation with her, her name is Natalia. Knowing her real name might help with what we are trying to do. Don't call her by any title she may give; always call her Natalia."

Ulrick pulled his ring out and started describing the demon as he remembered, but added the bindings and gag like he had done before. Then he whispered her name, just before he put on the ring.

Ulrick had his eyes closed, but he could clearly see, and standing before him--just as he had imagined--was the demon,

Natalia. Her eyes blazed hatred. The emerald flames felt like they were blistering his skin. There was no scream; the gag seemed to be working. Ulrick was confused as to what to do next. The heat of virtual flames, as well as the heat building inside him as he looked at the naked beauty before him, was mesmerizing. He was so distracted that he didn't notice the rag gagging the demon was burning away, then it was gone. The Green Witch laughed, the inhuman sound cutting into Ulrick, driving a beautiful fear into him. "Boy, kneel before your new master."

Ulrick really wanted to do as she asked. At that moment, all he wanted to do was please the woman before him.

"What is going on? Are you alright?" Bob asked.

Bob's question broke the trance and gave Ulrick a moment of inspiration. "No... Natalia, kneel before your new master".

"Noooo..." The scream Natalia let out once again was deafening, but because it originated outside of himself, rather than within, it was less severe, which allowed him to imagine a large stone lodged tightly in her mouth. The scream stopped. Even the fury in her eyes was somehow arousing to him. He then imagined a modest dress for her to wear so he could think straight.

"Natalia, kneel before your new master," he repeated.

She just stood there, hatred in her eyes. The dress he put on her quickly burned away, and she once again stood before him clothed only in translucent flames.

"Do you have no shame, standing before me naked?"

Rock still in her mouth, she rolled her eyes at him. "If I remove the stone, will you promise not to scream?"

She nodded. Ulrick imagined the rock gone.

"How do you know my name?"

"Answer my questions and I will tell you how I know your name."

"Shame?" She extinguished the flames and gestured to her naked form. "What do I have to be ashamed of?"

Ulrick imagined her in another dress, this one even more modest than the first, going from the ground all the way to her chin, then he veiled her piercing green eyes. "What of modesty then?"

"Modesty?" She laughed. "I am not Modesty, I am Pride." Her tone was filled with derision. "When I resided upon your plane of existence, I found modesty rather foolish. Why would I veil my power over you? Why would I hide my greatest assets, confining myself to appease the opinions of lesser beings? Men hated me because I would not submit to them. Women hated me because men had no self-control around me. Women hated me because they had no confidence in themselves." She laughed again with more mirth. Her new dress burned away. "They hated me while I lived, then they worshiped me, after I died." She indicated the book sitting on the ground beside him.

"I have answered your questions. Now tell me how do you know my name," she ordered him.

He weighed his options. He wasn't sure if he should tell her the truth. He figured the less she knew the better his bargaining position. So, he simply gestured at the book she had indicated just a moment ago.

"The more you lie to me, dog, the more pain you will feel when I finally destroy you." She tried to get her hands free from the shackles. "Boy, if you behave yourself and just submit to my will, I will not seek out those you love. If, however, you continue to resist, once I do take control, which is just a matter of time, I will visit every person you care about and destroy them with words from your mouth and pain delivered by your own hand. Those you care the most about will come to despise you so greatly that they will seek your life, and when they do, I will give up control so you can defend yourself and kill them with your own free will."

Each word she said dripped with sincere malice. The green flames flared, sending waves of hot hatred at him. "You see, I am the Queen of Pain. I have never taken the life of a single soul. I never have to; they take their own lives, and you will dream of death with every breath. You will, however, live a very long life. When your body finally dies, you will join me in the next plane, because your broken soul won't be able to be without the lovely pain, I have given you."

"Enough... kneel before your new master, Natalia," he commanded, unable to hide the fear and anger he felt.

She laughed, a deep belly laugh. "I never knelt before anyone when I lived in the base plane; I never knelt when I resided in the first negative plane." Dark hatred replaced any humor there may have been and her voice lost most of its human tone. The change gave Ulrick the chills. "And I will not kneel before you."

The waves of projected fear made Ulrick lost as to what to do next. He needed her gone or he needed her constrained, at the least. He was unable to even keep a dress on her for more than a few moments. Finally, he had an idea. "Natalia, you and I have a problem. I believe you are stuck, somehow attached to my ring." Trying to hide the fear he felt, he indicated the ring on his left middle finger. "And I would like the use of my ring, which I can't use if I have to have a test of wills, every time I put it on. If we can't come to some sort of agreement, I am going to have to leave it in the box." He picked up the egg-shaped box and held it in front of her. He noticed the very slight change in her demeanor when he held the box. That is what he was hoping for. "I doubt the week you spent in the box was very exciting." He opened the box. "I bet it is dark in there.

In fact, I bet without my link to the ring, you can't see or hear anything. So, unless we come to an agreement, I fear you will spend eternity in quiet darkness."

She stood before him, the green flames died, her beautiful form nearly transparent. All the hatred and fear radiating from her disappeared with the flames. She whispered, "I will bow to no man."

Ulrick actually felt sorry for her. She had gone from a demon of power that had complete control of another soul and fed off the emotions of an entire town, to being a prisoner trapped in a tiny egg. Of course, she probably was manipulating his emotions. Either way he needed a solution. "I will not make you bow to me, if you can come up with some other solution."

He was caught completely off guard by the blur of motion, and then she was within him. His left hand had clamped shut and Bob was having difficulty prying his hand open to get the ring off. He finally managed to break the middle finger and remove the ring.

Bob put the ring back in the box. "What happened?"

"I guess she had to try," Ulrick managed to say through the pain of his broken finger. "I think we should just leave her in the egg for a while. Maybe she will be more cooperative after another week of silent darkness."

Ulrick and Bob returned to Bob's home, so Bob could do what he could to relieve the pain of Ulrick's broken finger and splint it so it would heal straight. Ulrick relayed the conversation he had with Natalia.

"You did well with the binding of the hands, but I think next time you should imagine her hanging by her feet from one of the high branches," Bob said as they climbed the stairs into the main room of his home.

Bob started making their lunch. Ulrick was glad; for the first time since he had arrived at Bob's home, he wasn't doing it. He was frying what smelled like ham as he spoke. "Well, we are a week behind schedule. We need to make up for lost time in regards to your study. I would normally throw a bunch of books in front of you and have you reading day and night, but most young people of your generation read slow and understand little, so I will not waste our time with you reading."

Ulrick let the insulting assumption that he could not read well slide. He was glad he was not going to spend the next month reading. "So, why am I carving wax? It seems a wax magical item is of little use."

Bob chuckled as he fixed Ulrick and himself a plate of ham, then poured them both a glass of water and sat it all on the table. "The wax will simply be used as a mold for the casting. Most of the items your family made in the past have been silver. I do not know if they cast them or carved them by hand. I also don't know if it matters, but we will find out. So why do you have three equal balls? What do you plan on carving?"

Ulrick, through a mouthful of very good ham said, "I don't know. It just happened that way, and I have no idea what to carve them into. Can they just be round balls?"

"I honestly don't know, but from what I have read of others that have had the talent, the more time and effort spent producing the item, the more useful they are, you may find round balls rather useless."

"When we were at the Golden Anvil, you had mentioned that the Green Witch was a demon from another plane of existence. She had also mentioned what she called the base plane and the first negative plane. If you knew her then, how, did she come to live in another plane of existence?" Ulrick asked.

Bob slowly finished his ham, then took his time to drink

his water. The slow manner and the silence from the wizard always annoyed Ulrick. Why couldn't he just answer a question, or at least acknowledge the fact he had heard the question.

He picked the ham out from between his teeth as he finally began to talk. "First, let me explain the nature of our existence--at least what I know from all the study I have done over my lifetime." He wiped something he had picked from his mouth on his robe. "Maybe it would be best if we find out what you know and how much of it is nonsense. What do you know?"

Ulrick was caught a little off guard by the very vague question, but he had already been thinking about what he had been taught as a kid, and what others in town had believed and come to the realization that he really had never cared about what superstitions people held.

Vincent had always been the one to philosophize. Ulrick had never really believed any of it anyway. He had never believed in ghosts or demons or angels. But now he faced a demon, so there must be more to it than he had previously thought. "I don't really know anything. If there wasn't a demon inhabiting my ring, I would have never believed you if you said such a thing existed."

"Damn, so I have to teach you everything." Bob started clearing the dishes. "I guess a clean slate is better than false beliefs." Bob sat back down, clasped his hands together and rested his elbows on the smooth oak table. "I will be giving you quite a bit of information; most is truth and some is my own theories. I will try to let you know which is which, even though I think my theories pretty sound."

"There are several planes of existence. The exact number was debated heavily during the last golden age of man," Bob was saying.

"What is the last golden age of man?" Ulrick inter-rupted.

Bob looked at him, annoyed. "The last golden age ended about two thousand years ago. It wasn't until the end of that age they discovered the existence of the other planes. The discovery was made after the breeding of the mages and the creation of the goblins." Bob could see by Ulrick's confused look; the boy really knew nothing.

"Okay, I can see this is going to be a bigger job than I had originally thought, so I will just start with how mages came to be, then you can go gather some eggs and ponder what I tell you. Then, tomorrow I will teach you of the creation of the goblins. After that, I can explain what was learned by those two things.

It was discovered sometime in the last golden age that certain people had within them the ability to see energy patterns. As you know, most people do not have this ability. Once this was discovered, there was a group of educated men that started breeding those with the talent. What started as the ability to see energy patterns, eventually became the ability to manipulate the energy they could see." Bob yawned. "Everything I have read from the time, which isn't much--most was destroyed in the Great War, nobody really knew how they could manipulate energy.

As you can imagine, those with the ability became both powerful and feared, but mostly they were sought after for what they could pass to their children. Most male mages during that time had ten to twenty wives, and female mages spent most of their lives pregnant, having fifteen to twenty children. Of course, not all children of mages were born with the talent, but all children of two mages were...and the offspring of the untalented children of mages--when coupled with mages--increased the chance of talented offspring. Within one hundred years of the first mage, the population of those with the ability had become quite large. Working together and setting up schools, they made great advances in magic."

"So, we are both related to those mages of the golden age?" Ulrick managed to ask when Bob paused to drink.

Bob looked at Ulrick seriously. "Yes, which brings up a different matter. During those days, everyone had two names. The first name was their name given by their parents, and their second name was their family name. Those with known mage family names, whether they had talent or not, were quite sought after for marriage."

"Why don't we use family names anymore?"

"The events that lead to the Great War were rightly blamed on mages. After the war, anyone with a mage family name was hunted and exterminated. So those with mage names stopped using them and some that just wanted to protect those being hunted for no reason other than their name, also stopped using family names. Eventually, everyone stopped using family names. Because of the hardships after the war and the utter destruction of the technology of the golden age, most people now have no knowledge of the war or what caused it. So, mages like us can live freely without fear.

"This brings me to the most important thing you need to remember. If you remember anything I tell you, you must not forget this one thing. The Great War was caused by mages. More specifically, it was caused by one overused ability of a mage. That talent was once called teleportation. It is now called "walking the veil." You must never do it... ever." He was deadly serious, reminding Ulrick of Bob's threat to kill him not that long ago.

"What does this 'teleportation' do?" Ulrick asked, breaking the uncomfortable silence created by Bob's last comment.

"Walking the veil allows a person to move from one

location to another location almost instantly." He paused, his demeanor pensive. Ulrick knew if he interrupted now, he would get the old man's wrath. It was several minutes before Bob continued. "Walking the veil makes it easier for our friend Natalia to enter this plane and cause her discord. I will not teach you how. If by some chance you learn how on your own, don't do it." Bob yawned again. "I am going to take a nap. Find something useful to do until I wake."

Ulrick went outside. He wandered south along the small stream that meandered past Bob's cave. Bob had a small chicken coop carved into the cliff face, a stone throw from the little hut that was his false home. Ulrick was about to gather what eggs there were, but decided he would get them on his way back. He did have all afternoon; Bob rarely woke from his naps until the next morning.

As he wandered south. He found several deeper pools of water along the stream that he thought he would come back to later and try to catch some fish. The further south he went, the more the stream cut into the sandstone, eventually becoming narrow with cliffs, rising on both sides, blocking the sun and cooling the air. Some areas became so narrow, Ulrick was unable to continue without walking in the stream. He walked down the slot canyon for several hours, then the cliffs gave way to an open meadow of knee-high grass.

A single, very large cottonwood was growing in the middle of the meadow, about a half mile from where he stood. He made his way to it. When he reached the tree, he noticed two other streams met the stream he had been following, becoming one, much larger, slow-moving stream just beyond the tree. He followed the larger stream for a while, hoping to see some fish.

Ulrick was contemplating continuing his trek or returning to Bob's home. He really wanted to keep exploring, but it would probably be dark before he got back as it was.

Some areas in the slot canyon had been difficult to navigate; in the dark they would be very difficult. That decided him. He turned back to return home.

On the other side of the tree, how he had missed it when he had walked by before, he didn't know. There was something metal, shining in the sun. Each step he took increased his unease. As he neared, the metal looked more and more like a helmet, and as he got closer, he noticed the helmet was worn, judging by the sunburst insignia on his shoulder--a soldier of the Southern Territory.

The soldier was dead or near enough. It looked like he had been injured some time ago and had made it to this tree and could not make it any further. His pants were caked in dried blood that had leaked from a wound in his gut.

Ulrick wondered what to do. He could not just leave him here, but he could not carry him as far as he had to go. He thought maybe he could look through the man's belongings to see if he could find something that might identify him. He started looking for a belt pouch when he moved the man to check under the side he was lying on. The man's sharp intake of breath startled Ulrick, causing him to fall on his ass.

The man opened his pain filled eyes. He coughed up some bloody phlegm, which just dribbled down his chin, death too near to be able to wipe it off. "Thom...T-t-t...," another cough of blood. "T-tell...Thom...," another cough of blood. "P-Petre..." another cough of blood, "betrayed...T-tell only Thom..." another cough. "K-k-kill... me." He held his shaking, blood-encrusted hand toward Ulrick. "P-p-please... k-kill me." Then he closed his eyes, tears making tracks through the dirt on his face.

Ulrick sat there, stunned. He had no idea what the man had tried to tell him. He did not know of anyone named Petre or Thom. Had Petre betrayed? Or was he himself betrayed? He thought to nudge the man to better explain, but he did not have the heart to bring the man more pain. Also, he had brought no weapons with him. How would he put this poor soul out of his misery? He could use a stone to bash his head, but that could take a couple hits to finish him.

Ulrick's stomach twisted just thinking about it. This man's plight reminded him of his friend Eramus whom he had left in Elk Valley. He wondered if his friend had survived and if he was asking someone to end his misery, like this man was. *Would he have been able to help Eram die if that is what he had wanted? Would he be able to help this man?*

He looked around the area to see if he could find the soldier's sword. He must have dropped it some distance away, because Ulrick found no sign of it.

The soldier coughed again and his whole body convulsed in pain. A high-pitched whine and more tears issued from the man.

Ulrick steeled himself. He could not let this poor man suffer any longer. He looked around for a rock small enough to fit in one hand, but heavy enough to do the job.

Finding a rock the right size, he went to the man, and as gently as he could, he removed his helmet. He picked up the stone in his right hand and steadied himself for the blow. The man opened his eyes and looked up at Ulrick, stone ready.

"Close your eyes," Ulrick said quietly, tears from his own eyes flowing freely. The man complied. Ulrick put every ounce of effort into the blow. Hot, feverish blood exploded completely covering his hand and splattering on his face.

Ulrick stepped back several steps, dropped the stone and knelt, head down. "Be at peace, my friend," his voice quiet, but harsh with emotion. He knelt, eyes closed for some unknown amount of time, all sensation lost. It was strange, releasing this man from his misery gave Ulrick a sense of kinship for him, and even though he had killed the man he was comforted. It didn't come with the guilt like the deaths of the men from the tavern had. He was still racked with sorrow every time he thought of it, which was frequently.

The first thing he heard was a Robin, singing in the tree above. Then, the pleasant gurgle of the stream to his right, then a cricket signaling the coming of night. The beauty around him was oblivious to the horror that sat in front of him. Ulrick stood and started home. He avoided looking at the soldier; he did not want to see the mess he had made.

When he reached the slot canyon, he knelt by the stream and slowly cleaned the blood from his hands and face in the cold water. Then he started his hike up the quickly darkening canyon.

He figured he was nearly three quarters of the way through the canyon when he could no longer see where he was going well enough to keep going. He had already twisted his ankle, and a stray branch from a bush had nearly taken out his eye. So, he found a dry rock to sit on and think of how he was going to make it home. If he stayed here, as wet as he was, he could die of the chill.

He was still emotionally numb from the trauma of a few hours ago, but several questions kept rolling through his mind. Who was the soldier? What was his mission, and what was the meaning of the message he was willing to put himself through so much pain to relay?

The sound of a rock being turned, as if something heavy had stepped on it several yards behind him, caused his heart to jump. He stopped breathing so he could listen, but the stream drowned all but the louder sounds and he heard nothing more. He knew, however, there was something there, and being in a slot canyon, it was most likely heading his way. He was fortunate the breeze was coming from behind and he had been in and out of the stream so it was unlikely he was being tracked by scent, but a mountain cat stalking him or happening upon him by chance, would probably end with him in its belly either way.

The shock got his mind working again. It occurred to him that while in Smithville he had been able to see the tavern room clearly when he focused on it with his eyes closed. He tried it, but he had no visual reference to refer to, so all he got was darkness. He kept concentrating; he was desperate. What at first seemed like darkness, was not. Within the darkness, there were flashes of light--sometimes yellow and sometimes blue. He could see a slight glow in the stream.

He concentrated in the direction of the noise he had heard. Sure enough, there was something there. In the shape of a large cat was a multi-colored mass. Yellow flashed along the outside, and as it moved, lightning fast flashes of blue raced from its head to its limbs while red flashes raced to its head from different parts of its body, mostly from its feet and face. Its internals pulsed with green flashes that ran along the spine and into its heart, which clearly had its own green glow.

The cat, the size of a very large dog, was leisurely drinking from the stream. *It must not be aware of me*, Ulrick thought, *but that won't last long. Then he will be dead. Unless of course he can scare it before it is aware of what it faces.*

Slowly, Ulrick bent and felt around for a loose rock, big enough to cause some damage, but small enough to throw accurately. Rock in hand, he quickly reared back and threw with all the force he could muster. Normally, he would have aimed at the large center of the animal, increasing the likelihood of hitting his target, but he was distracted by all the light coming and going from the head. So instead of a body shot, the rock flew toward the cat's head. Ulrick put all of his concentration behind the throw. His life depended on its success.

The stone hit the cat with a sickening wet thud. The cat did not run as he was hoping, instead, it simply fell to the ground. Red lights still flashed to the head, but the blue flashes had stopped completely and the red flashes were dying out. The green of the heart was still pumping, though the lungs no longer moved.

Ulrick inched closer to the cat, fascinated by the slowly dimming, green glow of the heart. Once he was nearly on top of the cat, he noticed the red flashes were still active, but they were dim and did not travel toward the head, but instead just flashed like millions of twinkling stars.

He accessed his situation, now that he was familiar with this strange sight. The dim flashes in bushes and trees became more apparent. He could plainly see the glow of the stream, which dimly shimmered a rainbow of color.

He also noticed that if he concentrated on the colors of the water, they swirled and reacted to his will. When they entered his body, he began to itch. Not an itch he could scratch, but an itch that infused his body with discomfort, centering on his sore ankle and his tight belt, but with the discomfort also came energy and strength.

He could never hold it in long, like Bob had once told him. He felt compelled to let it go, so every few seconds, what he pulled in simply spilled back into the water. Feeling a new excitement and energy, he hefted the large mountain cat up onto his shoulders, feet dangling to either side of his head, and started back up stream.

When he got to the small shack, he dumped the cat on the ground; he would deal with it in the morning. Then he climbed the stairs. Bob was still asleep, so he went to his bed and was asleep almost before he was lying down.

Ulrick woke. Blinding sunlight filled the room. Barely visible through the glare, Bob was sitting in a chair, staring at him with amusement in his eyes. "Why are you watching me sleep again?" Ulrick asked, then went to move and found each movement was pure agony, so he stopped.

"I'm not watching you sleep. I' am watching you wake up." Bob chuckled at his own wit. "You had an interesting night, didn't you?"

"What? Did you see the cat?"

"No, I haven't seen any cats. Did you bring home a stray?" Bob was still smiling.

Ulrick was in great pain; every muscle in his body was stiff and each slight movement made the agony worse. "What is so damn funny, old man?"

"You unlocked yourself...and you did it without dying. What is truly great, is that even though you did not kill yourself, you did, however, cause enough damage that I doubt you will ever forget it."

"What?" Ulrick asked, still annoyed and more confused.

"There are two stages to unlocking the abilities of a mage. The first stage is really more of the development of a minor mage sight and very slight, unconscious energy manipulation. The second stage is a true unlocking of your abilities. You can now fully see the energy type you are adept at manipulating, and you can control when you see it. You can also call it to your aid, which is why you are unable to move without causing great pain." Bob laughed again when he said great pain. "The second stage usually requires two conditions to be met. The first is, you must be physically mature enough. Children cannot develop to the second stage. The second requirement is severe need or perceived need. Fear or great anger is usually the catalyst, but occasionally great sorrow can do it. I have been racking my brain trying to think of how I was going to unlock your abilities without killing you...or getting myself killed in the process. Your particular talent can be fairly volatile, if not tightly controlled."

Ulrick thought of the events of the previous day and concluded he had a pretty trying afternoon. "So why am I so sore?"

"You must have used electrical energy to increase the command to your muscles," Bob explained.

"What?" Ulrick was confused again.

"What did you see last night? You mentioned a cat."

Ulrick described his encounter with the mountain cat. He described the different colors of flashes moving through the cat's body.

"The flashes were electrical impulses the cat's brain sends to its muscles. Those impulses tell the muscles to move and how much to move and with how much force. Usually your body has controls on how much force your muscles are told to use. These controls keep you from tearing muscles and breaking bones. By utilizing the charged ions from the water, because you were carrying the cat, you added to the energy of the impulses from your brain, bypassing your normal physical controls. Now your muscles are sorely used. I have checked, and you are lucky none are so severely torn to keep you from a full recovery, but however, you will be in very much pain for a couple weeks." Bob chuckled again.

"Why do you think my misery is so funny?"

"I am not laughing at your pain...well okay, I am. But mostly, I am glad I don't have to waste my time teaching you this lesson only to have you ignore it because you are young and know better than I do. We have arrived at the desired location without the need for me being frustrated by your stupidity."

Ulrick didn't know whether to be glad or insulted.

Bob started filling a tub that was against the inside wall. The water flowed from a pipe that had been driven deep into the stone wall and was capped with a valve. Ulrick felt the air chill a little, then the water in the tub was steaming.

Bob returned to Ulrick's bed. "Let me help you into the tub; the hot water will help loosen the cramped muscles."

The hot water was almost scalding, but after a few moments, the heat did relieve some of the soreness. While soaking in the tub, Ulrick relayed his encounter with the dying soldier. Bob did know who Petre and Thom were, but he had not been to Southport in over a year and was not sure what to think of the message of betrayal. They had decided to go bury the man as soon as Ulrick was up to it, if the body was still there, anyway. Bob had already planned to go to Southport in about a month, so they would relay the message when they got there. Hopefully Thom would be able to make sense of it.

Ulrick spent the next week hobbling around the cave. Bob had refrained from any more tutoring; he had said there was no point--the pain would cause him to forget the lessons. The stairs were beyond his strength most of the week. By the seventh day, however, he managed to make it down the stairs and outside. Once outside, he noticed the cat had been skinned and the skin was staked out drying in the sun. Bob was walking up the stream with a basket of eggs. "I'm glad you killed that cat. I think the chickens are also glad." Bob set the eggs into the shade of the hut, then came back outside. "I think we should try to get that witch in your ring to cooperate again today. Do you think you are up to it?"

"Might as well. Me being weak might make getting the ring off easier. Maybe you won't have to break another finger to get it off," Ulrick said, strangely up beat at the prospect of getting another finger broken.

They both assumed the same positions they had before: Ulrick sat cross-legged against the tree, Bob sat next to him. "Put the ring on your little finger this time. Perhaps the loose fit will make it easier to get off, if needed." Bob took hold of Ulrick's arm.

Ulrick took the ring out of the egg and began imagining the Green Witch in all her sinister beauty, hanging upside down by her ankles, from one of the branches of the cottonwood, hands shackled...and a rock firmly lodged in her mouth.

He put on the ring.

There she was, hanging before him. The green flames radiated the heat of her hatred and contempt. Ulrick realized he truly had control of her so long as he kept her in her place. If only he could trust her to not try to take control. He pulled his arm free of Bob. "It's alright, she is bound." He got up and hobbled over to the shack, retrieved a small bucket and filled it with water. He walked back over and mentally adjusted the steel cable he had imagined into place around her ankles so that her face was even with his. He then imagined her in a modest dress, and before the dress could start to burn, he threw the bucket of water on her. The flames went out and her dress steamed.

Ulrick was quite fascinated by the dual nature of what was before him. On one hand, imaginary bindings kept her bound, but she hung from a real tree and real water put out her flames. By the look in her eye, the dichotomy was not lost on Natalia either. "As you can see, I have complete control of your world. The ring is tuned to me; you have no power over it. Your continued resistance is pointless. As I see it, you have two choices: one is to continue to try to control me, forcing me to leave you like this." He gestured to her situation. "Or you can make some sort of promise to me that you will not try to negatively interfere in my affairs. If you choose the second option, I will commit to you that I will seek a means of removing you from the ring. If you choose to continue to be a pain in the ass, I will grow to despise you and imagine more and more humiliating circumstances for you to manifest in." Ulrick turned his back on her, walked back to the tree and sat back down.

The dress he had put her in was nearly dry and starting

C L Larson

to smoke. He wondered if she had heard anything, he had just said to her. Her continued rebellion against his will was starting to infuriate him.

Bob put his hand on his arm. "Relax, she can use your anger to her advantage. Whatever she is doing to annoy you, let her. You are right; she has no true power here. If she did, we would be wrestling the ring off again."

"Can you see or hear her?" Ulrick asked Bob.

"No, but I can see a slight spirit energy signature where you have imagined her."

Ulrick exhaled his anger, took a deep breath and smiled at the Green Witch, as her dress burned away and she once again hung before him naked. The green flames flared, then went out and the two of them simply stared at each other. Ulrick found himself admiring her naked form, but he caught himself and did not fall into the trance as before. He continued to stare her in the eye.

After nearly an hour, she finally closed her eyes and nodded her head. Ulrick took that as at least a desire to talk, so he got up and physically removed the imaginary rock from her mouth. He tossed the rock aside--it disappeared before it hit the ground. He lengthened the cable and let her down from the tree and he physically helped her stand on her shackled feet. He marveled at the softness of her smooth naked flesh, but he kept control. He took two steps back. "Well, what do you have to say?"

Softly, her voice very human and feminine, "How do you know my name?"

"From the book," Ulrick lied.

"Why, if you have no fear of me, do you continue to lie? I read that book when I possessed that lump of putrid flesh in Smithville. My name was never mentioned. If you seek trust,

170

then tell me the truth," she said, her anger smoldering.

Ulrick really did not want to compromise Bob, but at this point, it really was just a matter of his control. She could do him no harm. "Bob here, told me your name." He did not say it out loud, but she seemed to hear him. He did not want Bob to know he had told her. He didn't think Bob would care, but he did not want to take any chances.

She looked at Bob in shock. "Robert still lives? He was a handsome fifty when I last saw him. The last two hundred years have diminished him, but not as much as one would think."

Ulrick looked at Bob. Bob returned his look, a question in his eye. Ulrick ignored the questioning look and turned back to Natalia. "How could he be two hundred and fifty years old?"

"The mage ability, when utilized sparingly and with control, can actually prolong one's life. Using it unwisely, like you have recently, will shorten your life. Speaking of the ability, you have unlocked since we last spoke, how long was I in that cursed egg?"

"A week and a day."

"What did he do to unlock you? I am impressed with his training; most lightning mages usually cause some permanent harm to themselves or others when they unlock." Her tone was conversational.

"He actually had nothing to do with it. Apparently, I just got lucky when I encountered a mountain cat the other night."

"Lucky indeed, for both of you," she commented casually. Then her tone suddenly became serious. "I have a couple demands if I am going to become compliant. Will you honor my wishes?"

"What are your 'demands?'" His tone dismissive of her

ability to demand anything.

Anger flared, but she controlled it. "You must never ask me to bow to you. You must never put a dress on me again. And, you must never call me crazy. If you do not honor these conditions, I will always be trying to destroy you. You may think you have complete control, but I will always be here, and in that moment of complacency, my interference will be your death or the death of one you are trying to protect."

Ulrick thought her demands were 'crazy.' Nothing she had demanded seemed difficult to comply to. In fact, other than the distraction of her being naked, he really could care less. "I don't see why I can't honor your request. We have a deal then? You will no longer try to control me; you will not negatively interfere with me or mine, and in return I will not make you wear clothes, ask you to bow to me, or call you crazy. How can I trust you to hold up your end of the deal?"

She looked him in the eye. "I have tortured, tempted and corrupted, but I don't lie, and I never murdered. I understand your hesitancy, however, being a dishonest man makes it hard for you to trust others. Are you going to unshackle me now?" She smiled innocently.

"Do you promise?"

"So long as you uphold your end of the bargain, I promise to bring you no harm." When she finished, she dimmed and fell to her knees.

Ulrick hesitated. "Unshackling was never part of the bargain."

Her look was ice. Chuckling he removed the shackles. She knelt down in front of Bob and looked him over curiously.

Bob looked at Ulrick through Natalia. "Have you come to some sort of agreement? I can tell she has moved and is sitting right in front of me. To be honest, it is kind of giving me the heebie-jeebies."

"We have come to an agreement. Judging by her reaction when she finished making her promise, the ring will hold her to it." His tone was pensive.

Later that day, Ulrick was sitting in his usual place under the cottonwood. Three balls of wax sat on a piece of leather. He picked one up and began absently molding the wax. It first became oblong. Then he started flattening the bottom. Sitting in the shade of the tree with the sound of the stream reminded him of his times under the pine with Eram, trying to catch trout. He wondered if Eram was doing okay. Bob had assured him Eram would survive his injuries, but would he survive Elk Valley without Lisa?

Thinking of Eram and Lisa brought Naomi to mind. His time with her last winter was the best two weeks of his life. He could see her brown hair blowing in the breeze. He could almost smell the sweet bread she baked, and feel her small soft hands as he held them to keep them warm. He longed for more of the long hours spent in front of the fireplace, just sitting close. He only had a few more weeks and would be heading back to her--and the rest of his life by her side.

He hoped Vince had not gone back to complicate things.

"Who do you think of that brings such a content smile to your face?" Natalia asked in a very subtle mocking tone.

Ulrick's mood couldn't help but darken with the question. "It doesn't matter. I'm sure you will find out soon enough; until then you can just wonder." The comment came out poutier than he had intended. He instantly regretted the response. He should not allow Natalia to get to him.

"A skull...not very original. You could have done better than that," she continued to taunt him.

Ulrick looked down at what he had been absently carving. Sure enough, the first ball had become a skull; he had even started hollowing out the center. He looked at Natalia. "I did not realize I was carving a skull until you mentioned it. Why not a skull? It will match the ring and the sword."

Natalia's face contorted with sudden surprise. "I should have realized who you were the first time I saw the ring and the fact that sword cut clean through that gluttonous pile of goblin shit I had possession of."

Ulrick paused his carving and asked, "Who do you think I am?"

"I have yet to hear your name, but if your family tradition held out this long, then your name is Ulrick. Am I wrong?" Her tone betrayed just a little of the fear and anticipation she felt.

"You are not wrong."

She knelt down beside him. Her green flames produced a pleasant warmth in the cool evening air. "I was there, you know. It was before I had started experimenting with the spirit magic. Your great, great...I have no idea how many greats it would be, but a grandfather of yours, the first one with ability--he made the ring. We were friends, not close, but friendly. Like you, he did not like how I flaunted my body. He thought I should save my beauty for whomever I fell in love with." She laughed bitterly. "Love is lie."

She laughed again, this time with more mirth. "It is quite ironic, really; here I am trapped in a ring made by a man I once knew, held by a distant relative being taught by another man I once knew, though I don't think Robert and Ulrick ever met. All this happens two hundred years after my life in this realm. Fate is playing a cruel trick on me."

Ulrick found he really didn't care about his great, great whatever grandfather. He felt he should care, but he didn't. "I think it is time for bed. I hope you don't mind, but you are going to spend the night in the egg. I will let you out again in the morning." He did not wait for her to respond. He took off the ring and put it away, put away his wax sculptures and made his way to his bed.

Ulrick woke to the racket of a large flock of starlings outside in the trees. Bob was sitting at one of his workshop tables reading something. He lifted his attention from the book when he noticed Ulrick sit up. "I will tell you a little of what I know of how goblins came into being while you get ready for the day." He closed the book and continued. "Wear one of your robes today. I want you to practice some manipulation as we travel today."

Ulrick rubbed the sleep from his eyes. "Where are we going?"

"We are going to see if there is anything left of that soldier you met." Bob got up and made his way to the kitchen area of the cave and started boiling some eggs. "Okay... where to begin...? Before the Great War, there of course were your standard wars between different countries, territories and what have you." Bob got another pan out and started frying some eggs for breakfast. "The somewhat constant conflict kept each faction searching for some weapon to give them the edge. One of those weapons was the creation of the goblin. Goblins were created in a laboratory. The traits of different animals were 'spliced' into humans. The traits they focused on, of course, were traits that made them better soldiers--and they wanted them to be able to reproduce and mature much faster than normal."

Ulrick put on one of his robes. It felt strange walking around without any constrictions. "How long does it take to get used to just flopping around down there?" He looked at Bob expectantly.

Bob looked at him sideways. "How long did it take for you to get used to always being squished down there? As I was saying, they wanted them to mature faster," he continued, annoyed by the interruption. "Those man-sized goblins we fought in Elk Valley were no more than three or four years old. They begin to grow slower as they age, but they never stop growing; a goblin your age would be seven to eight feet tall. Back in the old days, they called the larger ones Ogres, but these days it is rare to see one that has lived that long, because one of the traits they bred for was aggression. Left without a strong commander or an enemy to fight, they resort to killing each other. They reach sexual maturity at two-to-three years and the gestation period is four-to-six months, depending on the traits of the female."

Eggs done, Bob put half on a plate for Ulrick and his half, he just ate out of the pan.

Ulrick had a few questions, but realized if he did not want to have a miserable day he was just going to have to silently listen until the old bastard was done. He retrieved his ring from the egg-shaped box and put it on. Most of the emotions of the men he had killed in Smithville had bled off, for which he was thankful. He did not imagine Natalia before him this time and she did not immediately appear, giving him a pang of anxiety. When she did finally appear, she was somewhat clothed. She was wearing form-fitting white leather pants, made from the skin of some scaled reptile and printed with green vines with small blood red flowers. They laced up the outside of her legs. She still was not wearing a shirt and instead of green flames covering her entire body they covered only her arms. Feet bare, she didn't wear shoes.

She gave him a devious, half smile. "Good morning, Ulrick."

"Good morning," he responded mentally so as not to interrupt Bob. He was pretty sure the partially clothed look was just as, or more distracting, as the all nude.

"So, a strong disciplined commander could turn a small

force of goblins into a great horde in a matter of a dozen years," Bob was saying while, packing the boiled eggs gently into his pack. "The attack in Elk Valley and the situation in Smithville, and the fact that we have had very few goblin incursions from the north for nearly twenty years, tells me we may be facing that horde sooner than we will be ready for."

The last comment gave Ulrick a sick feeling. "What do you know of what evil is being planned?" he mentally, asked Natalia.

She shrugged. "Not everyone from the negative planes has some concerted agenda. My possession of the wretch in Smithville was simply a moment of opportunity. If there is some great plan, then my taking of that opportunity has probably muddied the water for them a little. Unless of course, a little chaos was all they were looking for, then it wouldn't matter."

"If the goblins were created to serve as soldiers, why don't we just capture some and breed our own army to counter what may be being bred?" Ulrick asked Bob.

Both Bob and Natalia answered at the same time. "That would be impossible."

"Why?" Ulrick asked innocently.

"I was going to get to that," Bob responded. "Like I was saying before, goblins are creations of man, they are unnatural. This is how they discovered that there are other planes. Once the veil had been weakened by excessive use of teleportation, demons started possessing the unnatural, intelligent, creations of man. Mankind learned a lot the first couple years after the possessions began. Most of what was learned was how much we had messed things up. No more questions until we get on our way." Bob shouldered his pack and headed for the stairs.

When they got outside, Ulrick started heading down

stream. "Hold up. Get the horses saddled. We are not going through the narrows. It is quicker to walk through the narrows, but it is just as quick to ride around the narrows, and a lot easier." Bob headed toward where the horses were corralled.

Saddled up and riding, they headed mostly south, up into the hills east of the gorge. The hills were mostly brush, with the occasional stands of short growing oak and the occasional tall pine. The morning was cool, but the breeze was dry and slight, promising a hot afternoon. They rode in silence. Bob led. The lay of the land was such that riding side by side was difficult, so Ulrick remained far enough behind to keep from eating the dust kicked up from Bob's beautiful white stallion.

Natalia started out walking beside his horse. But she could not walk fast enough to keep up and there seemed to be a maximum distance she could lag behind before her link to Ulrick's ring would pull her along. Both Ulrick and Natalia found the sensation of her being pulled uncomfortable, so she ended up riding behind Ulrick on the horse.

Ulrick found the whole experience disconcerting. On one hand, she was not physically in this world, but on the other, he could touch her and she was affected by the physical world as he willed it--or not so much as he willed, but more by how he perceived it. She, however, could not affect the physical world in anyway. Except, she was able to the affect him physically, as she occasionally did whenever she leaned against him, her naked breasts pressing against his back. The situation brought several questions he needed to ask Bob to mind. It took just a few moments to catch up to Bob. "I have a couple questions I need to ask you."

Bob looked at him quizzically. "The demon rides behind you?"

Ulrick glanced at Natalia, as he responded. "Yes. Her nature and the relationship she and I have with the ring are what I wanted to ask you about." He waited for Bob to reply for a few moments. He never knew how to talk to the old man. He was sure if he started asking, he would be interrupted, so he remained silent.

"Well, what are these questions?" Bob asked, annoyed.

It was several moments before Ulrick could come up with a question that he hoped would shed some light on what was going on, and not seem stupid to the old wizard. "You had mentioned that the ring was the first item made by my ancestors, and that each of the other items were made by other ancestors later. What was the ring used for before the sword was made?" he asked, then quickly added, "As far as I can tell, the ring has no purpose, other than holding and utilizing the energy captured by the sword."

Bob seemed pleased by the question. "The ring served absolutely no purpose for your father, but the man that made the ring was a mage like yourself. The ring in the hands of a mage is very useful. It is what we call an energy sink."

"So, I can put energy into the ring...without killing something?"

"Yes, but don't try it yet. That is one of your future lessons. You must first learn how to discharge the energy you gather safely, before you can safely store it. The ring stores the energy in the same form that it is inputted. Heat energy remains heat energy. Life energy remains life energy. So, the energy gathered by your sword being a derivative of life energy, gives you energy and makes the sword lighter. This is obviously a very simplified explanation and does little to explain the complex way in which the sword, you, and the ring interact. I am not sure anyone truly understands the Silverskull artifacts. They are truly unique." Bob's explanation stopped suddenly. he pulled his horse to a stop and he looked around a little uneasy.

Ulrick pulled his horse to a stop. "What is it?"

"Shhh," Bob exclaimed, eyes closed searchingly. "Look out!"

Bob's warning, came just as a fist sized stone struck, nearly knocking Ulrick from the saddle. Pain exploded in his left arm. Several other stones flew by, narrowly missing the two.

Without thinking, Ulrick had his sword in hand and was searching for the source of the thrown stones. He spotted one man as he stood up from behind a boulder several yards up the hill, as he let-fly another stone. Knowing the stone's course, it was easy to avoid, but several more men suddenly stood, also throwing stones. Most were easily avoided, but one managed to graze Ulrick's already sore and swelling left arm.

One of the stone throwers burst into flame. Screaming, the man ran south, then started rolling on the ground before coming to a convulsive, silent stop and continued to burn.

One man, shocked by his burning friend, started running further up the hill, he was nearly to the top when he also burst into flame. Ulrick spurred his horse toward the hiding place of the remaining men.

"Leave one alive, if you can," Bob called, just as Ulrick drew close to their attackers hiding place.

Not being the best horseman, and not wanting to get the animal killed, Ulrick dismounted and ran around one of the boulders he had seen one of the men throw from. He just managed to avoid the man's sword as it swung for his head. He stepped back two steps to get out of range of the man's follow up swing. Then he stepped forward with his counterattack. The speed and power of Ulrick's swing caught the man off guard. He managed to keep Ulrick's sword from killing him, but he lost his left hand. Before he could recover, however, his head was flying in a spray of crimson. Ulrick looked for his next opponent. The next boulder was cover for two men. One was cowering, obviously unprepared for the power of their prey. The other, however, was not daunted and faced Ulrick, ready.

Ulrick's swing was aimed at the center of the man. He hoped that the speed and force would end the fight as quickly as the last one. It became obvious, however, that this man was far more skilled than Ulrick's previous opponent, when he easily redirected Ulrick's swing and stepped forward with his counter nearly disemboweling Ulrick. After his close call, Ulrick was more careful and kept the superior swordsman just outside of the man's reach with quick controlled slashes.

Ulrick was not skilled at fighting; his experience was the usual stick fights with Eram and Vincent when he was young. His opponent, however, was skilled. Ulrick was sure he would be dead right now, if not for the extra foot of steel and his supernatural speed. As it was, the man was easily counter- ing everything Ulrick tried. Ulrick just hoped to continue, to keep the man outside of striking distance until his opponent tired enough for him to take advantage.

He did not have to continue long. A fist sized rock knocked the man to the ground. Ulrick was about to finish him.

"Stop!" Bob yelled "We need to find out what these men's purpose was."

The man was still conscious, but he lay prone, both hands holding his head, one covered in the blood leaking from his head. Bob grabbed one of the man's hands and twisted, for- cing the man onto his stomach. He then put his knee into the man's back, causing the man to wince in pain. "Get the rope from my horse."

The man tied up and tied over Ulrick's horse, they con- tinued to the meadow with the dead soldier. Ulrick had tried to continue his questions about his ring, but Bob had simply looked to the man tied over the horse and shook his head.

When they arrived, they found all that was left of the soldier was what was covered in his chain armor. His legs were gone and most of his innards had been eaten out. The soldier's head was still there, but had been torn from his body. All that was left of the head, were teeth marred fragments of bone.

They had tied Ulrick's horse to a large bush some distance away so they could speak freely. "Well, we are not going to learn much from what is left of him, we had best get to work burying what is left," Bob said as he removed the shovel he had brought from his horse and tossed it to Ulrick. "You dig the hole. I will make a marker." Then he disappeared around the other side of the massive cottonwood.

Ulrick found a spot far enough from the tree to avoid large roots, but still close enough to be still under the shade of the tree and started digging. The ground was quite moist and rocks he dug out were not large, so he had a sizeable hole in short order. When he was satisfied with his hole, he went to see how Bob was coming on the marker and found the old wizard sitting up against the far side of the tree, asleep. "I thought you were making a marker?" he asked, loud enough to wake Bob.

Bob looked up, an innocent smile on his face. "I was, but I realized I needed you to cut me a log, and since you were getting along so well, I did not want to interrupt." His smile widened. "Will you cut me a log and bring it over? Preferably a green cut log."

Ulrick shook his head. "How big, and is there a particular type you want?"

"As big around as you can find and as long as you can carry...and oak would be best." Bob leaned back against the tree and closed his eyes.

Ulrick made his way to a stand of scrub oak that grew on the hills that surrounded the small meadow. It was taking Ulrick far longer than he wanted to find a suitable tree to cut a log from, and his frustration was plain.

"What are you looking for?" Natalia asked, her form more solid looking than usual.

"I am not sure, but the man deserves more than just an ordinary post. He had suffered great pain trying to deliver a message. His dedication was inspiring to me. His marker should be significant to any that see it," Ulrick explained, as he vainly searched.

"Maybe I can help. Just following you around is getting quite dull." She suggested, "I will wander aimlessly this direction and you can wander aimlessly that direction."

Ulrick could tell when she had reached the end of the invisible tether that kept her tied to him. She then began doing back and forth sweeps of the area between them. Picking up on her strategy, he began doing the same. When Natalia appeared before him, his heart skipped a beat, not out of fear, but because of her arousing beauty. This caused a pang of guilt, he loved Naomi. He should not have this reaction to other women, especially not a demon who had wanted to destroy him.

Natalia seemed to sense his unease, which gave her pleasure. She gave him a half smile, winked, and then motioned for him to follow. Ulrick chastised himself for noticing the sway of her lithe form as he followed her through the trees. She stopped and pointed to a large pine tree. "Behold Ulrick, is this not what you have been looking for?"

The tree was nearly fifty feet tall and easily three feet in diameter. The branches spread wider the closer to the top they got. The tree appeared to have been struck by lightning some years ago, causing the trunk and limbs near the top to twist into bizarre shapes. "I don't think I will be able to carry this back, and it is pine, not oak."

"Don't be a complete fool. Just cut the tree down and take your pick of twisted branches at the top," she said disgusted. "The lazy old man said 'preferably oak,' not 'it has to be oak.'"

"It would be a shame to cut down such a majestic tree," Ulrick mused.

"I thought this man's memory needed something grand?"

Decided, Ulrick studied the tree, trying to determine which side looked to be the heaviest, before he took his first swing. He took small chunks out, not wanting to get his sword stuck. Once he had a good wedge shape cut about a third of the way through the large trunk, he took a mighty swing at the opposite side, hoping the tree would fall toward the wedge side.

He quickly backed away. He left his sword stuck in the tree, imbedded nearly half way through. He stopped a dozen paces away. The tree initially did nothing. Then he could hear a slight cracking that grew to loud pops, and then a deafening roar as the large tree flattened everything in its path, as it fell.

He stood on the trunk of the large tree and started walking toward the top, cutting branches that blocked his path. When he neared the top, he started looking for a piece that looked like something people would notice as they passed. Not that many people traveled through this out-of-the-way-meadow, but if they did, he wanted this man's grave to be noticed. He found what he wanted. And, filled with the energy of the man he had killed, he hefted the large twisted log onto his shoulder and made his way back to where Bob slept, following Natalia's inviting sway, as he went.

Ashamed once again, he looked past her to see Bob awake and making his way toward him.

When Bob was near enough to be heard, he yelled, "I did not ask you to cut down the whole forest. One simple log would have sufficed." Then he noticed the twisted log was pine. "I thought I said oak!"

Using Natalia's words, "You said 'preferably oak,' not 'it has to be oak.'"

They got back to the hole Ulrick had dug. "Scrape all the bark off and carve a flat spot where you think an inscription should be," Bob instructed.

"I thought you were going to make the marker?" Ulrick asked teasingly

Bob's look was ice. "I am going to make the marker and it will probably take me most of the night. Do as I say and when you are done, put the soldier's remains in the hole and put only a foot of dirt on top of him for the time being." The old man's anger was piqued as he continued. "Then start a fire, set up camp, and make me some dinner...and don't forget to take some water to our prisoner." Ulrick didn't think he deserved the old man's wrath, but he also did not want to fight about it either, so he got to work.

Ulrick finished with the log, then grabbed both of the water skins they had and made his way to his horse. He lifted the man off of his horse and set him on the ground. Then he made sure his legs were tied too tight to untie quickly. Then he untied the man's hands and tossed him the water skin. The man drank deeply, then looked at Ulrick questioningly.

"Why are you here and what was your purpose in attacking us?" Ulrick asked the man as he crouched down to be closer to the man's level.

The man, in response to Ulrick's questions, simply shook his head and remained silent.

"So be it. Hold out your hands." Ulrick re-tied the man's

hands when he complied. Ulrick lifted the man up over his shoulder. Leading his horse, he made his way back to camp. When he got back, Bob looked at him questioningly.

"I asked him his purpose in attacking us and he was not forthcoming. Since I don't have the stomach to torture the information out of him and I don't want to have to watch you do it. I figured I could at least let him get warm by the fire and have some dinner before I remove his head and add him to the hole."

Bob looked at the man then at Ulrick, his expression unreadable. "That sounds good to me. I was hoping to get some information out of him, but the fact that he has been uncooperative means our little fight was more than just a little highway robbery. I don't think we need to waste any food on him, though."

"Don't condemned men usually get to choose their last meal? We can't give a choice, but we can at least feed him." Ulrick stopped and considered a moment, then looked the man in the eye. "Also, if he has anything, he would like to tell any loved ones, depending on how difficult...I may deliver his words to them."

Ulrick got out the frying pan from Bob's saddlebag, added some ham to it and sat it over the small fire. He then got another length of rope and tied the man around his chest, just under his arms, tightly to the tree. Then he untied the man's hands. He got a couple plates out and divided the ham three ways, putting the ham on the plates, one third on each. He was going to eat his out of the pan. He sat the plate on the man's lap. "We have some boiled eggs, would like one...what is your name? Never mind, it will be easier if I don't know." He got a couple eggs out of the bag, put one on Bob's plate and held the other up. "Egg?" he asked the man.

The man looked at the egg, then at the plate of ham. He then started laughing, only a hint of fear could be detected.

"Nice act, boy. You don't think I can tell when someone is bluffing?"

Bob's eyes turned upward from his plate, first looking at the man across the fire, tied to the tree, then to Ulrick. His chewing slowed in anticipation.

"Eat up," was all Ulrick offered for comment and started peeling his egg. The egg peeled, Ulrick took a bite. He did not really care for boiled eggs, but the day had taken a lot out of him, and dividing the ham three ways had left him with less then he wanted.

"Bob, why would Natalia be completely unable to affect the physical world, but feel completely solid to me," Ulrick asked through the last bite of egg.

Bob, not expecting the out of nowhere question, took a minute and a swig of water to wash down what was in his mouth before he responded. "Now that you have had some time to observe, tell me more of what you have noticed."

Ulrick hurried into the ham to get the taste of egg out of his mouth, then washed it down with a pull on the water skin. "Well, like I was saying, she can't affect the world, but she seems to be able to see with her own eyes and hear everything just fine. She also can't move beyond about a hundred yards from me. The ring pulls her along, if I move beyond that range. She also has complete control of her appearance unless I change it."

"I don't have complete control over my appearance. I can change my clothes, flames and hair styles at will, but I can't affect my body--this is precisely how I looked when I lived." Natalia interjected as she sat cross legged between Ulrick and Bob.

Bob noticed Ulrick look into the empty space between them. "Did she just say something to you?"

"Yes, she said she has superficial control over clothing and similar aspects of her appearance, but her body shape is how it was and she can't modify it," Ulrick answered then continued, "Even though she can't affect the physical world, the physical world affects her according to my will or perception." Ulrick picked up a pebble from the ground and lightly threw it at Natalia's head. The pebble bounced off her head and landed in the fire.

"Why the hell did you do that?" Her tone bordered on murder.

Bob and the man across the fire gasped. "That should not be possible. She should be in a form of pure energy. Let me ponder this for a while and then I will get back to you. Our prisoner is done with his meal," Bob pointed out, obviously curious to see what Ulrick intended.

Ulrick didn't acknowledge Bob's reference to the prisoner. He leisurely finished his ham and took another long pull on the water skin. Then he stood, retrieved his sword and returned. "Look, boy," the man began saying. "There is no shame in the attempt. You made a good show of it, probably as good as I've seen, but I have been around awhile. I'm not easily fooled. I called your bluff, now use that sword of yours and cut me loose. If you do, I may tell you something of what we were doing." There was just a little more hesitation in his voice this time.

Ulrick grabbed the rope tying the man's feet together, cringing from a jolt of pain from his broken finger. "I don't bluff. Your fate was sealed when you took the first bite of your last meal. You have heard too much of me. If you did not already know who I am, you do now and your purpose was our death. If I let you go now, you will probably try again," Ulrick said this too loud as he cut the rope tying the man to the tree and started dragging him by the rope around his ankles to the hole he had dug for the soldier.

The man, his hands still free, tried in vain to grab or claw something to stop his progress toward his grave. "I will tell you anything you want to know, just let me go!" he yelled when they reached the hole.

"Too late," Ulrick said as he removed the man's head and pulled the man's body into the hole. Before he turned back to the fire, he nudged the still blinking and gasping head into the hole. "Sorry for the unpleasant company," he said to the already covered soldier.

He returned to the fire and sat against the tree where the now dead man had been. Natalia and Bob were just staring at him. Bob's expression unreadable, Natalia's a little shocked.

He did not know how long he had been sitting there, when the tears started flowing and the sobs took him. He had killed in the heat of battle, but this was cold blood. The man was begging to live. Had he done the right thing? When he became aware of his surroundings again, Bob was at the hole, putting a layer of dirt on top of the recently added body.

Natalia was still staring at him. When she noticed he was returning her look, she said, "You did the right thing. He would have killed you, if given the chance."

"I don't mean to offend," he said sarcastically, "but being told I did the right thing by a half-naked demon, is really not comforting."

He woke with the morning sun bright in his eyes. A pair of ravens were speaking their strange harsh language to each other. Probably wondering where their breakfast had run off to. He noticed right away, his ring was not on. He did not remember removing it last night. Bob must have done it. The thought of Bob got him looking around for the odd old wizard. Bob was at the grave, still working on the marker.

Ulrick got himself up and made his way to the grave. The marker had been carved square, with a pyramid at the top like an obelisk. The square edges still followed the twist of the wood, creating a distorted and twisted obelisk. Somehow the old man had caused the wood to turn as black as night and as smooth as polished marble. "How did you do it?"

"After a quarter millennium, with the ability to manipulate thermal energy, one can come up with some interesting ways to utilize their skills," was Bob's only response to the question.

On one face of the obelisk, carved deep was the inscription: "Here lies two unnamed men. One was brave and honorable the other shameful and cowardly." Bob looked to Ulrick and asked, "Is there anything you would like to add?"

Ulrick thought a moment. "Yes. Add, 'The honorable man a soldier of the Southern Territory died bravely trying to fulfill his duty. The cowardly man, an unknown assassin, died begging for his life after failing to do his duty.'"

Bob concentrated for a moment, smoke rising from the marker. After a few moments, he blew black dust from the deeply inscribed message.

"The black inscription is impossible to see unless you are looking at it very close," Ulrick mentioned.

Bob turned exhausted eyes toward Ulrick. "I have a remedy for that, but I need to sleep for a couple hours before I can finish." Bob made his way to his bedroll.

"Did you remove my ring last night?" Ulrick asked before Bob had made it far.

"Yes, I should have had you remove it before you had your moment of justice yesterday, but what is done is done,"

Bob said sadly.

"Do you think I did the wrong thing?"

"No, if I had, I would have stopped you from doing it. He really left us with no choice. He was obviously the leader of the group that attacked us. If we had captured one of the men with less fortitude, we may have learned something, but anything out of that man's mouth would have been useless. We could have done it in a way that would have been easier on you, however." Bob continued to his bed.

Bob was asleep before Ulrick could walk the distance. Ulrick rummaged through his belt pouch and found the egg-shaped box that held his ring. He hesitated before opening it. He wasn't sure he was up to the foreign emotions that came with the ring when he put it on, and he was sure he wasn't up to the feelings the Green Witch produced, but a problem not faced today, is a bigger problem to face tomorrow.

He got out his leather pad and his two round balls and one nearly finished wax skull and laid them out on the ground in front of him. Then he removed the ring from the egg and put it on. He could not seem to sculpt anything of detail without the ring on.

The absence of Natalia did not cause him any anxiety today. He was now confident she had no ability to cause him harm. It was not long, however, before she appeared. Today's outfit was much like yesterday's, reptilian leather pants, red instead of white, with the same green vines with white flowers instead of red. Her blood red hair was left free with loose curls covering her shoulders. The shadows around her neck would occasionally light up with a flicker of green flame. Ulrick noticed the theme today, red to match her hair, green to match her eyes and white to match her milky smooth skin. The affect never seemed to diminish.

"Good morning." She smiled deviously. "What should

we call you? Perhaps Silverskull the Executioner? It has a nice ring to it, don't you think?"

"No, I don't think. Ulrick, just plain old Ulrick, will suffice." Ulrick forced his eyes from her beauty and focused on the little sculptures before him.

"Okay, good morning, just plain old Ulrick."

Ulrick could not help but smile, in spite of trying not to. "You should go look at what Bob created with our twisted tree last night, while I work on my carvings."

"I have already seen it, because you have seen it." She sat cross legged in front of him.

Her statement got his attention. "What do you mean you've seen it, because I have seen it?" She smiled again. *Damn she is good at manipulating men,* he thought.

"I could answer some of the questions about your ring and 'our relationship' if you just asked me instead of Robert. I think you forget, I was once a thermal mage of no mean talent myself. If he did not have two hundred more years of practice than I, I would surpass his skill and knowledge greatly. I was far more skilled than he was when we were contemporaries," she said with a slight reminiscent pout.

Ulrick looked at her like she had just lost her mind. "I just asked--and just like the old bastard--you went on about something completely off subject. As I become more skilled as a mage, will I become just as difficult to talk to?"

"He almost said it," she said to herself, smiling. Her tone lost all of the playfulness of before and turned academic. "My sight is somehow linked to your mage sight. I can see what you see and what you would be able to see with your mage sight. I don't think my eyes see anything; they are just my focus of your mage sight."

"You can hear and see everything I see...or have seen?"

"No, I can see and hear everything you see or hear and I have memory of everything you have seen very recently, but not what you heard."

"You were a thermal mage. I am a lightning mage. Do you see as you did as a thermal mage, or as I see?"

"I see as you see, or a combination of the two; I'm not sure yet. It has been two hundred years since I have had mage sight. Things in the first negative plane are nothing like this life. Memories from this life are mostly lost when you pass through the veil. This life seems like a distant dream that you have to concentrate on to remember. My memories of this life returned fully when I took possession of that gelatinous slop in Smithville, but he had no talent, so my vision through him was mundane." She looked at Ulrick and smiled again.

"What else can you tell me about our connection, and why do you always refer to the man in Smithville negatively?"

"Two things stand out. One, my ability to see and the distance I can travel from you is affected by the energy level of the ring. Each time you killed yesterday, I felt the surge of life energy. The other thing of note is that I, like you, feel the emotion of those that you kill. Those emotions affected your actions last night.

"The man in Smithville is only worthy of disdain. Any man that would willingly give his will to an unknown entity is the worst of the pathetic. He should have never been granted life to begin with." Her voice filled with utter contempt. "I was going to destroy the innocence of his only daughter, just to see if I could get any resistance worthy of a slug."

Ulrick found this new perspective fascinating. This demon from another plane was disgusted by the man's lack of fortitude and decency. Before this moment, he would have thought such a creature would find contempt in the honesty and goodness of a man, not the lack thereof. "Why, when you died in this plane, did you descend to a negative plane?"

"Descend?" She laughed. "Your ignorance is astounding. Do you even know how many planes there are?"

"No," Ulrick admitted. "Bob said the number of alternate planes of existence was a point of contention."

She laughed again. "That old fool--he should know the information is available to anyone who searches."

"So how many planes are there?"

"First, you need to know the base plane; the plane in which you reside is the lowest energy level plane. The energy level here is like the people that live here; it fluctuates between negative and positive with moments of neutral." She ran her hands through her long, soft hair. "There are three negative planes. Each plane's energy level increases the farther you get from the base plane. There are also three positive planes, the same as negative; each level has a higher energy level. There is one more plane of existence, but it is neither positive nor negative nor is it neutral. That plane harnesses the opposition of the positive and negative planes and turns it to pure light energy. The energy level of that plane is extremely high. The beings that live there are pure like the energy they use.

"Think of it like a horseshoe. The base plane is the bottom of the horseshoe. The negative and positive planes rise from the base plane and turn toward each other. The last plane, the apex plane, resides in the space between the high energy level negative and positive planes." She took a long deep breath, even though she did not need to breathe.

"So why did you ascend to the first negative plane, versus the first positive plane?"

She seemed annoyed by the question. "Apparently, soul

magic--or blood magic as some call it--is a negative energy source. Also, apparently taking away another person's free will is also considered a negative form of power."

She did not give any more details.

For the first time Ulrick thought his looking at her was making her uncomfortable. He thought it a fair exchange, since she usually made him feel ill at ease. "There are those that believe when we die, we are just reborn into this world. Based upon what you have told me, that was simply a myth, like I had thought," he said to change the subject and give her some relief. As much as she might deserve being made to feel uncomfortable, he found he did not like being the cause.

"You are mistaken. The next level of both negative and positive, are significantly higher energy levels than this plane. To move to the next level, you have to have increased in either positive or negative energy. If you are still neutral, or near to it when you die, you will be reborn into this realm," she said longingly.

"So, all the myths people ascribe to and fight about are not myth and are all true, in a manner of speaking," he said, reflectively.

"Yes, in a manner of speaking. It is a tactic of those seeking negative power to create conflict between different beliefs as means of control. My teacher was a master of this kind of manipulation. He was born to no magical ability, but he commanded greater power than any mage-born." Her voice changed into the harsher, not quite female tone, like the voice he had heard the first time he had seen her. Her anger was hot, as her whole being flared in green flame.

She stood, turned away from him. The anger and hatred radiated from her. When not directed at him, Ulrick found it hard not to join his hate to hers. "He is why I find myself here. If I had the power, I would destroy him utterly, over and over

195

and over. Then, when I tire of destroying him, I will suck the life from his soul until he exists nowhere!"

Her scream of rage was deafening. Flames flared higher; balls of flame roared across the meadow. Ulrick's ring flared with green flame.

Then all went quiet. She fell to her knees and cried.

Bob was sitting up, looking at where Natalia sat crying. "I heard and felt that one. What did you do to her?"

"Her rage was not directed at me." As he had felt her rage, he now felt her sorrow. He moved to her side and put his hand on her shoulder, hoping to lessen the sorrow that seemed to permeate the whole valley.

"Do not touch me!" she commanded. "I need no comfort or pity from you," she growled.

Ulrick pulled his hand away. He could feel her hate, sorrow, and embarrassment, radiating in alternating waves. He put his hand back on her shoulder.

She looked up at him and narrowed teary eyes.

"Need has nothing to do with it," he responded as he knelt and put his arm around her. She put up no further resistance. They both remained as they were for some time as she regained control of her emotions.

When she finally got control of herself, Bob was back to work on the marker. Ulrick went over to see what he was doing.

Sitting on a couple stones was the pan Ulrick had used to cook the ham the night before, and in the pan were several silver coins. Bob was concentrating on the coins, and as Ulrick watched, the coins liquefied. Bob then poured the molten silver into the holes of the inscription. There was just a little bit of wood smoke, then the silver was hard once more. The inscription was now a very visible silver in the black wood.

They stood it up in the hole and filled the hole. When finished, the marker stood nearly five feet tall, with nearly that much of the twisted obelisk buried, it was quite fixed in position.

Done with their work they packed up their things.

Ready to return, Bob sat back down next to the cold campfire. "Before we head back, I want you to try gathering some energy and discharging it. I would rather you destroy something out here, rather than my home."

"Okay, what do I do?" Ulrick was a bit excited to finally get to the training the old man had promised.

"First, move further away from me and closer to the small stream," Bob instructed. "There is electrical energy available all around, but most streams and bodies of water contain charged ions. From what you had told me of your experience on your last trip, you had easily pulled energy from the water, so we will start with an energy source that has already worked for you."

Ulrick walked to the small stream. "Now what?"

"Stand in the stream."

Ulrick removed his boots and stepped into the numbingly cold water and looked to Bob for more instruction.

"Hold your hands about a foot apart and close your eyes. You should be able to see the different colors of energy in the stream. Don't pull all the colors, just pick a color and pull it into yourself, like you did the other night. Focus on putting the energy in your right hand and not your left. Don't try to hold the energy, just don't let it flow back to the water." Bob had just a little nervous anticipation in his voice.

Ulrick closed his eyes and started pulling. Of the rainbow of colors flowing around his feet, he started pulling the blue up into his right hand. As it flowed, the itch became more and more intense, and the pain of his broken finger started to become almost unbearable.

"When you have gathered enough energy, the energy will discharge itself. You should not have to do anything but gather..."

As Bob spoke, Ulrick could see the blue energy brightening around his right hand. It was starting to separate from his right hand in the direction of his left hand.

There was a loud pop.

Ulrick was thrown back several feet. He could not move his left arm; smoke and the smell of burnt flesh rose from his left palm. Then the extreme pain flared past his initial shock, causing him to scream and roll about in agony.

It was several minutes before the pain had reduced enough to become aware of Bob standing over him, laughing.

Ulrick would have tried to kill the old bastard, but was not even able to sit up from the pain of cramped muscles and burned flesh.

Bob stopped laughing and said seriously, "That, my young friend, was your second lesson in pain. That much energy would have killed any man without your talent. I think this lesson will definitely give you a respect for the energy you can control and its potential to kill not just others, but yourself."

Through teeth clenched in pain, "You could have just told me."

"Just telling you would not have had the lasting effect this will. Just telling you would not have been nearly as much fun. You know, being born a lightning mage is rare...and surviving long enough to safely control the electrical energy, is even rarer. The only lightning mage I know of, is the man that made your ring, and I never actually met him." Bob paused for some effect that made sense only to him, then continued. "To see it in action was quite thrilling. I am still seeing spots!"

Natalia walked up to him and held out her hand to help him up. "Bob is right, it is quite dangerous and quite thrilling to see. The Ulrick that made your ring, was indeed, quite impressive. The amount of pure power at his command was..." She shuddered in what Ulrick could only call pleasure. "Well, there really aren't any words to describe it." Reminiscing she continued. "He was probably the only..." She looked back at Ulrick. "Never mind."

Ulrick, seeing her hand still out for him to take, said, "I think I need to just lay here for a while longer."

"Yeah, no worries. Take whatever time you need, but when you are ready, I want you to try one more thing before we head home. I am mostly sure what I have in mind, will leave you completely unharmed." Bob did not know Ulrick wasn't talking to him.

"I don't know if your 'mostly sure' is really good enough for me." Ulrick laid there for a couple hours before he felt good enough to get up, and good enough was far from good. He walked around, trying to loosen the cramped muscles on the left side of his body. Ulrick noticed Bob's next experiment somehow involved the assassin's sword, stuck into the stream bottom.

Bob looked up from his preparation. "Some of the color has returned to your face. I think maybe we should try this last experiment and then get heading home. Get into the stream like you did before. Instead of pulling the energy into your hand, pull it into your sword. Also, instead of being held apart, start just letting the energy flow into your sword and back out through the other sword. Then, once a good flow is established, you can slowly add distance between the swords."

Ulrick hesitated as the flow started. Fear of the pain from earlier definitely had its effect. Gritting his teeth, he started the flow. He harnessed the energy that flowed by and also what flowed out of the other sword. He brought back around the circuit, slowly adding more and more current.

Because he was not actually holding any of the energy, he found the itch was quite mild and the increased flow did not increase the discomfort nearly as much.

"Good. I think you have enough flow going. Slowly start pulling the swords apart."

Ulrick did as he was told. He found there was some resistance to the initial separation, and as the swords separated, they seemed to want to remain in contact. Once contact was ended, there was a very fast snapping sound, and blue sparks filled the space between the swords. As the space widened between the swords, the discomfort also increased. The frequency of the sparks that filled the space decreased and the snapping sound increased in amplitude.

When the swords were separated by about a foot and a half, the sound of the snapping was deafening and the flash from the arc of energy was blinding. The discomfort was intense. the only thing that made it possible for him to continue was his exhilarated fascination with what was taking place. He finally had to stop the flow because his wrist was getting hot. When he stopped the flow, he sank to his knees from exhaustion and pain.

Bob, from about ten feet away, said, "That was quite spectacular. I am sure as you learn to control the flow, the discomfort will decrease, and with enough practice, be able to maintain a continuous connection."

It was midafternoon when they got back to Bob's home. Ulrick exhausted, went right to bed and did not wake until late in the morning of the next day.

The next couple weeks were a blur of practicing his talent. He found that he could control several aspects of the flow of energy. He also found he could control the attraction between objects he had energy flowing through--he could cause items to pull together or repel each other. He also found the more he manipulated the energy, the easier it flowed through him.

He had finished his wax skulls a couple days after returning. Bob had wanted him to use electrical energy to melt the metal for the casting, and he had wanted Ulrick to be better practiced before attempting it.

Natalia, during this time had been a mixture of pleasant company, bitter disdain, open ridicule, and rage mixed with long bouts of silence. Ulrick had learned to appreciate the silence.

Sitting in his usual spot under the trees by the small stream, Ulrick absently added small details to the wax skulls. He felt he was ready to finish his project and then they could get going. They could head to Southport and do whatever Bob needed to do. He did not know why he had to go with him.

A part of him wanted to see how Lisa was doing, but his real desires lay in the opposite direction. Ulrick felt he had enough training to keep from killing himself...and he just wanted to go to Naomi. Whenever he thought of her, he wondered how she was taking his absence and whether Vince had beaten him back.

"What is she like?" Natalia's question, pulled him out of his musing.

"Who?" he asked.

Natalia raised her eyebrows and sat cross legged in front of him. Ulrick was still mesmerized by her allure whenever she appeared after a period of absence. Her beauty was exhausting, draining him of his will. It was an exhaustion he never tired of. "The girl you think of, whenever you get anxious to leave."

Ulrick wasn't sure he wanted Natalia to know anything about Naomi, but since he was stuck with her for the foreseeable future, she was going to see her for herself sooner or later.

He thought of Naomi for a while trying to put words to how he saw her. "She is pretty, not beautiful like you, but the more comfortable beauty of home. You are snow-capped peaks framed by a fiery red sunset. She is a warm fire on a cold night. She has long brown hair and happy, brown eyes."

"Happy brown eyes?" Natalia asked, almost mocking.

Ulrick looked at her disapprovingly. "Yes, she has happy, brown eyes. Her eyes always smile, even when she isn't. She never has anything bad to say about anything. She finds joy in making others happy." He smiled as he continued. "She usually does this with her cooking; she can make the most unappetizing foods taste good."

"She seems wonderful. I can see why you chafe and want to leave," Bob said from behind.

"How long have you been standing there?" Ulrick asked, startled.

"Long enough. I think you are ready to turn that wax to silver."

Natalia stood first and offered Ulrick her hand. He took it and she pulled him to his feet. They both felt energy drain from the ring.

"That was interesting," she said.

"You may not want to do that in mixed company," Bob said. "The image of you being pulled to your feet by nothing is disconcerting in the least."

The cave was cool compared to the afternoon heat outside. Bob was mixing a large bowl of some type of plaster. "Make three funnel shaped pieces of wax and attach one to the top of each skull. Try to make the attachment as small as possible, while still being able to allow the flow of the silver."

Once that was done, Bob put each of the skulls in a deep square pan with the wax funnels sticking up. Ulrick kept each one upright as bob poured the plaster into the pan. "You are going to have to get the air out of the hollowed centers, or you will have to re-hollow them, which will be much more difficult once they are made of silver," Bob instructed.

Ulrick moved each around until he saw some bubbles emerge from the thickening plaster. Once the plaster was hard, Bob used his thermal talent and baked the plaster burning the wax out leaving hollow cavities in the now hard plaster. Bob put a dozen silver coins into a small stone crucible. "If you put enough current through the metal, it will heat up and melt."

Ulrick concentrated on pulling enough energy to melt the coins. "There isn't enough energy in the cave for me to draw on."

"I was afraid of that. I guess we are going to have to go see how much energy you can put into that ring of yours." Bob made his way outside.

Once they were outside, Ulrick knelt by the stream and started drawing current from the charged ions in the water and letting it sink into his ring. He sat by the stream for several hours gathering energy; the stream only provided a trickle.

After several hours Natalia's voice filled with wonder, "This is astonishing. I can feel the power--it is like my very being is filling with the energy."

Ulrick looked at her. Her normally semi-transparent form looked fully solid and seemed to radiate electrical energy. "I think I have enough energy to finish, should we go?" Ulrick made his way back into the cave.

Once back in the cave, Ulrick tried to melt the silver.

"Do you have some other type of crucible? I can't get the current to flow through the ceramic."

"I think I have an iron one." Bob went off looking for it. He returned. "This one is a little bigger, but it should still work."

It took some time for Ulrick to work out the flow. The current flowed through the silver much easier than everything else, so it took far more energy to heat it than he would have thought after some time the silver was still solid. He then tried to modify the flow by imagining a resistance to the flow within the silver. This seemed to work. How it worked, he had no idea.

Bob added some sort of paste to the molten silver. "Don't breathe the fumes." He then ladled a skin from the top and quickly poured the silver into the molds.

"You will need to vibrate the mold while I keep it hot," Bob instructed.

"I will keep it hot," Natalia said. "My energy is coming from the ring; if I keep it hot it may help the process. I still can't affect the physical. You are going to have to add your will to mine, Ulrick." She took his hand in hers.

Several hours later, the process was complete. Sitting in a pile of broken plaster were three skulls, each one looked different from the other. Ulrick broke the funnels off and examined each one.

He was disappointed. They just seemed normal, not the extraordinary workmanship of his ring and sword, and he couldn't sense any energy from them. He sent some energy into them and it just drained back out--like ordinary lumps of metal. He could sense nothing from them, unlike his sword and ring that had a profound effect on him. "I don't think it worked. Whatever they did to make the ring and sword, I failed to do with these. It was a complete waste of time."

"Why did you make them hollow?"

"I don't know. I really wasn't even paying attention when I carved. It was just something I did."

"Don't get discouraged--the ring and the sword both have crystals within them. There is a cave, three days south of here, that has a good deposit of quartz. I will draw you a map. You can leave in the morning."

The next morning, Ulrick loaded his horse up with supplies to last him six days: three down and three back. He was glad to be going. He did not think he could spend another week here. There were places he needed to be, and if he couldn't be there, he at least could be doing something.

He would have preferred to go to the cave with the crystals and then continue south to Southport, which was only a little over day further south. Bob said he needed more time. He would not be ready to head south for a week. Ulrick was confused as to what 'preparing' the old man was doing; all Ulrick had seen him do for weeks is eat and sleep.

"I should be ready to go to Southport when you get back. Then you can go to your lady love and I will bother you no more." Bob handed him a bag of foodstuffs. "Remember, keep the sword hidden and your ring as inconspicuous as possible. The Southern Territory is not a safe place for you yet."

"Yet?" Ulrick asked.

"Over time, we'll be able to overcome your father's reputation and you will be welcome in any land, much like I am," Bob answered. "That is why I want you to come to Southport. I can introduce you to the governor and you can insure him you want no part in Territorial conflicts."

"I don't really care how Silverskull is viewed. I am not going to be a public figure. I plan on taking my father's final advice to me, by living a simple life, helping Naomi and her parents run their inn, having a few kids, and eventually taking over the business for my family." Ulrick was serious, turning to look Bob in the eye, to make his wishes clear to the old man, he said, "You can visit occasionally, but I want no part in changing my reputation in the territories. If they don't know where I am or even if I exist, then my reputation will not matter."

Both Bob and Natalia were looking at him with the same odd look. "Ulrick, there is nothing I would want more for you and the memory of you father, than for your wishes to become a reality, but I fear you will not get the peace you seek. Power attracts power--there is no avoiding it. I have tried to separate myself from the troubles of the world, but something always falls at my doorstep, no matter where I hide. Your power far exceeds mine. The problems that have fallen in my lap are small compared to what is already moving to keep you from your 'simple life.'"

Natalia chimed in. "I am afraid Bob is right, Ulrick. It is obvious to us, because we have experienced it. Your power will not only attract those of power, but it will affect those that are close to you. Everyone close to you will become more than they would have, rather for good or bad is impossible to know."

Ulrick hardly heard Natalia, he did not want to hear it. He would find a way, but something Bob had said raised his anger. "What do you mean, 'what is already moving to keep me from my simple life?' What have you been up to?" Ulrick said just below a yell.

Bob shook his head, his sadness for Ulrick's plight, quickly turned to anger of his own. "I have done nothing but help shield you. Don't be stupid. Look at the events that have happened since you returned from your trip to the west.

"The day you received your father's ring, a small out of the way village is attacked by no fewer than fifty goblins. Goblins haven't been seen this far south in twenty years and those were in numbers of one or two. Coincidence? I don't think so.

"Then you happen to find a dying soldier with a message of betrayal. Then we are attacked, not on the road, but in the middle of nowhere. By who? Not bandits. There aren't any caravans or merchants out here for bandits to prey upon. Coincidence? I have lived long enough to know there are no such thing as coincidences." Bob took a deep calming breath.

"That is not all that is odd. Melisa told me of the Ogre, that was part of attacking goblins. He made no attempt to kill Melisa, but made it plain he intended to make your friend Eramus suffer before he killed him. Why? Eram is a simple blacksmith's son. Let me tell you what has transpired in Elk Valley since you've been gone. Your uncle David kicked Melisa out. She plans to travel to Southport with that serving girl you gave that gold coin to. Your friend Eramus is mostly recovered. He is also leaving Elk Valley."

"Does he leave with Melisa?" Ulrick asked hopefully. If he was headed to Southport, he could perhaps find him and Lisa. "How do you know any of this?"

"No, he doesn't. From what I have been able to find out, he is heading north into the dragon peaks." Bob was annoyed by the interruption. "I have my ways of knowing things. Let's just leave it at that."

"What would cause him to attempt a suicidal journey like that, to what everyone knows is nothing?" Ulrick asked almost to himself. They had talked about searching for lost treasure as kids but those were just childish fantasies. *It must be because everyone else is leaving. There is nothing left for him in Elk Valley*, he thought to himself. "I need to go back and talk some sense into him. He will listen to me."

Bob's comment had finality to it. "You will not be able to. He has likely already left. Continue on your path, Ulrick.

Let those you love choose their own destiny. You can't walk two paths at once."

Ulrick did not like it, but if Eram had left, there was no way he could reach him in time to stop him.

With a troubled heart, he started for his horse, but before he could mount, Natalia said, "You should fill your ring with energy before we leave, just in case we run into trouble."

He did as she suggested, mounted his horse, and thought her behind him as they started south.

The trip south was quiet. They spent the days silently riding. At night, Natalia asked him about his friends. He noted Natalia's mood swings lessened when they traveled.

He did not know why Bob had insisted on drawing a map; his path south followed the stream; there was no way to get lost. The climate and terrain changed drastically as he dropped in elevation on the second day. The air became hot and humid; the scrub oak and pines gave way to large, live oak and sumac along the stream that had grown larger the further south he traveled.

It was early afternoon of the third day when he arrived at the top of the waterfall Bob had described. The cave would be halfway down the cliff and hidden from view from below by the falls.

Ulrick nervously inched his way toward the edge overlooking the emerald pools the waterfall fed. Bob had said the pools were a popular spot for people from Southport to come to swim. There was one large pond directly under the falls. The large pond fed two smaller ponds over terraces of calcium deposits. The pools were surrounded by palm trees.

The pools and the stream they fed were in a canyon a couple hundred feet wide, with cliffs on both sides as far as Ulrick could see. It looked like the only easy way to the pools was up the canyon from the south. Bob had said the cave was more easily accessed from above than from below, however.

Ulrick could only see two people. They were sitting halfway in the water, talking. The girls were too far for him to see well--they appeared to be naked. One had long blonde hair and the other had shorter dark hair.

"Look at your good fortune, Ulrick. You arrive at a place of great beauty and the only other people here to share it with are two naked young women." Natalia laughed and flicked his ear.

Ignoring the comment and the flick, Ulrick said, "You should go get a closer look." He had found that when he closed his eyes he could see through Natalia's eyes and she could quite safely get down the cliff.

"Of course, I will get right on that, Master." Natalia said, but did not move to comply. "Go take a closer look yourself."

Ulrick felt something cold and sharp press against the back of his neck.

"Who are you talking to, boy?" The man's commanding tone expected to be answered, quickly.

Ulrick startled, would have jumped out of his skin, if the jump wouldn't have included a hundred fifty-foot fall to his death. Ulrick decided the best solution was as much respect as he could muster. "I was talking to myself, sir." *I need to remember to keep my conversations with the Green Witch silent,* he thought.

"It didn't sound like you were talking to yourself. Who are you, why are you here and where did you come from?" the man asked.

Natalia's tone was mocking. "Just roast him and be done with it. Or if you don't want to kill him, it won't take much to put him on his backside."

Ulrick didn't like Natalia's suggestion. He couldn't build good will by killing everyone that threatened him before he found out who they were. He didn't necessarily want to build good will but he didn't want to make enemies either. "Can I step back from the edge?"

His voice took on a dangerous edge. "When you have answered my questions and I find them satisfactory."

"My name is Ulrick, sir. I have come to gather some crystals from the cave below, and I have come from the wizard Robert's home. I am his apprentice, sir." Ulrick hoped his respectful compliance would negate the need to harm this man.

"The robe does look like something the old man would make his apprentice wear. Alright, turn around slowly and step away from the edge. Don't move quickly or you will find your head separated from your body."

Ulrick backed away from the edge and turned around. The man before him was a little taller than Ulrick, with a very military posture, and his clothing, though not a uniform, was military in fashion and had the sunburst emblem of the Southern Territory on his right shoulder. His sword was still leveled at Ulrick's neck, his arm slightly bent, allowing for a very quick and deadly thrust.

"Do you have any proof of your relationship with Robert?"

"He doesn't give out certificates as far as I know. So, I don't... wait." Ulrick remembered the map and started to get it from one of the many pockets sewn into the inside of his robe.

"Slow down, boy. What are you going for?"

"He drew me a map from his house to the cave. It is in my pocket, just inside my robe." Ulrick held up his right hand and slowly moved it into his robe and retrieved the map.

The man whistled two short bursts and two other men in military uniforms stepped out of the trees. "Take the map from the boy and hold it out so I can read it," he instructed one of the soldiers.

He studied the map for a moment. "That is indeed a map following the river right to Robert's home." The man chuckled a little. "The old bastard even signed it. You know boy, you are lucky I know how strange that man is or I would find this all too strange to believe."

And you are lucky I did not take the advice to kill you, Ulrick thought.

The man put his sword away. "Continue your patrols," he told the soldiers. They quickly left.

"I was expecting a visit from Robert a couple weeks ago. Can you tell me why he is late?"

Ulrick was suddenly suspicious. "Who are you?"

The man eyed Ulrick. Ulrick's question was not the response he was expecting. "I am Thom, former General of the Southern Territory, current protector of the governor's household." Thom paused then asked, "What trouble have you seen?"

Ulrick was stunned to temporary silence. He tried to make sense of what was revealed by the man's simple declaration of identity. Bob was expected to be traveling to Southport when he was attacked on the road to bury the man who had born the message to be delivered only to Thom. Not to mention he had been only moments away from seeing the famed beauty of Amber, the daughter of the governor, naked, no less.

Ulrick finally over his shock, said, "Yes, we ran into a little trouble a couple weeks ago. But more importantly, I have a message for you." Ulrick paused, trying to decide how he would continue. "A few weeks ago, I was in a meadow north of here, where three streams meet. While I was there, I came across a dying soldier. He told me to deliver a message to you and you only." Ulrick took a deep breath. The memory of that day and the days spent making the marker still weighed heavily on him. "His message was hard to understand. He was in extreme pain. The only thing I could make out was 'Petre... betrayed.' I don't know if he meant Petre was betrayed or if Petre betrayed him."

Thom was silent as he digested the information. Ulrick's message created more questions than it answered. "What happened to the soldier?"

The question brought images of him smashing the soldiers head to mind. "He begged for death. His pain was sickening to see" Ulrick took a shaky breath. "I honored his request."

Thom looked at Ulrick appraisingly. Ulrick had no idea what Thom's assessment was and neither did Thom. "I will sit right here with you until the girls are ready to leave. Then once we leave, you can do what you came to do."

They sat in an uncomfortable silence for nearly an hour before Ulrick finally got the courage to ask. "So, is that the governor's daughter I saw down there?"

Thom eyed him suspiciously. "Yes, and her friend, Lisa. No, you can't meet her. I assume you will be returning when Robert finally makes his appearance. I am sure you will get the chance then, and the circumstances will be more appropriate."

Ulrick was stunned once again. "Lisa...Lisa from Elk Valley?" He didn't think it possible, but stranger things had happened.

"Well, the surprises never end, do they? You aren't the boy her parents sent her away from, are you?"

"No, that is my good friend, Eramus. He didn't take it well," Ulrick answered. "I understand your position about meeting Amber, but is there any way I could talk to Lisa?"

"No, a conversation with Lisa would include a meeting with Amber. You can catch up with Lisa when you return with Robert." Thom seemed a little annoyed.

"Could you at least give her a message for me?"

Thom nodded.

"Tell her Eramus was heartbroken when we returned. She should have at least left a letter of explanation. Also, tell her he was nearly killed by goblins the day after we returned. He was recovering, but now he has left Elk Valley on a suicidal trek into the Dragon Peaks." He paused. There was something else he wanted to tell her. "Oh yeah, tell her Bob the wizard is also unhappy with her departure. He was planning on taking her on as an apprentice as well."

"You want me to relay a message that is designed to make her feel terrible about leaving Elk Valley, when you yourself are sitting here, having left your friend to face his suicidal trek without you as well?" Thom asked.

"Yes, I want her to feel terrible, like I have felt since I left. Will you tell her?"

Thom exhaled his annoyance. "I will, but only because she will be angry if I don't and she finds out I had talked to you."

A soldier came out of the trees. "They are ready to go sir."

"Farewell, Ulrick, I hope to see you in a week or two. Stay where you are for at least an hour, then you can collect your shiny rocks." Thom was unable to hide his annoyance at, unwittingly agreeing to be Ulrick's message boy.

10 - Lisa

The breeze was slight and warm, but it still brought a chill to Lisa's wet skin as she leaned against a large grey granite boulder, waiting for the 'all clear' signal from Thom. She watched Amber brush out her wet hair. She had a brief pang of jealousy. Amber never looked anything but beautiful, even wearing a simple cotton dress, her hair wet and tangled from swimming. Lisa could not imagine ever being able to travel anywhere with this woman without drawing attention. Of course, she understood this was one of the reasons for Amber's near imprisonment within the governor's keep. Trips like this happened very rarely.

Amber had been having nightmares and had insisted that Thom let her come here. The falls were one of Amber's favorite places. Lisa could see why. The canyon and falls were a hidden paradise. Although hidden, it was well known by the people of Southport. Thom had to send a contingent of soldiers ahead to clear the area before they could make the trip themselves.

Amber noticed Lisa staring and smiled at her. "What are you thinking?"

"I was just thinking about how nice it was to be able to get out of the keep. I have only left the keep twice since arriving in Southport, over two months ago. Once to the vegetable market with my aunt and now here. I can only imagine how it has been for you."

Amber stood up straight and brushed sand from her dress. Still smiling, she said, "It has only been the last month or so that I have been restricted. Before Petre's disappearance, I could come and go as I pleased, as long as I had a half-dozen guards with me. Now that I have you to protect me, I should be able to have a little more freedom again."

Lisa doubted Thom would see it that way.

"We are ready to leave," Thom said as he came out of the trees, his posture tight. "We should probably try to keep our pace brisk; it will be nearly tomorrow when we get back as it is." He quickly picked up the small pack of supplies they had brought.

Amber's eyes narrowed and brows creased. "Out with whatever is bothering you. I don't mind being brisk, but I don't want to do so with you fuming the whole way."

In the short time Lisa had been able to observe Amber and Thom together, she had been amazed at how well Amber could read Thom's mood. Most of the soldiers she had trained with found Thom unreadable. If she had not seen the subtle change in his aura color, she would have not thought he was annoyed or at least no more annoyed than usual.

Thom pointedly looked at Lisa, then looked back to Amber. "I ran into a 'stranger' up at the top of the waterfall." He started off down the canyon toward Southport.

"And," Amber prodded.

"And, I finally got the name of the boy that causes Lisa to mope about." Thom looked Lisa's way again.

Lisa now fully interested. "What are you talking about?"

"The man I spoke to was a one of Lisa's friends. Ulrick was his name." Thom watched Lisa's reaction to help verify the man's identity. Though he had little doubt Ulrick was telling the truth, it was always best to be fully sure.

"You met Ulrick up on the waterfall! Why didn't you have him come down and see me?" Lisa nearly yelled. *What was Ulrick doing here?* she thought.

Thom raised his brows and gestured toward Amber. "Do I really have to explain why I could not let him come down to talk with you?"

Lisa calmed herself, remembering who she was talking to and what her purpose was. "No, I understand. I just got excited, I have not seen Ulrick since the end of last summer and would have liked to have heard of how their trip into the Western Territory went. You obviously talked with him and he knew I was down here, so what did he tell you?" Her tone was soft, taking the edge off her words.

Thom paused and looked pointedly at Lisa, his eyes a little sad. "I don't want to relay the message he gave. His message is meant to make you feel bad. If I had not agreed before he gave it, I would have never mentioned I met him. That being said, I tell you I have a message for you, but I also tell you, you will not like it. So, if you don't want to hear it, I will not relay the message."

Lisa found Thom so much different around her and Amber. He would have never considered the feelings of the soldiers under his command when delivering a message. Lisa could deduce what Ulrick had to say. He was probably mad at her for leaving Eram, but she had left a letter explaining her reasons. Eram would have had a hard time with her words, but she thought Ulrick would have understood. "I would like to hear his message, but tell me what he was doing here first. Did he know I was here?"

"No, he did not know you were here until I unwisely mentioned your name. He was not seeking you out to give you a message." Thom cleared his throat. "He said that Eramus was..."

Amber stopped walking and gasped. She was looking at Thom, her face looked as if she had just seen a spirit of the dead.

"Are you alright?" Thom was concerned.

Amber shook her head to clear her thoughts. "Yes, I am alright, let's get going." She walked on, ignoring the worried looks from Lisa and Thom.

Lisa was worried about Amber. She had lost all color in her face, and the look of shock she had given Thom was something not easily forgotten. Amber was always so self-assured and that look was different she could not place it. It was not fear, but it had her somehow more worried than if it had been fear. Lisa thought Amber's distress would have been linked to something Thom had said, but he had not said anything of consequence.

They walked in silence for a while. Finally, Amber said to Thom "I am alright; finish telling Lisa your message." All of her poise returned.

Thom looked at her, concern still in his eyes. Then turned to Lisa and spoke, "He said Eramus was unhappy when he returned, and you were gone and you had not left a letter." Thom ran his hands through his short grey hair. "This next part is a little odd. I think I should have gotten more details. He said Eramus was severely injured in a goblin attack, but he is okay now. Then he said something about Eramus going into the dragon peaks." Thom had left out the terms heartbroken and suicidal, hoping to soften the message a little.

Lisa wiped a tear from her face. "I left a letter with my mother to give to him." She looked to Thom. "He must have been heartbroken; that could be the only explanation for a suicidal trip into the dragon peaks. I should have given the letter to his mother." Lisa had felt bad about leaving, but now she felt terrible.

"Why do you say a trip to the dragon peaks is suicidal?" Amber asked. Lisa barely heard the question. Amber had slowed and fallen behind while Thom had given Lisa the message.

Lisa and Thom stopped to allow Amber to catch up. "There is only one person that I know that has gone into the mountains and returned. Every couple of years, another group of adventurers head into the mountains to find the supposed dragon treasure and they never return," Lisa answered, once Amber had caught up.

Now Lisa saw fear in Amber's eyes, though she quickly tried to hide it.

Thom had noticed also. "It has something to do with the dreams, doesn't it?" Thom asked.

"Yes." Her voice low.

The pieces finally fell into place. Thom had said something of consequence. He had said 'Eramus.' "You have had dreams of Eramus?" Lisa asked.

"I think so." Amber's voice was still low. "What does he look like?"

Lisa, still awed by the odd series of events, tried to picture Eram in purely the physical sense. This was difficult for her because when she thought of Eram, she saw who he was-- a young man with knowing eyes and honest words. A picture finally in mind. "He is tall--of the same height as Thom, but slimmer. He has dark hair that curls to his shoulders and brown eyes."

"That description accurately describes the man I have seen by the name of Eramus, but does he have a spider web of scars around his right eye?"

"No...," Lisa answered thoughtfully, then added, "Thom mentioned he was recently injured though." *Goblins in Elk Valley*? Lisa thought. How can that be? She had never even seen a goblin. All the revelations of the day caused her stomach to twist in a knot of anxiety. Eram trekking into the mountains, goblins, and the most disturbing, Amber dreaming of the man she loved.

Amber must have noticed her stress. "I don't like to

speak of my dreams, but I will tell you this: I set him on his path. I don't know why, and I did not consciously do it. I do not have control of what I do, but I do know there is a chance he could succeed where others have failed." She put her arm around Lisa to comfort her.

11 - Vincent

The slight breeze blowing from the south was pleasantly warm. Vincent looked to the southern skies expecting to see the building thunder heads that rolled through the mountains most afternoons during the summer. It must be too early; the skies were clear.

Sitting on the bench under the large pine in the center of Elk Valley, Vince wondered how Eram and Ulrick spent so much time here--he was bored and anxious. He had things that needed to be done. It was his fault, however, that he was sitting here instead of traveling south. He had told Melisa if she wanted to travel with him, she would have to wait a couple days. He had to make arrangements to keep his planned traveling companions out of her sight and after hearing that Eram had left Elk Valley, he had to make arrangements for his disposal. He was quite upset with Eram. Why couldn't he have just stayed here and been miserable?

"Good morning to you, Vince," Higgin called as he crossed the bridge a little downstream from were Vince sat.

"Good morning to you, Higgin, and a pleasant evening also," Vince called back, thinking it funny that the local pig farmer looked and smelled like a pig himself. His thoughts made it easy to smile and wave pleasantly.

Vince wasn't sure how he felt about sending a goblin to kill Eram. He did hate him, but Eram had once been a good friend. He couldn't help but think that perhaps it was this weakness that had stopped him from killing Eram before. He also would have preferred to do the job himself--that level of pleasure and pain is not easily found.

He also wasn't too happy with the loss of Abby. She was fairly nice to look at and was most likely being poorly used by Stink--the goblin Headsmasher had sent--or would be soon anyway. What a waste of a beautiful woman. What would have possessed her to go with Eram anyway?

The sound of someone's approach brought him out of his musing. A bald man sat next to him on the bench and began nervously chewing the ends of his fingers and spitting the skin into the creek. Vince unconsciously ran his hand over his freshly shaved head; he did this every time he saw Lice. He did not know how or why the bald man had gotten the name. "Lice, I thought I told you to stay out of town."

"Headsmasher told me to let you know that a Lemurian woman was overheard asking about Ulrich in the Tidal Pool tavern about a week ago," Lice said around something he had bitten off his thumb.

A week ago? One thing goblins were good at is traveling fast; he would have expected a message to take nearly two weeks by normal messenger. "Tell Headsmasher to keep at least two tails on her at all times."

Lice got up to leave. "Anything else, sir?"

"Yes... make sure he sends the best. I don't want the Lemurian to know she is being watched, and I don't want her molested." A Lemurian? It looks like the rumors about Ulrick's father having contact with them toward the end of his life were true. Most people knew nothing of the Lemurians, and the few that had heard of them believed them to be myth. Vince didn't know much about them, but he did know they existed.

His master Titan's, purposes, included the destruction of the Lemurians. The Lemurians' willingness to send someone out from wherever they hide doesn't bode well. They must suspect his plans.

Vince concentrated on his master and yelled in his mind. "Master, I have a message." He repeated his effort three times, then waited.

Several minutes later: "I have already been informed of the presence of the Lemurian. What are you doing about it?" The voice in his head was muffled and quiet.

"I am having her watched, but nothing more, Master," he yelled silently.

After several more minutes, the quiet voice responded. "That is sufficient for now. I will let you know if I require anything else from you."

"Yes, Master." The conversation was over.

"Are you alright?" Melisa asked from behind him.

"Shit!" Vince exclaimed as he stood and faced her. "Yes... I'm fine... at least I was before you scared the shit out of me."

"Who was that you were talking to?" She seemed suspicious.

Startled again. *She couldn't have heard, could she have? No of course not, she meant Lice.* "Um... just some guy wanting directions."

"What was his name?"

Caught off guard again. "Uh... I didn't ask... What difference does it make?"

The suspicious look she had disappeared. "It probably doesn't. He just looked like someone I once knew."

Vince thought about it and realized there was a good chance she had met Lice before. Lice had spent some time in the west, soldiering with Ulrick's father. He was going to have to make sure Lice didn't make any more appearances. "Are you ready to go?"

"I've been ready for two days. I was just looking for you, hoping to prod you into leaving."

"I have to pick up a few things at the house, then we can go."

"Well, stop sitting there and get to it. If we leave now and push the horses a little, we can make it to Smithville before it's too late." She was annoyed.

Vince didn't much like Melisa. Sara had been much more pleasant. He also didn't like taking orders from people like her. He had sacrificed too much to get where he was in the Brotherhood. Most in the Brotherhood took orders from him now, and it irked him when someone beneath him thought to tell him what to do. It especially irked him that he had to bite his tongue. It wouldn't be long now and everyone would know the realities of the world...then he would have the recognition he deserved.

"I will meet you back here in an hour," he told her. He did need to make sure Lice knew to stay hidden; unfortunately, this made his correspondence with his goblin slaves difficult. Lice was usually his go-between, since his appearance in civilized areas didn't induce torch and pitchfork-wielding mobs.

12 - Eramus

The biting cold of the wind made his eyes water, distorting the view of the distant town he had left the day before. Eram could not see any homes or other signs of civilization; he could just see the meadow and the large tree he and Ulrick had spent so much time. Behind him was another meadow. He had been here several times over the years. The last time he was here was a little less than a year ago. Lisa, himself, and Ulrick had come to the falls that fed the small pond that was the center point of the small pine-surrounded meadow. The thought of Lisa caused a pang of sadness.

"We should get a fire started before it gets dark." Abby's voice seemed distant. She was facing away from Eram, admiring the spectacular falls.

The small stream that flowed through the town of Elk Valley started somewhere high in the dragon peaks. Its path down the mountain included several waterfalls, but this was the most spectacular of them all. Most residents of Elk Valley had been here at some point and many made the trip every couple of years.

Even though most of the people Eram knew had been here, Ben was the only person he knew that had gone further into the mountains, at least the only one that had returned to tell about it. The falls were several hundred feet high, creating a continuous rainbow mist. Thick moss covered the cliff face. The scene, especially in the late afternoon, held such beauty it invoked a spiritual awe.

"I will go get some wood." He headed into the trees. Deadwood was plentiful, so he was back with a large armload within a few moments. He deposited the wood into one of several stone-ringed fire pits that had seen an uncountable number of fires over the millennia. He retrieved flint and steel from his pack and began sending a spray of sparks into the dry grass he had put under the wood.

Abby shivered. "It is colder than I thought it would be." She rubbed her hands together.

Eram blew into the smoking dry grass, causing it to flare into flame. He added some more dry grass and positioned some of the smaller pieces of wood over his fledgling flames. "It is only going to get colder," he said without looking up from the fire. "I will set a snare on one of the game trails. Hopefully we can catch a rabbit while we sleep."

Abby spread an oiled canvas blanket out for them to sleep on. She tried to find a flat spot without any stones. Last night had been miserable. Sore from a day of hiking, she spent the night vainly trying to find a spot to lay without a root or stone jabbing into her side.

Eram got some dried fruit and meat from his pack and handed it to Abby. He then grabbed their packs and hoisted them up into the nearest tree. Too tired to say much, they ate silently, then rolled up together under the blankets they had brought. They had found the night before that sleeping separately increased the discomfort of the cold; halfway through the night Eram had woke to Abby snuggling up to his back.

They were asleep in moments after lying down.

Eram woke to a severe ache in his right arm. He was lying on his left side with his right arm draped over Abby. The cold made his head and arm ache. He didn't want to tuck his arm between them, because having any pressure on his arm also made it ache. He also didn't want to disturb Abby.

He could still feel some heat from the fire that was behind him, but there was no flickering light, so he knew he had been asleep for several hours. He wondered how long he had until dawn. Without moving he looked to the sky. The sky was perfectly clear and moonless, making the stars stand out brightly; the vastness of numbers always had amazed him. A slight breeze blew a strand of Abby's hair onto his face, tickling his nose. He didn't want to disturb her, but he wasn't going to be able to resist much longer.

A twig broke somewhere in the trees in front of him. He strained to see, but it was far too dark in the shadow of the trees, so he focused on trying to hear. For several minutes he heard nothing more, increasing his anxiety; if it had been a night critter, he should have heard some more movement. His fear built as his imagination started getting the better of him and the silence became deafening. His fear peaked as he realized it was far too quiet. All of his previous nights in the woods through the years had taught him the forest was quiet at night, but there were always a few sounds here and there--a squirrel digging in the leaves, an owl making its eerie call, but there had been no sounds for several minutes now.

Another snap, still somewhere in the trees, he knew he was in trouble now because whatever was out there was moving very slowly trying to stay quiet but was obviously circling the small meadow. By the pitch of the snap, it wasn't something small like a squirrel or rabbit. Also, he suspected it was some type of predator because the direction of its movement had put it down wind from them.

He very slowly ran his hand down Abby's arm and squeezed her hand until her breathing changed. "Don't move or say anything. I think there is something in the trees that means us harm," he whispered against her ear. "You have your knife close?"

Abby nodded slightly.

"Good, very slowly get it. We don't want whatever is out there to know it has been discovered until we can defend ourselves," he whispered as he let go of her hand and slowly reached for his dirk that he had put under his coat that he was using as a pillow.

Dirk in his hand. "Do you have it?"

She nodded slightly.

He swallowed his fear and steeled himself. Eram threw the blankets off and jumped to his feet. "Aaarrrrgggggghhhh!" he yelled as loud as he could, hoping if it were a bear or mountain cat the quick movement and noise would scare it off.

Nothing, no movement or sound after his yell. Abby stood behind him with her left hand on his back. "Are you sure, there w...," she started asking, when a goblin nearly as tall as Eram walked calmly out of the trees.

It carried a long-spiked club and wore a thick layer of dark furs making it nearly invisible against the darkness. Its skin was pale, making it look almost like its head was disembodied--floating above the ground. Its eyes were close set and shined in the dark like a cat's. He could see them, far better than they could see him. The goblin walked slowly toward them, obviously sizing up his prey.

Eram started backing away. The goblin smiled at him. "Run, it will make it more fun. You won't lose me, I can smell you from miles away, especially her, she smells tasty." It laughed.

Eram continued to back away, trying to come up with some plan to survive the next few minutes. He was discouraged by the way the goblin studied him; it showed a higher intelligence compared to the goblins he had encountered before. As they continued to back away, he noticed the goblin was trying to hide the fact that it was favoring its left leg. That could give him a chance.

Eram was contemplating his attack when a fist-sized rock flew past, narrowly missing his head. The goblin dodged right, but the rock still hit his left shoulder.

"Bitch, when he is dead," he pointed his club at Eram. "I

am going to enjoy you for a long, long time."

Another rock flew toward the goblin, but the creature was not caught off guard this time and he easily avoided the missile. Eram saw this as his chance though, and charged at the goblin. The goblin prepared to meet the charge, but Eram swerved right at the last moment forcing the goblin to put all its weight on its left foot if it was going to hit him. The goblin did not take the bait, however, it just turned to face Eram. Either way Eram had gotten what he wanted: the goblin was now positioned between him and Abby. Eram stayed out of easy striking range, but close enough that if the goblin went for Abby, he could strike before it reached her.

The goblin realized it no longer had the advantage when another rock hit it square in the back. The goblin turned so it could keep both Eram and Abby in sight.

Eram started circling right, making the goblin have to choose who to look at, and at the same time, feeling with his feet for a rock he could throw. "Whoever sent you should have sent more than one of you." Eram was hoping to distract and get information at the same time.

The goblin didn't respond. Eram's foot dislodged a suitable rock. He picked it up when the goblin was dodging another throw from Abby, but was surprised when it was just pelted with gravel and dirt aimed at its head. Eram was quite impressed with Abby's resourcefulness. If she hadn't been here, Eram was pretty sure he would be dead by now.

Rock in hand, Eram waited for Abby to throw again. When she did, he put everything into his throw, aiming at the goblin's lower left leg. Eram wanted to keep his throw low so he would not accidently hit Abby if he missed his mark.

The goblin, distracted by the second barrage of dirt and gravel from Abby, did not see Eram's throw and made no move to avoid it. The stone hit the goblin's ankle squarely with a sickening crunch.

The goblin cried out in agony and went down on its left knee.

Abby started throwing whatever she could grab as fast as she could. The goblin was completely caught off guard when the barrage suddenly stopped. It looked up just as Eram stabbed down into the center of its back with all his strength. Eram left the long blade in the creature's back and backed out of range of the wild swings of its club.

Unable to stand, the goblin, in a last effort, threw its club at Abby. She ducked. It looked to Eram that it had missed, but just after the club had passed, she put her hands to her face and went to her knees.

Eram ran to her side; he could see the blood seeping between her fingers and his heart wrenched with fear. He grabbed her wrists. She looked at him with tear filled eyes. "Let me see how bad it is," he said as he pulled her hands away. There was a deep gash on her cheek just below her left eye that ran all the way to just above her ear. It was bleeding badly like all head wounds do, but it didn't look life threatening.

Eram picked Abby's knife up off the ground, cut a piece of cloth from one of their blankets, and pressed it to the gash in her cheek.

"Eram." Abby was looking past him with fear in her eyes.

Eram turned to see the goblin had managed to get to his feet and was shambling toward them. Eram stood and cautiously approached the goblin. The goblin coughed and blood ran out its mouth and nose and dripped from its chin. He had punctured one of its lungs. The goblin just stood there staring at Eram with eyes filled with hate, pain and fear. Eram punched it in the chest. Agony replaced any emotion as it went back to its knees.

Eram retrieved the goblin's club and returned. Standing in front of the goblin, club in hand, Eram asked, "Who sent you?"

The goblin coughed, more blood dripped from its chin. It didn't look up, either unable or unwilling to talk, it just sat there.

"Abby, turn you head, don't look."

"No... I want to see it die."

Eram looked back at her. She was just staring at the goblin, her face devoid of any emotion. "Whatever." Eram swung the club, connecting with the goblin's head with a wet crunch.

Neither moved or said anything for some time; the shock of the attack made them numb. After an unknown amount of time Eram threw the rest of the wood in the fire along with the club. The embers were still hot enough that it didn't take long for flames to take hold. He then gathered their blankets and laid them out next to the cliff face. Then he pulled his dirk from the dead goblin and wiped it in the grass. He helped Abby to her feet and led her to the cliff face, he sat first then pulled her down in front of him, pulled the blankets up over them, and put his arms around her. "With the fire bright, and us sitting here in the shadows of the cliff, I will be able to see anything before they see us."

"Do you think there will be more of them coming?" Her voice betrayed her fear.

"I don't know." He pulled her in closer. "I will stay awake and watch. You try and get some sleep."

She didn't respond, but after a few moments she was shaking and sobbing. Eram didn't know how long she cried, but he was relieved when she finally fell asleep.

He woke when the first shaft of sunlight cleared the eastern mountains and rested in his eyes. When his vision had adjusted enough to see, he was surprised by what he saw. Abby had made a small pile of stones to hold a wrist-thick branch erect and mounted on top of the pole was the goblin's head, facing the trail they had come up on. He stood and noticed the goblin's body was laid out in front of the pole.

Abby was naked, washing the blood from herself and her clothes under the waterfall. In spite of the situation, he could not help taking a moment to admire her beauty.

"You should take this opportunity to get cleaned up also," she said without looking at him.

"I can wait until you're done."

She looked at him seriously. "I have already seen you naked. I helped Melisa when you were still unconscious."

Eram chuckled, self-consciously he cringed to think of how compromising his situation had been. "You have never seen me naked after I have seen you naked though."

The corner of her mouth twitched up slightly. "I'm done." She picked up her wet clothes and moving slowly to avoid sharp and slippery rocks, made her way to dry ground. He watched her lay out her clothes on a dry rock in the sun then began to dry her hair with a blanket. "Are you really going to just stand there and watch me all day?"

"No, but I don't think there is a man alive that would blame me if I did," he answered, after turning his back to her to hide his embarrassment.

He yelped in surprise at how cold the water was, but after a few minutes he grew numb to the cold. He stripped off his clothes and did his best to clean everything, then covering his unmentionables with his wet clothes, made his way to the nearest dry blanket. He dried himself quickly then wrapped the blanket around his waist and sat across the fire from Abby. She was clad the same as he was, and her nakedness caused him to take longer than it should have to notice the gash on her cheek that was still split open and seeping watery blood.

He got up and knelt down beside her and examined the wound. The worst part was about an inch long, right on her cheek bone. "I am going to have to find a way to tie that closed," he said as he got up to look for something he could use as a needle.

He found a fish skeleton on the shore of the pond. He took the largest rib bone he could find, made a needle out of it and cleaned it in the flames. Then extracted a fine thread from one of their ropes and returned to her side by the fire.

The gash was deep enough to see her cheek bone. As gently as he could, he pinched the wound closed. Abby gasped and her eyes watered. "Why did you do that?" he asked, pointing with his chin to the head on a pole.

She whimpered, tears welling up again as Eram pushed the fish bone through her skin. Through a gasp she answered. "If there are any more of them following us, I want them to think twice about continuing."

"Thanks, by the way." He pushed the fish bone through a second time.

"I just did what I thought would help." She seemed a little confused.

He pushed the fish bone through a third time. "I don't mean that." He nodded to the pole. "I mean thanks for not letting me come here alone. If you hadn't been here, I would be dead right now."

Done stitching he got up and cleaned the cloth he had used the night before and began gently cleaning the blood off her face. When he was done, he stood and checked his clothes.

"Thanks for fixing me up." She checked her own clothes. "It is going to be awhile before our clothes are dry."

"Maybe we should try and get some more sleep. I will find a hidden spot a little away from the falls," Eram suggested as he brushed a lock of her hair behind her ear to keep it from sticking to the still seeping wound on her cheek.

It took some time, but Eram found a fairly hidden spot that would also allow them to see the meadow without anyone seeing them. He called her over and they crawled behind some vines that were growing loosely against the cliff. Eram was vividly aware of both of their nakedness as Abby pushed her back up against his chest. Her warm soft skin set his heart pumping. He started to move his hand to take advantage of the situation, but then stopped himself. This was not the time or the place. He should be ashamed of himself. With nowhere else to put his hand, he put it on her shoulder and closed his eyes and tried to go to sleep. A couple minutes later Abby took his hand in hers and pulled his arm tightly around her and held his hand tight.

He didn't know how long he had slept, but he knew he didn't want to spend another night in close proximity to the dead goblin, so he extracted his arm from Abby's grip. "I think we should try and get some distance between us and the falls before we make camp again," he said as he got up and made his way to their clothes.

Up to the falls they had used a trail that had been kept clear and had ropes and makeshift ladders to get over the more difficult spots. "I haven't seen a trail that leads higher from the falls. Do you know where it is?" Abby asked as she struggled to pull her still slightly wet leather pants on.

Eram had been trying not to watch Abby dress, but he turned toward her when she asked her question. Distracted by her struggle, he nearly forgot to answer. "There is no trail further into the mountains. If we get lucky, we will find some game trails that go in the right direction," he managed to answer and avert his gaze before she turned and caught him staring again, even though she did not seem to really mind, it still made him uncomfortable.

"Do you have some defined location you are trying to find, or are we just wandering north?"

Eram looked briefly in her direction. She was facing him now and bouncing up and down trying to get her pants up the last couple inches. She gave him a half smile and a wink. He quickly turned and faced away from her, took a deep breath and let it out slowly trying to cool his blood. "I don't know precisely where I am going. According to the treasure hunter's stories, there is supposed to be a valley before you reach the last peak with a cave where there is a dragon's treasure."

He pulled his shirt on and began buttoning it up. "I don't necessarily think I will find a treasure or a cave for that matter, but I do know the anxiety I was feeling when I was just wasting time, has subsided. If there is no cave or treasure, I will cross the last peak and see what the imperial city is like. Maybe that is where the dream meant for me to go anyway. I only mention the treasure because for a lot of years Ulrick, Vince and I have been planning to go find the truth of the treasure once we were old enough. This was the summer we were supposed to go but Ulrick left, and the only reason I would go anywhere with Vince now is the hope I would get an opportunity to push him over a cliff."

"And what if there is a cave, treasure and... a dragon?" Abby asked, only half serious.

"Dragon?" Eram laughed. "I don't believe in fairy tale creatures."

Abby looked at him sideways with a mocking smile. "So, you think there could be a cave full of treasure, but no dragon. How could there be dragon treasure without the dragon?"

Eram shrugged. "I don't know. I figured enough people

came through town over the years looking for the treasure, there had to be something to the story and whoever put the treasure there made up the story of the dragon to keep people from looking for it."

Buttoning her cotton shirt, top down. "Huh," she grunted. "I definitely think we had better plan on crossing all five peaks."

Done dressing, Eram shouldered his pack and went to check the snare he had set the night before. They still had some dried meat and some hard flatbread but he hoped he could save the dried food as long as he could. He was pleasantly surprised to find his snare had successfully snared a large squirrel. As he approached the squirrel, it doubled its efforts to escape, bouncing and flinging itself wildly against its tethers. It took Eram a minute to get his hands on the frantic critter. Once he had hold of it, he quickly snapped its neck and began gutting it. Done with the bloody work he headed back to the falls.

Holding the small animal high and with a big grin on his face, he entered the clearing saying, "It looks like we get fresh squirrel for dinner tonight."

Abby smiled, shouldered her pack and gestured toward the sheer cliffs of the falls blocking their northern route. "Which way?"

Eram looked at the cliffs, his smile fading. "Let's see if we can find a way around to the west. That way we don't have to risk getting wet again, crossing the stream." They headed west; the forest varied from sparse to nearly impenetrable. The cliff also varied, but after walking for nearly an hour they still had not found an easy way up--if anything it looked to be getting more difficult. Frustrated, Eram stopped. "Maybe we should go back and see if there is an easier way to the east. After walking another couple hours east, they were no better off, and after their nap they were running out of daylight.

"Maybe we should just camp back at the falls again tonight?" Abby commented.

"It is at least an hour back to the falls. I don't want to risk spending another night there. We need to just figure out how to get up the cliff." Eram was frustrated with the lack of forward progress.

Abby walked back and forth along the cliff. "I think I could possibly climb up this section here." She pointed to a cleft in the stone that gave a few more hand holds but was still nearly thirty feet of vertical cliff. "But I don't know how you could do it with your arm still weak." She looked at him, questioningly.

Eram looked at the section she indicated, trying to see if he dared to attempt a climb. "I don't think I can climb that." He dropped his pack, frustrated, and began to pace hoping to find a solution to his problem. He knew if this small cliff was proving this daunting and they had not even made it past the first peak, there was no way he would be able to make it over four or five peaks. He knew he did not have to actually climb the peaks, but even going around there was going to be near impassable sections and cliffs higher than this one. He sat on the ground staring at the cliff thinking. "What are our options at this point?" he asked Abby. He had not given up yet, but his tone was that of defeat.

She looked back the way they had come then looked further west along the cliff. "You could give up."

He looked at her, confused.

She looked at him, her expression unreadable. "We could just sit here on the ground feeling sorry for ourselves, or we could camp here and continue east in the morning."

Eram knew she was just trying to make him angry with the first two comments, but he did not have the energy to get angry, but her attempt had made him realize he had not really even thought about a way up. He had been only been thinking of an easy way around, but he realized there was not going to be an easy way to where he was going.

The cleft she had pointed out was as good a place to climb up as any they had seen, but he could not climb. He stood and looked at the cleft from several different angles. No, he definitely wouldn't be able to climb that. He walked away from the cliff a few strides then looked back to the cliff. The forest was sparse to non-existent close to the cliff, but as he moved away from the wall of stone, the trees increased in both number and size. Then it hit him; he knew how to get up the cliff. He looked for what he needed eyeing several trees, not more than ten feet from him, was a tree that was perfect. He went back to his pack and retrieved the small hatchet he had brought and returned to the large pine and began hacking into it.

"What are you doing?"

"I am going to chop this tree down so that it falls against the cliff and then we will have a steep ramp up the cliff, instead of a strait up climb," he answered as he chopped. The hatchet was small and the tree was at least as big around as he was. With a full-sized ax and a right arm that did not throb with pain with every stroke, he could have felled the tree in about a half hour, but with what he had, he figured it was going to be well over an hour. If he hurried, they would have just enough light left when they reached the top to gather wood for a fire.

"What if the tree falls the wrong way?" Abby watched him work with her hands on her hips.

Eram paused and looked at her like she was crazy. "Elk Valley is in the forest. All our homes are made from logs. If by ten you don't know which way a tree is going to fall, you had better leave town because you aren't going to make it." He started chopping again switching back and forth between his right and left hand to reduce some of the pain of chopping.

The sun was well below the horizon when the first pops occurred, indicating his job was nearly finished. A couple final well-placed swings and the tree was falling toward the cliff. He held his breath, hoping the force of the tree hitting the cliff didn't snap the trunk, leaving them short of the top.

The large pine bounced when it hit, but stayed whole.

The climb up the tree was not easy. Eram had to remove several branches blocking the way, but with other conveniently located branches for hand holds they got to the top with just a few scratches, and a lot of sap covering their hands and arms. The top of the cliff was solid stone for thirty feet or more before there was tree cover again. Picking up fallen dead wood for their fire, they made their way into the trees, not wanting to spend the night exposed to the cold wind that was both colder and stronger than down by the pond.

Abby laid out their blankets while Eram cooked the squirrel. The squirrel was good and greasy. Eram was gleaning every bit of meat he could from the bones when he noticed Abby's blue eyes staring at him from across the fire.

"How does your arm feel?"

"It feels like it has been pounded on by a forge hammer and as it gets colder the pain increases. You may have to hit me over the head with a rock so I can sleep," he responded with heavy eyes and a tight smile.

"Speaking of sleep, we should try." She stood and headed to the bed she made. "Get over here, we are going to have to see what we can do to keep your arm warm."

Eram laid down in his usual position on his left side making enough room on the blanket for her to lie in front of him.

"If you leave your sweaty, wet clothes on we are both

going to freeze." Eram just raised his eyebrows at her. "I'm not joking, do it. I am not going to lie next to you if your clothes are wet; your shirt is soaked," she said, her face stern, but her eyes smiled.

Eram removed his shirt and lay on his back. "Well get over here, I'm freezing."

Abby straddled him, sitting on his thighs. "Put your arm on your chest."

Confused, Eram hesitated, but did as she said. Abby then removed her shirt and pulled the two thickest blankets they had up over her head and rested her head under his chin, his sore arm cradled between her warm soft breasts.

Eram wasn't very experienced when it came to women, in fact women usually ignored him or ridiculed him, but he was smart enough to realize, Abby had been practically throwing herself at him since they left. He did not know how to deal with her. On one hand he was quite attracted to her and looked forward to the nights so he could be close to her, but on the other hand, the woman from his dream occupied a large amount of his waking and sleeping thoughts. He did not even know if she was real or just his imagination, but he knew that if she turned out to be real, he would leave any woman he was with for her. He also knew he cared too much for Abby to bring her that kind of pain. "Abby?"

"What?" Her breath was warm on his chest.

"I don't think I can give you what you want." His voice was quiet with regret.

She sat up just enough to look into his face, she wore a mocking smile. "And what exactly do you think I want?"

Her response was not at all what he expected. Caught off guard, he did not know what to say, so he just stared at her.

She gave him plenty of time to wallow in discomfort,

then asked, "Well?"

"I'm not sure, but you can't look as good as you do and lie on top of me nearly naked and not be expecting something. Can you?" he finally asked.

"Actually, I know exactly what I can expect. You will be a complete gentleman." She chuckled lightly, then sighed. "You are thinking about this too much. We are traveling together for who knows how long, and based on what you have said we probably won't survive, so what is wrong with enjoying each other's company?"

"I care about you Abby. I don't want to hurt you."

She laughed at him. "What makes you think you have the power to hurt me?" Then more seriously, "I saw the look in your eyes when you described the woman in your dream, but listen to me Eram. You don't even know she is real and not just a figment of your imagination. I listened to your dream and I believe there is something to your quest, but that does not mean what your mind put before you as motivation is real." She shook her head. "How many years would you live without love and companionship before you gave up on this dream girl?" Abby put her head back on his chest.

Eram was silent for quite a while thinking of what she had said before responding. "You are right, she might not be real, but if she is, I don't think I can be true to whoever I am with when I find her."

"Eram, I think you are a nice-looking man and you have a good heart but, I don't know that I like you enough for any of this to matter. You are too serious for me." She leaned up and kissed his chin. "Now go to sleep."

Eram didn't know whether to be happy or disappointed by her comment.

Eram woke the next morning sore from the previous

day's labor, but he had slept better last night than the previous nights. Abby was still asleep on his chest. He didn't want to wake her, but lying like this on the hard ground all night had made his back sore, and nature was calling, so he brushed the hair out of her face and lightly rubbed her shoulder until she started to stir.

Abby sat up and stretched her arms behind her head. Eram waited patiently for her to move off him so he could get up. While he waited, he marveled at how much beauty and pain had entered into his life the last few months.

When he returned from relieving himself in the woods, Abby had most everything already packed up. "What is the plan for today?" she asked when she noticed he was back.

"From what I can see from here, straight north looks pretty clear, but I think we should angle back toward the stream as we go so, we don't run out of water. I don't know of any other streams up this high." He picked up his pack.

It took over a week of mostly steep uphill climbing to get past the first peak. During that time, they had managed to bypass the rocky cliffs they encountered. Eram was glad he had had that talk with Abby, because after that they had been 'enjoying each other's company,' making the trek a little more bearable.

He now stood on a cliff overlooking the downhill side of the first peak. Abby came up behind him and stepped in front of him; his body shielded her from some of the cold wind coming down from the peak. Her presence did nothing to obstruct his view of hills and forest before him. Once she was there, Eram slouched a little and rested his chin on the top of her head and wrapped his arms around her.

"Now what?" she asked.

"I don't want to go down any more than we have to.

241

Every step we take down is just one more step up when we start up the next peak. I think we should head east and see if we can stay high up on the western side of that ridge." He pointed to what looked from here to be a thin ridge connecting the two peaks.

"Sounds good to me." She headed off in the direction he had indicated on what looked to be a trail used by a fair number of deer or elk.

His plan to stay high up on the ridge paid off. They managed to skirt around the eastern side of the second peak in just three days. The only down side was they had stayed more exposed to the wind, so it was three days of muscle cramping cold. He also had no luck catching any food. That, combined with the need to eat more to stay warm. had depleted their food supply to just a few scraps of dried beef.

Once they got far enough around the peak, they hiked up to what looked like a good place to survey the path ahead. Reaching the summit of the small treeless hill first, Eram exclaimed with joy, "From here it looks like we can take an almost flat valley all the way to fourth peak." He reached down and helped Abby the last few feet to the top.

"Hopefully we can find something to eat down there." She sounded too tired to get excited about what was before her.

Eram put his arm around her. "That valley appears low enough to have berries if I can't catch anything, but I should be able to snare something down there." Eram's excitement increased when he noticed what looked like a game trail that led right to a snow field that sloped down the northern side of the second peak. "Look, if we take that trail, we could probably slide down that snow field on the oiled blanket and be down to the valley by night fall and finally be out of this damned freezing wind."

Abby patted his arm. "Let's get to it then." Her voice still held none of Eram's excitement.

Eram's plan worked better than expected; they were walking off the snow field an hour before dark and they only had a quarter mile or so of walking through soggy grass to get into the trees. It was also far warmer here than either of them expected, and halfway to the trees they were shedding their coats. Abby smiled at Eram for the first time in at least two days.

When they got to the trees, Eram set a couple snares while Abby got the fire going. Their actions had become routine by this point, so they no longer had to speak of their intentions. While Eram was searching for a good spot to set his snares, he stumbled upon a spring lined with blackberries. He finished his snares, then spent a while picking berries there wasn't very many ripe berries, so it took nearly an hour to pick enough for dinner and breakfast.

When he returned all that was left of the sun was a slight glow highlighting the silhouette of the western mountains. Abby had a fire going and was pacing, her face aglow--fire light betrayed her fear which quickly turned to anger when she saw him. "What the hell took you so long? I would have come searching for you, but I didn't pay attention to which way you went."

Eram's only response was to hold out his blackberry-filled coat and smile.

Her eyes lit up at the sight. "Okay, you are forgiven for letting me think I was going to have to finish this trek alone." Several berries had made it to her mouth before she finished talking.

"Don't eat too many. After days of jerky and hard bread, too many berries could leave us squatting in the bushes all day tomorrow," he cautioned.

She set the berries aside after just a handful.

The waxed canvas blanket shielded them from the moist grass. Eram sat with his back to a spruce, with Abby leaning her back against him his arms wrapped around her midsection both his hands held in hers. Her head under his chin, he breathed in her scent and was surprised that in spite of nearly two weeks without anyway to wash, he still found it pleasant. This reminded him of advice his mother had once given him. "Find a girl that smells good to you even when she stinks and you will have the makings of a long, happy life." He couldn't remember what Lisa smelled like.

They had been dozing as they watched the fire burn down to glowing coals when the first distant howl jolted them both awake.

"Was that a wolf?" Worry marred Abby's voice.

The single howl turned to a chorus. "No... not *a* wolf, that is at least six wolves."

She tensed. "Are we going to be alright?"

"Wolves rarely attack people, although we had better be more vigilant going forward." He extracted his hands from her grip. "I had better put more wood on the fire. A larger fire should add to their hesitation to bother us."

"I will get it." Abby stood and added several arm sized pieces of deadfall to the coals.

"There is one encouraging aspect of the wolves' proximity however," Eram continued when Abby returned to her spot in front of him. "With wolves close, we are less likely to encounter a bear or mountain cat and they are more likely to decide we are food than wolves are."

After a few minutes Abby asked, "I have been meaning to ask you about Vincent."

"What do you want to know?" Eram's mood darkening

far more with the mention of Vince than the thought of being eaten by wolves ever could.

"Melisa said you two once were good friends. What happened?"

Eram sat in reflection for a while before answering. "I don't know. Before his mother was killed, we were far better friends than Ulrick and I are. After she died, however, he started ignoring me and over time his animosity increased. I have actually thought about it often and can't come up with anything I could have done to make him dislike me, let alone want to kill me."

Abby turned and faced him surprised. "I never heard him say anything good about you, but what makes you think he wants to kill you?"

"When I was laid up, he came to see me. He said he had come to kill me, but had changed his mind because he looked forward to making my life in Elk Valley a miserable hell." Eram's voice held no malice only sadness.

Abby sat pondering for a moment. "Do you think he had something to do with the goblin that was after us? I only ask because I keep replaying the night we were attacked in my mind. You asked it who had sent it, as if you already knew, but wanted confirmation and it refused to answer, as if the answer would be significant."

Eram looked at her critically. "I would have never said it out loud because I haven't connected all the dots and I hate to think he could be involved, but the more I think about the circumstances of the attack on Elk Valley, the more I believe he at least knew something was going to happen. Why else would that giant goblin say he was there to ensure Melisa wasn't harmed."

The fire had died to a faint glow and the moon was high enough to bathe the forest floor with a sparse patchwork of silver light when Eram woke, shivering. The wolves had long ago ceased their complaints to the night. He still sat against the tree. Abby was curled up, wrapped in a blanket at his feet only a couple feet from the fire. Something had woken him, but he could not place it. He sat quiet, breathing shallow for what seemed like an eternity trying to hear anything that could have woke him.

Then he heard it...there was some rustling not too far off. A jolt of fear leapt from his feet and through his gut. He held his breath, trying to identify the cause of the noise. He sighed in relief when he realized the rustling was coming from where he had set one of his snares. It sounded like he was going to eat fresh meat for breakfast.

He was about to get up and stop his prize from thrashing so as not to attract other predators, when he saw movement in that direction. It stopped almost as soon as it started causing him to question whether he had seen anything. It was impossible to make out any details in the obscured moonlight. He had just about discounted it to his imagination when he saw it again and another much more powerful jolt of fear flashed through his whole body. What looked like a man in a grey robe moved silently through a patch of moonlight toward the rustling sound. Moments later the thrashing of the trapped critter stopped.

Eram, paralyzed by fear, sat for the rest of the night, straining to see or hear the mysterious personage again. Normally he wouldn't have been this frightened, but there shouldn't be anyone here. Nobody inhabited the mountains. Also, what was he doing out here in the middle of the night? Had he been watching them and for how long? And if he was, why?

The normal sounds of the much-awaited sunrise finally allowed him to relax enough to relieve his tension-induced muscle cramps. It wasn't much longer when Abby started to stir.

Eram stayed where he was until the sun's approach brightened the eastern horizon enough for him to see without struggle. Abby had been up long enough to get their fire going, spitting sparks into the morning mist. When he did finally rise to his feet, he made his way slowly checking for footprints or any other signs of last night's silent visitor. He saw no indication anyone had been where he thought he had seen the man or whatever it was he had thought he saw. He was just beginning to think he had just imagined it, when he got to the snare, and sure enough, it had caught a large cottontail. Kneeling down, he inspected the rabbit; its neck had been broken. His gut twisted. "What is going on here?" he said quietly to himself, then added only slightly louder. "I guess I should thank whoever you are for doing what I would have had to do. At least you left me my meal."

He quickly gutted the rabbit, then went back to camp. "More good luck, rabbit for breakfast." He held up the limp rabbit by the ears. He sat on a fallen tree not far from the fire and skinned the rabbit then, spit it on a long, thin branch. Using some nearby stones, he propped it up over the fire, then sat back on the rock to wait for it the cook. Abby watched him silent, absently poking the fire with a stick. After turning it several times, and an hour of cooking, the rabbit was ready to eat. Still saying nothing to each other, they began their feast of rabbit and blackberries. It was the best meal they had had since leaving Elk Valley.

Eram was nearly done eating when he was disturbed by the harsh language of a raven. It wasn't cawing, but was speaking its strange garbled raven tongue used between other ravens. It sat alone on a branch not far from their camp and looking right at Eram, bouncing its head up and down as it spoke, as if it was speaking to him. Eram looked at Abby questioningly. She looked from him to the bird then back. Her mouth was full, so she just shrugged and continued to eat.

Looking back to the bird, "What... are you hungry" he asked. The raven bounced its head more quickly. Eram picked up the rabbit skin and tossed it so it landed just below where the raven perched.

"Caw... caw." The raven spread its wings, hopped from its perch, floated to the ground and started eating the skin.

Abby swallowed what was in her mouth and licked her fingers as she looked from the raven to Eram. "I guess it was hungry." With a strange look on her face she got up and started packing up their packs. "Are you ready to get going?"

"What's the hurry?" Eram was still watching the raven pick at its meal.

"This," she waved back and forth between Eram and the raven, "is freaking me out."

"I need to check my other two snares, then we can get moving." He smiled. It was strange, but the appearance of the raven had actually settled his raw nerves.

"I will be right back." Eram was heading toward his other snares.

"Hold up... you are not leaving me here with that." She pointed to the raven. She jumped when the raven cawed at her. "I'm coming with you!"

"I'll check the snares on the way." He started helping her pack up. The first snare had a rabbit; its neck broken, and so did the second. Eram tied the rabbits to his pack.

"How are the rabbits dead when the snare only latches onto its foot?"

Eram looked at her seriously, he hadn't wanted to worry her, but he wasn't going to lie to her so he told her of the mysterious man.

"Shit! Shit! Shit! Son of a goblin whore! Mother of all that is good! What is going on here?" Fear laced every word. "We have to get out of here."

Eram took hold of Abby's shaking hands. "Whatever I saw last night did nothing to harm us, if anything it possibly saved us from predators that would have been attracted by the distress of the snared rabbits. This place is very strange, but I don't think we need to panic yet." He pulled her close. "We only have one way to go now anyway, north over the last two peaks."

Abby didn't let him pull away for a long minute. "I know, but this all is just too strange for me to comprehend. My old grandmother used to say ravens are the messengers of god and that one back there was talking to you."

Eram chuckled. "I don't believe in all that nonsense. Even if ravens are the messengers of god, the only message I received today was that he was hungry."

She laughed nervously and let him go. "Okay, let's go."

As they traveled, Eram was amazed at how strange this place was. The further they got from the ice field the warmer it got, and it got harder and harder to tell which direction they were traveling. At home he could tell which way was north by the dusty orange and green lichen on the trunks of the trees, here moss covered everything and hung in long streamers from the branches. The forest wasn't particularly dense, but the trees were massive--spruce that were two hundred feet tall or more. Oak that weren't the gnarled short trees he was used to but great trees with limbs spread a hundred feet from the massive trunks. The maples he saw weren't the spindly trees that grew along creeks back home.

The only similarity was the shape of the leaves. The ground between the trees was covered in low growing ferns and a large variety of shrubs, covered in sweet smelling flowers and berries. Rock and dirt appeared only in small stream beds and ponds, which they encountered more and more frequently. Insects swarmed in the rare shafts of sunlight and small colorful frogs bounded from their path as they made their way through the forest.

It was early afternoon when they came to a large pond, and for the first time that day they could see the sun. Eram was pleased to see they were still moving north, but now their path was blocked. They walked around the pond, but both the inlet and outlet were too wide and the current too swift to cross.

"Any ideas?" Eram asked as he sat on a moss-covered log.

"Yep, I do. We can throw our packs over the stream here, then we can swim across the pond." She took off her pack.

Eram shrugged, removed his pack and threw it over the fast-moving stream, then grabbed Abby's pack and threw it. They made their way back to the pond and began swimming.

Abby made it across first. "I think we should camp here tonight. I want to bathe and wash my clothes."

Eram retrieved their bags and they made a fire using the hanging moss to ignite dead limbs they cut from the trees. Any fallen limbs were too wet to burn. Once the fire was burning good, they both stripped out of their wet clothes and hung them up to dry. Abby watched as Eram skinned and cleaned one of the rabbits and started cooking it.

They were almost done eating when a raven landed on a tree limb not far away from their camp and started bobbing its head and speaking its garbled language. Eram and Abby shared a long look, then Eram looked and pointed toward the gleanings from the rabbit. "Go ahead, they are all yours." To their amazement the raven glided to the pile of entrails and skin and began to eat.

Abby and Eram shared another look and Abby pulled a blanket up over her naked body. Eram raised his eyebrows questioningly.

"I don't want that thing looking at me while I'm naked."

The raven looked at her and cawed.

She shivered and moved closer to Eram.

The next morning, they took a dip in the pond, then got out and rubbed ashes on their wet skin, hair and dirty clothes, then rinsed everything off back in the pond. After their bath, Abby with a blanket wrapped around her waist, sat cross legged in a patch of sun, braiding her long blonde hair.

Eram watched her. When she was nearly finished, he said, "I think we should stay here another night."

"Why, what are you thinking?" She didn't look up from her hair that was draped over her shoulder as she worked.

"I was thinking that we could 'enjoy each other's company' for a while," he said smiling.

She looked up now. "Another bath in the morning would be pretty nice." She winked at him.

The one extra day by the pond turned into a full week. By the end of the week, they realized how much they had needed the rest and good regular meals. Eram hadn't felt this good since before his unfortunate encounter with the goblins. Other than the occasional ache in his arm and the itchy scars around his eye, he felt better than he ever had.

The vision in his eye had markedly improved, in fact, he thought his vision in that eye was slightly better than the uninjured eye. Abby had gotten used to the raven that hadn't left and ate the leftovers from their meals.

The first night Eram hadn't put out any snares, but he had used their ropes to set up trip lines that would alert them to anyone coming close. Nothing tripped his lines, and by the third day they relaxed. Even the distant howling wolves at night had become a comfortable routine.

During the warm humid days, they wandered the forest naked, or near to it; there wasn't anyone but the forest animals to see after all, and the animals, didn't seem to mind. They gathered fruit and berries of types neither had ever seen, letting the raven try the unknown fruit first, if it ate it, they would try it, if it didn't, they left it alone. During the cool misty nights, they kept each other warm.

Eram had never felt so free and content.

Abby was lying on her stomach in a rare patch of sun. Eram lying on his side absently ran his fingers lightly on the back of her thigh. "Abby?"

"What?" She turned her head toward him.

He smiled warmly. "I wanted to tell you that this has been by far the best week of my life. I could stay here with you forever." Then more seriously, "No matter what happens in the future, I want you to know, I will always love you and appreciate what you have done for me."

She turned onto her side, head resting on her palm. "Really?" Her brows rose. "What is this all about?" Her voice was serious, but her face was jovial.

"It's just, as much as I would like to stay here with you, I think we should get going in the morning."

Smiling big and with a chuckle, "You know you don't have to get all serious and sentimental to convince me of the importance of moving on."

"I'm serious about everything I said." He was saddened by her lighthearted response to his feelings.

Her tone mocking, "I know you are serious. You are always serious." Then, with a warm smile, she ran her hand along the side of his face, tracing some of the scars around his eye. "This place is more beautiful than I could have imagined a place could be, and I couldn't think of anyone I would have rather been here with than you."

Eram was still just a little saddened by her first response, but did not want to make the rest of their time here uncomfortable, so he decided to give her a more lighthearted tribute. Standing with arms wide, "I agree this has to be the most beautiful place in the world and a place this special can't be seen and left without a name." He stopped turning and looked down at her. "I name this place, Abigail Forest."

Abby, lying on her back, was now momentarily speechless.

"If I live through this, whenever I tell of our harrowing journey into the dragon peaks, I will say, we came upon Abigail Forest, the most beautiful place on earth." He smiled big down at her.

She recovered from his show. "How do you know this place doesn't already have a name?" She mirrored his grin. "If this is Abigail Forest, then Abigail Forest is within Eramus Valley."

He laughed. "You know that just doesn't work. It would have to be Eramus Forest lies within Abigail Valley. The valley is insignificant, however, since the forest covers several small valleys and hills. So, this place from this day forward is Abigail Forest."

Sobered by his show of devotion, only her eyes continued to smile. "Since you are naming things, what are you going to name the crow?"

The raven cawed.

"Raven," he answered.

"I know it is a raven. What are you going to name it?" she

asked looking at the raven still a little ill at ease by its ability to know when they are talking about it.

"Raven is his name," he responded.

"You can't name a raven, Raven," she snorted. "It's like naming your son Boy and your dog, Dog, and how do you know it is a he, not a she, anyway?"

Eram sat back down next to her. "If I had other ravens to name, I guess it wouldn't work, but since it is the only raven, I have had the pleasure to talk to," the raven cawed, "it works just fine, especially because I don't know its sex. Raven works either way." He lay down next to her and leaned his body against her warm, soft skin, ending their conversation.

They continued north the following morning, just after dawn, while the mists were still heavy in the air. Both were quiet, not wanting to leave this place, but knowing they could not stay forever. Winter starts early high in the mountains.

After three slow moving days the land started sloping more and more upward, and the forest began to thin, allowing them to see what lay before them. Getting around the fourth peak was going to be the most daunting of their journey, so far. It was going to be hundreds of feet of near shear cliffs, or miles of hiking on a glacier that wrapped around the east side of the peak. Eram had never been the best mountain climber, so he was leaning toward the glacier route, but they still had a least a day of travel before they reached the need to decide.

It was nearing dark--the air had grown noticeably colder since leaving the rainforest and the bite of thin, cold wind was a shocking contrast to their days of naked leisure. Abby led the way to a hollow in a rock out cropping that they hoped would offer some shelter from the wind and cold when Eram saw a grey blur heading straight toward Abby. With no time to think, Eram grabbed Abby by her pack and pulled her back hard, while shielding his face and neck from the approaching fangs.

The wolf's jaws clamped down on Eram's left arm and its momentum knocked him flat on his back. Like the last time he had a beast on top of him with the intent to kill, time slowed. He knew his only hope to survive was to sacrifice his arm to the wolf's attentions while he attacked. He tried grabbing the side of the wolf's face and stick his thumb into its eye, but the beast's face was covered in blood and he could not get a tight enough hold to leverage his thumb into its eye, hard enough to do any damage.

That couldn't be all his blood, could it? he thought. He did finally manage to jab its eye, doing little to no damage, but it did cause it to release his arm momentarily before trying to go for his neck again. Eram barely managed to get his arm in its path.

The eyes weren't working; he needed to get his dirk. Frantically he reached for his long-bladed knife, but had difficulty keeping hold of it because of the back and forth thrashing of the wolf. Finally, he managed to get a hold of his dirk and thrust it as hard as he could into the bloody beast's neck.

Eram had sank the blade to the hilt--a full hand of blade was sticking out the other side. The wolf, with the blade through its windpipe, tried desperately to remove the blade from its neck, managing only to cut its paws.

Not taking any chances, Eram--gritting through the pain--got to his feet and pulled the smaller knife he used for gutting and skinning and cautiously approached the wolf. Its breath was labored, trying to pull air past the dirk and blood filling its lungs. Each exhale sprayed blood from its nose in a mist. Eram stayed back, watching for an opportunity to finish his foe. The wolf, still on its feet, watched him warily for a few moments, then slowly settled to the ground. Eram pounced, plunging his skinning knife into the wolf's eye. The wolf jerked back, but sank back down to the ground, a second knife imbedded in its skull. It stopped the struggle for breath a few moments later.

The battle over, Eram sank to his knees, nauseous from the pain in his arm and the smell of blood. The shakes started shortly before the tears. He sat back on his heels, struggling to stay upright and keep from emptying his stomach. He did not know how long he sat there alone watching blood drip from his coat sleeve before he realized he was alone. "Abby?" he called weakly. There was no response.

Gut clenching with fear, he struggled back to his feet, then he saw her lying on her back. He hurried to her side. There was a pool of blood under her head. "No... no... nooo!" he cried. He cradled her head with his blood-soaked hands and pressed his face against hers. "You can't die, not here, not when we are so close, not when I need you so much," he whimpered into her ear.

She exhaled, he felt it. She wasn't dead. Feeling no pain, because he was invigorated with new hope, he picked her up and made his way to the hollow in the rock they had been heading to. Once he was there, he gently laid her down. Using a blanket, he wrapped her head the best he could. He then lay down and pulled the rest of their blankets over them and he was out.

Eram stood, looking south over Abigail Forest. The mists were heavy, obscuring any details of the forest.

"Eramus?"

Eram turned toward the sound of his name. Standing before him was the most beautiful woman he had ever seen. Her amber colored hair shone in the rising sun, her green eyes held both sadness and fear.

"Eramus, you must wake." Her voice held the same fear he saw in her eyes.

"Why?" he asked, even though seeing this woman afraid nearly made him weep.

The mysterious, but somehow familiar woman pointed at the ground, and lying before her was Abby in a pool of blood--much larger than what could be possible. "Eramus, you must wake."

Eram looked upon Abby. "I have no power to save her."

"Eramus." The woman tried to mask her fear with firm resolve. "You must wake."

"What can I do? I am nothing."

"Eramus, you are dying. Eramus, you must wake." Each command to wake was made with more fear-tinged force.

The vision before him began to waver. "But I don't want you to leave."

"Eramus, if you die, this woman before you will die." Then, with even more desperation, "Eramus if you die, I will die. You must save me."

Eram woke with a start, shivering, but Abby was shivering more. The left side of his body felt wet. Panicked, he quickly checked Abby's head; her head had stopped bleeding. He pulled the blankets off himself. The blood was his. When he sat up, he nearly blacked out--his arm was still dripping. He took off his coat, not daring to look at the damage. He quickly wrapped his coat as tight as he could around his arm. Dawn was still dim in the east when he went looking for wood for a fire.

"Caw... caw," Raven called from above his head.

Not far from where he and Abby slept was the dead wolf,

whimpering and growling were four wolf pups, wondering what was wrong with their mother. Eram reached for his dirk before remembering both of his blades were still embedded in the mother wolf. He started to look for a rock big enough to kill the pups.

"Caw... caw," Raven called.

"Oh... right, Abby is freezing. I need to start a fire. She needs me." He said to himself, delirious. "I will kill you after I start a fire," he called to the wolf pups.

He got the fire going and pulled Abby further under the shelter of the rock, then he was out.

13 - Lisa

The east wind blew hot from the hills, drying her sweat before she could feel its wetness. Most of the time the breeze blew in from the bay, keeping the temperature pleasant and filling the air with the scent of the ocean, but the last week had been unbearable. Of course, normally Lisa spent her days in the stone keep where the moisture in the thick stone walls kept the inside of the building comfortable most of the year. Over the last week, however, she had been tailing Zeek, learning his habits so she could safely dispatch him...as she had been directed by Thom.

As of yet, she was unable to see a pattern to his routine. If it could be considered a routine at all; the only place he went consistently was a tavern in one of the less savory parts of Southport. The one revelation of consequence they had discovered since tailing Zeek was that he was secretly working for Andarus while posing as a captain in the army. This revelation had galvanized Lisa to the need of disposing of Zeek. Both Thom and Amber believed Andarus was either responsible for or involved in the disappearance of Amber's brother.

Having spent most of her time since being in Southport in the keep, she was finding the rest of the city a mix of wonderful, distasteful and utterly disturbing. The city was laid out in a series of semicircles; the keep and the bay were at the center. The first couple of sections were mostly shops and food markets with a few homes of the wealthy. The further she got from the Keep, the more degraded the homes and populace became. Once you got to the outskirts, however, the land turned to vineyards, orchards of oranges, avocados, pistachios and the mansions of the owners of the orchards. She imagined the city would look like a giant spider web if viewed from above. Most everyone in Southport either worked in the fields picking and processing fruit, or at the docks loading fruit onto ships.

259

Zeek leaving the goldsmith shop, brought Lisa back to her purpose. When he exited, he looked around to see if he were being followed. Anyone that concerned about being followed was up to no good. He was like this whenever he left the Keep, though. She assumed by his actions, Andarus had him doing something nefarious. Of course, he never spotted Lisa, because she did not have to be visible to see and follow him. She was currently absently checking the quality of some oranges around the corner from the Goldsmith shop. She could clearly see him with her mage sight. As long as she kept him within about one hundred feet, she could track him anywhere.

He would have led Lisa in a meandering circle, punctuated by abrupt turns down less trodden alleys, if she hadn't recognized his one pattern of evading imagined pursuit to the one place he went regularly. Knowing where he was going, she simply walked the quarter mile to the Sea Serpent tavern and waited around the corner for him to show up. Zeek arrived right on time an hour later. *Paranoia must get exhausting,* she thought. Knowing he would spend most of the evening there, she went back to the Keep to report to Thom.

"So, today he went to the north winery, then to a silversmith and a goldsmith shop?" Thom asked.

"Yes sir," Lisa responded, still standing at attention in Amber's parlor. She always gave here reports to Thom and Amber here. Thom was no longer general commander of all of the Southern Territory troops, he was the personal protector of the governor's daughter, so his command center was Amber's opulently decorated parlor and his troops consisted of Lisa and six other body guards.

Amber was sitting on one of the overstuffed sofas. She smiled at the 'yes sir,' but kept quiet.

"I trained you too well. It is going to take me months to un-train your 'yes sirs' isn't it?" Thom asked, exasperated.

"Yes sir." Lisa's smiled warmly for the old soldier.

"Yesterday, he didn't go out." Thom was pacing, trying to figure out what Zeek could be doing.

"It appears Andarus is expecting a guest. Either some woman he expects to seduce with fancy wine and jewelry, or someone important he wants to impress. Since the only women he could be wooing would rather just get their money and leave, he must be expecting an important visitor." Amber twirled her golden hair with her finger.

Since becoming Amber's bodyguard, other than her time spent tailing Zeek, Lisa had spent every waking and sleeping hour with Amber. She had quickly realized that Amber, in spite of trying to look the innocent fool in public, was actually the brains of their little group. Thom was the muscle, and his former position brought a bit of clout. Lisa was still trying to figure out what she brought to the group, but she found she was enjoying her job. She also realized she was looking forward to ending Zeek's time alive. While following him, she had discovered everything he had achieved was achieved by bullying others. As a captain in the army, he enjoyed abusing new recruits. His romantic life consisted of getting women too drunk to resist or occasionally forcing some poor woman that found herself in the wrong place at the wrong time.

"Have we found out enough? Can I kill him now?" Lisa asked.

Thom sighed. "How do you plan on doing it?"

"I think I will simply be a poor woman caught after a night of drinking."

"I don't like it," Thom said. "I would prefer if you simply stab him in the back and steal his coin to make it look like a robbery."

"After getting to know him this last week, I want him to know it was me, a young girl that killed him. He told me while he was beating me, that if I were to ever beat him, he would deserve to die. I want him to know, he does deserve to die!" She realized she was letting her emotions get out of control, she took a deep breath. "Also, this way if I get caught, I can claim he was trying to rape me in the alley, which he will be."

"You are letting him get to you. I think I am going to have Sam do it." Thom was worried.

Lisa came to attention. "Sir, I will do as you command, but I need this experience to harden me to what I may be called upon to do in the defense of the governor's daughter. If you have someone else do this, I will never forget you took this away from me." She took a cleansing breath "As you command, sir."

Amber laughed.

Thom looked at Lisa seriously for a long time. "Fine, but Sam is going with you. Post him somewhere out of sight, but close enough to back you up if you need it."

Lisa smiled, there was no joy in it.

"I am going to let Sam know he is at your disposal." He made his way out. Then he paused. "Don't abuse your new-found command." Then he was gone.

Still chuckling Amber said, "And you tell me not to play with his feelings." Then more seriously, "You need to be careful, Lisa. I don't think you have thought through what could go wrong and the repercussions if it does."

Lisa sat in one of the many alleyways Zeek could choose

to use on his way back to the army barracks. This one he had chosen several times before. Lisa and Sam had followed Zeek around all day. He had spent his time buying vegetables and fruits that were harder to get in the south. He didn't take anything with him, so he must have arranged for delivery. After several hours, Zeek finally made his way to the Sea Serpent tavern.

Now she sat bored, waiting for him to decide if he was drunk and belligerent enough to return home. Sam was stationed a street over. If she needed him, she would whistle twice.

Two hours must be the amount of time for belligerent to set in, because Zeek was on the move and he was loudly assaulting a woman's dignity on his way out of the tavern.

As luck would have it, Zeek headed toward the alley one street over; this would put her further away from Sam, but she wasn't worried. It was a dark, moonless night and the alleys were near pitch and she had spent some time studying the alleys so her mage sight would be an accurate depiction of her surroundings.

She headed away from the tavern so she could cut him off before he could reach the end. She got there with plenty of time. She slowly made her way down the alleyway, careful to move silently. Zeek was standing motionless, facing the wall. *He must be relieving himself,* she thought. Lisa moved to within ten feet of him, then waited. A lantern lit and Zeek walked toward her, a lewd smile on his face.

"You're not drunk." Lisa was surprised--a jolt of fear tore through her.

"Nope, I never would have thought you the type to look for thrills in dark alleys." He laughed "If I would have known, I would have suggested a meeting a long time ago."

Taking control of her fear, she drew two long blades just

slightly shorter than a sword. "I doubt you are going to enjoy the thrills I have in mind."

Without further comment, Zeek attacked, his sword sped toward her. She easily blocked his swing, but she was surprised by the power he had put behind it. She spun with the blow to keep from losing her knife and ducked low and slashed with her other knife. He had anticipated her move. Zeek easily blocked her slash in such a way that her knife spun out of her hands. One knife left, she took a defensive position.

Zeek launched into a blur of attacks. She had trained in this style and knew how to defend against such attacks. His last blow, however, had left her over-extended. His left fist filled the space left in her guard. She wheeled backward, blood streaming from her swelling lips.

He laughed. "I bet you can't whistle. No help is on the way. If you had trained with me a little longer, tonight may have went a little better for you, but it looks like my thrills are going to hold sway tonight."

Fear gripped her as she put up her guard, she hoped he would get over confident and make a mistake.

"What, no witty banter? No oaths of violence and death? I must say, I am a little disappointed." His arrogance was infuriating.

Lisa attacked. His defense was almost dismissive as he sent her second knife flying, and before she could run, he had a hold of her arm. She punched, kicked and thrashed against his grip, but he had her held tight. She realized how much training she needed, but she also realized now that none of that mattered, she was not leaving this alley alive.

Holding her with his left hand, he tossed his sword aside and tore her shirt open, exposing her to the warm night air. He then grabbed her by the hair and pulled her face close to his, he licked the blood from her lips. "You have no idea how much I have wanted to see you like this. I am going to make this last all night...No, I think I will make this last much longer than one night. I know a guy that would be happy to keep you hidden for me. All he would want in return is a turn every now and then."

As Zeek spoke, Lisa was aware of the breeze against her skin, drying her sweat causing an involuntary chill. Knowing she was going to die, she thought of the one thing that came to mind, the one regret. "I'm sorry I hurt you, Eram," she whispered. Then she saw it. Zeek's aura was red, but there was something else, a red glow that emanated from within him. Instinctively, she knew it was his life. She imagined pulling it out, sucking it from him.

Zeek's face went from perverted glee to terror; somehow, he knew what was happening. He tried to pull away. Lisa grabbed hold of his arm with both hands. He started pounding on her with all the strength he had. She felt her jaw break, then several ribs broke--the pain was mind-numbing.

She just took his violence, but didn't let go. She knew if she let go, she would die, so she held with every ounce of strength she had--which increased as the power of Zeek's attempts to get away decreased.

During his fight to survive, Zeek had managed to break Lisa's jaw and a few ribs, but in the end, she prevailed. Zeek lay on his back, eyes staring blankly at the millions of stars covering the night sky. His skin was slate grey. He was dead.

"I killed him," she whispered to herself.

"Yes, you did," someone said behind her.

Sam, she thought. No, it wasn't Sam. She knew the aura of the man behind her. Andarus's black-tinged yellow aura was familiar to her. Her heart sank as she turned to face the employer of the man she had just killed. The gravity of the situation was not lost to her. Whatever she had done to kill Zeek would not work on Andarus. He was wise enough and powerful enough to not let it.

Andarus laughed--it wasn't a happy laugh or a mocking laugh it; was a laugh of irony. "Next time you decide to spy on a man in the employ of a mage, you should be more careful." He pulled his hood back away from his face. His face now deadly serious. "What did you learn of me during your short career as Thom's spy?"

Lisa's mind was racing. "After what Zeek had done to me in training, I wanted to kill him. I wasn't spying for Thom. I was spying for me, with Thom's okay."

Andarus's pale eyes seemed to look through her. "And what did you learn about me while spying?"

Lisa took a deep breath. "I didn't know he was working for you until I started spying. Once I did, Thom said I was allowed to kill him because he had abandoned his oaths as a military officer."

"Don't play me a fool, girl," Andarus growled. "Tell me what you learned of ME!"

She played like what she had learned was damning, if it got out. Looking up at him meekly, "I learned you have a girl you want to impress because Zeek was buying fancy wine and jewelry."

His laugh was jovial this time. "Indeed." He shook his head. "You know we could have made a pretty good team--with your talent, my talent and experience, we could have ruled this world. Unfortunately, I'm afraid that ship has sailed."

Andarus walked past Lisa, giving her a wide berth and knelt beside Zeek. He rummaged through his clothes and removed two pouches. He tossed Lisa one of the pouches. "That is his coin. This," he held up the other larger pouch, "is my coin. You know that," he indicated Zeek's body, "is not supposed to be possible. You used his life energy to heal some of your injuries as he inflicted them. Impressive, to say the least."

"You're not going to kill me?" She was looking dazed at the pouch in her hands.

"No, I'm not going to kill you. In fact, because of my respect for fellow mages, I am going to give you some advice. Make sure you take any evidence putting you here is gone, because by tomorrow afternoon. Some of the more superstitious in the city are going to think we have a vampire on the loose."

Andarus rifled through Zeek's clothes some more and removed a piece of folded up paper. "If you had found this before I arrived, you would be dead." The paper burst into flame and was gone in an instant. "You are a rare woman, Lisa. You should not be playing bodyguard to the spoiled daughter of the governor. A life mage is born maybe once every hundred years. You are above this petty servitude to lesser beings. The sooner you realize this, the sooner you can start living up to your potential."

"You are just an advisor to a short-sighted governor." Lisa regretted the comment as soon as she had said it.

Andarus's joyless chuckle sent chills down her spine. "If that is how you see it, then you have a lot to learn. I forgive your ignorance though. I was once young like you."

He picked up the lantern and put it out. "You are on the losing side of the coming conflict. Thom's ignorance of what is plainly before him speaks of how out-played all of you are. There is a change on its way, Lisa. When you realize you have chosen the wrong path, come see me. I will help you find your way. You're welcome by the way."

"What should I be thanking you for?" She closed her eyes to more easily use her mage sight. The alleyway was now aglow with dots of life of varying sizes. She could also see energy in everything around her--the colors and shades confusing, but indescribably beautiful.

"Because of my willingness to facilitate this little encounter, you are now a fully unlocked life mage." He turned his back on her and left.

Traumatized by her encounter, she had made it halfway to where Sam was before she realized she was wondering the night bare-chested. She covered herself the best she could with her torn clothes and continued to where Sam waited.

Sam had a shielded lantern with him. When he caught sight of Lisa hobbling toward him, he exclaimed, "Damn it, Lisa, Thom is going to kill me!" He quickly removed his jacket and draped it over her shoulders. "Let's get back to the Keep. We should probably see the army medic before we report to Thom."

"No, I will be fine. And this," she indicated her beat up face, "is entirely my fault. I will make sure Thom doesn't hold you responsible." Once at the Keep, they took the less used route to Amber's rooms. Sam took his leave before she entered.

Lisa entered Amber's parlor. Thom stopped his pacing and Amber gasped.

Thom came to her and gently looked her over. "What happened?"

"They knew." She had managed to keep her emotions in check when talking to Andarus and during her return trip with Sam, but now alone with people she trusted, she fell apart. Crying openly, she embraced Thom.

He held her while she cried. Then the 'they' in her statement dawned on him. He began to shake with rage. "Andarus did this? I am going to kill him." He started to pull away.

"No, Andarus didn't touch me." She didn't let him go.

Amber was now at her side. "Thom, maybe you should let me take her and get her cleaned up. She can give her report tomorrow."

"Okay, I will be out here if you need anything." Thom reluctantly, let her go.

Amber led the shaking Lisa into her bath and began filling the tub, then she helped Lisa remove her torn and bloody clothes. Lisa gasped as she entered the hot water that turned a watery red. Amber softly cleaned the blood from Lisa's face. "Zeek did this?"

"Yes," she responded quietly.

"Is he dead?"

"Yes."

"Good," was all Amber said for the rest of the night.

Lisa woke alone in Amber's bed. Judging by the angle of the sun outside the windows, it was midmorning. She got up and looked at herself in the mirror. Her face and chest were a mass of bruises. Andarus was right, she had healed herself. Her jaw wasn't broken and neither were her ribs, but the bruising suggested she should have broken ribs. She found one of her robes and made her way to the parlor.

Thom stood when she entered. "Hopefully it looks worse than it is." He chuckled, but it didn't work for him.

"It looks far worse than it is." Lisa smiled at him warmly. She sat at the table and began eating the breakfast that they had left for her. She told them what happened the night before. While she recounted the events, neither Amber nor Thom said anything, and when she finished her tale, they both remained silent for a long time.

When Lisa finished eating, Amber asked, "How did you

kill Zeek, again?" There was something in Amber's tone that made her feel nervous talking about her ability for the first time.

"I sucked his life energy out of him." She was a little taken back by the look on their faces.

"Could you suck the life out me, if you wanted to?" Amber asked, unable to hide the underlying fear and revulsion on her face.

Lisa saw her life crumbling before her. If Thom and Amber no longer trusted her, what would she do? If they didn't trust her, who would? Andarus? No, she could never side with that snake. She knew, though, she had to lay it all out before them and let them decide.

"Probably, but it would be easier to just stick a knife in you. It would have been easier to just stick a knife in Zeek also, but he wouldn't let me...then, when he threatened to keep me so he could use me as he wished, I... never mind." Her anger burst forth into tears. Even though tears flowed freely down her face, she would keep her chin up. She would meet their revulsion head on. She looked them both in the eye confronting their opinion of her.

Thom looked away. She didn't know what that meant, but it broke her heart. He should be standing with her, not looking away. She looked at Amber.

Amber stared at her with those too knowing, unnaturally green eyes. Her face no longer held a look of revulsion, but one of shame. But she did not look away from her shame. Instead, she stood and embraced Lisa. "I'm sorry," she whispered, "but I had to know."

Lisa pulled away from her. "What do you mean you had to know?" Anger replaced her tears.

"I had to know what your true motivations are," she

answered, shame still painting her face. "Don't hold it against Thom. He did not want to go along with this."

Thom still looked at the wall.

Lisa was mad with indignity. "How does this prove my motivations?"

"The look of fear and anger, but most importantly, betrayal at our reaction to your ability, told me what you care about most. Trust is what you care about most, to be trusted, and to be able to trust those closest to you. I know that my methods may seem like a betrayal, but I hope you will eventually see the wisdom in what I did. I am truly sorry, but Andarus is right, change is coming, and if I... no, if *we* are going to survive this, we have to be able to count on each other completely."

Lisa just stared at Amber, shocked and confused. She was having difficulty just grasping everything Amber had just said, let alone being able forgive her for it. "So, let me get this straight, you didn't trust me before?"

Amber sighed. "I trusted you, but you can never truly know for sure until that trust is tested. What motivates a person's actions says a lot about how far they can be trusted. My father told me once to trust no one, especially those closest to you. The betrayal of those close to you is the most damaging and the most painful. From that day forward, I never trusted my father again. You sleep in the same room, you eat with me. If I can't truly trust you, I am already dead because I will always be looking over my shoulder, always sleeping with one eye open, always wondering if my food tastes funny, because of a mistake, or because of poison.

"This test was not for you because of some potential flaw in your character. This test was for me. I will sleep better tonight because of it."

"How did you know I had used my ability to kill Zeek?"

Lisa Asked.

"If you had killed him with your knives, you would not have been beaten--stabbed maybe, but not beaten. I also knew if it had gotten to the point of simply hand to hand, there was no way you could have overpowered him without using some sort of mage power," Amber answered. "However, the description of you sucking the life from him obviously made our charade easier to pull off."

Lisa was still confused, but it was starting to come together. "You haven't been telling me everything, have you? Now that I have your trust, will you be letting me know everything that's going on?"

Amber twirled her hair around her finger. "See, Thom? I told you she would get it." Then she looked at Lisa seriously. "No, I will not be telling you everything. If you knew everything I know, Andarus would have killed you last night. I am not a friend that shares with you all her secrets. I am your friend, but I am your commander first and your friend second. I will tell you what you need to know and leave out the things that could get you killed. I am your commander, though; you will tell me everything."

Lisa looked at Thom then back to Amber. Amber was better at her act than she had previously thought. "You are brilliant. I had actually thought that you were unhappy by your father's insistence you have more protection. I also thought that Thom's removal from the army was your father's idea or Andarus's, so that Thom would be out of the way if they went to war with the west. I just realized, however, that it was you all along. You wanted Thom as your protector... no... not protector, advisor and his ability to garner the loyalty of the troops if things go bad. You are the commander, aren't you? Was my involvement your idea also?"

"No, you were Thom's idea." Amber looked at Lisa sternly. "Thom is the only man I trust in Southport. You see now why trust is important. If we are going to survive what is coming, Andarus and his ilk need to think they have the upper hand. They need to overlook their strongest opposition, because honestly, Lisa, they do have the upper hand, and we have to stay below their attentions until we can do the most good. Remember, I'm the spoiled daughter of the governor, not high up on their priorities right now; we need to keep it that way."

Lisa looked at Thom. "I forgive you." She then looked at Amber "I'm still mad. You made me cry. It might be awhile."

Amber smiled. "Take whatever time you need, but you are still on duty."

A thought occurred to Lisa. "Speaking of trust, you need to reassign Sam. He can't be trusted. He had little concern for me, but was quite concerned for what you would do to him." She told Thom.

"You are saying his governing motivation is self-preservation?" Amber asked.

"Uh… yeah, that is what I'm saying." Lisa was still a bit confused.

Their conversation was interrupted by a light knock at the door. Thom went to the door, Lisa and Amber stayed seated at the small table. "It is Andarus." Lisa said.

Thom opened the door. Andarus stood, arms behind his back, hood pulled over his head concealing most of his face. What could be seen was his thin lips and weak chin covered with two days of gray stubble.

"May I come in?"

Thom moved aside. "Sure, come in, have a seat." He motioned to the sofas. "What brings you unannounced to Amber's personal quarters?" His comment and tone made it clear to everyone he thought the visit inappropriate.

Andarus chuckled. "I have a couple items your… um…

Lisa left out in the street last night." He pulled her two long knives out from under his grey cloak. "I told you to make sure to remove all evidence of your involvement in Zeek's death." He set the knives on the small table in front of Amber and Lisa. "I did notice, however, you were a little delirious, which could be expected under the circumstances, so I waited around just in case...and a good thing I did. Rumors of the death are already top of the list for gossip this morning."

"We still have some fruit left from breakfast, would you like some?" Amber indicated the bowl of fruit on the table.

"No thanks." Andarus moved over to one of the sofas Thom had offered. "I'm not much of a fruit-eater, but I will take you up on the seat. There are a few things I need to discuss with your team." Andarus pulled back his hood, revealing his bald head, and sat.

"Is this going to be some long drawn out discussion where you two," she pointed toward both Thom and Andarus, "argue and want to kill each other by the time we are done? Because if it is, I will be in my room." She got up to leave.

"Please stay," Andarus asked. "I am merely here to share some mutually beneficial information and I want to be sure you hear it firsthand. I hope to keep this civil."

Amber, already up, moved to the sofas and sat across from Andarus. Thom stood to her side, making it obvious he was ready if Andarus tried anything.

Andarus looked toward Lisa, still sitting at the table. "Your bodyguard seems a little lax in her duties."

"She had a rough night, so she is not yet on duty," Thom answered.

"I know she had a rough night, that is the primary purpose of my visit." Andarus leaned back and rested his arm on the back of the sofa. "She explained the motivation behind her encounter with Zeek. I believed most of it. Has she told you of my conversation with her?"

"She has given a full report," Thom answered.

"I believe she probably told you everything she thought was important, but I doubt she included that what she did to Zeek last night is supposed to be impossible. There was a lot of debate over the ability to steal energy from an unwilling life two thousand years ago. After a lot of experimentation, the experts of that age concluded that it was impossible." Andarus leaned forward, expression intense. "But that is not even the truly amazing part though. She used that stolen energy to heal herself. As she pulled Zeek's life from him, he fought valiantly to live; during his fight he had broken Lisa's jaw and no fewer than eight ribs." He gestured to where Lisa sat. "Yet there she sits, bruised, but whole."

"You must understand, Thom," Andarus continued. "I wasn't going to tell you any of this, but after a night of no sleep trying to understand what I saw, I could not let this discovery go unrecognized for what it is."

Lisa could see the irritation building in Thom. "Andarus," Thom hid none of his irritation, "would you get to the point? What do you want?"

Andarus sighed. "Thom, you always have to make things more difficult than they have to be. What I want, is what you should want. I want to train Lisa. I want her to live up to her potential." He stood and paced behind the sofa he had been sitting on. "Last night Lisa was very nearly killed. If Zeek hadn't been obsessed with abusing her, and had just gutted her from the start, she would be dead. However, if Lisa had entered that alley as a trained life mage, she could have pulled the energy from around her and turned the air around Zeek into a poisonous cloud that melted his skin and lungs."

"I thought a life mage only manipulated life energy?

How could I change the air?" Lisa asked from across the room.

"You see?" Andarus waved in Lisa's direction. "She has no idea what is possible. The term 'Life Mage' is deceptive. It is really the manipulation of the energy of bonds. The bond between body and spirit is just one of the nearly infinite bonds that can be broken or reformed. As an example, a fire is simply the energy released from the bonding of carbon and oxygen. A Life Mage is the most complicated of the disciplines, but as such she has the potential to be the most powerful. She could potentially turn those knives of hers into piles of rust, then use that energy to neutralize poison in someone's blood. But without training, she will just be a knife wielder with the novel ability to see who is at the door."

No one said anything; they just watched Andarus pace.

He stopped and looked at each of them, exasperated. "Well, at least think about it." Then he started to go, but then stopped. "One more thing. It has come to my attention that Master Robert and his apprentice will be arriving in South-port possibly tonight or early tomorrow--just thought you would like to know." He pointedly looked at Lisa, then left.

Once the door closed behind Andarus, Lisa jumped up, unable to contain her excitement. She had not seen anyone from home for months. "Amber, you will like Ulrick." Then she was off to get ready for the day.

The rest of the day had been spent discussing Lisa's education. They all admitted she needed to learn more of her talents, both physical and magical. Her encounter with Zeek had highlighted her deficiencies. Thom had mentioned that Robert could possibly be of some help, but he had no idea if he would be willing to stay at the keep for an extended period of time. They all agreed they did not want Lisa to leave with Robert. They had discussed what she had learned from the book Thom had gotten her. She, at that point, had to admit that though she could read, she was not as proficient as she would like, and that the words used in the book were also outside of her ability to understand. She admitted that she would not have learned at all, except Eram had insisted on teaching her. At that point, they decided that before they would consider Andarus's offer, they would bring in a tutor to teach Lisa how to read better. Until then, however, Amber would read the book with her and they could at least try to learn what they could.

A cool breeze was fluttering the curtains silver moon light pulsed with the motion. Lisa had grown to love this time of night. She sometimes stayed up late, other days she woke in the middle of the night; she kept the schedule as random as she could. She knew it was nearly dawn by the sounds of birds beginning their morning songs. She expected the eastern sky to start to lighten with the coming sun anytime now. She heard Amber moan in her sleep; Lisa was not alarmed by this. Amber had bad dreams most nights. She was surprised, however, when she appeared in the doorway to her bedroom, tears on her cheeks glistened in the silver light.

"Eramus is dying."

14 - Ulrick

The sound of leaves fluttering in the warm afternoon breeze and the gurgle of the small stream were the only sounds. Ulrick sat with his back to the large cottonwood he liked to sit under. Three small silver skulls, along with several pieces of quartz crystal, were sitting on the piece of leather he kept them wrapped in. He had gotten back from his trip to the falls late the night before, and after completing a list of items the old mage had assigned him, this was the first chance he had gotten to see if he could get his carvings to be something other than lumps of silver shaped like skulls.

None of the crystals fit tightly in any of the skulls--they were either too large or too small. Something told him that chipping the larger faceted crystals to fit wouldn't do him any good, so he simply placed smaller crystals into the hollow of the inside of the skulls and there they sat upside down, with crystals sticking out of the bottom of the skulls. And there he sat just staring at them, at a complete loss as to what to do next...if there was even anything to do next. This whole thing was probably just a project the old man had come up with to kill time.

Natalia was sitting cross legged on the leaf covered ground a few feet in front of him. He had finally grown accustomed to her continuous presence. He had even grown used to her continuously bare chest. He still could appreciate her physical beauty, but it no longer caused his pulse to race--or at least it usually didn't cause his pulse to race.

Ulrick became aware that she had stopped doing whatever she had been doing and was now staring at him. "What?" he asked, palms held up and out to either side.

She shrugged.

"Do you know where Bob went off to? I could really use some advice about now," Ulrick said frustrated.

"You do realize, I am only here because I am unable to leave. I really could care less about you or the senile old bastard." She gave him a mirthless, sarcastic grin.

Ulrick had also gotten to know the pattern of the Green Witch's moods. She hated just sitting around doing nothing, and she also hated it when Ulrick asked Bob questions instead of her. "What would you suggest I do next?"

Her brows pulled together. "I know you are asking just to humor me."

"I've been sitting her for nearly an hour and you have yet to offer any advice or suggestions. Then you get your feelings hurt when I want to ask Bob for suggestions. I only go looking for advice because I figure by your lack of input you have nothing to say." Ulrick's temper snapped. "By the three hells, if you have a suggestion, why don't you just give it?"

She smiled an evil grin. She always got a perverse satisfaction when he lost his temper. "Ironic curse you just used."

"Well?" He wasn't going to play her game.

"The representative from the first of the three hells advises you run some energy through them. The representative from the first hell believes the fact you have yet to at least try that, proves you are an imbecile." Her smile widened. "I, however, don't have any idea what the other two hells would suggest."

Ulrick glared at her, but did as she suggested. He started slow, only running a trickle of electrical energy through the skulls. Nothing was happening. He made eye contact with Natalia questioningly.

"Try forcing the energy through the crystals. Don't let it just flow around them."

As soon as he did what she suggested, he detected a slight vibration from the crystals. "Keep adding more energy."

Forcing the energy through the crystals was far more difficult than just letting it flow, and there was a greater energy loss. To be able to add more energy, he arranged the skulls in a triangle and forced the energy to flow through each of the skulls, recirculating what was left back into the circuit, and as he did this, he slowly added more and more energy. The discomfort of the effort was becoming agonizing. He didn't think he could keep going, then he noticed the crystals had begun to glow.

"Keep adding energy. I will make sure the skulls don't melt from the heat." Her eyes glittered with excitement. "Add as much energy as you can. This is the time to push yourself, use this as an opportunity to see how much energy you can handle. Embrace the pain."

Ulrick almost lost his concentration when he noticed the crystals beginning to melt.

"Don't stop now. Keep the flow going, let the crystals melt some so they fit into the skulls but don't let them melt entirely, leave a seed for them to recrystallize otherwise they will just be glass when you're done. Start reducing the energy slowly, let it cool slowly. See if you can look into the structure and manipulate the quartz as it begins to re-crystallize. I have some experience with this so I will help regrow the crystal structure."

Ulrick's whole body was shaking and sweat had drenched his shirt. He had completely lost all track of time; he could take no more and he let go of the flow. He closed his eyes and nearly passed out. When he finally opened his eyes, his vision was blurry with tears. The skulls had burned through the leather pad they had been sitting on.

"You can pick them up. I have removed all the heat."

Ulrick Picked one of them up. The quartz had filled the interior space completely and the bottom was sealed over with silver; the only visible quartz was through the eyes of the skull. He looked at Natalia questioningly.

"While it was still hot, I let some of the silver along the bottom edge melt and it flowed across the bottom, sealing it off. It seemed like the right thing to do."

Ulrick proceeded to pick each one of them up and inspect them. As he did, his frustration began to build again. He felt nothing from them. He could feel his ring when it was off and he could feel his sword the whole time his ring was on, but he could feel nothing from the three skulls. "It didn't work." Ulrick sat looking into space. He was too frustrated and tired to think straight. He sat thinking nothing

Natalia, also, was without comment. She got up and paced a slow circle around the tree and Ulrick. It was around the tenth trip around the tree when she finally asked, "You said once that only you could use the ring. How is that possible? Your father used the ring?"

As tired as Ulrick was, it took him several moments to even realize Natalia had said something, and a few more moments to understand the question. Once he understood the question, however, the next step occurred to him almost instantly. "Blood. We have the same blood," he said quietly as he pulled out his sword and ran his finger across the blade, opening a cut on his finger. He then smeared his blood liberally on each of the skulls.

Nothing happened. His frustration from before turned to anger. He reached to pick up the skulls, but was shocked, the electric jolt made his arm useless. Then the blood on each skull flowed and pooled in a line across the forehead of each skull. The blood smoked, then flowed into the eye sockets. The eyes of two of the skulls began to glow a light red. As they did, Ulrick felt energy drain from the ring into them. The red in the skulls and the ring evened to the same intensity. The third skull did nothing for a time. Then the eyes in the third beganto glow slightly, but instead of red, they were green. The strangest change, however was the skulls had compressed. Instead of the size of an un-husked walnut, they were now the size of a shelled walnut. The two skulls with the red eyes had the inscription, Honor, Family, Peace. There was no inscription on the green-eyed skull.

Natalia gasped. "I feel it."

"Well, something worked, but what exactly, I don't know," Ulrick was saying when the green-eyed skull lifted off the ground and appeared to be looking around.

"I can see through its eyes. Not like I see using your mage sight, but as I once saw when I was alive." Natalia was giddy with excitement. She looked at Ulrick with both the green-eyed skull and Ulrick's projected image of herself. "Just think them into motion."

Ulrick did as she suggested and the other two skulls rose into the air. He quickly realized controlling them was nearly instinctual, as soon as he had willed them into motion. He willed one in front of him and had it settle in the palm of his hand. Unfortunately for Ulrick, the process of activating the skulls also used a fair amount of energy that added to the exhaustion from the earlier work.

Ulrick fell forward onto his face unconscious.

He woke suddenly, his cheek stinging. Ulrick opened his eyes. Kneeling before him was Bob with a look of concern on his face...his hand poised for another slap. "Good, I was starting to worry. You were out for quite a while."

Rubbing his cheek, Ulrick asked, "How long?"

"I wasn't here when you passed out, so I don't know exactly, but you have been out since yesterday. It is mid-afternoon now." Bob stood and held out his hand to help Ulrick to his feet. "You need to get yourself cleaned up. I want to get going as soon as you are able and hopefully that will be now."

"Where...?" Ulrick, with Bob's help got to his feet. "Uh... Southport, right?"

"Yes, Southport. I was hoping to leave early this morning, but I have been unable to wake you all morning."

"I...," Ulrick began, but was interrupted by the old man.

"Just get going. I already have all you will need packed and, on the horse," he said as he headed to the two already saddled and packed horses.

He was still lightheaded, but he knelt at the stream and splashed the cool water on his face and rubbed his eyes. He then got up into the saddle of his horse.

"Good, now let's go." Bob, already in the saddle, kicked his horse into a gallop south.

Kicking his horse into motion himself, Ulrick barely managed to stay in the saddle. It was dark when Bob finally came to stop and started getting a fire started. Ulrick dismounted and started setting up his bed. "What do we have to eat? I don't think I will wake up tomorrow at all if I don't get something to eat tonight."

"I've gathered all the eggs and I brought all the cheese we had left. I will cook it all up for you tonight." The look he gave Ulrick was worried. "I'm sorry about making you ride all afternoon, after whatever traumatic experience you had yesterday. I received some disturbing information from one of my informants yesterday, combined with a gut feeling something bad is going to happen, if we don't get to Southport soon."

The fire going, Bob cracked nearly a dozen eggs into the pan he had over the fire. "What happened to you yesterday?"

Ulrick, for the first time, noticed he didn't have his ring

on. He looked in his bags for it. Coming up short he asked, "Where is my ring?"

Bob fished around in the inside of his robe. "I took it off, hoping that would help get you to wake up." He handed Ulrick the egg-shaped box. "Are you going to tell me what happened to you yesterday?"

"It will be better to show you," Ulrick answered as he slid the skull shaped ring over his middle finger. He did not know where the skulls he had finished the day before were until he had the ring on. Once the ring was on, however, he was shocked to realize while two of the skulls were in his bag the other one was not. It was quite some distance behind them. He closed his eyes and concentrated on the missing skull. He could see through the eyes of the missing skull and what he saw shocked him.

The skull was obviously lying in the dirt because his view was partially obscured. He willed it up and looked around. What he could see, though, sent chills down his spine. Under the large cottonwood, under which he did his best thinking, was a large campfire and roasting above the fire, was what appeared to be the lower half of a man. Around the fire were no fewer than fifty goblins. Another jolt of fear ran through him when he noticed one of the goblins. A small, pale skinned creature looked at him and started pointing.

Ulrick willed the skull to him. He opened his eyes.

Bob concerned, "Are you alright?"

"It is good we left when we did. There are fifty goblins eating what looks like a man, camping right where we stood not five hours ago." Ulrick was shaking with both fear and lack of food.

"How do you know this?" Bob did not look too surprised by Ulrick's revelations.

Ulrick reached into his bag and pulled out two small skulls. "When you packed up my stuff you must have missed picking up one of these." The two skulls in his hand with red eyes floated into the air. "I can see through the eyes of the one you didn't pick up, back at your home."

Bob was staring open-mouthed, amazed at the floating skulls. "Tell me how you did it."

Awe struck by how fast the third skull must have been moving, Ulrick turned toward the third skull as it slowed and took its place beside the other two.

"Are you sure that skull was just at my home? The goblins must be closer than you thought, because there is no way that thing," he pointed at the newly arrived skull, "could possibly get here that fast."

"I am sure." Ulrick would have been just as disbelieving as the old mage if he had not seen what he saw.

"How did you do it?" Bob asked again.

Ulrick explained the process he used to finish the skulls.

"The green one is linked to the witch?" Bob asked.

Right after Bob finished asking his question, the green-eyed skull started flying around Bob's head. "Tell the old man he needs to refer to me with a little more respect," Natalia demanded

"I am not your slave to be ordered around," Ulrick said silently, so only Natalia could hear.

"I believe so," he answered Bob

"Do you have any control over it?" Bob asked, trying to hide his fear at having a small fast-moving metal object under the witch's control, flying around his head.

Ulrick concentrated on the green-eyed skull, and without much effort, brought it back in line with the other two.

"Yes, I have control over it. I believe she can only control it if I don't think of it."

"You are no fun. If you would have given me a few more minutes, I could have had the old man pissing himself." Natalia was beautiful in the firelight.

Bob finished cooking their dinner. He took a small portion for himself and handed the rest to Ulrick. Ulrick knew he was hungry, but once he started eating, he didn't stop until he had cleaned every last bit of food from the pan. His hunger satiated, he wondered what Bob's information was and why he had not been surprised by the goblin presence. "You didn't seem surprised that goblins had overrun your home."

Bob looked up from his still unfinished, meager meal. "I knew they were coming. That is why I did not let you wake on your own. I was just contemplating dragging you behind the horses, when I was finally able to wake you." His eyes tracked the skulls as they darted around their camp. The red and green glow of the eyes made them visible, even out away from the fire. "Are you doing that?" He pointed to one of the skulls as it drifted past.

Ulrick watched as it passed. He was not consciously controlling any of the skulls. They seemed to him to have their own will, each one had its own pattern of movement. If he thought about what he wanted them to do, they would respond, but once he stopped giving them direction they went back to drifting on their own. "Natalia are you controlling the skulls when I'm not?" he asked silently.

She was sitting across the fire from him her green eyes reflecting the fire light. She seemed to be concentrating on something.

"Natalia?"

She looked up "What?"

"Are you controlling these?" he asked, gesturing to the skulls moving around the camp.

"No, I have no control over the other two skulls," she answered absently, her mind obviously somewhere else.

"They seem to have a mind of their own, when I am not consciously directing them," he answered Bob. Ulrick could, when he concentrated on the skulls, tell that they were using energy from the ring. It wasn't much, but they were slowly draining the stored energy, much like his sword did whenever he had it out of its scabbard, and Natalia did also when she was out and about.

He experimented a little with the energy flow between the ring and skulls and found that the hovering skulls could hold their own energy also, but since he had not filled the skulls, they were pulling what was in the ring. He figured after sometime the ring would empty and start pulling energy from him or through him from the world around him.

Ever since he had first started pulling energy from around himself, he had started finding more and more sources of electrical energy that was readily available to him. The air around him, especially during inclement weather held a vast amount. He began filling the ring and the skulls with energy. He was not aggressive with his harvest, because he didn't want to induce the severe discomfort of large energy transfers. He just let it trickle in, which only caused a slight itch that could only be scratched by ending the transfer.

Then he had a moment of inspiration. He directed the skulls into his hand. Once the items were all touching, the discomfort was negligible. He had no idea how much his ring, and now his three skulls, could hold, but he figured he should find out, especially since there was a small horde of goblins on their tail. As he filled the skulls, the glow of the eyes became darker in color, but somehow increased in brightness. The effect was strange and counterintuitive.

"I will take watch while you get some sleep," Bob said after he finished eating.

Ulrick didn't hear him because he was already asleep sitting up.

Ulrick woke, body sore, to the sound of a robin's morning song and the faint smell of a dead campfire. The sun was yet to rise, but the glow from the eastern horizon was bright enough to see by. He hadn't moved from where he fell asleep the night before. Bob was already moving about somewhere in the trees.

"We had better get moving soon. Pushing the horses yesterday gave us some space, but you would be surprised how fast a hunting party of goblins can travel." Bob was somewhere behind him.

"Are you sure they are after us and not just roaming randomly?" Ulrick asked through a yawn.

"Oh, I am sure they are after us. The only question is whether they are after me, or you." Bob was leading the already saddled horses. "I guess there is one other question, and that is whether there is only one group or if they have planned ahead and there is another group ahead waiting to cut us off." Bob mounted his horse. "Leave one of your new toys here so we can know how far they are behind us. Let's get going." He started south.

Ulrick mounted up. He pulled out the green-eyed skull from one of the interior pockets in the grey robe he was wearing and let Natalia take control. He watched as she directed it into the crook between a limb and the trunk of a nearby tree, its eyes were facing out over last night's camp. Ulrick took a deep breath and nudged his horse into motion.

They weren't pushing the horses like they had the night before, but they did gallop whenever their path flattened out. The sun had just fully risen above the eastern hills when Natalia nudged him. "There is something at the camp."

Ulrick concentrated on the skull they had left and looked through its eyes. A lone goblin was squatting in front of their dead fire smelling the air. Ulrick caught up to Bob. "There is a goblin in our camp."

Bob reined to a stop. "Shit, how many?"

"Just the one so far. It is small, hairy, with big eyes and a thick snout," Ulrick described.

"A scout, not that it matters. Our trail is easy to follow; the rest won't be far behind him. They must have started out sometime last night to have already reached our camp." Bob sighed and looked around. "I doubt we are going to make it to Southport without a fight."

A thrilling fear laced excitement settled into Ulrick's gut. The feeling struck Ulrick as odd; he could not think of why he would be thrilled to have to fight a horde of goblins.

"I know how to slow them down a little." Natalia was thrilled.

Now Ulrick knew where that foreign feeling came from. "What do you have in mind?" he asked her.

"Watch."

Ulrick looked through the eyes of the skull they had left at camp. The skull was moving. The strange perspective and the flowing motion made him nauseous. The goblin had spotted the skull and was looking at it. It appeared to Ulrick it was looking right at him. Then almost instantly the skull sped toward the goblin. Ulrick's vision blacked out, then a moment later it was a blurry red. The vision slowly cleared and what he saw now made his already nauseous gut clench, and he nearly lost what little was in his stomach. The small goblin's head looked as if had exploded. Its forehead had a walnut sized hole, but all that was left of the back of its head was a gooey mass of blood and pieces of skull.

"Now they will think we are closer than we are, and they will slow down so they are not caught unaware, like their little scout just was." Natalia was giddy with what she had just done.

Ulrick relayed what had just happened to Bob. Bob just looked at him, his expression unreadable. Ulrick had seen that same look from the old man on a few occasions now and each time he wondered what the mage was thinking. Each time was when he had done something that should have evoked an emotion of some type, but instead, he just got that analyzing flat stare.

"Keep an eye out for a good place to make a stand. We don't want to be caught in a place that gives their number an advantage." Bob kicked his beautiful white horse into a gallop. "Let's go."

They traveled south through juniper and oak covered hills. The last couple weeks had been dry, so their horses kicked up a cloud of dust as they went. Ulrick crested a hill to find a large flat meadow of tall grass, dried yellow gold. Bob had reached the center of the field already and was dismounting. Ulrick slowed his pace, dismounting, when he reached Bob's location.

"We will make our stand here." Bob started flattening the grass in a circle. "Help me flatten the grass in about a fifteen-foot circle."

Ulrick was not a military strategist by any means, in fact he had only been in conflict twice, and both times were strictly reactionary, but he would have never thought a flat grassy meadow would make a good spot for them to make their stand against fifty goblins. He would have thought maybe a slot canyon, so they could only come at them a couple at a time. "Why is this a good place to make our stand?

Won't they be able to surround us out here?" he asked as he trampled the grass down.

His hood pushed back, exposing his tangle of white hair and sweat dripping from his chin, Bob looked at Ulrick from the corner of his eye. "With our particular talents, open spaces like this one are an advantage." He turned to face Ulrick, straightened his back and continued. "As soon as they arrive, you can start to pick off as many as you can from a distance. They will keep their distance as they surround us. Once they have us surrounded, they will attack. That will be awhile, though, so let's have a light snack and rest while we wait."

"Shouldn't we make a better plan or something?"

The grass tramped down how he wanted it. Bob pulled some dried beef strips out of his saddle bag and handed one to Ulrick. "I have a plan. You should just do as I said--pick off as many as you can from a distance." Then he looked at Ulrick pointedly. "Whatever you do, however, don't leave the circle." He sat and started chewing his beef.

They did not have to wait long before the first goblin appeared cautiously over the rise of the hill. It paused and looked at them.

Natalia jumped to her feet. "Watch." The green-eyed skull raced from the circle of stamped grass, by the time it reached the goblin on the hill, it was moving so fast they could hardly see it. It slammed into the goblin's head. Its head exploded. It was obvious to Ulrick that the skull must have been moving considerably faster when it hit this goblin than it had when it hit the one back at camp, because this goblin's head simply disappeared in a spray of red splatter.

Bob whistled. "I doubt we have anything to worry about."

It was a few minutes before they saw anything else on the hill, and when they did the goblins they saw were just barely peeking over the ridge of the hill. Obviously, the bloody end of their comrade had them nervous. Once they noticed that there were only two men, and they were quite some distance from them, they stood.

Natalia chuckled as another head exploded.

The goblins on the hill squealed and ran to the high grass and dove, becoming invisible to Ulrick. There was another yell and soon after a large number of goblins crested the hill and sprinted for the cover of the tall grass. Two more heads exploded.

Ulrick had yet to do anything and with all the goblins now crawling through the grass; he was trying to come up with a way to stop the inevitable. The goblins were crawling fast toward them. They were trying to reach their prey before all of their heads exploded.

Natalia giggled with each kill.

Ulrick drew his sword in anticipation. Then the grass behind the goblins caught fire. The goblins stood and started running toward them. Ulrick made ready. Then the grass right in front of him burst into flame. He stepped back from the intense heat of the towering flames. Most of the goblins stopped now, completely surrounded by flames they had nowhere to go. Most stopped, several ran, screaming through the flames.

His extra-long sword glinted in the sun as it passed through the first goblin that came running through the flames. The goblin's forward momentum caused the top half to continue further into the clearing than the bottom half. Blood and entrails covered the ground between the two halves. Three other goblins met the same fate, then it was over, other than the continued screams of the burning goblins.

Several of the goblins had made it through the outer wall of flame, but only one made it over into the hills. Natalia managed to explode the heads of all the others, but not without cost. Ulrick noticed that his ring and sword were quite drained. If he hadn't received energy from the goblins he had killed with his sword, he believed there would be no energy left. It seemed the faster the skulls moved, the amount of energy used greatly increased. And he had no way to replenish the energy in the skulls while they were more than two hundred feet away--which was about the distance he could see with his mage sight.

Now that it was over, the look and smell of the carnage caused Ulrick to wretch the contents of stomach into the trampled grass.

Patting Ulrick on the back, "You see now why every military commander in the empire will be seeking you out to join them and you have yet to learn to use your true talent to its potential." Bob mounted his horse. "The exploding heads was the work of the Green Witch?"

Ulrick wiped his mouth, grabbed the reins of his horse and started walking. "Yes, she enjoyed it immensely." Then he spoke to Natalia, silently. "I thought you told me you never killed anyone before?"

Natalia skipped in front of him, turned and faced him walking backward with a big grin on her face. "I still have never killed anyone. Those were goblins; they have no soul. Their death should bother you less than stepping on an ant-- an ant at least has a soul."

"I am not bothered by their deaths," he responded to her, though he was not sure he believed himself. "I have always had a weak stomach. The smell and sight of the blood makes me sick."

Now that they had dealt with the goblins following them, they traveled slower, keeping an eye out for a potential ambush.

"Goblins are bred for war; simple combat strategy is instinctual," Bob called from a few yards ahead. "If this group is being directed by someone that will allow them to, they would have sent a group ahead to cut us off. The group behind us was most likely hoping to push us headlong into a larger group, hoping to surround us."

"Why did they attack then?"

"The blood, unless they have a strong commander with them, once they get the scent of blood, they have difficulty not acting on their instinctual blood lust. Also, we had stopped and confronted them," Bob responded.

Feeling a bit nervous about what could be lying in wait ahead, Ulrick stayed alert using his mage sight to learn all he could about what lay around and ahead of him. As he did, he could not help but notice the myriad of colors of the electrical energy around him. As they traveled, keeping out of dense vegetation and trying to stay on the ridges of the hills as much as possible, he started experimenting with the energy around him. He started by just pulling certain colors to him. As he did, he noticed different colors had different properties. The most apparent was that some types created far more discomfort than others. He found that a pinkish-purple color caused very little discomfort as he drew it in.

He pulled in different types of energy. He did not discharge it or try to hold it, he just pulled it in and then let it bleed back into the environment around him--like he was breathing energy. As he did, he seemed to develop an intuitive understanding of the energy, and he was able to, if he concentrated, pull in one color and change it to a different color, then let it bleed out. After breathing the energy for a while, he started pulling different colors and creating a small arc between his thumb and forefinger.

He noticed that different colors flowed through him differently. Some seemed to flow deep within him, which caused far more discomfort, others tended to flow on the outside, through his skin with almost no discomfort. Once again, he found the color that flowed the easiest, with the least discomfort was the pinkish-purple color. Also, the arc of this color didn't create a loud erratic pop when it arced, instead it created a more continuous arc that buzzed and flickered along any surface it was directed to. He found he was able to easily direct the arc to different objects and the ground with little to no damage to the object it was directed at.

In a moment of inspiration, he sent his three skulls out in a line a few feet apart from each other, the farthest one was about fifteen feet from him. He started pulling energy from around him. He created a pink arc from his hand to the first skull and then to the next creating a continuous pink arc between himself and the skulls. He then converted the pink energy into one of the harsher colors in the last skull. As the energy built in the last skull, the air around it began to shimmer.

After several minutes of letting the energy build, it arced in a bolt of white energy, hitting a small tree several feet from the last skull. The boom from the discharge thundered across the hills causing his horse to bolt.

Ulrick was lying on his back in a cloud of dust, blind from the flash and deaf from the concussion of the energy discharge. He stayed where he was, trying to catch his breath and clear his vision.

It was several minutes before his vision cleared enough to see anything. His first vision was that of Bob looking down at him with a slight grin, hand held out to help him up. Once he had helped him up, Bob got on his horse and went to track down Ulrick's horse.

Ulrick sat on a rock in awe at the destruction caused by his little experiment. The small tree was split in two and burning. There were chunks of bark and wood from the tree over a hundred feet away. After the initial shock wore off, he noticed a large sliver of wood was stuck in his arm. He pulled it out, glad the damage was minor.

Bob returned several minutes later with his horse in tow. "While I was hunting your horse, I realized why you made three skulls."

Still mostly deaf, it took Ulrick a moment to piece together what Bob was saying. "Why?"

"I believe a small part of the soul of each of your ancestors resides in the ring you wear. Each of your ancestors that had the ability to manipulate energy created an item. You created three because your father and his father before him did not have the ability." Bob was excited by what he seemed to think was a profound discovery.

"If that is the case, why did I create three instead of two?" Ulrick rubbed his eyes.

"Because you made them after the inadvertent capture of your crazy demon friend."

"I will show him 'crazy demon friend.'" Natalia brought the green-eyed skull speeding toward Bob's head. It stopped inches from his forehead.

"I guess she didn't like my comment." Bob's voice was shaking as he stepped back from the hovering skull.

It happened so fast Ulrick did not even have a chance to register what just about happened. "Thanks for thinking better of killing him," he said silently to Natalia.

"I didn't stop it, I thought you did. He was going to be the first person I killed and I was alright with it." Natalia's voice had taken on the not-so-human tone, an indication of her unrestrained hatred.

After a moment of thought, "I guess the ring is holding you to your promise not to harm anyone I care about."

They got back to their journey south. Ulrick pondered what Bob had said about the souls of his ancestors being trapped in his ring or at least a part of their soul. He didn't know how he felt about it. Did that mean a part of him was going to be trapped within the ring when he died? Maybe a part of him was already trapped; perhaps that is the uncomfortable pull on his heart when it is off. He decided he needed to know how Bob came to that conclusion. He rode up alongside Bob. "What brought you to the conclusion that a piece of the souls of my ancestors are trapped in my ring?"

Bob did not acknowledge the question for several minutes. "I had suspected that it could be the case for some time now, but now I am sure. There are three factors that prove my theory: First, your ring has the ability to trap fragments of souls as evidenced by..." He looked around nervously then continued. "By the beautiful woman that is now your continuous invisible companion."

Natalia chuckled at his more favorable reference to her.

"Second, the number of Silverskull artifacts is equal to the number of owners of the ring: the two skulls, the sword, the helm, the shield, the breast plate and the ring. You are the eighth named Ulrick. The third factor is evidenced by that little show you just performed. Mastering the manipulation of electrical energy is very difficult. At least it is for most with your talent. What you just accomplished would have taken most decades to achieve. The fragments of souls trapped within the ring must contain memories that you are somehow, without realizing it, tapping into. You were never able to carve on your skulls without the ring on, correct?"

Ulrick was long to answer. "Yes, I was only able to carve when the ring was on and I never really paid attention to what I was doing, it just seemed to happen. So, does that mean a piece of me is also trapped?"

Bob never answered him and Ulrick knew if he didn't

answer the first time, he asked that meant he was not intending to ever answer. It was what Ulrick hated most about the old man, not that he really hated him, but he did hate that about him.

After a couple hours, Bob broke the silence between them. "Explain exactly what you did back there. Don't leave anything out."

Several minutes passed as Ulrick went over in his mind what he had done, then he explained the process he had followed to get to the result he had achieved.

Bob reigned in his horse and faced Ulrick. "When we are sure we are clear of any ambush, I want you to repeat what you did, except instead of building the energy in the last skull with a highly resistant color of energy, try using a type only slightly more resistant to the one you said flowed easiest. The amount of energy you released was far greater than you need if you are using that technique in battle. In fact, the least resistant type is probably enough to kill ordinary creatures. You have to remember having the ability makes you more resistant to the affects, not immune, but more resistant." He kicked his horse back into motion.

A couple hours before sunset they crested a small hill, Bob stopped. Ulrick stopped beside him. Before them the elevation started dropping steeply, which reduced the number of routes they could take to get to Southport. They were several miles from the easiest, and the route they would have most likely taken. The route from Bob's home to Southport did not follow any roads. The road most travelers take to Southport was ten to fifteen miles further east.

"If we are going to encounter an ambush, it will be down there between those two hills, in that dry streambed. We could avoid that route, but if we do, it will add at least one extra day to our trip." Bob looked at Ulrick, a question in his eyes.

Ulrick knew what he was asking with that look. He was asking if he wanted to add another day to their trip or battle an unknown number of goblins.

"Just so you know, there is no guarantee the other routes will be clear. There is also no way of knowing if this route isn't clear."

"Yes, there is." Natalia sent the green-eyed skull speeding away toward the most likely location of ambush.

"We should know shortly if we have friends down there," Ulrick said as he looked through the eyes of the skull. The view of the ground speeding by, and the wavy, too smooth motion, made him light headed.

"Keep the skull in the trees to keep it from being seen," Bob mentioned.

Both Natalia and Ulrick looked annoyed at Bob for stating the obvious.

After several minutes of silence, Ulrick describe to Bob what he had discovered. "Around the first hill and up in a small slot canyon, there is a hidden camp of what looks like at least twelve men, wearing Southern Territory uniforms. It seems they have been camped there for quite a while. Further down the streambed, under the shelter of some large trees, is a group of seventy-five or so goblins. I don't think the men are really soldiers. I would not have found them if I hadn't noticed one of the larger goblins come out of the canyon, they are hidden in. It doesn't look like the goblins have been there very long."

Bob was thoughtful. "Draw it here in the dirt."

Ulrick complied, making a crude map of the area in the dirt. "Has the large goblin made it back to his camp yet?"

Ulrick eyes closed. "He is about fifteen feet away. He doesn't seem to be in a big hurry."

"Explode his head, just as he enters his camp."

ble to stop the skull before it had gone through a second goblin head.

Ulrick watched as the goblin camp came to life with panicked action; several goblins ran out trying to locate where the attack came from. Most picked up weapons and hunkered down in anticipation of another attack. There was some yelling, and one of the smaller goblins--a particularly ugly thing with wide spread eyes and sickly yellow skin--ran off toward the camp of soldiers.

The skull followed.

The goblin ran into the camp of soldiers, yelling and waving its arms. Ulrick chuckled when it used its hands to try to describe what had happened to the large goblin's head. One of the soldiers got up and smacked the small goblin, open handed to the side of its head, hard enough he nearly knocked it to the ground. Then he grabbed it and pushed it forward and followed it out of the hidden slot canyon.

Ulrick relayed what happen to Bob. As he did, he noticed the skull he was using for reconnaissance was starting to lose energy and was moving slower, and the vision he saw through it flickered and blurred. Apparently, he could not use it endlessly. He figured he had better bring it back to recharge.

300

Once it was back in the range of about two hundred feet of him, he felt the drain when the energy levels of the ring and the skulls evened out. He could put more energy in one of the artifacts, but he had to consciously maintain the uneven storage of energy making it not very advantageous.

He realized his total energy savings would deplete if he kept sending a skull out to see what was going on. He also realized the skulls did not recharge when they took a life; only the sword had the ability to draw energy from death. He also noticed the faster the skull moved the energy consumption increased greatly, looking through the eyes also increased energy use and energy he pulled from the environment versus energy stolen from killing tended to bleed off quicker. He related all he had discovered to Bob.

"What you're saying is that we aren't going to be able to sit back here and kill all our foes without getting our hands dirty." Bob's look was grim.

"I probably could, but it would take a couple days." Ulrick responded. "It would probably be quicker to find another way to Southport."

"I would agree if it were just the goblins, but I would like to know what that company of soldiers are doing."

"So, what is the plan?"

"First we are going to get off this ridge and find a hidden place to spend the night. Our friends down there are going to have a restless night wondering where their attackers are and whether more attacks are coming. Perhaps you can fully recharge and cause some more agitations in the middle of the night. I will look around a bit before it gets dark and see if I can find a place, we can draw them to that will give us some advantage." Bob moved down and away from their enemies.

They found a copse of trees that would keep them hidden from a distance. They made no fire, cold, dried beef for dinner. Ulrick concentrated on refilling his energy store. It was nearly dark when finished.

He sent out the green-eyed skull to make sure there wasn't anyone sneaking up on them. Once he felt sure their camp was not discovered, he sent the skull out to check on their friends in the canyon. The goblins had not moved. They had several fires going with several types of game cooking over the fires. They seemed more agitated since the last time he had looked in on them, and it appeared they had killed several of their own. To Ulrick's horror one of the fires was cooking the dead goblins. He set his skull high up in the crook of a tree and stopped looking through the eyes to conserve energy.

Bob had not gotten back from his search for a likely place to meet their foes, so Ulrick found a hidden spot in the trees and tried to get a few minutes of sleep.

It was well after dark when Bob woke Ulrick. "I think it is time to make sure our friends aren't getting a restful sleep," Bob said once Ulrick was roused.

Ulrick was about to move his sight into the skull he had stashed, when Natalia interrupted. "If you want, I can relay what I see; it will probably use less energy if I have complete control than if you are also looking in."

Ulrick couldn't see a reason not to. "Okay, but wait a minute. I want to make sure we do what Bob has planned," he relayed to her silently.

"Bob, what exactly do you want me to do?"

"How many do you think you can kill before you start getting too low on energy?"

"That depends. Are we just causing disruption in the goblin ranks or am I going to be bothering the men also?"

"Just the goblins, since it seems they are reporting to the soldiers anything we do. The goblins will keep the men up also, and I don't want to kill any men if we can help it, until I know what is going on."

"What do you think?" Ulrick, silently asked Natalia.

"I am sure we could kill five to seven if we don't make too much of a show of it, but I think the show is what you want, so four should be easily doable."

"Four," he told Bob.

Bob paced back and forth, hands clasped behind his back. "I think it will be best if we kill some that are relaxing or eating. We don't want to kill any of the sentries. They need to feel threatened in the center of their camp. If there are any that stand out as leaders kill them, if not, kill the biggest of the bastards."

"You got that?" Ulrick asked Natalia.

"Got it." Her somewhat translucent form faded completely from view.

A few minutes passed. Ulrick had difficulty refraining from looking in on what was going on. He was relieved when Natalia's form reappeared in front of him. Before she spoke, Ulrick couldn't help but wonder how an incorporeal being's eyes could still shine with reflected moonlight. "It is done. I found one that looked like some sort of leader and the other three were just larger than the rest. I probably could do another, but I really made a mess of the four I killed. One more really will just reduce the number by one." She smiled big. "It definitely had the desired effect, though. They are running every which way, trying to find where the attacks came from. I made sure to hit in different locations and from different directions. I am pretty sure some have resorted to killing each other, thinking it had to be one of them."

Ulrick took a brief moment to look in on the goblins and bring his skull back, then relayed the results to Bob.

"Good, now let's try and get some sleep. I will show you what I have planned in the morning."

Ulrick slept poorly, thinking of the battle in the morning. With the sound of birds and a slight glow to the eastern horizon he gave up on getting any sleep and got up. The morning was cool, but warmer than he was used to. He swished his mouth out with some water, drank deep then checked on the horses they had tied them up some distance from where they had slept. Everything in order, he woke the old man, who judging by the slight snore he heard most of the night, had had no problem sleeping. "The earlier we get this over with, the sooner we can get to Southport."

"Eager, are you?" Bob was somewhat grumpy from being woken.

"Not at all, just unable to rest until it is done" He responded with no small amount of anxiety.

"Okay, I see your point." Bob began drawing a map of the area in the dirt. "Do I have the locations of the goblins and soldiers correct, and did you happen to see if they have any horses?" He continued to draw the surrounding area, including where they were now.

"Close enough. I saw no horses, but I was not looking for them specifically."

"Good, here is what we are going to do." Bob pointed with the stick he had used to draw with. "You are going to head down to the narrow point in the draw. I will be here," he indicated a spot that was shielded by some boulders "with the horses. I will be close enough to cover you if you get into a bind. Once you are in place, you will need to draw them to you. Kill as many as you can. If you start to get bogged down, retreat to my location and we will ride to here." He indicated another location on the map. "You will once again kill what you can then retreat to here. I will keep the horses with me."

"Hold on, this plan has me doing all the work," Ulrick complained, unable to hide his underlying fear.

"Don't worry, I will be quite busy making sure you don't get surrounded and covering your successive retreats." Bob patted Ulrick on the back. "You have no reason to fear, I will make sure you don't get killed." Bob's reassurance didn't help Ulrick's nerves. "I don't know how many times you will have to retreat, but I think we need to keep myself and the horses away from the battle. If the horses go down, we have no escape options, and I am useless in a hand to hand brawl," Bob said matter-of-factly.

Bob was in place, so Ulrick made his way from Bob's position to the narrow section of the stream bed. He was wearing leather pants and cotton shirt--he was going to be running a lot and did not want to be tripping over a damned mage robe.

Natalia walked beside him, her manor upbeat. "Pay attention to the terrain. Remember, you are going to be running back this direction with goblins on your tail. Knowing the obstacles ahead of time so you can use them against your pursuers, is the only advantage you will have, unless that sword of yours makes you faster than a goblin."

Ulrick started paying attention to the land around him as he made his way toward the draw. Natalia skipped out in front of him. He thought he had gotten used to her near nude form, but with his heart already racing in anticipation of the coming battle, the sight of her prancing, giddy for violence, made his face flush and his hands sweat. "Why do you care if I manage to outrun the goblins?" His voice betrayed his fear of battle and the annoyance of how she was affecting him.

She turned, but continued to walk backwards toward their goal. "I don't care if you survive. I care about being trapped inside that ring of yours for the rest of eternity. You have no little Ulrick's to pass the ring to, so if you die today, I end up trapped forever."

He chuckled lightly, trying to calm his nerves. "Here I was starting to think you might actually care about something other than yourself."

She smiled big and faced forward, away from him. "Nope, still just looking out for myself, don't forget it."

Ulrick stayed away from the direct route to his destination so he would not be spotted until he wanted to be. Once he was there, though, he wiped the sweat from his hands and made sure he had a good grip on his sword and stepped out into the middle of the dry stream bed.

He could see the goblin camp from where he stood. He even picked out three goblins facing his direction, probably watching for their prey to make an appearance, strange though, it took several minutes of anxious waiting before he was finally spotted. Once seen though, the response was quick. Ulrick's hands began to shake with fear and his legs felt weak. The goblin that saw him, yelled, and without waiting for the others, started running for him.

Ulrick hadn't consciously gotten his skulls out but he noticed they had started spinning around him just outside of his sword's striking distance. The green-eyed skull started for the lead goblin, the other two remained spinning around him. "Let me kill the first one. You can't kill them all, and I can't kill them all so just try to thin them out as they come. If too many make it past you for me to handle, that is when I will retreat," he told Natalia before she started killing, his voice sounded more composed, than he felt.

The small goblin that had first spotted him slowed and raised a short sword before attacking. Ulrick didn't have a chance to swing his sword. The small goblin didn't notice the skulls spinning around Ulrick and walked right into their path. The first skull slammed into the goblins face, ripping its jaw off, then a split second later the second skull tore through its stomach, leaving a gory splattering of blood and entrails on the ground.

Ulrick stepped back. The spinning skulls took out the next three goblins that made it past the Green Witch. He took two more steps back. The goblins that came after that were wary of the skulls and tried to avoid them. Since Ulrick was not consciously controlling them, some of the goblins started to get through. The first goblin, through, died quickly--split in half before he managed to get into its shorter striking range. Ulrick felt the surge of energy from the kill and the increased need for violence.

Ulrick killed three more in quick succession. With each kill his energy level increased as did the desire for blood he inherited from the dead goblins. He stepped forward with each new kill. He willed the skulls out further and above most of the smaller goblins. The large ones would still have to duck and weave to get through, giving Ulrick, with his extra-long sword, an advantage but allowed him to fulfill his increased desire to kill. Blood splattered all around him as he continued to wade into the battle each stroke of his sword brought death. He barely managed to avoid a thrown spear, as it was, his left arm was still awash with blood, his mixing with the goblins'.

After an indeterminate amount of time and death, there was nothing left to kill, at least none that dared to get within reach of his sword. Several spears came his way. His sword was beyond light at this point, it weighed less than nothing. It pulled his arm where his mind willed it to go, faster than his arms could ever accomplish. He easily knocked the spears from the air with the flat of his blade.

His blood was pumping hot and angry. He charged into what was left of the goblins, but most managed to get out of his way and then stayed further from his wraith. He roared a challenge. He needed their deaths, nothing else mattered. The green witch had stopped her killing and was just watching him.

Frustrated, he took control of all three skulls and sent them out over the goblins that refused to run, but also refused to come meet the death they deserved. He began sending energy into the skulls in the form of purple lightning, and doing as Bob had suggested, he let it discharge in arcs of a more potent blue. The arcs started slowly, but he pulled all he could stand then more. It felt like his skin was boiling, but it was distant in his mind. All he wanted was more blood.

Blue arcs of lightning began arcing into goblins. He did not direct it so the effect was random hitting goblins with metal weapons raised first. Each bolt killed. It only took about half a minute and ten dead goblins for what few were remaining to realize death was standing before them.

They each ran in different directions, hoping they would not be the focus of the horror that stood before them. Ulrick managed to pick off several more before they got out of range.

He caught movement out of the corner of his eye, or he sensed it with his mage sight he did not know which. Ulrick turned to see a man standing in the opening to the slot canyon--the crest of the Southern Territory a blazing sun on a field of turquoise on his chest. He started after him.

"Ulrick!" Bob called from somewhere behind him. Ulrick turned and looked at the old man. He could kill him--end the annoying bastard's life. He wanted to kill him.

"Ulrick!" Natalia called from his right. He looked at her. Her beauty called to him, fueled not only violence but lust. He could abuse her in every way imaginable. She looked at him with a half-smile. She knew what he wanted, it spoke to the evil in her soul, but her eyes still held fear. He took a step toward her then stopped. He could, but he knew he shouldn't. His hands began to tremble--not from fear this time, but from restrained violence. He tipped his head back and roared his frustration to the world.

He moved to take off his ring. "Ulrick wait," Bob said before he managed to get his ring off. "If you can maintain some control, we still have some men to deal with, but follow me and don't do anything until I say."

They made their way into the slot canyon. Ulrick was still on edge, but the prospect of more violence ahead had a slight calming effect, as long he was moving and focused on the next battle. They came around a slight bend in the canyon to where the soldiers' camp was. Every man was standing facing them, weapons at the ready. Several in the back had spears ready to throw.

"Stay back or die!" one of the men yelled, fear tainted his words.

Bob chuckled lightly. "Don't do anything stupid. You all know you are in over your heads. Drop your weapons unless you want to die."

All the men gaped at Ulrick, not daring to move-- afraid to drop their weapons and become defenseless, afraid not to and earn his wrath. For the first time, Ulrick noticed how he must look. He was covered from head to toe in blood, not just blood, he noticed as he looked at his arms. There were pieces of flesh and bits of bone as well. He looked back up at the men before him, a lust for mad violence in his eyes, his hands still shaking with barely held restraint.

Chuckling lightly again, "I take that back, we won't kill you all, we will need one of you alive to torture some information out of," Bob said with an almost jovial air, which came across as eerily demented.

One of the men in the back spoke up. Ulrick recognized him as the man who had gone to the goblin camp the day before. "We are soldiers of the Southern Territory doing the will of our governor. If you kill us, you will be outlaw, hunted until caught, then hung a traitor's death."

"I am not a citizen of the Southern Territory. I am only subject to imperial law, which all of you are guilty of violating." A couple of the soldiers looked at each other confused as Bob spoke. "As soldiers, you should be aware that working for, or using the services of, goblins is punishable by death."

One of soldiers nervously said, "We are just following orders." He looked to the first man who had spoken. "We have done nothing wrong?" His tone was questioning.

Bob's tone became angry. "Young man, I really doubt your governor ordered you to meet up with a company of goblins and ambush travelers on their way to Southport." Bob sighed. "Even if my young friend and I were some sort of threat to the realm, do you really think Governor John and General Thom would resort to using goblins to annoy us on our way to a meeting they are expecting us to attend?"

Ulrick was tired of waiting. He sent his three skulls out over the men and let them fly in lazy circles, covering the whole area the men were in. "I don't know how many of you saw what happened to your goblin friends, but I would strongly suggest you drop your weapons and kneel down so we can tie you up and take you to Southport for judgment." His throat felt dry and raw from yelling, making his voice sound harsh to his own ears.

"Men, the monster before you, is none other than the Reaper's Hand. If we were able to kill him and bring the governor his head, we would all be heroes," the man who had spoken first said, trying to sound confident.

Since the same man had spoken twice and with some attempt at authority, Ulrick figured he must be this group's commanding officer. Ulrick acted before the small group of soldiers managed to find the courage to die on his sword. He sent a purple arc of energy into the closest circling skull, then made it flow into the next, then the third, creating a harsh buzz and bathing the shadowed slot canyon in purple pulsating light. He then sent as little energy as he could manage and still maintain the arc into the man, he assumed was the leader of this small group of soldiers. The man made a high-pitched yelp, then fell to the ground silently convulsing in agony for a moment, before groaning in agony and laying still. The closest man to him ran and checked on his commander and found him still breathing, but unconscious.

The second man who had spoken, was the first to throw down his sword and kneel. Seeing their comrade comply, encouraged the rest to see the wisdom of continuing to live.

Bob held his hand up to Ulrick, signaling him to stay put as he went and started gathering the soldiers' weapons and putting them out of reach. Ulrick kept the purple arc pulsating between the circling skulls to help make sure none of the soldiers started feeling brave, while bob searched each one. Once he felt he had adequately disarmed the men, Bob checked on the man Ulrick had electrocuted.

"Will he live?" Ulrick was not sure he cared, but for some reason asked anyway.

"I think so." Bob got up and went to get some rope off the horses.

Bob threw the rope to the man who had surrendered first. "Tie all your friends in a long row make sure the rope is tied tightly around each man's waist and then wrapped around their belt. Leave about two feet between each man." Bob watched him closely from a few feet away, to make sure it was done how he wanted it. By the time they were done being tied, the man who had been shocked was awake. Bob tied the man that had tied the others, then he tied their commander, knotting it tight around his waist then wrapped around his neck just loose enough for him to breath, then he knotted it behind his back, out of reach of his hands.

Once the soldiers were secure, Bob asked just loud enough for Ulrick to hear, "Are you alright?"

"I don't know. It is all I can do not to gut these men where they stand." His hands were still shaking with barely maintained restraint.

Bob tied another rope around the lead soldier's neck. He gave himself about fifteen feet, then tied it to his horse. Then they started off down the canyon.

"By all that is damned!" one of the men exclaimed as they exited the slot canyon and beheld the slaughtered goblins. There were nearly sixty dead goblins, but there was no way to easily count them. Most were in multiple pieces--body parts were strewn far and wide. The smell of blood and torn open bowls filled the air, attracting the already arriving crows.

Ulrick brought up the rear of the column, and when he entered the battlefield, he did not feel sick like he knew he normally would--like he knew he should. Instead, the smell of blood caused his heart to race and his rage nearly took control. His whole body started to shake. His horse, sensing his distress, became skittish. He roared. Somehow his pent energy amplified his voice and the narrow stream bed echoed with his rage.

The man he had shocked pissed himself, and the rest of the men tried to put distance between themselves and the gore covered nightmare. Being tied together, they did not get far before tripping each other up, some falling to the ground, bringing the rest to an abrupt halt.

Bob rode up to Ulrick. "You need to ride on up ahead. Get some distance between yourself and the smell of death. Our path crosses a small stream a couple miles ahead. Go get cleaned up. I don't want you breaking down in front of the prisoners, so don't remove your ring until you get out of sight," he said quietly.

"What if they try to escape once I'm gone?" Ulrick's voice was low and menacing.

"I doubt they will give me trouble, but if they do, I can handle it. Go."

Ulrick rode off at a gallop. It didn't take him long to get to the stream Bob had mentioned. He stripped down and let his clothes float downstream, then started scrubbing the blood off. It took him longer than he thought to get the crusted blood out of his hair and out from under his fingernails. Once he felt he had most of it off, he removed his ring. He fell to the ground in exhaustion. The instant absence of hatred and rage, on top of the visions of the horror he had just perpetrated, destroyed him emotionally. Face in his hands, he cried great wrenching sobs.

It took him nearly half an hour of sitting in the grass beside the stream before he felt emotionally stable enough to get up. He had sat there too long. He tried to rise, but all his muscles protested. His thighs cramped and he fell back to the ground. It took another several minutes of torturous agony to get his legs straitened and un-cramped. Once he did, he tried again to rise; this time he succeeded, barely.

He was sitting on a large stone in one of his grey mage robes, wondering how long he should wait before he went back for the old man. During his wait he had put his ring back on several times, trying to get control of the hate he had received from all the goblins he had killed. He was just managing to get some control, when it had occurred to him it had been nearly an hour since he had left Bob with the prisoners. He should be here by now.

He mounted his horse and started back. He got to the top of the first small hill and he could see Bob leading the prisoners slowly toward his location. Ulrick rode out to meet him. When he got close, he identified the cause of their sloth. Each man held a rock large enough to be difficult to carry; each man struggled with the load. He looked at Bob questioningly.

Bob waved him close. "By the time we make camp for the night, none of these men will have the energy to try and escape. Not only that, having to hold those rocks all day will make their hands and arms so weary they would not be able to effectively use a sword if they managed to get a hold of one."

"With the way you tied them, and now the rocks, I'm starting to think you've done this before."

"Ulrick, I've been alive for two hundred years." Bob grinned. "In that much time you find you have the opportunity... or misfortune, to experience nearly everything. That includes leading a group of prisoners to justice. Unfortunately, leading twelve prisoners carrying large stones is probably going to add another day to our trip."

The long day of downhill travel brought a significant change to the environment in which they now traveled. Instead of juniper and scrub oak, they now walked amongst Eucalyptus and Manzanita. The sun was low in the west when Bob lead them into a large copse of towering Eucalyptus and they made camp for the night. Bob tied the end of the rope to a tree, then made the soldiers pull tight against the tree and each other, then he tied the other end to another tree.

They made camp. Ulrick was glad to be able to have a fire; he was looking forward to a hot meal. They gathered wood and made their fire a good distance from their prisoners. Bob managed to kill a large cottontail for dinner. Ulrick ate nearly all of it and was far from feeling satisfied.

Morning came too soon for Ulrick, even though Bob let him sleep well past first light. As it was, he woke to the old man quietly, but forcefully prodding him. "We need to get going if we are going to make it to Southport sometime tomorrow," Bob said once he saw Ulrick stirring.

They traveled, agonizingly slow, south. It was nearly midday when one of the perpetually silent soldiers asked Ulrick, "Are you really the Reaper's Hand?" Several of the other soldiers looked his direction, obviously interested in his answer.

"No," he answered. He did not want any of these men to know anything about him so he offered nothing more.

It was a few minutes later when the man trudging at the end of the line, limping heavily and unable to carry a stone because his left arm was useless after being electrocuted, spoke up. "It doesn't matter who you are or aren't; you are still going to pay for what you have done."

"Keep making stupid impotent threats and I doubt you will survive the day," Ulrick said without emotion. After that nobody spoke, for which Ulrick was thankful.

By late afternoon they started passing through citrus orchards. Several workers in the fields stopped what they were doing to watch them walk by. It wasn't long after that Ulrick saw a company of soldiers heading their way from the east. Bob rode out to meet them. Ulrick kept an eye on the prisoners to make sure they didn't get any ideas. After conferring with the patrol, Bob rode back with the patrol behind him. "I am glad to say Sergeant Addicus here is willing to take the prisoners off our hands."

Leaving the prisoners, Ulrick followed Bob east from where the patrol had come from. "The main road south into Southport is a couple miles east of here. There are several inns on the road we can get a good meal and spend the night. We should be arriving in Southport before midday tomorrow, if we get an early start."

After leaving the prisoners in someone else's care, they

made good time. The further south they went, the hotter it got. The heat combined with the increase in humidity was an uncomfortable change to their circumstance.

The inn they decided to stay at was nicer than any Ulrick had ever stayed before. When he traveled with his uncle, they tried to stay within a strict budget, so his experience was that of the inns of middle to low quality.

When they entered, it became obvious the proprietor knew Bob and he immediately got them seated in a private booth. "I have a particularly good selection of red wine from the eastern coast vineyards I am sure you will enjoy, Robert."

"Bring me a bottle of whatever you think best, would you? Also, I would like to order a triple portion of whatever you have that is fresh. The boy, has had a rough couple of days and could use a good meal," Bob said to the proprietor.

"A new apprentice?" The man motioned to Ulrick.

"Yes."

"I thought you told me you were done taking on apprentices." He pulled up a chair and motioning to one of his servers over to relay their order.

"Empty threats I'm afraid." Bob motioned to Ulrick. "This here is Ulrick from Elk Valley. He is a special case I really could not pass up...a favor for an old friend."

"Ulrick, my name's Janus, it's good to meet you." Janus had a pleasant look, slightly overweight, with a little grey in his dark hair. He extended his hand.

Ulrick shook his offered hand. "Good to meet you as well."

"If you don't mind me asking. What's your particular specialty?" Janus asked conversationally.

He didn't think Janus was being anything but friendly,

but the last couple days had started making him paranoid. He contemplated not telling him, but Bob's look told him he had no reason not to say. "Lightning," he finally answered.

"Lightning mage, uh… special case indeed." Janus's kind look turned a little sad.

Janus stayed and talked with Bob until their food was ready, mostly about crops and the state of his business. "Well, I will leave you two to your meals; don't hesitate to holler if you need anything else," he said as he left.

Their meal consisted of a wide range of fruits, most of which Ulrick had never seen before, and cold strips of sweet seasoned meats. Ulrick ate twice as much as he thought was possible, and there was still a fair amount left when they finished.

Leaning back with a sigh of contentment, Bob said, "Janus is the best kind of man. He has become very successful over the years. He does business honestly. He keeps his prices as low as he can and treats those that work for him with a great deal of respect; most have been with him since his early, lean times. Once you get settled with Naomi and get started in the inn business, I would suggest you make a trip out here and get some tips from him. He really is the best at what he does and I'm sure he would be happy to give you advice."

Bob's mention of Naomi brought to mind that he was nearly done with his time with the old man. Excited butterflies fluttered through his gut at the prospect of seeing her again. It had been too long since he had last seen her. A few more weeks and she would be in his arms and he could put the nightmare of this summer behind him.

"You're thinking of her, aren't you?" Natalia asked, startling him out of his pleasant thoughts.

He looked at her, she had a sad look. "Why does that make you sad? Are you jealous?"

"Ugh… Don't be stupid. It is just disheartening that you think there is a possibility for you to find happiness down that path. If you truly cared for this girl, you would stay far away from her. Do yourself a favor and try to forget about her."

Ulrick did not like what she had said and he did not want to think about it, so he remained silent and turned away from Natalia's judgmental look.

"Fine, ignore what is plain to everyone, but you. I will try to refrain from telling you so, when you finally realize it yourself." She faded as she walked away.

Sweat ran down both his back and chest beneath his grey robe. It was nearly midday when they topped the hill overlooking Southport. The city was larger than any Ulrick had seen, and just past the expanse of humanity was the endless ocean. A river ran through the city, ending in the crescent port, that was busy with the coming and going of ships, some moving up and down the river others heading out to sea with the receding tide. The air smelled of citrus and magnolia blossoms. Date palms lined the main road that lead to the Keep that overlooked the bay.

The building was massive, but plain. The rectangle building was five stories high with one square tower on each end. The first two stories were windowless. The only design element that gave the building any beauty was the long balconies and large arched windows on the upper floors. A large wall encompassed an immense area of land around the keep. No trees grew between the wall and the Keep.

Bob noticed Ulrick had stopped and was staring at the city. "There is over a hundred thousand people that live in Southport, over five hundred that live in the keep and the barracks built into the walls that surround it. Just the keep houses nearly three times the population of Elk Valley."

"It is hard to imagine that many people so close together," Ulrick responded.

Bob chuckled then became serious. "Remember, your father was hated here. Make sure you keep the hilt of that sword covered and you might want to remove your ring so as not to draw attention. Once we are inside the keep, we will make your identity known to Thom and the governor."

It took over an hour to get to the walls that surrounded the keep. Up close, Ulrick could not help but stare at the thirty-foot-high walls that were nearly as thick as they were high. He couldn't imagine an army large enough to assault the walls and win.

The massive gates were open and the two guards on duty waved them through. "Master Robert, you are expected. Thom is waiting for you in the foyer of the keep. We will make sure your horses are taken care of and your baggage will be delivered to your rooms." The guard who had spoken looked at Ulrick with suspicion as they rode through the gates and dismounted.

The guard at the keep opened the door for them when they arrived. The inside of the keep was a stark contrast to the outside. Instead of rough grey granite, the interior walls were paneled in mahogany; any stone that was visible was grey granite, but it was polished to a mirror finish. The floors were a dark veined cream-colored marble. The hall was lit by oil lamps interspersed every ten feet.

Two men greeted them when they entered. One he recognized as the man he had met overlooking the falls, Thom. Bob had mentioned he was the High General of the Southern Territory, but he was not wearing a uniform, at least not a military uniform. The other man shorter than Thom wore a resplendent uniform, the blazing sun crest large in the center of his chest, golden pins adorned the collar of the black overcoat.

"Master Robert," the man in the uniform stated formally. "We expected you a couple weeks ago."

"Punctuality has never been one of my virtues." Bob almost hid his confusion.

Thom noticed Bob's confusion. "I guess you have not yet been informed, I am no longer High General. Let me introduce you to High General Mika. He has served as one of my best officers for over twenty years and I was quite pleased to recommend him when I retired."

"I was under the impression you would die as High General, Thom. I am glad you are finally getting a long-deserved rest," Bob commented.

"Honestly, I was a little hesitant at first, but I have grown to see the wisdom of the decision to make a change. Although, I don't seem to be getting anymore rest. My new duties are far more demanding than I would have thought." Thom's manner was conversational and his tone spoke of the familiarity he had with the old mage. He then turned to Ulrick. "It is good to see you again, Ulrick."

Ulrick was unsure how he should address men of such importance, but he figured he was required to acknowledge the general in some manner. "High General Mika, I am honored. Thom I am pleased to find you well."

Thom smiled, amused.

The general looked briefly at Ulrick, but did not in any other manner acknowledge his existence. "Master Robert, the governor is impatient to see you. Will you come with me?" It was not a question. He motioned to one of the guards at the entrance and turned and left expecting to be followed.

Thom leaned in close to them both. "Forgive Mika, he is a little nervous greeting two mages, and unfortunately for you Ulrick, your father's identity has just recently been discovered. I am going to have to ask you to turn over your sword to one of the guards. The guard will show you to your room."

Ulrick looked at Bob questioningly.

"Don't worry, we will get this cleared up. I will make sure the governor understands he has nothing to fear from you," Bob assured.

Ulrick found the prospect of handing his sword over much more daunting than he would have ever thought. Until now, he would not have thought he would have any problem with it. He then felt inspired to have Thom take it. "Thom, I am hesitant to hand over my sword. I am sure you understand." He saw the guards with his mage sight tense up and put their hands to the hilts of their swords. "I will however turn it over, as long as you take it. You are the only man here I have met before. You treated me fair and I get the impression you are a man I can trust." He then unstrapped the sword from his back and held it out for Thom to take.

Thom reached to take the sword; he hesitated for a moment. There was a slight tremor in his hand just before he took the sword. Thom nearly dropped it when Ulrick let go. He was not prepared for the weight of the over long sword. "I thought it would be light." He chuckled nervously, then lead Bob off in the direction the General had gone.

The guard the general had summoned stepped up beside Ulrick. "Sir, I will show you to your room."

They did not go far. The room the guard took him to was windowless and was furnished with a sofa two chairs and a short table in front of the sofa. This was obviously not the room he was going to be staying in. "Sir, if you would be so kind as to stay here until Master Robert returns. Lunch has already been served for the day, but I will have someone bring you some refreshment." The guard left, shutting the door behind him.

Mage sight allowed him to see the energy patterns in a large radius around him and what he saw was both disconcerting and a little flattering. Positioned outside his door were two guards, another two had positioned themselves across the hall, and the rooms to either side of the room he was in had ten guards each. He pulled his ring out of one of his robes inside pockets and put it on.

Natalia materialized in front of him. She looked around. "Pretty nice place, I guess we are in the Keep of Southport. You know I visited here once, a long time ago." She looked around a little more and then chuckled softly. "So, you are a prisoner in the Keep of Southport. They are a little naive if they think twenty-four soldiers will keep us prisoners for long. Are you contemplating escape?"

"Not yet. Bob has assured me he would be able to clear up any misunderstanding. Not only that, they took my sword; without it I think twenty-four is more than sufficient to keep me locked up." Ulrick was not as amused at his current circumstance as the Green Witch.

"Twenty-four is only sufficient because you lack confidence in what you are capable of. I saw what you did to the goblins, less than half were actually slain by your sword. Not only that, we would not have to fight the men in the two rooms. We could simply melt the hinges so the doors would not open. The other four would be dead before they could even think there was a threat. Then we could simply walk out the front door, no one outside would even think to stop you until we were clear of the outer walls." She smiled, her eyes were asking for the go ahead.

"Like I said, Bob is taking care of it. I don't think making the entire Southern Territory my enemy is the answer." Ulrick, however, started going over the plan in his mind anyway.

There was a light knock on the door, followed by a timid voice. "Sir, I have cheese and wine, if it pleases you."

"Come in." Ulrick remained seated on the sofa. He did, however, remove his feet from the short table before the servant came in.

The guard opened the door for the servant, but stayed out of sight, trying to give Ulrick the impression he was not being guarded. Natalia was laughing and Ulrick had a hard time not joining in. The servant couldn't have been older than fourteen. She was going to be a beautiful woman in a few years, with long dark brown hair and dark tanned skin. Ulrick couldn't help but see the fear in her dark eyes as she set the tray of cheese on the short table in front of him. He was impressed with the variety, and they had included a full carafe of wine. "Is there anything else you need, sir?" Ulrick was impressed by her ability to keep her fear out of her voice.

Ulrick wanted to ask her several questions, but did not have the heart to cause her more anxiety. "No miss, I have more than enough." The girl was nearly to the door when Ulrick had a moment of inspiration. "Excuse me."

She turned and faced him hands clasped behind her back. "Sir?"

"I was wondering if you happen to know Lisa of Elk Valley?"

Her eyebrows furrowed in confusion.

"She is about this tall." He indicated Lisa's height with his hand. "She has brown hair and blue eyes."

She still held the look of confusion. "How do you know Lisa?"

This is good, Ulrick thought. "Lisa is a good friend of mine. We grew up together in Elk Valley. I was wondering if you could let her know Ulrick is here."

"Let her know Ulrick is here. Your name is Ulrick?" She still had a look of confusion on her face.

She was obviously terrified of him. He wondered what she had been told about him. Obviously, what they had told her did not include his name. The fact that so many people were terrified of him, suddenly made him sad. He had never envisioned himself as a scary man, and he had never wanted to be considered as such. "Yes, my name is Ulrick. Would you let her know for me?" He tried to convey kindness in his tone. It was one thing to have the soldiers outside, that was somewhat humorous and flattering, but it hurt him to know this poor girl's perception of him caused her fear.

"Yes, sir," she answered, then hurried from the room.

"Apparently they think you will be easier to manage if you are drunk." Natalia scoffed. "That cheese and wine look good. I think for the first time in a long time I wish I could taste. The food you and Robert usually eat makes me glad I don't have to."

Ulrick realized he was quite hungry. He had had a very good breakfast at Janus' inn, but they had left before dawn and hadn't eaten anything since. So, he dug into the food with gusto. So far, he hadn't cared much for the wine Bob had ordered in the past, but a few sips of the nearly purple wine, that was sweet with the flavor of some kind of berry, was enough to change his opinion of wine. He drank nearly half the carafe. A little light headed, he decided he had better stop.

15 - Lisa

Amber was standing tall in the doorway of the balcony. Her long, amber-colored hair shimmered as it waved in the cool afternoon breeze blowing off the ocean. She was wearing a simple green cotton dress, but somehow, she still looked more regal than her position as the governor's daughter.

Since becoming Amber's bodyguard, she had had many opportunities to meet with the governor and every time she did, he diminished in her mind, while Amber shined all the more brightly. Lisa marveled, the daughter, even at her young age, surpassed her father so greatly. Lisa could not help but be envious of her beauty, even though every time she was, she then felt guilty. It was a strange dichotomy--her envy followed by guilt; her jealousy felt like a betrayal. Amber was everything Lisa could ever hope to be: beautiful, wise, and just.

Distracted, Lisa had not noticed the arrival of someone at their door until she heard the slight knock, followed by a timid voice. "Lady Lisa, I have a message for you."

"Maybe the friend you have been eagerly awaiting has finally arrived." Amber turned from the balcony. "Come in."

The door slowly opened. Lisa recognized the girl from her time in the kitchens. She was a daughter of one of the cooks, but she could not remember her name. "I have a message from the son of the Reapers Hand," she said, once she had entered.

Lisa looked at her confused. "What... Who?"

"The son of the Reapers Hand," the girl said again, paused for a moment, then continued. "He said his name is Ulrick."

Lisa jumped up from her seat at the small table, excited.

"Ulrick is finally here. So, what is the message he asked you to give me?"

"Oh... just that he is here. They are holding him in one of the rooms off the entry hall. They even took his demon-possessed sword."

Lisa was even more confused. What was this nonsense about the Reapers Hand? She had heard of the legendary warrior from the Western Territory, that it was said had killed ten thousand men. She had never really believed such nonsense. And what did any of that have to do with Ulrick? "What are you talking about? And why would they be holding him?"

The girl had become confused herself. "So, you really do know him? He said you grew up together. Did you ever meet his father the Reaper's Hand?"

"That's enough, thanks for the message, Marie," Amber said, letting the girl know it was time for her to go. Marie left disappointed.

"What are you thinking?" Amber asked her.

Lisa thought a moment before answering. "I guess it is possible his father is who they are saying, but he never knew his father. He frequently would mention that he had no father. He felt since he was not around, he did not care, therefore he would not care about his father. I'm sure he never even knew his father was who they are saying he is. If he had, everyone in town would have known. Regardless of whom his father may or may not be, Ulrick is a good man. He should not be treated this way."

Amber seemed deep in thought for a moment. "No, he should not be treated this way, especially if his father is who they think. To make an enemy of a man that could potentially kill ten thousand men is utter foolishness, and my father should know better."

"Why would you assume that because his father was such a great warrior, he would then also be a great warrior?" Lisa sighed. "Vincent and Eram would go hunting and fishing and play at war, but Ulrick never had any interest. He couldn't even gut a fish without sicking up."

"Have you ever heard of the Silverskull relics?" Amber asked her.

"Wasn't he called Silverskull the Reaper's Hand?"

"Yes, he was. For generations the Silverskull relics have been passed down from father to son. Each man has been notable in their power. Only a direct descendent can use the relics, since Marie said they had taken his sword, we can assume Ulrick's father has died and he has received the relics. More notably, didn't Thom say he was apprenticed with Robert the mage? Lisa, your friend could very well be the most powerful man to currently walk the earth. We definitely don't want him to be our enemy." Amber slipped on some shoes and headed for the door. "Let's go fix this before we can't."

Even without her mage sense, she would have had no problem figuring out which room he was in, but with her mage sense, she could see not only four men in the hall guarding the door, but she also could see the twenty men in the adjacent rooms.

When they reached the door, the guards blocked their way. "I'm sorry ladies, but I have been given strict orders to let nobody in."

Lisa was disgusted by the audacity of the guard talking to the governor's daughter in such a way. "Shawn, isn't it?" Lisa asked.

He nodded in the affirmative.

"Do you realize, the man you are guarding is a mage?" Lisa stepped close to the guard, looking up into the large man's eyes.

"Yes, we were informed," he answered blandly.

"Well, what you probably don't understand is that as a mage he is able to see that you have twenty-four men guarding him, four in the hall and ten in each of the rooms to each side. I am also sure he knows you are trying to make it look like he is not being guarded." Lisa's anger at the situation was unhidden.

Looking a little embarrassed by Lisa's revelations, "How do you know all this?" he asked.

"Shawn, if you are tasked with guarding someone, you should know something of what they are. Mage sight is quite well documented in several books on mages in the library." Her tone was condescending. "Not only that, if he is half as powerful as the man you think his father is, do you really think you could stop him if he decided to leave?"

"What you say may be, but either way, we are not letting either of you in," Shawn said.

The door behind Shawn opened. Both soldiers turned, stepped back and drew their swords, so did the men on the other side of the hall. Before any of them could do anything, Ulrick held up his hands showing them he meant no harm. "I also know of the fifteen soldiers that are now guarding the front door and the twenty further in the keep. That being said, I don't intend to leave until Bob gets back, but I would be very appreciative if you let me talk to my good friend here." He motioned toward Lisa.

Since the guards had taken defensive positions facing Ulrick, Lisa was free to just walk into the room. Amber made to follow but, Shawn grabbed her arm. "I can't let you go in there with *him*."

Amber looked down at his hand. "Shawn, you are lucky Thom is not here or you would currently be without a hand."

Embarrassed by her rebuke and knowing she was right, he let her go. Amber closed the door behind her once she was in the room.

Lisa gave Ulrick a long, tight hug. "I have missed everyone from home so much. I'm glad you are here, Ulrick."

"It is good to see you too, Lisa. Uh... who is you friend?"

Lisa gave him a disparaging look. "I'm sure you know who this is, but I guess I should have introduced you. Ulrick, this is Amber the governor's daughter."

"It is an honor to meet you," Ulrick said.

"Likewise."

Since her encounter with Zeek the other night in the alley, Lisa's mage sight had changed drastically; most of the change was confusing. Instead of people glowing with distinct colors and the rest of the space, if it was unknown to her, was void of any details. Now everything glowed with energy--with so much variety she was seeing colors she had no name for, and she was sure, did not exist visually. Even the air around her radiated visible energy that swirled as it flowed.

Air exhaled had a different hue, then dissipated into a more homogenous shade as it mixed with the air in the room. The profusion of all the colors made her more confused, by much around her, rather than enlightened so much so she frequently blocked out her mage sight entirely. Even as confused as she had been lately, there definitely was no confusing what she saw pacing the far corner of the room.

It was a near nude woman.

Lisa looked from the woman to Ulrick, then back to the woman, then back to Ulrick. Ulrick did not seem to notice her distress, because he had not taken his eyes off Amber since their introduction. The woman, however, had noticed Lisa looking at her.

"Ulrick, I think your friend here can see me," the half nude woman said, finally pulling Ulrick's attention away from Amber.

"Yes, I can see you." Lisa's tone was anxious.

"Oh, and apparently she can hear me as well. Not sure how that is possible," the woman added.

"Lisa, what is going on?" Amber interjected.

Lisa looked at Amber. "I'm not sure." Then she looked at Ulrick. "Ulrick what is going on?"

Ulrick motioned to the two chairs. "It is a little complicated. Have a seat, eat some cheese, drink some wine and I will try to explain. Unfortunately, Bob is not here, he is better at explaining these types of things." Ulrick sat on the sofa opposite the two chairs and waited for the two girls to sit before he started his tale.

Ulrick explained what had happened in Smithville and the subsequent days of struggle for control. He left out a lot of the details of that struggle, and finally, that he and demon had come to an agreement.

When he was done, Amber got up and opened the door. "Shawn, can you please have someone bring some water and a few more glasses." Then she closed the door and sat back down. She did not seem that interested in Ulrick's tale.

Lisa didn't wait for Amber to return to her seat to ask, "So, was part of your agreement that she had to walk around half naked?"

Ulrick's brows scrunched in frustration and anger. "Out of all that I told you, the one thing that is bothering you, is her lack of clothes. Yes! That was part of the agreement, but not how you are thinking. I had to promise not to make her wear clothes." His face softened. He took a deep, cleansing breath. "I am sorry for my tone, but I'm a little on edge. This is the first time I have been held against my will and I am also having a hard time with the fact everyone is afraid of me, everyone except the two of you, that is."

Lisa, taken back from his outburst, remained silent.

Amber finished a piece of cheese and cleared her throat. "Ulrick, I would like to apologize for my father's lack of foresight. I am sure, however; Thom and Robert will manage to bring some sanity back to this situation. Until then, I would like to know a little more about the goblin attack on Elk Valley."

Lisa was surprised Amber did not seem to have any interest in the demon attached to Ulrick. She had noticed while Ulrick had told his story that the demon was indeed attached to the ring he wore. She could see a thin translucent thread of energy running from the demon's heart to the ring. The ring also was quite fascinating; the myriad of colors that radiated from it was quite fantastic. She had yet to see anything else produce that effect. She also noticed three more thin lines running into Ulrick's robe, and upon closer inspection, there was another line that ran further into the keep and several more, thinner, almost invisible lines that were running somewhere to the north.

Lisa's attention was brought back to Ulrick's story of the goblin attack when she heard him mention Eram.

"... Eram was lying on the ground. A goblin was pounding on him with a club. Once I had removed the goblin that was on top of him, I was relieved to find most of the damage had been dealt to the other goblin," Ulrick was saying.

Amber interrupted. "Ulrick, I know it will sound uncaring, but can you shed any light on why the goblins attacked and who may have been behind it? It is the answer to those two questions I am hoping you have some insight."

Ulrick looked annoyed. "I don't have any idea who, but

since Kramdon, the man who had brought the message of my father's death, had been attacked on the road. The fact Bob and I have since been attacked by no fewer than one hundred of the bastards. I am or more accurately this," he held up his hand with the skull ring on it, "is the why."

"You have been attacked since Elk Valley?" Lisa asked.

"That's what I just said. I am surprised you haven't heard anything about it. The soldiers we captured with them should have been brought in late last night." Ulrick's annoyance was growing.

"Ulrick, I am going to do both of us a favor and get right to the point of my purpose here." Amber's tone was commanding, but diplomatic. "I would like to hire you..."

Ulrick interrupted before she could finish. "No. I don't want anything to do with the petty conflicts between territories."

Amber's look was disappointed, but undaunted, she continued, "Ulrick, I can understand and respect your reluctance to get involved..."

Ulrick interrupted again. "No, I already have plans that have been postponed for far longer than I wanted as it is. After Bob's business in Southport is concluded, my apprenticeship is over and I am leaving this nightmare behind me."

Amber sighed. "I will honor your desires and advise my father to do the same, but since you are currently being held by my father and have some time on your hands, at least hear me out."

"Fine. I will listen, but you will be wasting your time," Ulrick said with resignation.

The light knock, at the door, stopped Amber from continuing.

"I have the items you requested, Lady Amber," Marie's

meek voice came from the other side of the door.

"Come in," Amber responded.

Marie brought in a tray with a carafe of water and several glasses and set them down on the table before them. She did not take her eyes off Ulrick as she backed back out of the room.

Amber chuckled lightly as she poured herself a glass of water. Then seriously began, "Ulrick, what do you know of our form of government? I don't ask to be condescending, but because I found Lisa's education in regards to Empire governance quite lacking and don't want to waste my time explaining things you already understand." Lisa was struck by Amber's candor with Ulrick. She usually played naïve.

"I understand enough to know I don't want anything to do with it," Ulrick responded.

Amber shook her head in annoyance. "Ignorance does not save you from the ravages of war when it arrives. I see you Ulrick, you don't have the heart of a warrior. If your father wasn't who he was, you probably would have become a merchant... No, not a merchant, an innkeeper. Your family would be your priority, having four or five kids to help run the growing business."

Ulrick looked at her surprised, but said nothing.

"But Ulrick, your father was Silverskull the Hand of the Reaper. You can try to hide from that legacy and I will even be willing to help you as long as I can, but it won't be long." She paused, ate a piece of cheese and sipped her water. "As I am sure you know, there are four territories North, South, East and West all governed by governors, appointed by the Emperor. What you probably don't know, is that the emperor has not contacted my father in nearly ten years. We still send our quota of boys required by the empire's army and pay our share of taxes. Edward, however, declared himself king of the west when the Emperor failed to appoint a successor after the previous governor came to a premature end...some suspect poison. It is also reported that Joshua of the East has become a religious fanatic."

"The lack of Empire intervention of border disputes has resulted in bloody battles along the borders of the territories. My brother has been missing for months, either dead or kidnapped, we don't know. Nobody has taken credit or sent any demands. Because my brother is gone, and the Emperor is not showing any interest, I am the current heir of the Southern Territory. The guards have already caught several suspected assassins in the Keep, but they were caught early, so whether they were coming for me or my father is unknown.

"Now, there have been goblin attacks in the Southern Territory, in groups according to you, of over one hundred goblins. There haven't been goblins this far south in many years, let alone in those kinds of numbers. Tell me Ulrick, how do you think one hundred goblins managed to travel from the islands off the coast of the Northern Territory? Then all the way down here without being stopped and killed?" Amber's look was intense, as she looked into Ulrick's eyes.

Lisa knew Ulrick pretty well and could tell Amber's last statement had him thinking, but he did not respond to her question.

Amber filled the silence. "Ulrick, I am going to assume the plans you have made are either in Elk Valley or somewhere in the Western Territory. If you decide to live in the Western Territory, how long do you think it will be before Edward insists you take your father's place in his army?"

The last statement finally broke through his barriers. "What are my choices? I can either try to have a normal life or I can spend my life killing people at the whim of one of the governor's. I really don't see which governor I kill for matters."

Amber looked grave. "There is a war coming that is bigger than governors and territories. I suspect the outcome may affect even more than the Empire. Which side you stand in the coming conflict is important, Ulrick. My and hopefully your enemies, are able to send large companies of goblins anywhere in the Empire. That would not be possible without an organized network all working for the same goal." Amber stood and started to pace. "I don't know where the other governors stand. I also don't know what the goals of the opposition are."

The look Ulrick gave Amber was perplexed. "If you don't know who the enemy is, what good is there in hiring me to kill them?"

"Oh… now I see the issue. Ulrick I don't want to hire you to kill anyone. I want to hire you to help me find out what in the three hells is going on and how we can stop it."

Ulrick still looked confused. "I have no idea how I would do that."

Amber chuckled lightly. "You don't have to know anything. All I want you to do is tell me who comes to you with offers and what those offers entail. You can go live your life as you see fit. I will send someone on occasion to get information. Simple enough?"

"You're not going to send me off to kill once you know who is behind what you seem to think is coming?" Ulrick didn't try to hide his skepticism.

Amber sighed. "War is coming. I doubt there is anything any of us can do to stop it. When it does, I would hope you will be willing to help defend your friends."

Ulrick was silent. He was obviously deep in thought. Amber, having made her case, waited for a response. Lisa knew her well enough to know she wouldn't press any further until Ulrick said something.

Lisa, uncomfortable with the silence, "Can you choose whatever you want to wear? Is your appearance the same as when you were alive?" she asked Natalia

Natalia stood, faded from sight, then reappeared, her clothing changed. She was still not wearing a shirt, but the pattern of her pants had changed from white with green vines and red flowers, to red pants, green vines and white flowers. Her dark red hair had changed from long curls to short, combed back flat against her head, green flames slowly burned from her legs up and over her body. "I can change everything, but my physical form. What you see is how I looked when I was alive. I can change my hair color, but this is the color my hair was and how I prefer it."

Lisa marveled. "What I wouldn't give to be able to change my clothes that fast. I really like your pants. Are they something you just imagined or is that a real type of leather?"

Now interested probably because she was frustrated with Ulrick's silence, Amber asked, "What does the demon look like?" Lisa described what she saw and included what Natalia had told her.

Amber's attention was now piqued. "I think I know her. There is a book in the library about the Green Witch. Ask her if she is the Green Witch?"

Ulrick spoke up. "Yes, she is the Green Witch. Bob knew her when she was alive."

"That can't be possible. The Green Witch lived nearly two hundred years ago," Amber said.

"Apparently, Bob is over two hundred years old. He says there have been mages that have lived almost three hundred years, but most don't live as long as he has because they usually get murdered. He says life mages are typically the longest living."

Three hundred years...Lisa was flabbergasted. Until now, she had never heard that mages live longer than everyone else. It was a strange revelation--she just realized she would probably outlive everyone she knew by two hundred years. She wasn't sure she liked the idea.

"I will do what you ask. I don't plan on telling anyone where I am going, but if you somehow find out where I am, I will tell your agent whatever you feel will help," Ulrick finally decided.

Amber laughed and shook her head. "Ulrick you are so naïve. I already know where you are going. I would bet anyone who knows you also knows where you are heading. The only questions really are whether those that know you, also know who your father was, and whether you stay where you are going or moving on afterward."

Ulrick didn't seem to believe her. "If you know where I'm going, tell me."

"I believe I remember Lisa mentioning the young daughter of an innkeeper by the name of Naomi that you are smitten with. Also, if I remember right, she lives in a small crossroads town too small for a name, just on the other side of the pass into the western territory. I am also sure that if you decide to leave after you marry her, she will surely tell her parents where she is going." Amber sighed. "You see Ulrick, if you can't even hide from me. What makes you think you can hide from Edward or whoever sent the goblins?"

Ulrick, with a look of defeat looked to the floor. "I already agreed to tell whoever you send whatever information you want to know." There was a long moment of silence then he leaned forward, put both hands on the table between them and looked up. The look in his eyes sent a chill through Lisa. "But know this, if you or anyone else sends someone that is in anyway threatening to my family, I will kill them and if any harm comes to Naomi, I will hunt down and kill everyone involved."

Amber unflinchingly held his gaze, reached across the table and put her hand on his. "Ulrick, I promise you no one intending your family harm, will come from me." She took a long deep breath. "Because if for some reason we end up on opposing sides, those I send will not bother with your family, they will be coming for you alone."

Lisa cringed and held her breath while Amber and Ulrick sat staring at each other.

Amber finally broke the tense silence. "I think we understand each other."

"Yes, I think we do." Ulrick leaned back on the sofa and put his hands behind his head and smiled. "I may not know much about politics, but I am pretty sure if by chance you become governor, the Southern Territory will be in capable if not good hands."

Amber smiled back. "I will take that as a compliment."

"As you should." Ulrick chuckled. "The only other person that has so easily been able to read me is my friend Eramus." He looked at Lisa apologetically. "I think he would like you."

His comment sent a jolt of jealousy and fear for Eram from her heels up through Lisa's spine and caused Amber's composure to crack for a moment.

Ulrick did not notice Amber's reaction, but he did notice Lisa's. "Why did you leave? He might have been too stupid to realize how much he cared for you until he had left, but I know you cared deeply for him." Ulrick shook his head, his eyes moist and asked again. "Why did you leave him? He needed you."

Lisa couldn't stop the tear from flowing down her cheek. "I left a note with my mother, explaining everything.

My parents expected me to stay here and find a more suitable suitor" She glanced at Amber, hoping she didn't take this the wrong way. "But I intended to return after a year. Like you said, he did not see our relationship as I did. I was hoping my absence would help him discover his feelings, but if they didn't change, at least I would know for sure." She sighed. "But now he is no longer there for me to return to anyway."

Ulrick poured himself a glass of wine and took a long sip of the dark red liquid and spoke quietly, almost like he was speaking to himself alone. "When we were younger, we would talk of the treasures and adventure we would find in the Dragon peaks. I knew they were just childish fantasies. We would never really take the suicidal journey and there was not any treasure to be had anyway. Eram is a smart guy. I assumed he had come to the realization of the foolishness of our fantasies, but I guess I was wrong. I really can't imagine what would have possessed him to go, especially since there was no way he could have been fully healed from his injuries."

Lisa looked from Ulrick then to Amber and was about to say something about what she knew, but Amber spoke first.

"Ulrick when forks in the road of destiny present themselves, we have the choice between continuing on as we have or stepping into the unknown. Knowing only that the path will contain pain and sacrifice, your friend stepped onto that unknown path. It is only the great among us that have the strength to take the more difficult path. Whether foolish or inspired, he nor we, can know until the end."

Ulrick stared at Amber a moment then looked at Lisa, his look perplexed.

"I know, sometimes I think instead of being the daughter of the Southern Territory, she should be an old woman living in a shack in the woods, making potions and giving advice to lost travelers." Lisa smiled at Amber. "Or cooking lost children for dinner."

The door opened and Thom entered, followed by the mage, Robert. Thom looked at those present, one side of his mouth turned up in amusement. "Ulrick, Robert and I have spoken with the governor about your service to the Southern Territory and the need for all of us to remember there is no need for animosity. He has agreed his actions were short-sighted. He apologizes for his distrust. As a token of good will, he asks if you would join him and his family for dinner to-night." As Thom finished, he handed Ulrick a very long sword.

Lisa could see the connection between the sword and Ulrick's ring. She was amazed by the amount of energy held in the sword, not just in the crystals in the skull, but also in the metal of the sword itself. She was not sure what she was see-ing, but it was similar to the energy she could see in any blade or piece of metal but it seemed far more compressed. The scabbard also was different from anything she had seen before. As she pondered what it meant, she realized a silence had per-sisted since Thom's statement. Ulrick had stood to retrieve his sword from Thom and now everyone was just waiting. "Ulrick, I think Thom is awaiting your answer to the gov-ernor's invitation," Lisa whispered, even though everyone in the room could hear her anyway.

"Oh...uh...okay, sure, that would be great."

Thom cleared his throat. "Okay, I will let the governor know you have accepted his request." Thom opened the door. "Shawn, please show Ulrick and Master Robert to their rooms. Ladies, shall we let them get cleaned up and..."

"Actually, Thom, is there any way I could steal Lisa away for a few minutes? Her particular talent as a life mage gives her far better mage sight than any other discipline. Young Ulrick could use some insight into the workings of his sword, and I'm sure I could give Lisa here some insight into what she is seeing, which should help in her capacity of her employment." Bob's tone did not really leave room for denial, of what he asked.

Thom looked from Robert to Lisa then to Amber. "Lisa works for Amber; she will be the one to give you the permission you seek." Lisa noticed Thom made it clear to Robert that indeed he did need permission, contrary to his expectation of acceptance.

Bob's brow furrowed. Lisa figured a long life of getting what he wanted, then having to ask permission from a woman just out of her teen years did not sit well with him. Bob did not re-ask the question, he simply looked to Amber and raised one eyebrow.

Ulrick chuckled lightly at the exchange.

Amber patted the old man's shoulder. "You have my permission, as long I get to come along."

"We don't have to go anywhere, we can do it here," Bob replied.

Ulrick cleared his throat. "Actually, I have been cooped up in this room for a while now. I could use some fresh air."

"We can go to the rooms; we have sent your things. It will have a balcony overlooking the bay." Amber looked at Shawn. "Their things have been taken to one of the suites with a balcony, have they not?"

"Um... of course, please follow me."

The room they came to was three stories up. The three-bedroom suite was larger than Amber's rooms, though not nearly as nicely appointed. The balcony faced south with a good view of the river that emptied into the bay.

Lisa watched Ulrick as they walked into the room, and she watched as he checked his saddle bags, making sure everything was there, then he opened the doors to the balcony and took a deep breath of the cool sea breeze. Lisa noticed he looked at the demon and seemed to communicate something to her and was waiting for a response, but instead of replying, the demon just looked to Lisa and nodded.

Ulrick looked to Lisa, then turned back to the view of the bay. Ulrick had definitely changed since the last time she had seen him. The look he had given Amber as he threatened her had scared her. He was more serious, darker, more reserved. He was no longer the light-hearted boy she had grown up with. The change was unnerving and she couldn't help but feel sad. The easy sheltered life they had had in Elk Valley was gone. None of them were the same. She wondered if she had changed as much as Ulrick had. How much had Eram changed?

16 - Vincent

A breeze blew in from the open door, bringing a temporary reprieve to the aroma of spilt alcohol and stale tobacco smoke. Vince only knew the man responsible for the open door by reputation and correspondence through intermediaries, but he did know enough for him to know the black leather pants, loose fitting black shirt and wide brimmed hat, was a disguise. The man in black was an older man, but Vince could not tell his age. The only other person present in the room was a serving girl that made herself scarce once the man entered.

Vince stood and motioned for the man to sit, then sat back down. "It is good to finally be able to meet you."

"I am also glad to finally be able to meet one of the favored of Titan, however, before we go any further, I will need proof of Titan's favor." The man spoke quietly, even though they were alone in the room and they sat removed from the vicinity of the doors. He seemed in control, but Vince could see through his attempted confidence.

Vince smirked, pulled his dagger out and laid it on the table. The blood-stone on the pummel was nearly black, attesting to his high skill as a blood mage. Then he opened his right hand revealing the scar on his right palm. The scar was not so large as to be readily noticeable, but for anyone that knew what to look for, it was obvious.

It became clear to the man Vince was not offering any more proof. "I will need more proof than that. Anyone can scar their hand and own a dagger with a dark stone in the pummel."

Vince's smirk died and was replaced with annoyance. "Trust, it is such a fickle thing, is it not? I sit before you undisguised and incriminating myself, while you sit before me in disguise, having offered no proof of your identity, but demanding further proof of mine. Prove you are the man I was supposed to meet and I will bare the truth you seek."

The man in black smirked, then all the oil lamps in the room went out. The Sea Serpent tavern's main room was windowless, so when the lamps went out the only light in the room was a sliver of noonday sun coming from under the door. The darkness lifted slightly as the candle at their table lit. The man's eyes glittered eerily in the flickering yellow light, then one after another a candle on each table in the room lit.

Vince was well aware of the power of naturally born mages, but he had never actually seen the use of the power. The demonstration left him sour with jealousy. According to his sources, there was only a handful of mages alive in the empire, so the demonstration was all the proof he needed.

He undid the buttons on his shirt and revealed the mark of the serpent. The mark was an intricate pattern of different symbols, all contained within a circle scarred into his flesh by the great serpent, Titan. His God had dipped its razor-sharp claw into acid, then slowly cut the pattern into his skin. The searing pain of the acid was beyond agonizing and he had to remain motionless throughout the process. Thinking about it now brought on an involuntary shudder. "Now that we are done with the ridiculousness, can we get to business?"

"I have one more thing before we get to our purpose. As you know, I don't subscribe to your religion, so as a token of good will between us, I brought you a gift." The man untied a pouch from his belt and emptied its contents on the table.

Sitting before Vince was a medallion connected to a heavy silver chain. The medallion was made of a flawless, clear round stone, about the size of a walnut. It was intricately faceted. The back of the stone was cut flat and into the back was an exact replica of the symbol etched on his chest. Some of the symbols within were inlaid with gold, while others were silver. Vince looked at the man questioningly.

"I don't know how much your teacher taught you of the power of symbols, or if you know how different metals affect the storage and projection of energy, but once you fill up that stone you will find that medallion far superior to that knife." The man leaned back and watched Vince's reaction.

Vince didn't know how he should feel about the gift; it was obviously very expensive. He had no idea how much the labor to create it would have been, but the stone alone was quite an item. Blood stones were easily found, but one that large and perfectly clear was quite rare. He was only marginally aware of how different shapes affected power. Jax had told him the dagger was a good focus because of the emotion an instrument of death brought. It was also the knife he had used to cut his mother's veins to allow her blood to drain. He knew the symbols were meaningful, but he didn't know how it would affect his projections. Not knowing if he should be thankful, insulted or... He nodded to the man, put the medallion over his head and buttoned his shirt up, covering both his raised scars and the medallion.

"The reason I have asked to meet with you is because my master wants me to confirm directly that everything you promised is going according to plan." Vince wasted no more time getting to the purpose of their meeting.

"What part of the plan is your master most concerned with?"

"First, is Petre prepared to do what is required of him?"

The man seemed to be debating how to answer, then came to a decision. "He is prepared to try, but I am not sure of his ability to succeed."

"Why don't you think he will succeed?"

"It is not that I don't think he can succeed, it is just the protection within the keep may be more capable than we previously anticipated."

"Don't worry about that aspect of the plan. His potential failure has been considered and it has been determined the attempt is more important than success. Even if he fails, we can make that work for us. What is important, however, is that in the event of failure, he dies in the attempt. When will he do it?"

"You are aware, Ulrick is at the Keep? I don't want to do anything until he leaves--his presence may create problems we can't plan for." The man paused for a moment. "Ulrick, you know him, don't you?"

The man was fishing. Though Vince didn't know how he didn't already know. He did not think knowledge of his relationship with Ulrick was important. "I know him. He is my cousin."

"Cousin?"

"On his mother's side, unfortunately. What about our mage problem? Have you figured out how to take care of it?" Vince asked.

"Should be done sometime this afternoon. He has a weakness for young women; he won't recognize the danger until it is too late. I am a little disappointed this was not handled by those in your employ. The girls I am using could be compromised."

Vince ignored the reference to the multiple failures. "Everyone involved is unmarked I expect? We are not quite ready to reveal ourselves just yet."

"Yes, of course," the man responded.

Vince had verified everything needed. "Thanks for the gift." He got up to leave.

"Where are you headed now?" the man asked before Vince made it to the door.

Vince stopped. "I'm to meet with the immortal." Then

he left the man in the dim empty tavern.

17 - Abigail

Wind-blown ice burned any exposed skin, so did the harsh sun--both from above and what reflected off the surface of the glacier. She kept her watery eyes nearly closed. Her view was a small slit of white desolation. It had been three days of absolute misery and Abby didn't know if she was going to survive another night in the cold wind. Luckily, Eram had skinned the wolf he had killed before he lost all sense of reality. It took some of the bite out of the cold ground when they slept.

Abby vaguely remembered a wolf lunging for her, then darkness. When she woke Eram was fevered and incoherent, a wolf pup licking white puss off his shredded left arm. The wolf he had killed must have been the mother to the pup, because she had seen several more hanging around the overhang they had used for shelter. None of the others would come close though. She had tried to run the pup off, but Eram growled at her when she did. He must have been waiting for her to wake before heading out because the next morning he set off. He did not say anything to her, he just gathered his things as he mumbled incoherently and started up the slope of the glacier.

Three days later, here she was drudging along behind him. He hadn't said more than ten words to her in three days. She did not blame him; his fever was intense and seldom did his eyes look clear of delirium. He did, however, in his more dire times, talk to the wolf pup that followed them and licked his wound every time they stopped. Sometimes during those talks he would apologize for killing the wolf's mother, but most of the time, it was incoherent mumblings. He also had long talks with Raven that made no sense to her, but seemed profound with meaning to both Eram and the bird.

They were not traveling during the day and sleeping at night however. Eram would just walk for a while, then lie down and sleep a few hours. Later, he would be on the move again. Day and night were the same: a few hours walking, a couple hours sleeping, on and on they went. She was sure his fever was keeping her alive--lying next to him was the only warmth she felt throughout the long days.

Her feet and hands ached to the bone from the biting cold. They had eaten very little and what they had wasn't satisfying, consisting primarily of frozen, uncooked meat she suspected was wolf. Each step was agonizing. She would have described her feet as numb if the pain did not lance up her leg with each step. Her hands were no longer able to grip even the lightest objects. Unbuttoning her shirt would have been impossible, not that she would have considered such a thing in the freezing wind.

She should have considered the whole venture an utter mistake, but she had felt so strongly that she needed to come with him. When Melisa had told Abby of her plans to go to Southport, she should have been overjoyed. As a young girl she had gone to Southport once and she had loved it. The food was delicious and it never got that cold, and being on the coast tempered the southern heat. But for some reason, the thought of going south had created a deep anxiety that made her gut clench. Then Eram had shared his dream with them and she knew then why she could not go south. When she decided to go with him, it was an instant relief all her anxiety had melted away.

Until now she had been glad, she had come. Sure, climbing the first couple peaks was difficult, but she had made a difference, helping kill the goblin early on, helping set up camp every night, cooking. And she liked to think their nights together helped keep him from despair. She knew it helped her. She had meant what she said when she said he did not mean enough to her for him to hurt her. She even believed the words herself, but after the week with him by the river, lying naked on the moss-covered ground together, she now regretted those words. That week was the best week of her life--she had never felt so free and perfectly contented.

Like Eram, she wished they could have stayed, built a small cabin and lived out their days there. She knew life was not that simple, however. Certainly, it was beautiful in the summer, but what was winter like? There had to be some reason no one lived there. No, looking back she now knew he did have the power to hurt her. In fact, he had her heart completely. Watching him now drag himself through the snow and ice, with each step he seemed closer to death, was breaking her heart.

The sun was low in the western sky when Eram fell to the ground and curled up in a ball. Abby hurried to his side. She laid out the oiled blanket, then the wolf skin, and rolled him onto it.

He opened his eyes and looked at her. She could tell he was actually seeing her for the first time in days. "I'm dying," he whispered, then curled back into a ball.

She looked at his arm bandage she had made. It was mottled yellow and rusty brown. She wanted to replace it, but she had nothing else to use. She didn't like letting the wolf pup lick it, but every other time, it seemed to sooth Eram, so she unwrapped his arm, exposing it to the air. She had to turn away from the sight of the wound. Most of his forearm looked like ground meat oozing yellow pus.

She called to the wolf. She kept her distance from her since she tried to chase it off, but after some coaxing, it finally came. It looked up at her and whined. "Go ahead do your job," she said, then stepped back from the scene before it made her sick.

Abby curled up, her back to his. Eram slept to Abby's crying and the sound of the wolf licking pus.

It was fully dark when Abby felt Eram getting up. She

had not slept enough, but it was good he was getting up. Traveling at night was a mixed bag. On one hand, it was colder than during the day, but on the other, there wasn't the biting wind. Judging by the position of the stars in the moonless sky, it was halfway between dusk and dawn. He had slept nearly six hours this time. She gathered up what Eram had left lying. Somehow, in spite of his current mental state, he carried more than his share of the load. He also traveled in what seemed the right direction. Abby just followed.

She didn't know how Eram knew where he was going or that he even did. For all she knew, in his delirium he was leading them both off a cliff. Abby followed close anyway, trusting his delirious sense of direction over her own inability to see anything, but his barely visible silhouette in front of her. Sounds in the night would have had her heart racing, but after what seemed like an eternity of pain and darkness, she did not care what could be out there. A part of her actually longed to be eaten by some great beast. She could not imagine the pain of having a bear eat out her insides would be any worse than how she felt now. Being killed would end her torment. She hoped the next life was at least more comfortable than this one.

It was times like this that caused people to contemplate death and what becomes of your consciousness once your body dies. Abby was not different. There were those that believed once dead your soul would be reborn into another body and that how you lived this life affected the circumstance of the next. She had never really known what she thought of that. Some of it made some sense to her. Others believed that your soul would be bound to a greater being in another realm. If you lived your life well, the being would be benevolent. If you lived poorly, then you would be bound to a being of malice, spending eternity in hate filled torture. The problem she saw with both of these philosophies was the disagreement with what constituted a good life. Still others believed there was no soul and when you died the body turned to dust--you simply ceased to exist. She sometimes hoped that ceasing to exist was her fate, but something deep and undefined within her, knew that was not the case. Not only that, those that professed to believe the end was simply that, did not live in such a way. They tended to be the most superstitious, holding to luck as the reasons for things they could not explain. Or they denied the existence of anything outside of what they knew, calling those that had seen or done the unexplainable liars or insane.

No, she could not believe there was nothing after this, even though on some level that is what she wanted. An end to everything, the restful state of oblivion, spoke to her, but how could she explain the illogical drive to follow Eram into these mountains? The only thing she could come up with was that some greater power than herself had pushed her to follow him. The nature of that higher power was the true question in her mind. Was she sent to help him on some important task that would better the world? Or was she already in hell, and a demon had sent her just to play with her, causing agony of the mind, heart and soul--knowing she would first fall in love, then have to watch that love slowly fade away into madness and death?

There was one thing she did know for sure, evil existed. She had watched it destroy her once loving father, turning him into a spiteful and cruel man. She had watched Ulrick liberate her father from that evil, then battle it for control of himself.

Deep red tinted the bottom edges of the eastern clouds, lightening to pink at the top. Deep in thought, Abby nearly ran into the back of Eram when he stopped. She stepped up beside him. She had not noticed, but sometime in the night they had left the glacier behind and they now stood on the ridge of a rocky saddle between two high hills.

Before them was a nearly round valley surrounded by the steep walls of the mountains. Forest hugged the steep hills around the valley, but the valley itself was barren. The only thing growing was short brown grasses sheltering in the shadows of boulders that littered the surreal landscape. The boulders and scattered stones seemed out of place lying on the flat ground with no apparent explanation has to how they could have gotten there. In the center of the valley was the strangest feature of the landscape. Swirling dust and debris created a pillar that covered a small patch of ground, then disappeared high into the sky.

They had made it. The final valley before the final peak, but only desolation and death awaited them. Abby despaired, tears flowed from her blue eyes leaving tracks on her dusty face, then falling dirty to the ground. She had no idea what she had expected to find, but this was definitely not it.

Without acknowledgement or word, Eram started down the steep slope, dislodging dirt and small stones as he went. The large cloud of dust he kicked up during his falling slide down the hill flowed toward the center of the valley and the tower of spinning dirt. The wolf pup whined for a moment before following.

Abby waited, not really seeing the point of continuing. Once in the valley there was no way they would be able to climb back out. She did, however, know she would be following anyway. What else was there? She couldn't go back, especially not alone. So, she waited until she figured the stones she would dislodge as she slid down, would not hit Eram, then she stepped off.

It took less time to get down the slope and through the forest than she thought it would have. She had gotten used to the immensity of the mountain landscape. Early on, what she had thought was hours away, sometimes had turned to days of travel, but here, what looked like hours away, was closer to reality.

She stepped out of the forest. Eram was stumbling some distance ahead. He fell several times, each time he crawled for a few feet before struggling back to his feet. Watching him broke her heart. She wanted desperately to help him, but she knew she was not much better off. Each step took extreme effort and she knew once on the ground, she lacked the energy and more importantly, the will to get back up. So, she stumbled along in his wake, unable to do anything but put one foot in front of the other.

Eram stood about three paces in front of her at the edge of the swirling mass of dust. Up close, the column appeared to be spinning much faster than it had appeared from a distance. The blowing sand looked like it would blast the flesh form her bones. The air being pulled into the vortex whipped around her, making it difficult to see past her blonde hair being continuously blown into her face.

Slowly, he stepped into the blasting vortex. His hands went to his face to protect it from the blowing sand. Abby stood motionless, watching. He moved continuously, but slowly into obscurity. Then one moment he was there, and the next he was gone.

Abby's gut clenched with fear, but she was too tired to give it much credence. She stepped into blasting sand, eyes shut tight to the onslaught, she pushed forward. About the tenth step in, her foot met nothing but air. She fell, spinning head first into open air. The jolt came quick, knocking the breath from her lungs. On her back, she slid head first down a slope of small cold stones, then settled on what felt like flat cold stone.

"Abigail, get up." The voice that spoke to her was smooth and masculine, but it seemed strange. "Abigail, get up." She identified the strangeness with the second demand. She was not hearing the voice; it came from within her own head.

"Who are you?" she asked, her voice loud and harsh from dehydration.

"You only have moments before Eramus is dead. He will only live if you do exactly as I tell you," the unknown voice exhorted. "Get up."

Abby climbed to her feet, she worked her dirt filled eyes open. Eram lay at her feet, his breath fast and shallow.

"Go through the door directly in front of you. Once inside, there will be cabinets to your right. In the first upper cabinet there are several blue bottles. Drink one of them, only one though, you will want to drink more, but it is deadly to drink more than one. Then, three more cabinets down, there are small pink bottles, you must get Eramus to drink as much of one of them as you can. Hurry, there is not much time." The voice was insistent.

Vision clear enough to see the door the voice had indicated and nothing to lose, she went to do as the voice had commanded. She found the blue bottles, drank one. The thick liquid burned as it slowly made its way to her gut. Her body began to tingle and she felt energy and warmth spread through her body, clearing the cobwebs of fatigue. She almost reached for another bottle before remembering what the voice had said. Quickly locating the pink bottles, she brought it to Eram. She propped him up, tilted his head back, and poured the pink liquid into his mouth.

"Now, back in that same room toward the far end, there is a large rack of bottles. Take two of the large brown bottles and come back." The voice was now only slightly less urgent.

Doing as the voice said, she returned with the bottles. "Now what?" she asked.

"Follow the wall to your left, go through the third door.

Inside you will find a pool of hot water. Pour the contents of the two bottles into the pool, then come back and get Eramus. Strip off all of his clothes and put him into the pool. You will need to do the same yourself. Stay in the pool until I say."

18 - Ulrick

The late afternoon breeze was coming from inland through the balcony doors, making it far warmer than the refreshing sea breeze from earlier. He must have dozed off after everyone left. The heat of the day now had him sweating and awake, his mouth dry. The bed he laid in was the most comfortable he had slept in for months. Actually, it was the most comfortable bed he had ever been in. In spite of this, his sweaty body had him itching all over. Miserable, he had to get up.

Bob and Lisa had discussed his ring and sword for nearly an hour before they left. Bob said something about having business in the city he wanted to take care of before dinner. Of course, without a good reason to stay, Lisa and Amber left soon after.

Ulrich was both relieved and disappointed they had left. Disappointed because Amber was by far the most beautiful woman he had ever seen. How could he not just want to have a woman like that close by? It wasn't just her appearance. She had a force of will that left you captivated and once their confrontation was over, she seemed light-hearted, with a witty sense of humor. He was relieved because Amber was the most beautiful woman he had ever seen. When she was around, he forgot about Naomi, the woman he loved more than anything in the world. He did not want to forget about Naomi.

Ulrick did not learn much about his sword and ring. He could not see what Lisa saw and neither he nor Lisa really understood what Bob was saying about it. All he did get from it was something about Lisa being able to see the energy of bonds that held materials together and the visibly higher energy levels in the metal of the sword meant the small particles that made up the metal of the sword were compressed tighter making it heavier and far stronger than any normal metal. He also didn't learn much because Amber was the most beautiful woman he had ever seen.

Sitting up on the end of the bed, he removed his dirty robe and tossed it toward his saddle bags. He noticed Natalia through the sheer curtains as they rippled in the breeze. She was standing completely naked on the railing of the balcony with her arms spread like she was going to dive off the edge and try to fly. The breeze was blowing her hair. He stood and stepped into the doorway behind her. "Can you feel the breeze against your skin and hair?"

She looked over her shoulder. "No, I feel nothing." She looked back over the bay.

Ulrick imagined the breeze, warm as it caressed her skin, her hair tickling her face and neck as the air gently filtered through each strand. "Can you feel it now?"

"Yes… thank you." She sighed. "In Hell there is no wind. There is no taste. There is no soft caress and no harsh whip. There is no sweet and no bitter. There is no sensation at all. This and the apex plane are the only places of physical existence. There is only a memory of the strong hand of a lost lover whose name you have forgotten. Hell is knowing you will never feel again."

"How long was I asleep? How much time do I have before dinner?"

"About an hour." She turned around. "Please keep imagining for just a few moments more."

He had just finished getting ready, when there was a knock at the door. Lisa was waiting when he opened it. She looked good in a form fitting dress the same color as her light blue eyes. Her shoulder length brown hair was pulled back into a tail with fragrant magnolia flowers around the base of the tail. The dress was slit more than halfway up her left thigh. He realized why as soon as he noticed the long knife strapped to the inside of each thigh. If not for his mage sight they would have remained hidden to him.

She smiled. "I knew if I was going to have any chance of you looking at me, I would have to come without Amber." She grabbed his left hand and put her arm through his. "Let's get going. We don't want to be late."

They had walked arm and arm for about a hundred feet when Lisa came to a stop. "I forgot about Bob. Was he ready to go?"

"He hasn't gotten back yet. He will just have to meet us there. Don't worry about it. I never really know where he is or when he will be back from wherever he goes. I wouldn't be surprised if he was asleep in a closet somewhere."

They entered the dining room without any ceremony. Everyone was just mingling in groups of two or three, talking quietly. Everyone in the room was dressed as nice as or nicer than Lisa was. Ulrick felt uncomfortable wearing only a grey mage robe. He had left his sword in the room, but he did have the three skulls tucked away.

Mika noticed them and made his way over. "Ulrick, I apologize for how I treated you earlier. It is not every day the son of the most infamous man in the empire shows up at your door. I may command thousands of men, but standing in the entry hall with you and Robert made me feel impotent, and it is my responsibility to keep everyone here safe. I know it is a thin excuse, but I hope you find it in you to forgive me." He held his hand out.

Ulrick was taken back by the complete change in the man. "General, no harm was done and it all worked out, so I don't see anything to forgive. You did your duty as you felt was necessary. I can't fault you for that." He smiled and clasped hands with the general.

Lisa pulled him further into the room. That is when he

saw her. She was in a dress similar to Lisa's, but instead of blue it was a cream color that was nearly the same color as her skin. The curve of her hips as they smoothly transitioned into her long legs caused his heart to skip a beat and his hands to sweat. It took him a moment to realize everyone had stopped talking and were all looking toward the end of the room.

A man strolled into the room, he was tall with graying blonde hair. Ulrick could tell the man had once been muscular, but now his stomach was more pronounced than his shoulders. He was obviously the governor. Ulrick was surprised someone hadn't announced him or something. He was under the impression that is how things were done. The governor scanned the group before him, his eyes stopped on Ulrick for only a moment. "Please everyone, be seated."

The tables were set in a U-shape. The governor and his daughter sat on the outside of the bottom of the U. Everyone else just found a place somewhere on the outside of the other tables. The servers worked the inside.

It wasn't a large group: it was just the governor, Amber, Thom, Mika, Lisa, Ulrick and five, judging by the uniforms high ranking officers. All the seats closest to the governors table were taken, but the room could easily handle hundreds of guests. Ulrick noticed he was seated farthest from the governor's table. He was pretty sure Lisa had done that on purpose. Obviously, they did not really trust him yet.

There were several empty place settings to his left and across from him. He assumed one was for Bob and some other guest not here yet. Just as he thought it, another man entered. He was wearing a black mage robe. At least he no longer felt under dressed.

"Sorry I'm late." The man stopped before he reached the tables.

"Please be seated Andarus." Apparently, that was the

only formality. No one could sit until the governor gave them permission. "Ulrick, is Bob going to join us or should we start without him?" the governor asked.

Ulrick shrugged. "I haven't seen him for several hours. It is my experience he keeps his own time."

"Yes, it seems that is the habit of wizards." He glared at Andarus. "Okay, bring in the food, I'm starved."

Everyone sat silently while servers brought in plates of mixed fruit and greens and placed them in front of each guest, starting with the governor and progressing outward. The young server that had brought him his refreshment earlier, placed a plate in front of him.

"Marie, right? It looks like you have drawn the short straw again," Ulrick mentioned, as she filled his cup.

She only curtsied and left.

Ulrick looked up from his plate and noticed everyone was looking at him. Lisa patted his leg under the table. Natalia grinned at him from the other side. Then she made her way to the head of the table. Lisa squeezed his leg under the table. Ulrick had a hard time keeping a straight face as the bare-chested demon sat in one of the two empty seats at the governor's table. He could tell Lisa was about to come apart. He put his hand on hers reassuringly.

The governor picked up his fork. "I think we can forgive Ulrick his poor etiquette. He is from Elk Valley, after all." He took a bite of his food and everyone else followed suit and started talking quietly amongst themselves.

Lisa glared at Ulrick. "Can't you control her?" she whispered as quietly as she could and still have him hear.

"Yes, I just choose not to. Don't worry, Lisa, everything will be fine." He tried his food; all the fruit wasn't really his thing, but it was good.

"It looks you have Lisa there, all flustered." Andarus held out his hand. "The name is Andarus."

"I know."

Andarus looked at Lisa then back to Ulrick. "Don't believe everything you've heard."

"I know your name because the governor said it when you walked in. I don't know anything else about you, other than based on the robes, you are a mage or maybe you just like playing dress up." Lisa squeezed his leg again. He pulled Lisa's hand off his leg and set it on hers. He leaned into her. "Really, relax, will you?"

Andarus chuckled. "You know, Ulrick, I think I like you." He popped a piece of apple in his mouth and took a sip of his wine. "Sometimes I think I am the only one with a sense of humor around here." He smiled at Lisa.

Ulrick had barely had a chance to eat any of his food when Marie and the other servers showed back up and started clearing plates. Once again, Ulrick noticed the whole meal seemed to revolve around the governor. If he was ready for the next course that meant everyone else was ready whether they really were or not. The next course was thinly sliced seasoned sweet meat, much like what Janus had served him yesterday. When Marie sat the plate in front of him, he asked Lisa, "Am I allowed to speak to the help now?"

"You are certainly allowed to, but it may be considered rude if you only talk to the servers." She sighed. "Marie did not pull the short straw. She asked if she could serve the Son of the Reaper's Hand."

Ulrick smiled and winked at the young girl. She hurried off. "At least she isn't afraid of me anymore."

"I don't think her fascination indicates a lack of fear," Andarus said through a bite of meat. "It is like standing next to the mountain cat cage at the menagerie."

"So, I am a monster in a cage? Is that why I have a mage to either side of me? Are the two of you the bars of my cage?" Ulrick was able to keep his tone light, but he as growing irritated at the situation. It was at this point he noticed the number of guards in the room exceeded the number of guests by double. He couldn't help but smile at the absurdity of it. He knew he could kill the governor or his daughter before anyone could even think of stopping him.

Andarus noticed his smile and guessed at the reason. "I am glad you can see the humor in all this. All this for one young man barely starting his training with your sword maybe, but without...I agree it is a bit overkill."

Ulrick's smile widened and Natalia laughed, startling Lisa. "Overkill...Is that what is humorous?"

Andarus looked like he was going to respond, but was interrupted by the governor. "Ulrick, I understand you are what they call a lightning mage?"

"Yes, sir."

"I hear the power of a lightning mage can be quite spectacular to witness."

Obviously knowing where the governor's question was going, Andarus spoke up before Ulrick could respond. "Sir, I don't think that is a good idea. At his level of experience, his lack of control could be deadly to himself and everyone in this room."

"I'm not talking about a large demonstration, just something small like when you light candles."

Before Andarus could say anything more, Ulrick spoke up. "Sir, I would be glad to give you a small show." Ulrick figured they already didn't trust him, he might as well give them a reason to fear him and make sure their lack of trust was unfounded. After all, if he meant to bring them harm, he could at any time. He stood and walked into the inside of the U at the end where no one was sitting.

"You don't have to do this, Ulrick," Lisa said.

Ulrick ignored her and pulled out his three skulls. "What are those?" someone said just as they rose into the air.

"I don't recall hearing anything about floating skulls in the stories of your father. Thom you met his father, did he have floating skulls?" the governor asked.

Before Thom could answer. "My father did not have these. I made them."

Andarus looked uncomfortable as the skulls widened their lazy circle further into the room. "Sir, I still don't think this a good idea." Everyone was mesmerized by the floating skulls; nobody responded to Andarus's concern.

The ring and the skulls had nearly a full charge so he converted it into the least dangerous form and had it start flowing between the skulls, the pulsating arc brightened the room drastically. The buzz and occasional snap of the arc filled the room with sound. Ulrick then changed the form slightly and had the energy return to the ring with a near deafening pop, followed by deafening silence.

Ulrick wasn't done yet. After making sure no one was outside, he turned toward the door at the end of the room. He sent all three skulls speeding through the thick wood door. The door disappeared into a spray of pieces of wood. He turned back to those seated as the skulls slowly returned to his hand. Every face was grave, some even quaked in fear. He looked at Andarus

"Overkill?" Then he looked to the governor. "I have never meant to bring you or any of your household harm and as long you feel the same toward me, I never will." He gestured at the guards around the room, most had drawn weapons waiting for the order to attack. "If I had meant you harm, none of these men could have stopped me, even your pet mages would not have had time to save you." He took a deep breath and let it out slow. "Trust me so I can trust you."

All were grave, but Amber, she smiled. "Well that makes lighting candles look childish."

The focus of the tension shifted from Ulrick to the sound of a commotion outside one of the side doors. Before anyone could do anything, the door burst open and a guard ran into the room, but before he managed to say what the commotion was, two more guards ran into the room with Robert supported between them. Blood saturated the bottom two thirds of his robe. "Why are you bringing him here? Get him to a medic!" the governor yelled, as he made his way to the injured old man.

The guard that had come in first, trying to catch his breath, responded. "Sir, he insisted we bring him to his apprentice. He said he would turn us to ash if we failed."

Everyone gathered around as the guards laid him on the cold marble floor. Eyes wide with pain, Bob looked to Andarus, then his eyes locked on Ulrick. He tried to say something, but it turned into a bloody cough. His eyes more panicked, he tried again to speak, but all he managed was a wet cough.

"Stop trying to talk!" Lisa was kneeling over him. She had torn open his robe and was frantically trying to stop blood from exiting his body through a knife wound in the side of his chest. The fact that every time Bob exhaled, the blood would spray from the wound didn't help.

Lisa was crying. "I am a life mage. I am supposed to be able to heal, but I don't know what to do." She was getting frantic.

Bob lifted his hand and put it on Lisa's shoulder and looked at her with sad eyes. He didn't try to talk; he must have realized it was pointless, he just patted her shoulder. Ulrick thought he was trying to let her know it was alright. Then the old mage coughed again, spewing a large spray of blood into the air, struggled for another breath but failed. Soon after his eyes glazed and his hand fell from Lisa's shoulder.

"No! No! No!" Lisa was frantic again.

"Lisa, his injuries were severe. Even if you were properly trained, which you are not, he probably would have still died, and at this point there is nothing that can be done, even life mages can't bring people back from the dead," Andarus said calmly.

"I should have been able to do something," she whispered.

"Lisa, could you move back? I would like to see if I can make sense of his injuries." Thom knelt by the dead mage, pulled his robe down to his waist and examined his wounds.

The governor came up behind Thom. "What do you make of his wounds?"

Thom rolled the mage over onto his stomach. "I would say there were two attackers, and knowing Robert's skills and caution, he knew and trusted both. It looks to me, he was stabbed here in the kidney first. You can see here how the wound is elongated to the right of the initial entry point. He must have turned as he was attacked and then the person he was facing originally, stabbed him here in the chest. I suspect by the angle the second attacker meant for the blade to hit his heart, but the knife was too short or they didn't manage to get it in all the way." Thom turned the body back over and pulled Bob's robe back up and pulled his hood over his head, covering his dead eyes. "Since he made it back here, I bet his attackers are dead."

The governor motioned for Mika. "We will want to follow the blood trail back to where this happened. Try to find out who did this."

"I will get on it personally." Mika left, taking a handful of guards with him.

Thom motioned for the guards that had brought Bob in over. "Take him to the morgue. Bring any personal items he has on him to me and I will make sure Ulrick gets them before he leaves. Ulrick, I assume you will be staying around until we have had a chance to make some sense of what happened and have a funeral service for Master Robert."

Ulrick wasn't sure yet how he felt about what just happened. On one hand he had spent the better part of two months with the old man and the death of any person you know is a sad thing. On the other hand, he had wanted to stick a knife in the old bastard himself many times in that time. Mostly he was just still numb, yes, he had killed quite a few men the last couple months. Something until just recently he never imagined he would have ever done.

He had never wanted to really kill someone. Sure, there were times people made him mad, but to really kill a man had never been something he had seriously considered. He couldn't say he actually hated anyone enough to kill them. Yet here he stood, looking at the dead body of someone who could be considered a friend, and he felt nothing. It wasn't real… yet.

"We aren't staying here that long, are we?" Natalia asked.

"No."

"No?" Thom asked confused.

"No, I will not be staying. I will be leaving first thing in the morning." Ulrick noticed Lisa give him a look. He wasn't sure exactly what it meant, but she didn't look pleased. "I never had reason to be here. Bob had business here and he wanted me to meet the governor." He looked to the governor and nodded. "I have met the governor; I no longer have reason to stay. Can someone show me back to my room? I'm not sure I can find it."

19 - Eramus

Darkness...Black covered everything. Then liquid blue flowed into the black over taking it. Then liquid red flowed from the right, overtaking blue. Liquid yellow from the top overtaking the red, purple flowed from the left before it covered red; blue again on and on it went color after color flowed over each other.

Awareness...He felt like he floated, feeling nothing but nothing. Then the smells unknown, never before had, he smelled them. He was in water of no temperature. His fingers twitched. Awareness...He had fingers. Awareness... He breathed; slowly in and out the waters moved with each breath, colors still flowed. Awareness...Hands wrapped around him. Awareness...Eramus was his name. Awareness... Abigail's hands. Awareness...The memory of feeling something he could not remember; colors still flowed.

He had been asleep, no, he had been far deeper than sleep. There was no memory, there was no dream, and there was no light. Time was meaningless; colors still flowed.

Eram opened his eyes; still colors flowed in the darkness. He lifted his hand out of the water; the air was cool on his wet skin, but not cold. He lifted his other hand; both rested on the edge of the pool in darkness. Where was he?

He pushed himself up to stand. Pain flashed up his left arm as bright light flared to life, forcing his eyes closed. Slowly his eyes adjusted to the light outside his closed eyes. Once that was not blinding, he cracked one eye then slowly the next.

The room was small; the walls were white, and the floor was alternating black and white tile. He stepped out of the untarnished steel tub. Other than the pipes protruding from the wall over the tub, the tub was the only thing in the room. The source of light, was round, brightly glowing globes attached to the ceiling. He looked to Abby, she still slept or perhaps she was someplace deeper, like the place he had just been. The water in the tub was dirty and so was Abby's face. The trails through the dirt that ran from her eyes to her jaw sent a jolt of sadness into his soul. Dipping his hands in the water, he brought his wet hands up and slowly washed the dirt and trails of sorrow from Abigail's face.

His left arm ached fiercely. His arm was a mass of scarring with pits where flesh had been torn free, but it was all covered in skin; the open wound had been closed. The memory of what had caused the ugly mess was just flashes of violence and sadness. He noticed his naked body was thin, almost skeletal. He walked to the door. He needed to know where he was.

The room he entered was immense. The wall to his right and left both ran off into darkness. A small wolf whined and licked his hand. He remembered he had named her Destiny. Why, he could not recall. Raven glided and landed softly in front of him.

"Caw... caw..." Bobbing its head up and down, Raven seemed to be saying welcome back.

Then Eram saw it: a tower of gold coins and grains piled high, nearly to the ceiling beneath a round hole nearly thirty feet up. Then a mound of gold moved, separating itself from the pile. The shape at first was hard to distinguish because whatever it was, was composed entirely of brightly polished gold. When the shape became apparent, Eram's heart leapt with anticipation and fear, but more excited anticipation.

What moved before him was a massive winged beast fifty or more feet long. It was a golden dragon, and its eyes like globes of glass were focused right on him. Then it spoke, but not like any other being, it spoke within Eram's head, its voice a smooth masculine, and it said, "My name is Eternal, Eramus. Welcome to the past and future of Mankind."

The End of Book One

Printed in Great Britain
by Amazon

54168355R00210